NIGHT HUNT

Applause for L.L. Raand's
Midnight Hunters Series

"Raand has built a complex world inhabited by werewolves, vampires, and other paranormal beings…Raand has given her readers a complex plot filled with wonderful characters as well as insight into the hierarchy of Sylvan's pack and vampire clans. There are many plot twists and turns, as well as erotic sex scenes in this riveting novel that keep the pages flying until its satisfying conclusion."—*Just About Write*

"Once again, I am amazed at the storytelling ability of L.L. Raand aka Radclyffe. In *Blood Hunt*, she mixes high levels of sheer eroticism that will leave you squirming in your seat with an impeccable multi-character storyline all streaming together to form one great read."
—*Queer Magazine Online*

"*The Midnight Hunt* has a gripping story to tell, and while there are also some truly erotic sex scenes, the story always takes precedence. This is a great read which is not easily put down nor easily forgotten."—*Just About Write*

"Are you sick of the same old hetero vampire/werewolf story plastered in every bookstore and at every movie theater? Well, I've got the cure to your werewolf fever. *The Midnight Hunt* is first in, what I hope is, a long-running series of fantasy erotica for L.L. Raand (aka Radclyffe)."—*Queer Magazine Online*

"Any reader familiar with Radclyffe's writing will recognize the author's style within *The Midnight Hunt*, yet at the same time it is most definitely a new direction. The author delivers an excellent story here, one that is engrossing from the very beginning. Raand has pieced together an intricate world, and provided just enough details for the reader to become enmeshed in the new world. The action moves quickly throughout the book and it's hard to put down."—*Three Dollar Bill Reviews*

Acclaim for Radclyffe's Fiction

2010 RWA/ FF&P Prism award winner *Secrets in the Stone* "is a strong, must read novel that will linger in the minds of readers long after the last page is turned."—*Just About Write*

Foreword Review Book of the Year finalist and IPPY silver medalist *Trauma Alert* "is hard to put down and it will sizzle in the reader's hands. The characters are hot, the sex scenes explicit and explosive, and the book is moved along by an interesting plot with well drawn secondary characters. The real star of this show is the attraction between the two characters, both of whom resist and then fall head over heels."—*Lambda Literary Reviews*

Lambda Literary Finalist *Best Lesbian Romance 2010* features "stories [that] are diverse in tone, style, and subject, making for more variety than in many, similar anthologies...well written, each containing a satisfying, surprising twist. Best Lesbian Romance series editor Radclyffe has assembled a respectable crop of 17 authors for this year's offering."—*Curve Magazine*

In **Benjamin Franklin Award finalist** *Desire by Starlight* "Radclyffe writes romance with such heart and her down-to-earth characters not only come to life but leap off the page until you feel like you know them. What Jenna and Gard feel for each other is not only a spark but an inferno and, as a reader, you will be washed away in this tumultuous romance until you can do nothing but succumb to it."—*Queer Magazine Online*

2010 Prism award winner and ForeWord Review Book of the Year Award finalist *Secrets in the Stone* is "so powerfully [written] that the worlds of these three women shimmer between reality and dreams...A strong, must read novel that will linger in the minds of readers long after the last page is turned."—*Just About Write*

Lambda Literary Award winner *Stolen Moments* "is a collection of steamy stories about women who just couldn't wait. It's sex when desire overrides reason, and it's incredibly hot!"—*On Our Backs*

Lambda Literary Award winner *Distant Shores, Silent Thunder* "weaves an intricate tapestry about passion and commitment between lovers. The story explores the fragile nature of trust and the sanctuary provided by loving relationships."—*Sapphic Reader*

Lambda Literary Award Finalist *Justice Served* delivers a "crisply written, fast-paced story with twists and turns and keeps us guessing until the final explosive ending."—*Independent Gay Writer*

Lambda Literary Award finalist *Turn Back Time* "is filled with wonderful love scenes, which are both tender and hot."—*MegaScene*

By Radclyffe

Romances

Innocent Hearts

Promising Hearts

Love's Melody Lost

Love's Tender Warriors

Tomorrow's Promise

Love's Masquerade

shadowland

Passion's Bright Fury

Fated Love

Turn Back Time

When Dreams Tremble

The Lonely Hearts Club

Night Call

Secrets in the Stone

Desire by Starlight

Honor Series

Above All, Honor

Honor Bound

Love & Honor

Honor Guards

Honor Reclaimed

Honor Under Siege

Word of Honor

Justice Series

A Matter of Trust (prequel)

Shield of Justice

In Pursuit of Justice

Justice in the Shadows

Justice Served

Justice for All

The Provincetown Tales

Safe Harbor

Beyond the Breakwater

Distant Shores, Silent Thunder

Storms of Change

Winds of Fortune

Returning Tides

Sheltering Dunes

Visit us at www.boldstrokesbooks.com

NIGHT HUNT

by

L.L. Raand

2012

NIGHT HUNT
© 2012 BY L.L. RAAND. ALL RIGHTS RESERVED.

ISBN 13: 978-1-60282-647-2

THIS TRADE PAPERBACK ORIGINAL IS PUBLISHED BY
BOLD STROKES BOOKS, INC.
P.O. BOX 249
VALLEY FALLS, NY 12185

FIRST EDITION: MARCH 2012

CREDITS
EDITORS: RUTH STERNGLANTZ AND STACIA SEAMAN
PRODUCTION DESIGN: STACIA SEAMAN
COVER DESIGN BY SHERI (GRAPHICARTIST2020@HOTMAIL.COM)

Acknowledgments

Nothing is quite as exciting or as intimidating as creating an entirely new world and populating it with characters who are at once recognizable and more-than-human. Writing the the Midnight Hunters novels has challenged and rewarded me as an author, and along the way has been great fun. Hearing readers say they tried one even though "they don't like paranormal books" makes all the work worthwhile.

Thanks go to my assistant, Sandy Lowe, for her efficiency, skill, tireless support, and amazing good humor; to author Nell Stark for her keen eye to story and enthusiastic feedback; to Ruth Sternglantz for her tremendous job of editing; to Stacia Seaman, for ensuring a stellar final product; and to my first readers Connie, Eva, Jenny, and Paula for insight and encouragement during the early drafts.

And to Lee, who reads every story like it is the first—*Amo te.*

L.L. Raand, 2012

For Lee, everlasting

CHAPTER ONE

Just before sunrise, Lara pulled Niki beneath her and pressed her mouth to Niki's neck. "I hunger."

Niki arched her back and gave her throat to her Packmate, in submission and invitation. "Feed."

Through the haze of her bloodlust, Lara's heart constricted. Niki, the Pack *imperator*, the leader of the Alpha's elite *centuri* guard, had never submitted to anyone except the Alpha, but she offered herself willingly now for Lara's need. Daylight was coming, and Lara's newly turned Vampire physiology drove her to consume the blood that would keep her alive during her somnolence until the circadian cycle edged into night and the deadly ultraviolet rays of the sun were neutralized. Before her body became quiescent, she had to replenish the essential ferrin compounds that her system lacked. Without blood, she would die. When she tried to resist the urge, a terrible chasm of pain opened inside her, stripping her reason, driving her mad. Lara groaned and her vision hazed to red.

"Feed," Niki murmured, threading her fingers through Lara's hair, forcing Lara's open mouth harder against the bounding pulse in her neck. "Please, I need you."

Need, desire, all-consuming hunger rolled through Lara's mind and scorched along her nerve pathways, thrumming beneath skin so tight she feared she might tear apart. She was Vampire, but she was also Were. Claws erupted from her fingertips, canines—thinner and sharper after her change—shot from their sheaths. Her lips drew back in a snarl. Brown pelt feathered the trench between her abdominals, and her clitoris lengthened. She pulled Niki to her, scoring shallow gouges in Niki's chest that ran crimson in the dusky glow of almost-dawn. Lara licked the scarlet flow and Niki writhed, her swollen sex hot and hard against Lara's thigh. Lara rubbed her stone-tipped breasts over Niki's and sank into Niki's throat, injecting a flood of erotostimulants into Niki's system with her bite. Niki growled and her face morphed, her canines erupting, her jaw elongating. Lara pulled at Niki's throat and Niki released a torrent of thick, hot *victus*, roaring in an agony of pleasure.

Lara's hips pumped in time to the contractions in her throat, her continuous climax driven by the surge of blood into her tissues. She knew nothing but the blood. She drank, but the dark hollows within her never filled. Her clitoris pulsed, her sex glands emptied over and over, but she craved more. More, and never enough.

A faint whimper penetrated her lust-clouded consciousness. *Niki.* Niki strained in her arms, vulnerable and defenseless. Niki. Lara wrenched her mouth away, panting, her canines still throbbing, her abdomen so tight she could barely breathe. Niki shuddered in midshift, her eyes wolf-green, her red-gray pelt shimmering beneath her sex-sheened skin. Lara fell away and Niki threaded her fingers through Lara's hair and kissed her, licking the blood from her mouth.

"More," Niki growled, dragging Lara's head down to her neck. "Take more."

"I can't," Lara gasped.

"Yes." Niki slid her hand down Lara's belly, gripped her sex, and squeezed. "Drink me."

"No," a cool voice said from across the room.

Lara stiffened and flung herself to the far side of the bed. Away from Niki. Away from temptation. Away from the blood that called her like a lover. She wrapped her arms around her middle and buried her face between her knees. "Get away."

Heed her, little Wolf. The command slid through Niki's mind like a knife.

Niki whipped her head around, snarling as she came up on all fours, inching closer to a full shift. Her jaws ached, her heart thundered. Her pelvis throbbed with the pressure of sex hormones swelling her glands. She was ready to fight or fuck. She focused on the Vampire in the shadows. Gates, lethal as a blade where she leaned against the wall in dark pants and a white shirt open between small breasts, her eyes fiery red, her skin silvery pale in the glow of a morning she would never see again. Niki growled a challenge. "I can feed her all she needs."

Jody Gates pushed away from the wall and swung the shutters closed over the windows, blocking the daylight. Muted amber lights came on just inside the door. She regarded Niki with a chilly, dismissive expression. "You might be able to. You're *centuri*. If you were human, she would drain you. Even other Weres cannot give what you give and survive. She has taken enough."

Rage tore through Niki's blood. Need curdled in her stomach. Somewhere nearby she felt the Alpha running, running without her. But the Alpha's call still stirred her, and she had nowhere to turn, nowhere to go. No one to ease her terrible emptiness. She needed to lose herself in the addictive pleasure of Lara's bite. The Vampire watching her had taught her that pleasure the night Niki had first offered her blood to save the Vampire's life. Now she was left with the insatiable desire for the pleasure, and oblivion, only a Vampire's bite could bestow.

"You have fed her for the last time," Jody said.

Niki came out of her crouch with a powerful thrust of her legs and launched herself at Jody's throat. She would not be subjugated to the will of this Vampire or any other. She answered only to the Alpha. She would take her pleasure where she wanted, when she wanted, and no one would dictate to her or any other Were. She struck the thick log wall where Jody had been standing, her claws scraping timber and her jaws snapping closed on empty air. She'd shifted in midflight and her wolf fell heavily, rolling with a growl onto her feet. The Vampire had moved so quickly as to be invisible. Vampires carried no scent detectable even to a Were's heightened senses, forcing Niki to track her by sight. Whirling around, she scanned the room with a quick sweep of her head. Jody stood between Niki and Lara, who had fallen into her daylight somnolence, naked, blood-covered, coated in *victus* and sex sweat. Niki stalked forward, lips curled back, eyes fixed on her prey.

"You forget, little Wolf," Jody said softly. "I am Risen now. You are no match for me."

Jody's eyes darkened to the color of burning blood and Niki whined, the pressure in her skull from the Vampire's thrall forcing her down on her belly. She would not show her throat, she would die first. The pressure grew and she whined again. The Vampire was suddenly crouched in front of her. Cool fingers threaded through her ruff, lifting her effortlessly until her muzzle was extended and her throat exposed.

"I could take you now, little Wolf," Jody murmured, "if I wanted. There was a time when all wolves came to the call of their Vampire masters. I could call you to me again, but I won't." Jody lowered Niki to the floor. "Understand this. Lara is *centuri*, and she is Were. But she is also Vampire, and she is mine. She will not feed from you again."

Niki staggered on unsteady legs to the bed and crawled up next to Lara. She rested her muzzle on Lara's breast, shielding her. Guarding her. She had been born to guard and the Alpha had ordered her to protect Lara. This she understood. This she would do, or die.

❖

Jody slipped out of the room, satisfied her newling would be secure until Lara rose again at nightfall and she took her out to hunt. She glided down the wide hall of the Were infirmary toward the room where she had risen only a short time before. Becca was there. Jody's throat tightened. Becca.

A female stepped from the shadows and Jody slowed, misting into visibility. She nodded to the Were medic with the pale blond hair and haunted cerulean eyes. "Sophia."

Sophia murmured, "It is good to see you, Detective."

"Thank you." Jody didn't bother to correct her. The moment she had risen, she had ceased being a police detective. While she had been a pre-animate—what the humans called a living Vampire—she had appeared on the surface to be more human than Praetern, and even then, her colleagues distrusted her. Most feared her. There would be no place for a Risen Vampire in the human law enforcement hierarchy, especially not one with the level of power bequeathed by her ancient bloodlines. Now she had no choice but to take up the mantle of her Clan and prepare to rule the Dominion that would pass to her when her father stepped aside or the balance of power among the many families shifted and she would be forced to take his place. For now, her responsibility lay in ensuring the survival of her species.

Sophia glanced over her shoulder toward the massive wood doors at the far end of the hall. Doors built for a fortress, not a hospital. A sliver of sunlight glowed beneath them. "I know you must go. Niki—and Lara. Are they all right?"

"Lara is safe. Niki guards her."

"Has Lara fed?" Sophia asked. "We didn't send anyone."

"She has been cared for."

Sophia colored. "Of course. Niki. Thank you."

"Much has changed in a very short time," Jody said, her heightened empathic powers reading sadness verging on despair in the Were's psyche. "Everything will not always be as it is now."

"No one knows that better than I," Sophia said. "I won't keep you. I only wanted to let you know we have dispatched guards to your room and Lara's, although here in the Compound you are safe."

"That's not necessary. My soldiers will see to it." She had already called for her soldiers and her blood servants to come to the Compound. When she woke at sunfall, so soon after rising, she would be voracious, and she could not risk Becca being the only one nearby to host. As to how safe she was in the Were Compound, she trusted Sylvan Mir's word that she and her Vampires would be protected, but she was no fool. If Sylvan fell, the next Alpha might have a different view. Until her transition was complete, she would not be able to function well during daylight hours. Soon, she would not be so weak. Her powers were emerging quickly. Even now her body resisted the pull of the torpor ignited by the rising sun.

"Then you will be doubly guarded." Sophia smiled. "The Alpha has ordered it."

"Thank you, then," Jody said and left Sophia to join her consort.

Jody stepped into the room where she had risen. Becca had already closed the blinds and shuttered the windows. A lamp beside the bed illuminated Becca's shoulder-length ebony hair and made her coffee skin glint with mahogany highlights. Jody latched the door behind her and strode to the bed, unbuttoning her shirt as she walked, watching Becca watch her undress. Becca's eyes gleamed and Jody saw hunger there. She'd seen hunger countless times in the eyes of her hosts, males and females, human and Praetern, but no one's hunger had ever stirred her the way Becca's did. Becca hungered for *her*, not the pleasure her bite would bring or the chance for immortality.

"You show me worlds I never dreamed of," Jody murmured. Her

throat ached to taste her. Her need filled her until all she knew was Becca.

"I can see myself reflected in your eyes," Becca said. "You make me feel beautiful and desirable."

"You see the truth." Jody stopped at the foot of the bed and unzipped her pants. She stepped free of everything—clothes, preconceptions, old wounds—when she went to Becca. "I don't have much time."

Becca pushed the covers aside. "I know. Come to me."

Jody slid under the covers, lassitude spreading through her. "I'm sorry."

"Don't be. You're here with me. I couldn't ask for anything else."

Smiling, Jody traced the line of Becca's jugular, flowing hot and fast beneath her skin. "No?"

"You see the truth, as well." Becca caught Jody's hand and kissed her palm. "Lara? Is she all right?"

"Yes. She did well."

"Good." Becca's eyes were worried as she skated her fingertips over Jody's throat and down the center of her chest. "Will you be safe today?"

"Don't worry. My people are already here."

Becca glanced at the door. "I don't hear anything."

"I feel them."

"Are they in your blood, like me?"

Jody pressed her mouth to Becca's throat and let her incisors pierce the skin infinitesimally. "There is no other like you. You are my blood mate. My blood flows in you, and yours in me. We're bound, eternally."

"Eternally," Becca whispered, sadness swirling in her eyes. "But I am human—"

"Becca," Jody whispered. "When I rose this morning, my destiny changed forever, as did yours. I have much to tell you."

"I know. When you wake, there will be time for us to talk." Becca rested her hand beneath Jody's breast, her fingers trembling. "You're growing cooler."

Jody covered Becca's hand with hers. "You won't feel it beat until I feed again, and sometimes, not even then. Does that bother you?"

Becca kissed her. "No. I have you. That's what I need."

"I hunger for you."

"The Weres who hosted for you were not enough?" Becca said, the gleam of satisfaction in her eyes. "What else do you need?"

"You. I need you." Jody pulled Becca on top of her and pushed her hair back, exposing her neck. She licked the smooth skin over the pulse in Becca's throat. "I would drink you before I sleep."

Becca shifted and straddled Jody's thigh. She was wet, hot. "Would you?"

"You already fed me once. I shouldn't."

Becca smiled, rubbing herself against Jody's abdomen. She wasn't yet used to the crimson shards that had appeared in Jody's eyes when she had risen, but she loved the flames that leapt in them now, knowing she had put that need there. She loved knowing no matter how many others had fed her lover, she was the one Jody still needed. She slipped her fingers behind Jody's head and pulled Jody forward until Jody's mouth was against her neck. "Drink me. You're mine."

"Yes." Jody groaned and slid into Becca, flooding Becca's body with her hormones, filling herself with Becca's lifeblood.

Becca arched and cried out, her orgasm a burning tide streaming through her. Beneath her, Jody climaxed in deep, continuous waves until she licked the punctures closed in Becca's throat, shut her eyes, and fell away, lying still as death. Becca gathered her close, aching to see her so defenseless. She didn't care how many guards stood outside the door. Jody was hers to protect, and no one would threaten her while she lived.

She hadn't slept the night before, waiting for Jody to return from the night raid with the Alpha, and she wasn't planning on leaving Jody's side until she had risen again. Jody would need her bonded blood until her transition was complete, no matter how many others hosted for her. She drifted until a faint click jerked her awake. She sat up, putting herself between Jody and the door as the knob turned.

A blonde Becca didn't recognize—a soldier by the looks of her black leather pants, calf-high boots, black T-shirt, and the automatic weapon holstered beneath her left arm—entered and closed the door. Her gaze swept the room, lingered for a moment on Jody, then settled on Becca.

"The Liege rests comfortably?" Her voice was low and resonant, like the smooth register of a fine stringed instrument.

Becca drew the sheet over Jody's bare chest. "She's fine. Who are you?"

"I am Zahn Logan, head of security for Clan *Chasseur de Nuit*."

Becca mentally thumbed through her little-used French. "Night hunters. Jody's Clan?"

"Yes."

"The sun is up. How is it you're awake?"

"I am human."

Becca frowned. "I thought Rafaela was in charge of Jody's guard."

"She is head of the Vampire guard, and they answer to me."

"How is it that I've never met you before?"

"The Liege did not wish protection. Now that she is Risen and officially Heir, she has no choice." Zahn nodded and reached for the door. "I'll be outside, should you need anything. When the Liege rises, she will need to feed."

"I know," Becca said sharply.

"She left instructions that you were not to be the first to host tonight."

"Oh? And who will be first?"

Zahn smiled. "I will."

CHAPTER TWO

As the sun crested the mountains, Drake kept pace with Sylvan, racing beneath the forest canopy on a narrow trail through underbrush where only deer and fox had previously passed. Her mate never took the same path twice. Routine invited ambush.

The scattered shafts of summer sunlight highlighted the silver in Sylvan's coat and reflected in golden shards from her wolf-turned eyes. Drake's shoulder brushed Sylvan's with every stride and her heart pounded with exertion and unfettered joy. Sylvan was healthy again, and she was certain Drake carried their offspring inside her. Drake was afraid to hope. She wasn't supposed to be able to bear young. She wasn't born Were, but turned, mutated, transformed. Others called her *mutia*, but she couldn't remember a time when she hadn't been Were. She couldn't remember a time when Sylvan had not filled her heart and mind, when she hadn't been Pack. In another life, she had grown up alone, never having known her parents, left to defend herself in a system in which the outsider was more often than not abandoned and lost. She had survived, but she had never expected to be anything other than alone. Now her life was filled with the scent and the sound and the heartbeats of hundreds of other Weres, Sylvan's Pack. Her Pack now. If Sylvan was right, she carried the promise of the Pack's future in the young who would continue Sylvan's line. If Sylvan was right.

Sylvan bumped her shoulder and nipped at her muzzle. *You doubt me, Prima?*

I can't feel them.

You will. Sylvan circled her, growling and snapping at her nose, diverting her from her worries. *Run with me, mate.*

Sylvan streaked away, expecting Drake to give chase. Drake followed slowly until Sylvan disappeared into the brush, and once Sylvan was out of sight, cut into the forest, abandoning Sylvan's trail. Drake would give Sylvan her throat as easily as she'd given her heart, but she would never let Sylvan dominate her. Sylvan was the most dominant Were in the Northern Hemisphere. Drake trusted Sylvan's love and the power of their mate bond, but Sylvan needed more than her love and devotion to complete her. She needed challenge. Sylvan needed an equal to rule by her side and, even more importantly, to shield her, to protect her, to comfort her. Sylvan would never accept that comfort from anyone less than an equal.

Drake burst out of the trees into a clearing on top of a ridge that overlooked the Compound across the valley. Smoke curled from the stone chimneys of the log buildings surrounding the central complex. She could just make out the *sentries* standing post at the top of the stockade fence. Much closer in the forest, she sensed the *centuri* forming a protective circle around her and Sylvan, and others in the far mountains, guarding their perimeter. Even deeper, hundreds of miles away, lone scouts roamed the wilderness, protecting their borders. In these thousands of acres of Adirondack forest the Weres lived free, and she and Sylvan would die to protect their freedom.

Twenty yards below her, a silver streak glinted through the green leaves. Sylvan. Drake bounded down the mountainside, angling along the edge of the ravine, and burst out onto the lower trail just as Sylvan emerged from the brush. She launched herself at Sylvan, taking her to the pine-needle-covered forest floor with her jaws buried in Sylvan's ruff. Sylvan growled and snapped, thrashing to throw her off, struggling to mount her. Drake closed her jaws on Sylvan's leg, catching her paw, biting down hard enough to make Sylvan snarl. Drake backed off with Sylvan's leg between her teeth, careful not to injure, and lowered her shoulders, shaking Sylvan with a deep rumble. They were nearly the same size in skin, but in pelt, Sylvan was larger, heavier, stronger. She was Alpha.

Sylvan broke free and lunged, teeth slashing the air. Drake skirted away, abandoning her hold. Sylvan's canines grazed her flank, and she twisted in a tight S-turn and came at Sylvan from behind. When she jumped, Sylvan cut low underneath her, clamped down on her throat, and dragged her to ground. Drake's nose dug into the rich loam, and she sneezed a cloud of dirt and leaves in Sylvan's face. Eyes gleaming in victory, Sylvan rolled her easily and straddled her midsection with all four limbs. Sylvan closed her jaws around Drake's muzzle until Drake whined in surrender. When Sylvan released her, Drake licked her face and nipped at her neck.

Sylvan shimmered above her, the power and speed of her shift pulling Drake back to skin with her. In an instant, they were breast to breast, skin to skin, heart to heart.

Drake kissed her. "Have a good run?"

Sylvan supported herself on her elbows and grazed Drake's jaw with her teeth. "I felt you coming, you know. I let you catch me."

"Liar." Drake laughed.

"You think you can hide from me, Prima?" Sylvan's blond hair glowed in the sunlight, blue eyes deeper than any ocean. She nuzzled Drake's neck and kissed her. "I feel you always. Everywhere."

Drake ran her hands down Sylvan's back, tracing the heavy muscles along her spine and the strong arch of her ass. She opened her legs and drew Sylvan between hers. "I feel you in my body. In my heart. Always."

Sylvan's eyes glittered gold and the bones in her face grew heavy. Her wolf surged and she pressed herself more tightly between Drake's legs.

"You're sure, about the young?" Drake whispered.

"Very sure." Sylvan's voice had dropped, grown gravelly. She had perfect control of her shift and could transform partially, unlike any other Were in the Pack except for Drake. Now she let her wolf surface to claim her mate.

Drake readied to Sylvan's call, opening for her, lifting to her, accepting the firm length of Sylvan's clitoris into the cleft below her own. Heat swept into the depths of her belly, different than the agonizing fire of breeding heat—smoother, fuller, a steady burn calling her wolf to join. She seated Sylvan with her inner muscles and felt Sylvan tense. Her mate was close to release already—always so potent, so primed to claim her.

"I'm here," Drake murmured. "I want you over me, in me."

Sylvan thrust between her legs, her hot mouth covering the shadow of the mate bite on Drake's shoulder that never disappeared, only faded until her blood called for her mate. When Sylvan slid her canines into her muscle, Drake thrust hers into Sylvan's chest. Heat turned to flame, flame to fire.

"Now," Drake cried, her pelvis jerking in time with Sylvan's release, her essence pulsing over Sylvan's pelt-streaked belly and thighs, joining them, uniting them, marking their bond. Sylvan's ass tightened and she pushed deeper inside, swelling until they locked. Drake's claws emerged and she held Sylvan to her, raking her back, the pleasure-pain forcing Sylvan to empty with a roar.

"I love you," Drake gasped as Sylvan shuddered inside her, claiming her.

"Mine," Sylvan groaned, collapsing in Drake's arms, her hips still pumping as her orgasm trailed away. "You are my heart."

"Yes." Drake smoothed the damp hair at the back of Sylvan's neck. These were the moments she held most precious, when Sylvan's need for her comfort and protection was greatest. No one else would ever see Sylvan this way. To everyone else she was unapproachable, unassailable, unbreakable.

Drake kissed Sylvan's temple, a bright surge of pleasure followed by an incredible sense of peace rising from deep within her. Her loins stirred, not from need or desire, but from joy. She tightened her hold on Sylvan. "I feel them."

Sylvan's breath caught. "How many?"

Drake laughed. "Two."

"Can you tell what?"

"Not yet." Drake nipped at Sylvan's shoulder. "Do you care?"

"No," Sylvan said. "Every pup is precious, and male or female, I will teach them to lead."

"I know you will, but there'll be no need for a new Alpha for many years to come."

Sylvan nestled her cheek against Drake's shoulder. "We have unfinished business."

"I know," Drake said, tracing the scars on Sylvan's chest and abdomen where the assassin's bullets had torn into her. Whoever had attempted to kill her was still at large. They had yet to discover who was behind the abuse of the young wolves they had liberated only hours before from an experimental laboratory. Their enemies were everywhere, and Sylvan was still a target. "We need to speak with Katya and Gray. Hopefully they will have some clue as to who abducted them and why."

"I'm afraid there may be others still imprisoned," Sylvan said darkly. "Who knows how many other young they may have taken from other Packs or even from our own. Our adolescents often leave the Compound to roam for a year or two before they're ready to settle down and mate. Some leave to integrate into human society. We have young females in colleges, police academies, the military. Dozens if not hundreds beyond our immediate protection."

"Wouldn't you know if they were missing?" Drake stroked Sylvan's back, aching to ease some of Sylvan's burden. Sylvan bore a heavy mantle of responsibility safeguarding the well-being of an entire society, but Sylvan did not see her obligation as a burden. Her duty was the destiny she was born to, and Drake would never try to turn her from that path. But she would not let Sylvan's duty destroy her either.

"Their families would alert us," Sylvan said. "I can feel all of the Pack, always, but more as a collective consciousness—not individuals, unless I focus and try to reach out to them. Without knowing who might be in danger, I might not know until it's too late. And if their captors are capable of shielding them from us as they did Katya and Gray, then I would never know."

Sylvan's skin shimmered and her pelt slid like quicksilver over her sleek muscles, her anger and frustration pushing her wolf to the surface.

"We know now what to look for," Drake said calmly. "We've already sent out alerts to all the females outside the Compound. Everyone will be on guard."

"And what of the young from other Packs who might still be in chains?"

"Would you take on the responsibility for every Pack in the Northern Hemisphere?"

Sylvan growled. "If need be. There hasn't been a Supreme Alpha to unite all the Packs for centuries, since before my mother's time. But there was a time when one Alpha ruled all the Packs. Perhaps that time has come again."

"Suggest that," Drake said, "and you'll make yourself a target among the Weres as well as the anti-Praetern factions."

"I must do what needs to be done."

Drake sighed and threaded her fingers through Sylvan's hair. "I know. But will you at least agree to wait until we have more information? There's so much we don't know about why Gray and Katya and the others were abducted, and if we can discover what their captors wanted from them, we may be able to find out who they are."

"You ask me to be patient, when our enemies seek to exterminate our entire species?" Sylvan's blue eyes turned to ice.

Drake had never been afraid of Sylvan. There'd been a time when the sheer lethality of Sylvan's power overwhelmed her. But not now. She had seen Sylvan moments from death. She had seen her feral. She'd seen her helpless in the throes of orgasm. She did not fear Sylvan's wolf. She tugged on Sylvan's hair. "I would have you think before you bite." She grasped Sylvan's hand and pressed it to her abdomen. "They will need you, as we all do."

Sylvan rumbled and her eyes narrowed. "You don't fight fair."

"I fight any way I have to to protect what's mine." Drake relaxed her grip on Sylvan's hair. "You will lead us to freedom, but not at the cost of your life."

Sylvan pushed up, clouds rolling through her eyes. "You trust me?"

"In all things. Except…"

Sylvan snarled and Drake laughed.

"You tend to be a little overprotective. You must promise not to keep secrets from me. I need to be your mate in all things."

Another unhappy rumble rolled from Sylvan's chest, but she nodded. "And you must promise that you will guard yourself and our young no matter what happens to me."

"I promise I will guard our young and you as long as I breathe," Drake whispered. She slid her hand behind Sylvan's neck and pulled her down to kiss her. "Promise me the same."

"I promise."

"Then let's go home. You need to talk to Katya and Gray and find out what was done to them. Then I'll need to consult with Leo and Nadia." She sighed. "We're going to have to examine them, Sylvan— probably at the lab. It won't be easy for them."

"They are wolf Weres," Sylvan said archly. "They will stand."

"They're young," Drake said softly.

"They're *our* young, and you are their Prima. They will trust you."

"And what about the Vampires? They stood with us last night. Are you willing to ally with them now?"

Sylvan sat up, put her back against a tree, and pulled Drake into her arms. She rested her chin on top of Drake's head. In her lifetime, there hadn't been a formal Were-Vampire alliance, although she knew such agreements had existed in her mother's time. Over the years as the Praetern species had integrated into human society, the old alliances had fallen aside as each species maneuvered for power or privilege or protection. The Weres had carved out strongholds in remote, undeveloped terrains, quietly buying up acreage to establish their Pack lands. The Vampires had chosen the underworld, often skirting the edges of the law to establish their power base, rubbing shoulders with organized crime in their casinos and hotels and clubs. Those most able to pass as human, the Sorcerers and the Psi-gifted, were the most loosely organized, and the Fae had retreated to Faerie, emerging only when they needed humans to breed. She wasn't sure who to trust, even among the Praetern Coalition that she led.

"I trust Gates," Sylvan finally said. "And her soldiers fought well for us last night."

Drake said, "We share more than a common enemy with her. We share Lara."

Sylvan's lip curled, but she nodded. "When the Vampire wakes, we'll discuss strategy." She growled. "It seems we will have to get used to having Vampires in the Compound."

"And they'll have to get used to Weres in their lair."

Sylvan smiled and kissed her. "Good point."

Drake pressed Sylvan's hand more firmly to her abdomen. "When will we tell the Pack?"

"They'll know as soon as they scent you."

"Great." Drake sighed. "They know when you need to tangle because you broadcast to all of them. They know when we *do* tangle, because you're so damn potent. Now they know when I'm…"

"Pregnant."

Drake smiled. "Yes. Is there anything about us they *don't* know?"

"No." Sylvan kissed her again. "We are their leaders."

"I feel them all," Drake said softly. "It's amazing. You're amazing. I love you."

"I love you. Let's go home." Sylvan kissed her, and her wolf called Drake's.

Sylvan howled, calling their wolves to run with them, and Drake joined her.

CHAPTER THREE

Veronica Standish stood on the balcony of her 220-year-old brownstone facing Washington Park, sipping her black coffee, enjoying the cool breeze blowing through the thin satin robe she'd pulled on after her shower. Her damp hair curled on her shoulders, her nipples hardening pleasantly in the chill air. By noon the day would be hot, but right now, a few hours after dawn, the weather was perfect. Contemplating early-morning sex, and who she might call upon to accommodate her, she observed the runners streaming along the footpaths, wondering how many of them weren't human. She wondered too why more humans weren't outraged at the notion of creatures moving freely among them, imitating them, pretending to be human, while all the time endangering the human species. If the mutants weren't directly preying upon humans like the Weres and Vampires, they were compelling, enchanting, or mind-manipulating humans to their own benefit. Long before the Exodus and the unveiling of the Praetern species, she had been working to perfect and preserve the human genome, so when she had discovered the presence of these deviant species she had immediately adapted her work to find ways to control them. She'd always had to be secretive about her true goals—now more than ever. The assault on her lab last night was a setback but, as with all negative outcomes, also an opportunity to learn and improve the experimental model.

Her hand shook at a surge of rage and she calmly refocused her mind. She could not afford to be emotional. She had to regain control, and quickly. No one else could be counted on to protect her work. She had assumed the mercenary guards Nicholas had provided, some of whom weren't human, would be adequate security, but obviously she had been wrong to trust something so critical to him. The cat mongrels had been no match for the wolves, and the human guards even less so. What she needed was her own security force, and humans weren't sufficient. She didn't trust Weres—too primitive, and she'd never allow a Fae or Psi, who might be able to affect her mind, anywhere near her inner circle. But the Vampires—now, they were a real possibility. Her nipples tingled as she recalled the feeding she'd witnessed last night, a Vampire bleeding one of the wolf Weres, forcing the Were to orgasm. The Vampire had been breathtakingly powerful and had sexually dominated even the dominant Were. Just watching the Vampire feed had made her wet.

She'd speak to the Chancellor of the City about employing her own security going forward. She laughed quietly. The Vampires would have their uses, at least until the greater threat of the Weres—more numerous, more visible, and more organized—was neutralized. She'd deal with the Vampires later.

Turning away from the idyllic—and boring—early-morning scene, she strode through her bedroom to her office across the hall and settled behind her Louis XV desk. As she pulled several file folders toward her, she dialed Nicholas's number. He answered on the first ring.

"Yes?" he said tersely.

"Good morning, darling. I hope you don't mind me calling so early."

"Of course not," he said, although she detected an edge of annoyance in his voice. He had asked her not to call him at home.

She smiled. All the better for him to realize she didn't play by anyone else's rules. "How soon will we be able to convert one of the other labs so I can resume my work?"

"It will take some time, especially if we want to complete the conversion in secrecy."

"After last night, secrecy is even more important," she said. "The Weres have been alerted to our work now. They'll be looking for us."

"Perhaps we can create a diversion," he said. "Something to focus their attention elsewhere."

"I think that's an excellent idea. In the meantime, we have the problem of the remaining subjects in the compromised lab."

"We can move them temporarily," he said.

She opened the first file and scanned a few tables of results. "I don't think it's worth it. Thus far, the results have been less than promising with them, and now they're essentially contaminated specimens. I'd much rather start fresh."

"We could drop them off at the hospital again and try to stir up some public anti-Were sentiment that way."

"Ordinarily I'd agree," she said, "but after last night, I don't think we want to call attention to any part of our operation. Simple disposal would be better."

He sighed. "Easier said than done."

"Well, you know how frequent and devastating industrial accidents can be. If there was to be an explosion, for example, the lab would be destroyed and so would all the laboratory animals."

"Jesus, Veronica—that's a multimillion-dollar installation."

She laughed. "Darling, that's why you have insurance."

❖

After their run, Sylvan and Drake showered while the *centuri* circled their remote cabin, guarding them. Sylvan pulled on a pair of jeans as she watched Drake dress. Her mate had changed since her transformation. Her muscles had become more prominent, her cheekbones sharper, her gait more fluid. She'd been compelling as a human; she was breathtaking as a Were.

"Would you have loved me if I'd never changed?" Drake asked, pulling on a pair of charcoal camo BDUs. She caught Sylvan's gaze, held it. Another thing only she could do. "Because I loved you even before."

The uncertainty in Drake's eyes struck Sylvan's heart like a blade. Growling a warning low in her throat that would have put any other Were, wolf or not, on their belly, Sylvan leapt across the space between them and pulled Drake down on the heavy wood-framed bed, landing above her with her thighs caging Drake's hips. "I knew you were mine the minute I saw you."

Drake framed Sylvan's face, still searching.

Sylvan rumbled but allowed the scrutiny. "What do you see?"

"An Alpha who might not have let herself claim a human." Drake shuddered. "I'm sorry—I don't know why—"

"Ask your wolf what she feels," Sylvan whispered, kissing Drake's throat. "Weres grow up learning to trust that truth. Our wolves see the world differently than we do in skin. They aren't misguided by convention or pretense. They connect by instinct, choose by nature, love...*mate*...with certainty."

"I know." Drake rubbed her cheek against Sylvan's shoulder. "I feel our bond. I don't know why I even think about what might have happened if I hadn't turned."

Sylvan laughed and pushed down on the bed. She kissed Drake's tight stomach, noting the faintest swelling that hadn't been there the day before. "Maybe they have something to do with it."

Drake groaned. "Oh no. Not already. I refuse to be crazy this entire pregnancy."

"You can be as crazy as you like," Sylvan whispered, rising up to kiss Drake again, "just never doubt I love you. And to answer your question, yes, I loved you before. I would have had you, or no one."

"Ah God. I know that in my heart." Drake brushed her fingers through Sylvan's hair. "How long before they're born?"

"Leo and Nadia said you are physically indistinguishable from a born Were. So sixty days."

Drake jerked. "So soon?" She ran her hand down her belly. "Are they sentient?"

Sylvan nodded. "They will be soon. They'll know us, feel the Pack and each other."

"And they'll look like you."

"Maybe." Sylvan rested her chin on Drake's and grinned. "The hormones in my *victus* carried my DNA and the reproductive catalysts, but your DNA carries the Were traits. They might look like you."

"Hmm." Drake licked at Sylvan's mouth, kissed her. "I can't wait to see you with them."

Sylvan's chest tightened and a surge of adrenaline raced through her. "We can't let anything endanger them. You should stay here—in the den—where you'll all be safe."

"For two months?" Drake asked carefully.

"Even longer would be better. Until they can run fast enough to avoid predators."

"Predators?" Drake's eyes widened. "What predators?"

Sylvan's canines dropped and she snarled. "Other Weres. Humans."

"Weres? Not our Weres." Drake sat up, her body quivering.

Sylvan pulled Drake into her arms. "Wolves are territorial, and I don't trust Bernardo's wolves not to attack any of our young if they come upon them." She caressed Drake's back. "Nothing will hurt them. I swear."

"How soon will they be able to shift? They'll run faster then, be safer."

"I don't know. They won't have any control until they're adolescents. Before then, the pups will shift instinctively if threatened. The more dominant they are, the sooner they shift."

Drake twisted in Sylvan's lap, brushing her breasts over Sylvan's. "Since they're yours, they'll probably shift as soon as they can move."

Sylvan laughed. "Ours. They're ours."

"Yes," Drake murmured, tucking her head in the curve of Sylvan's throat. "And we have others to protect as well. I can't hide away for months, Sylvan."

"I know." Sylvan sighed. "I'm going to the infirmary to talk to Katya and Gray."

"I'd come with you, but I think they might be more comfortable with you alone. I'll talk to Elena about their medical condition and you can brief me after."

Sylvan wrapped her arms around Drake's waist. "Promise you won't leave the Compound without Jace and Jonathan."

"With Lara absent and Niki assigned to guard her, the ranks of your *centuri* are already depleted. You shouldn't reduce them further by assigning me your personal guards," Drake protested.

Thunder rolled through Sylvan's belly. "You are Prima, and pregnant. You should have *all* the *centuri* around you. By rights, I should confine you to the Compound."

Drake raised a brow. "Oh really. In which millennium?"

Sylvan growled. "Don't push me on this. I won't have you at risk."

Drake leaned into her and bit her chin. "I know, and I won't worry you unnecessarily. I'm not planning on going anywhere until I've talked to you, and then I'll take Jace and Jonathan with me. But I need to see the Revniks."

"All right," Sylvan said. "I need to go contact the rest of the Coalition. I want to find out if any of them had any inkling of what was going on in that laboratory in Vermont."

"You actually think they would tell you?"

"Perhaps not, but I can usually tell when they're lying."

"If you need me for any reason, I won't be far."

Sylvan pulled her closer and kissed her hard. "Good. Because I need you again soon."

Drake smiled. "That's a far better way of keeping me close than restricting me to quarters."

Sylvan rumbled. "Whatever it takes."

Sylvan found Elena, the Pack *medicus*, in her small office at the front of the infirmary. Elena looked up as Sylvan stepped through the door, her dark eyes rimmed with shadows. Small, fine-boned, and nondominant, she appeared nonthreatening, but Sylvan knew Elena would fight as fiercely as any of her warriors to protect those in her care.

"Have you had any sleep?" Sylvan asked.

"Not much. It took me most of the night to evaluate both of them, just to be sure there were no acute problems needing attention."

Sylvan closed the door behind her and leaned against it, folding her arms across her chest. "And?"

"They're in bad shape, Alpha," Elena said, sadness and fury streaking through her eyes. "They're both malnourished, as well as having been physically and psychologically abused."

"How?" Sylvan asked, her voice flat and cold as winter ice.

"They've been bound with silver—they have burns around their wrists and arms and waists. Probably chained to a wall."

Sylvan snarled.

"Katya has tears on her neck. They look like bite marks."

"Vampire?" Sylvan growled. Gates and her soldiers had all been outside the installation with her. She hadn't seen any other Vampires inside.

"I think so. And there's more," Elena said wearily. "They both have multiple puncture sites at various places on their bodies where blood and tissue specimens have been taken. They've also been… manipulated in some way—electrostimulants, I would guess—to force emissions."

Sylvan paced, her lips drawn back and her canines flashing. Silver streaked her bare chest and abdomen, hardened nipples tightened over the prominent muscles in her chest. "Are they permanently damaged?"

"Physically? I don't know. I don't think so." Elena came around her desk, shoulders drooping. "Psychologically? Quite possibly. The silver prevented them from shifting, and then when Gray did last night, after so long—you saw her. Her control is gone. She shifted again early this morning and was barely restrainable. Misha was in the building and was able to talk her into shifting back, but I'm concerned we're going to have to tranquilize her."

"Don't do that," Sylvan ordered. "She's already had too many drugs pumped into her, they both have. I could smell it on them."

"I know, but I can't let her attack someone. She's strong, Alpha."

"Why didn't you call me?"

"It happened quickly, and I knew you and the Prima were resting. She needs all your attention now."

Sylvan growled and halted a few inches in front of Elena. "I know what my mate needs. And I know what my Pack needs. Don't keep anything from me about any of them again."

"I understand," Elena said quietly.

Sylvan sighed, gripped Elena's shoulders, and pulled her close. She kissed her temple. "I don't doubt your medical decisions, but when one of us is hurt, they need me more than ever."

"We all need you more than ever." Elena rested her cheek against Sylvan's chest and held on with both arms around her shoulders. "Are you going to talk to them?"

"Yes."

"They'll want to please you. If they seem to be growing more agitated, more stressed, please stop. They've already suffered enough."

Sylvan stroked Elena's thick, tangled dark hair. "I know they have. But they're safe here. And we'll go at their pace as long as we can."

"Thank you, Alpha."

Sylvan nodded. "Call Misha to stand by. She, Katya, and Gray were all in the same *sentrie* training class. It might help them to have someone their own age around after."

"I will."

"And you should call your mate and spend some time with him. You'll feel better."

Elena laughed. "You're probably right. But then, you always are."

"Go call Roger," Sylvan murmured. With her Pack under assault, she needed to be right now more than ever.

CHAPTER FOUR

Sensing the Vampire approaching outside her inner sanctum, Francesca gave one last swipe of her tongue to the bite in the smooth, warm flesh and raised her head from the human's thigh. *What is it, Daniela?*

"I'm sorry, Mistress," Daniela said from the hall outside Francesca's boudoir. "A phone call."

The aide-in-training was a youngling, recently risen, and not yet able to telepath her thoughts consistently. She had barely matured enough to remain aware during daylight hours, even deep in the protected caverns of Francesca's lair. Sighing, Francesca turned away from the naked human stretched out on his back in the center of her bed. Her eyes met Michel's lust-laced gaze across his chest, and she smiled. "Go ahead, darling. I won't be long."

Her *senechal* exhaled, her small tight breasts streaked with crimson from the toying bites she'd scattered across the human's abdomen, her sensuous mouth compressed. "I await your pleasure."

Francesca ran her carnelian-tipped nail along Michel's jaw. She'd let her enforcer fuck her after Michel returned from the lab where the humans were studying captive Weres, but she hadn't let her feed. She'd discovered centuries past that the way to secure the fealty of her followers was to bestow favors—and pleasure—at unexpected moments. "I do love how loyal you are. You're still hungry even after having that young Were, aren't you darling?"

"I hunger for you."

"Do you." Michel was the oldest of her line, a powerful Vampire in her own right who could easily head a Clan—or lead a rebellion—but she continued to serve as Francesca's second. Francesca kissed Michel and loosed her erotic spell, letting her thrall wash over Michel and the blood servant. Michel shuddered. The human writhed, his erection straining between his thighs. "Feed. Your pleasure will be mine."

Snarling, Michel gripped the human's head and bared his throat. She lowered her mouth, plunging her incisors into his neck. She groaned and swallowed. He whimpered in ecstasy. Francesca stroked Michel's back, letting her fingers linger on her rhythmically thrusting ass, absorbing the tendrils of Michel's orgasm, the shared release flowing through her consciousness, augmenting her hunger. When the vicarious pleasure had honed her need to a razor's edge, she turned to the door. "Come."

The iron-banded, arched oak door swung open on soundless hinges and Daniela glided into the room. Cinnamon skin, mahogany hair, deep green eyes—she was beautiful, intelligent, and submissive without being fragile. She'd been a blood servant since she'd been twenty, had accepted Francesca's bond at twenty-five, and had petitioned to be turned immediately. Francesca had agreed to turn her as soon as the blood union was complete. Daniela's body was still temptingly fresh, bearing the last vestiges of her fading mortality in the softness of her lush breasts and gently curving hips, but her control was fragile. The scent of blood and lust that soaked the air enveloped her, and her eyes shimmered with scarlet flames. Her nipples probed her sheer white silk shirt like ice picks. She dipped her head, incisors gleaming and leather-covered thighs trembling. Her need was ambrosia on Francesca's tongue. "Mistress. There is a call from someone on your priority list. A Dr. Standish."

"Really," Francesca murmured, slowly massaging the human's cock. When he climaxed, the flood of adrenaline in his blood would spike Michel's pleasure. "Did she state her business?"

"Personal."

Francesca laughed. No doubt. Veronica Standish had called her just the night before, seeking assistance for one of her experiments. She'd been vague, but Michel had reported in detail. Dr. Standish was involved in some very secret and very illegal experimentation on Weres, and that knowledge was power. Now Standish was calling again, and the thought of having the doctor in her debt sent a frisson of satisfaction through Francesca's blood. After so many lifetimes, the lure of blood had taken second place to the thrill of power. She enjoyed feeding, but enjoyed feeding off the submission of others even more. She leaned over and kissed the host, the stimulants in her mouth adding to the ones Michel injected into his blood. He cried out hoarsely, his cock arcing violently. She let him go as he came, stroking Michel's midnight hair and running her thumb along the sharp blade of Michel's cheek. "You'd better stop soon, darling. He's close to depleted."

Michel groaned, an agonized gasp of need, but she pulled away, her flat red eyes blind with bloodlust, a trickle of scarlet coursing from the corner of her mouth.

Francesca kissed away the blood trail and pushed Michel onto her back. She kissed her throat and then her breasts, sliding her hand between Michel's legs. "I have to take a call, darling." She slipped her fingers into her, a deep hard thrust of ownership, and Michel orgasmed in her hand. "Rest now. We'll feed together when I return."

She left Michel staring at the ornate carved ceiling above the bed and crossed to where Daniela quivered in the doorway, her face contorted and her eyes glazed. Daniela would have fed with all the other Risen at sunrise, but any Vampire in Francesca's presence would be stimulated by her unshielded sexual thrall. And she hadn't bothered to shield herself. Daniela pressed her back against the doorjamb as Francesca approached, her agonized gaze taking in Francesca's nude body.

"You did well to come for me," Francesca murmured, pausing inches from her.

"Thank you, Mistress," Daniela gasped, her throat working convulsively.

"Kneel."

Daniela dropped to her knees and Francesca threaded her fingers into the thick dark waves at the base of Daniela's neck. She pulled the young Vampire's face to the cleft between her legs. "Drink."

Whimpering, Daniela closed her mouth over Francesca's sex and sucked frantically. Francesca threw her head back, laughing quietly as her orgasm rippled through her like sunlight washing down a mountainside. She had not seen sunlight in a hundred lifetimes, a trade she would make a hundred times over for the power she had now.

❖

Sylvan followed the scent of her injured young down the hall and knocked on the closed door. Any other time she would have entered unannounced, but she didn't want to startle them. Sophia answered immediately and stepped outside, partially closing the door.

"Alpha," Sophia said, dipping her head for an instant.

"How are they?"

"Restless. I can't get either of them to eat. They seem to have an aversion to food."

Fury roiled in Sylvan's chest. "Why would that be?"

"Elena could probably tell you better than—"

"I'm asking you."

Sophia straightened and the fatigue in her eyes dropped away. "The blood tests we've run indicate they've been drugged chronically, probably via their food and water. Their respiratory emissions also show breakdown products of silver. Their entire environment, from the food they ate to the air they breathed, was a prison. My guess is that their wolves will reject anything they haven't killed themselves, and they're too weak to hunt."

Sylvan's claws shot out and she threw her head back, struggling to contain a howl of rage. Sophia gasped, white pelt rippling beneath her skin, rising to the call of Sylvan's wolf. Sylvan leashed her wolf, her jaws aching with the effort of holding her back. "Prepare the food trays and bring them in. They'll eat for me. As soon as they're stronger, I'll take them out to hunt."

Sophia flicked her gaze away, then fleetingly met Sylvan's eyes. "Alpha, if I might make a suggestion?"

Sylvan's wolf paced in furious circles, demanding retribution. She wanted to track down whoever had ordered her young to be tortured, drag him to the ground by his throat, and tear him limb from limb. She would, before this was over. She growled.

"About the young," Sophia said gently.

A soothing hand brushed over Sylvan's wolf and she paused in her incensed stalking. Drake was the only one who could truly calm her, but Sophia was exceptional among all the Weres in the Pack. She was Omega—neither dominant nor submissive—a peacekeeper, and her presence would settle anyone near her. She was also likely to absorb the rage and pain of others until she risked being battered herself. Sylvan ground her teeth, forcing her wolf to heel. "Tell me."

"I know what it's like to distrust everyone, even myself. They're confused. They may fear you."

"I am their Alpha."

"Yes, and probably the only one they will be able to trust, perhaps ever—but until they can, they're dangerous. Especially Gray."

Sylvan snarled. "They are mine. I will care for them."

"Gray's shifts are unpredictable, but she's fighting them. I think she was forced to shift in the lab."

"She won't say?"

"She's not talking. Neither of them is."

"They need to." Sylvan cupped Sophia's cheek and lifted her chin. The skin beneath her eyes was purplish, her cheeks hollow, her color ashen beneath the summer bronze. "So do you. You're not well." Sophia tried to look away but Sylvan held her jaw more firmly. She breathed in, catching the subtle wave of pheromones on her tongue. "You're in heat and suppressing it."

Sophia shuddered. "Please. When you touch me—"

Sylvan released her. She was mated and usually mated Weres had no effect on Weres in heat, but her touch would always produce a physical response. She should have sensed Sophia's need instantly. "What are you doing to dampen the call?"

"Nothing prohibited. Just the hormonal blockers the soldiers use when they're posted alone for long periods." Sophia hugged herself, struggling for composure.

"More than you should be taking if I didn't sense your need instantly. Why?"

"I don't seek a mate. You know why."

Sylvan sighed and lightly caressed her cheek. "Why haven't you found one of the less dominant Weres to tangle with? They won't attempt a mating unless you offer."

"Hardly fair to them." Sophia smiled wanly.

"That's not true. Tangling with a female in heat is never a hardship." Sylvan caught her gaze. "If you don't, the buildup of hormones will weaken you. You know that."

"I'll be all right. I'll do what needs to be done, just not yet."

"Have you talked to your mother about this?"

"No. Please, Alpha. I'll be all right."

"We need you healthy, Sophia. Don't put this off."

"Of course." Sophia colored. "Thank you, Alpha."

"There's nothing to thank me for. You're mine. Don't forget that."

"I never will." Sophia sidled around Sylvan and headed down the hall. "I'll be with Elena if you need me."

Sylvan let her go, eased into the sickroom, and closed the door behind her.

A single shaded bulb in the center of the ceiling cast pale light on the two beds at right angles to each other at the rear of the room. Katya and Gray, both naked, had kicked off the plain white sheets. Katya lay curled in a ball, her arms around her middle, her eyes closed, giving no sign of sensing Sylvan's entrance. Shock, exhaustion, malnutrition had dulled her protective instincts. Gray sat with her back pressed to the wall and tracked Sylvan's movements as she walked toward her, eyes wary and just this side of challenging.

Sylvan crouched between the two beds, reaching to touch both young at once. "You are my wolves," she said steadily. "You're home now, and safe. Feel me, feel the Pack." She let her power rise and Katya whimpered, shifting in her sleep until a slender brown wolf with white-tipped ears and muzzle lay comma'd in the center of the bed, panting softly. Gray fought not to shift, rumbling in her chest. She absorbed Sylvan's call, her teeth grinding, claws erupting from her fingertips, a wash of charcoal pelt sliding over her abdomen. She pulled away from Sylvan's hand, her breath ragged and uneven.

"Come to me," Sylvan murmured and Gray snarled. She was strong, but she couldn't be allowed to defy the call of her Alpha. She needed to reconnect with the Pack. She needed the security of belonging. Sylvan held Gray's gaze, staring her down until Gray's gaze slid to the side. Still she did not shift. Sylvan unleashed the full force of her call. "You are my wolf. *Come to me.*"

Still struggling to resist, Gray shimmered in midshift, her pelt sliding and receding over her torso, her face morphing and changing back. She'd damage herself if she fought Sylvan's call much longer. Sylvan grasped her by the neck and pulled her from the bed, forcing her down on her back on the floor. She straddled her and stared into the wild dark eyes. "You *will* submit to me. I am your Alpha." Gray arched, a plaintive whine breaking from her throat. She shifted and a charcoal wolf shuddered beneath Sylvan.

You're safe, my wolf. Sylvan sank back on her heels and pulled the wolf into her lap, tucking Gray's head against her shoulder. She ran her fingers down Gray's back, over her muzzle, behind her ears. She rubbed her cheek against Gray's head. *You're safe with me. You're strong now, but I need you to be strong in skin. Find your strength, Gray.*

The wolf shivered and whined again.

Sylvan sat with her back against the bed, holding the wolf in her arms, letting Gray absorb her strength, letting her feel her connection to all the hundreds of hearts beating in the Pack. *It's time to come back, Gray. You're safe. Do it now.*

The wolf tensed, shimmered, and after a few convulsive seconds, Gray shifted to skin and lay curled up in Sylvan's arms, her breasts against Sylvan's chest, her cheek on Sylvan's shoulder.

"Alpha," Gray moaned, her mouth against Sylvan's throat. Heat poured from her skin and pheromones erupted from her pores. She was young, dominant, and aroused.

Sylvan lifted her and laid her gently on the bed, stepping back. "Look at me."

Gray focused on Sylvan's face, her eyes clearing.

"You're home. You're safe. Do you hear me?"

"Yes, Alpha," Gray murmured, licking her lips.

Sylvan nodded, bent over, and brushed her fingers through Gray's hair. "I need you. The Pack needs you. Can you stand strong, my wolf?"

Gray's stomach contracted, her thighs tight as iron bands. She sucked in a breath. "Yes, Alpha."

"Good. First you'll eat, then we'll hunt."

Chapter Five

Sophia hurried down the deserted corridor to the pharmacy and pushed inside. She halted abruptly when she realized the room wasn't empty. Elena and the Prima stood on the far side of the room, computer printouts in their hands. Of course. Reviewing the test results from the early-morning blood she had drawn from Katya and Gray.

"I'm sorry to disturb you." Sophia backed up quickly, reaching behind her for the doorknob.

"That's all right," Elena said. "I was just about to call you. Is there anything new?"

"No, I'm afraid not. I can't get them to eat anything, and they keep pulling out their intravenous lines."

An ominous rumble rose from Drake's chest. "The Alpha is with them?"

"Yes," Sophia said, shivering although the room was warm. She glanced at the locked drug case in the far corner, her stomach cramping, muscles quivering. The hormonal suppressants were wearing off faster and faster every hour. She'd hoped this time she'd be able to anticipate when she was about to go into heat and blunt the process with a megadose of drugs. She should have known by her urgent, uncontrollable desire to tangle with Niki yesterday that she was close, but she'd thought her irrational need was because *Niki* was in need. Niki, the only Were in the Pack who refused to answer her call when she couldn't hide it, was the one she could never completely deny. She'd been caught up in Niki and hadn't started the drugs soon enough. Not that they could completely control her biological urgency for sex. Nothing prevented the insistent need to tangle, but at least if the rest of her system was functioning normally, she could stand the unrelenting arousal. When her heart was racing, her skin drenched in sweat, her stomach tied into knots, she didn't have enough mental control to contain her need. And she had to, somehow. She'd tripled the dose of drugs the *sentries* took when they were alone for weeks at a time and went into heat, but she needed more. She needed more now.

"Is there any evidence of incisions?" Drake asked.

Sophia jolted back to attention, forcing her mind to what really mattered. Taking care of Katya and Gray. "Katya has a short vertical incision just above her pubic bone."

Drake's brows drew down and her growl intensified. "Laparoscopy?"

"Probably," Sophia said.

"We'll need to ultrasound their ovaries," Drake said. "If they've had a recent biopsy or harvesting, we should see swelling."

"I don't know that we can get close enough to them to do that," Sophia said.

"We won't force anything on them," Drake said, "but it has to be done. In the meantime, you both look like you could use some rest."

"You'll need help with the procedure," Elena said.

"We'll let the Alpha decide on the timing. If she doesn't think they're ready, we'll have to wait. I'll call one of you to assist." Drake slowed on her way to the door, her dark eyes moving slowly over Sophia's face. "You need more than sleep. Are you all right?"

"Yes, Prima," Sophia said, a featherlight sensation of heat passing through her, almost as if invisible fingers had stroked her. She held her breath, searching to recapture the feeling, and then a glow suffused her consciousness. She gasped, and a flood of joy erased her pain and disappointment. "Prima! You're…How wonderful!"

Drake smiled wryly. "I am, and thank you." She glanced at Elena. "I gather this is going to go on pretty much continuously?"

Elena nodded.

"Maybe we should just make a mass announcement," Drake said.

Elena grinned. "Oh no, Prima. We wouldn't want to rob anyone of that first exciting instant when they recognize a new member of the Pack."

"Two," Sophia whispered. "Two of them. And so strong already."

"You can sense them that clearly?"

"Yes," Sophia said, glancing at Elena.

Elena said, "Sophia is a very strong empath. She could sense her Packmates even when she was young."

"Hmm." Drake slid her hands in the pockets of her BDUs and rocked back on her heels, her eyes going distant as if she waged some internal debate. "How much can you tell about them?"

"I'm not sure I should say without the Alpha—"

"I understand, but you can be sure if you know, she'll know too. Just...are they healthy? Can you tell that?"

"Oh yes," Sophia said, her awareness heightened now that she was seeking out the young. Wonder such as she hadn't felt since the first time she'd shifted and run through columns of sunlight under towering trees streamed through her, and she reveled in long-forgotten pleasure. These young would bring the Pack new energy and vigor. "Very strong." She laughed. "I don't think I've ever sensed unborn pups so early before."

Drake rolled her eyes. "Well, of course. They are the Alpha's young after all."

"Do you want to know—"

"You can tell?"

"Yes, I think so."

"Not without Sylvan." Drake cupped Sophia's chin. "You've told me what I most needed to know. Now do you want to tell me what's wrong?"

"I..." Sophia drew a shaky breath. "With your permission, Prima, I'd rather not."

"We'll have need of you more than ever in the days ahead. We'll need you strong."

Sophia nodded. "I understand. Thank you for trusting me."

Drake drew her close. "I've known you for a long time, well before I was Prima. You knew me as human. If you need someone to talk to, I'm here. Friend to friend."

Sophia's throat tightened. She had friends in the Pack—but none who could really understand what it was to be an outsider, even if she could tell them what kept her apart. Drake, more than anyone else, would know. She rested her head on Drake's shoulder, allowing herself brief comfort. "Thank you."

"Not necessary. I know something of what you feel." Drake hugged her quickly and, grasping her shoulders gently, put distance between them. "The Alpha is coming. She's a little possessive these days."

Sophia's heart jumped into her throat. All Weres with pregnant mates became irrationally possessive, but the Alpha? She took another step back just as the door swung open with a bang. Sylvan strode in, a warning snarl reverberating in her throat. Drake intercepted her.

"How are Katya and Gray?" Drake asked.

Sylvan drew up short, her hot gold gaze sweeping the room. Her canines gleamed against her wide, cruelly beautiful mouth. "You are well?"

Drake caressed Sylvan's chest and angled her body against Sylvan's side, her bare arm nestled against Sylvan's breast. "I'm fine. Sophia tells me we're all very healthy."

"No one should touch you unless I'm present." Sylvan focused a predatory gaze on Sophia, who kept her place but lowered her gaze to Sylvan's shoulder.

"Sophia," Drake said calmly, continuing to stroke Sylvan, "tell the Alpha what you told me."

"The pups are broadcasting already." Sophia couldn't help but smile. "They're eager to run."

Sylvan glanced at Drake and grinned, her eyes shimmering to blue and her wolf calming. "You'll be busy with them."

Drake threaded her arms around Sylvan's waist and kissed her. "We'll be busy."

Sophia couldn't help but feel the bond of tenderness and passion between them, and her joy was tinged with heartache, knowing she could never share a mate bond, the final irrevocable joining. She backed away until her shoulder accidently touched Elena's. When Elena rested a hand at the base of her spine, the unexpected tenderness made her gasp. She had not been intimate with anyone in weeks, not even a casual tangle after a run. The absence of physical touch was a severe deprivation for a Were, and her body responded instantly. The blaze smoldering in her depths flared and she gritted her teeth to hold back a moan. She edged away. "I'm sorry."

"No," Elena said, "I am. I wasn't thinking."

Sylvan watched them from across the room, her eyes narrowed. "I need food for the young. And you two need to talk." She slid her hand around the back of Drake's neck and dragged her close for another kiss. "I'm taking them out for a run. Don't leave the Compound until I return."

Drake slipped her fingertips beneath the waistband of Sylvan's jeans and nipped her lip. "I won't. Stop snarling."

Sylvan snarled again, but a smile softened her mouth. "Once they hunt, they'll be stronger. You can talk to them then."

"Good. Be careful."

"Always." Sylvan kissed her hard, spun around, and pushed out through the door.

Drake said to Elena, "I'll be at headquarters if anything else turns up in the lab work."

"Of course. We'll let you know right away." When Drake had left, Elena said quietly, "What you're doing, it's not safe."

"I'm not taking anything the other females don't sometimes use."

"Not in the same quantities. And we don't really know how the drugs will react in your system. You can't be sure your body is metabolizing the chemicals. You could be inviting a dangerous buildup of toxins."

Sophia turned away, humiliated. "I don't have any choice."

"You do. I can think of a dozen unmated Weres who would be more than happy to answer your need."

"And what if I lose control?" Sophia dug her claws into her upper arms, focusing on the pain and not the terror flooding through her. "What if I bite? What if we mate?"

Elena came toward her, careful not to touch her, sensitive to how agonizing the slightest touch could be to a female in need. "And what if they welcomed your bite? What if you found a mate and you had to give up being alone?"

"You think that's why?"

"No, not entirely. I know why," Elena said quietly. "I was here when your parents brought you, remember?"

"I'm sorry," Sophia said. "I do remember. Of course I remember. I remember how kind you were to me. I remember you sitting by my bedside, wiping the fever sweat from my forehead, telling me over and over that I was going to be all right."

"And you are all right. You're a strong, healthy Were, and we all love you."

"Almost healthy," Sophia murmured.

"We're not certain. You know that. And what of your heart?" Elaine asked. "We are more than our instincts. Our wolves may choose by instinct, but we mate with more than our bodies. We mate with our hearts and our minds. What about that?"

Sophia thought of Niki, of the pain in her eyes and the power in her body. She shuddered, remembering the feel of Niki's arms around her, Niki's hard body pressed against her back, her hot breath against her neck. She'd wanted to give Niki her throat. She'd almost begged Niki to let her answer her need. She would have accepted Niki's bite, returned it. And she would've despised herself. "I can't take the chance."

Elena gestured to the drug cabinet. "This is not the way."

"I know," Sophia murmured. Her system was rebelling, rejecting the drugs and possibly compromising her at the same time. She'd been through unrequited heat before and survived. She could again. She'd have to. She would not draw another Were into a mate bond that could prove deadly. "I'll find another way."

Niki paced circles in the small room, aching to shift, needing to run. Her hunger had been sated by the release ignited by Lara's bite, but the Alpha's call still echoed in her depths. The mindless craze of bloodlust could never satisfy the needs of her soul. Her wolf craved the touch of another wolf. She paused, feeling the familiar tingle of her wolf rising. Pelt feathered the midline of her belly. Her clitoris tensed. She breathed deeply and quivered. The tang of potent pheromones teased her tongue. Not the Alpha's call. She rumbled, her canines lifting her lip. Beside her, Lara was deep in her daytime somnolence and defenseless. Sunset was still half a day away, but they were sequestered in the heart of the Compound. No harm would come to Lara here.

Niki strode to the door and slid out into the hall. Max leaned against the wall across from her. While she was safeguarding Lara, Max had taken her place as Sylvan's general. A necessary move, but a blow to her heart she could barely tolerate.

"Good to see you, *Imperator*," Max said, his craggy face breaking into a smile.

Niki bristled. "Shouldn't I be calling you that?"

He ducked his head at the challenge in her voice. Like all *centuri*, he was dominant, but Niki was subordinate only to the Alpha, and now the Alpha's mate. "I stand for you by the Alpha's command, but I will never take your place. We miss you."

"Just see that no harm comes to the Alpha," Niki snarled, "and guard Lara."

"I'll be here until you return."

Niki loped down the hall and out onto the wide split-log porch, drawn by a call that struck deep, inciting her wolf. Movement across the Compound drew her attention, and she sprang down onto the hard-packed earth, the ache in her belly exploding into furious need. Her heart hammered in her chest and her skin glistened with sex-sheen. Sophia leaned against a column on the barracks porch, her head tilted back, her eyes closed. Her arms hugged her middle and she trembled with need.

Niki leapt, clearing the distance between them in one powerful lunge.

CHAPTER SIX

*K*ill quickly. Kill clean.
The Alpha's voice resonated in her mind as Gray raced through chest-high grass in the upland meadow, bearing down on her prey. The Alpha was running nearby, and so was Katya, but all her senses were fixed on the shimmering form just ahead of her, leaping and jumping. She hadn't run free in weeks, hadn't felt the wind in her face, hadn't scented rich earth and pungent pine and the tang of fox and rabbit. Now she was strong again, and she was never going to let anyone catch her. Never let anyone chain her. She gathered all her strength and burst forward, striking her prey on the soft underside of its throat, biting deep, bringing it down swiftly and breaking its neck with a powerful twist of her shoulders. Quick. Clean. Her kill.

Gray raised her head and howled, claiming her victory. The Alpha loped down from the ridge and Katya drew up on her flank, coming to share in the kill. Gray swung her head around and snarled at Katya, warning her away. Katya showed her teeth. Gray bristled and crouched, her tail stiff. Katya was too dominant, a threat. The Alpha arrowed through the waving green stalks, the tips of her silver ruff gleaming gold in the late-afternoon sunlight. She growled and shouldered Gray aside and circled the kill. Gray held her ground, rumbling deep in her chest, and the Alpha snarled, pinning her with a fixed stare. Gray looked away and Katya crept nearer. The Alpha sniffed the kill and Gray rumbled again.

The Alpha whirled on her and charged, snapping and growling. Her jaws grazed Gray's muzzle and with a startled yip, she backed away. She raised her lip and the Alpha stalked her, ears stiff, hackles raised.

You'll eat when I'm ready for you to eat.

The Alpha's command struck a chord deep inside her, igniting a primitive need for her to obey. The Alpha was everything she trusted, everything she depended on to bring order to a wild and dangerous world. Gray lowered her tail. The Alpha circled the kill again and shouldered first Gray, then Katya forward. *Eat.*

Katya waited while Gray took the first bite, tearing off the choicest portion. Then Katya fell on the carcass, and together, they shared in the kill. Despite her hunger, Gray stopped every few seconds and checked over her shoulder, watching for danger. Nowhere was safe.

I'm here. I will protect you. Eat.

Whining softly, Gray acknowledged the Alpha's order, but she was still uneasy.

Sylvan sat far enough from the kill site to see in all directions, watching for human hunters or roving bands of cat Weres from the mountains to the east. She didn't eat. She'd hunted with Drake that morning. She watched Gray carefully, alert to a resurgence of her aggressive posture. Weres, regardless of their place in the hierarchy, were not usually aggressive over food. Gray had won the right to own the kill, but the natural thing would have been for her to share without contest. Her show of aggression toward Katya and reluctance to submit to her Alpha's authority were signs she was losing her Pack connection. If she could not find her place in the Pack, she would have to leave, and she would not survive as a lone wolf. Not many Weres could, and those who managed it were those who had never formed strong Pack bonds to begin with. Those circumstances were rare and usually a result of a very young Were having no access to the Pack at a critical stage of development. Every few generations, a very dominant Were would leave to start their own Pack, but as territory was scarce, they often failed. Even the most dominant wolf Weres usually remained with the Pack, content to serve as *centuri* or *sentries* or to perform some critical function in human society. It was always hard to let one of the Pack go, and Sylvan and her mother and the Alpha before her would do anything possible to prevent losing one of the Pack to the wilderness. If Gray broke with the Pack, Sylvan could not allow her to stay in Timberwolf territory, and she was too young to command her own Pack. She would die alone.

Sylvan grumbled, reminding the young hunters she was nearby. Reminding them they were not alone. Reminding them they were hers. She was not going to lose Gray.

❖

Sophia felt the air change, as if the atmosphere was suddenly charged with electricity. The hairs on her arms and the back of her neck lifted the way they did when a high wind blew down from the mountain, carrying storm clouds and rain. Her muscles tingled and blood rushed through her veins, stirring her wolf, calling her out to run. Her pelt streamed to the surface, pressing against the undersurface of her skin, threatening to burst free. The urge to tangle, to thrash and bite and fuck and join, knifed through her so sharply she wanted to howl. Moaning, she squeezed her arms tighter around her middle as if that would dull the churning desire. Her wolf coiled within her, ready to spring, ready to launch herself at the wolf careening down on her. Her wolf was demanding she tangle, demanding to be filled, to be tied. To mate.

Her call was answered with a resonant growl.

"No," Sophia gasped, her eyes snapping open. The porch shuddered under her bare feet and a blur of red-gray dropped into a crouch in front of her. Niki. Frenzied, coated in pheromones, her wolf riding her hard, unleashed and dangerous and so beautiful. The muscles in Niki's legs bunched, absorbing the shock of her landing, and Sophia imagined those strong hips pumping between her spread thighs, Niki's clitoris sliding along her hot cleft, making her come, forcing her *victus* to explode in torrents down the carved columns of Niki's legs. Her canines burst out and she fixed on the sculpted muscles in Niki's shoulders. She wanted to bury herself there, leave her mark. But she couldn't. She *couldn't*.

"Oh God, Niki," Sophia whispered. "What—"

"You called me," Niki growled, her cheekbones standing out in sharp relief, her eyes half-wolf, slanted and sharp, the dense green of a forest after a storm. Her breasts were tight, her nipples hard, dusky discs, her abdomen a staircase of stone painted the color of blood. She straightened to her full height and stalked a step closer. "You've been calling me since yesterday."

"No." Sophia stumbled back and felt the porch post at her back. Her sex tightened and she couldn't stop the whine breaking from her throat. She fought to contain her wolf, but she was losing the struggle. The drugs were useless, overpowered by the hormonal storm of her heat. She'd denied herself too many times. But she was too close to abandoning all control. She'd never be able to contain her need to bite, to join and finish completely, and she couldn't risk inciting a bond. Somehow she had to drive Niki away. "No, no. I didn't mean to call you, I—"

"You never do," Niki snarled, bearing down on her, seeming so much larger even though she was only an inch or two taller. And then she was up against her, one arm high up on the post above Sophia's head, the other sliding around her hip, pinning her in place. Heat poured from her naked torso. Fire raged in her eyes, and her mouth—oh God, her mouth—was so gorgeous. The tips of her canines gleamed like pearl daggers and Sophia wanted them against her skin. "You never mean to call me, but you do."

"Oh," Sophia gasped, arching into her, tilting her head back to bare her neck. She couldn't help herself. She couldn't hold back, couldn't chain her wolf or her need.

"Why is it you never want to call me?" Niki's canines extended fully, her words now only a guttural growl. She sniffed Sophia's neck, licked the column of muscle running from her shoulder to her ear. "Why?"

"Please," Sophia whispered. Niki's teeth scraped along her throat and Sophia's legs went weak. She ached, mindlessly, and Niki was all she could feel. All she wanted. Her claws extended, ready to hold Niki to her, over her, inside her. "Please, Niki. I can't—"

"You can't what?" Niki rumbled. She kissed Sophia's jaw and thrust her pelvis into the valley between Sophia's thighs. "You can't tangle with me? Who, then?" Niki growled and nipped Sophia's lower lip. "You called *me*."

"No," Sophia said desperately. "No, I couldn't help—I couldn't stop—"

"I want you. I've always wanted you." Niki rubbed her breasts over Sophia's, her claws lightly scraping Sophia's belly.

The tiny scratches shot tendrils of pleasure between Sophia's legs and she whimpered. "I can't. Not now. I can't—"

"I can smell you, taste you," Niki said, licking her again. "You're ready."

"Just let me go," Sophia moaned, but she opened for her inside. Filled for her. "Not now...not now—"

A furious roar resounded across the clearing. "Get away from her!"

Niki whipped her head around, snarling a warning. Dasha Baran charged across the Compound, growling a challenge. Niki coiled to attack the dominant *sentrie* lieutenant, putting herself between Sophia and the challenger.

"Niki, no!" Sophia grabbed her, tried to hold her back.

Niki was past hearing. She was done bending to the will of others. She would give her throat to the Alpha, but only the Alpha. She had already given up her place leading the *centuri*, had subjugated herself to a Vampire's bite, but she would not give up this female to another. She'd given up too much already, everything that mattered to her, everything she thought she understood about herself and her life and her place in the world. She was done surrendering. She would have this female, and she would have her now. Niki reveled in the raw edge of pain as she shifted, snarling as her bones morphed and her wolf ascended, roaring with the glorious surge of power. She launched from the porch, eager for combat. She wasn't much older than Dasha, but she was stronger, more dominant, and Dasha was a few seconds slower in her shift. Niki hit her midshift in the center of her torso with all four legs, claws extended and jaws snapping. She rolled the smaller brown wolf and clamped onto her throat before Dasha could protect her vulnerable, soft underbelly. But Dasha was strong and agile, and her claws emerged as they fell onto the hard-packed earth. Claws dug gouges into Niki's belly, tearing through fur and skin and shredding muscles. Niki ignored the pain, closing her jaws tighter on Dasha's windpipe, shaking her head, trying to crush the air from her lungs. Another wolf struck her shoulder out of nowhere and dislodged her hold just enough for Dasha to break free.

In a fury, Niki rolled away and swung around, ready to tear into the interloper. A white wolf with turquoise eyes planted herself between Niki and Dasha, offering no challenge, emitting no growl, telegraphing only calm strength. Sophia. Niki lifted her lip, growled a warning.

She wouldn't hurt her, but she would not let herself be calmed. She would not be neutered now, and not by this wolf. *She* would answer Sophia's call, her, her and no one else. Dasha was on her feet again, blood soaking her ruff, her eyes wild with pain and sex frenzy. They both wanted Sophia, and one of them would die here. Niki lunged at Sophia, feigning an attack, trying to drive her away, but Sophia held her ground. She whined, not a frightened submissive cry, but a coaxing, imploring plea.

Sophia wanted mercy, but Niki had no mercy left. Only rage. Niki bunched her shoulders, growled a warning.

Sophia dug her claws into the earth, holding Niki's gaze, no anger in her eyes, only pain. Niki's heart tightened, but her wolf clamored for blood. She wanted to hurt the wolf that challenged her. She didn't want to be the one hurting anymore.

Dasha circled out from behind Sophia, lips curled back, hackles raised, rumbling in continued challenge. Dasha would not back down. She was too lost in the frenzy, wanting to claim Sophia, wanting to displace Niki from her position in the Pack. No more. Niki would give no more. Niki charged and Dasha leapt. They crashed in midair, jaws clashing, claws raking, filling the Compound with wild roars. Somewhere in the distance, a door slammed open and another wolf vaulted into the center of the Compound, huge, black, midnight eyes as hot as molten lava.

Enough! Drake growled. *Stand down.*

Niki snapped her jaws closed on Dasha's foreleg, and Dasha whimpered, thrashing and struggling to escape. Claws raked Niki's muzzle, tearing open the flesh beneath her eye. Pain exploded through her, but her fury blunted the agony. She was close now, close to a kill.

Drake charged. Sophia tried to intercept her, racing into the melee, but the other wolves were larger, heavier, and she was no fighter. Drake landed heavily on Niki's back, her huge jaws closing on Niki's neck. Her weight rolled Niki for an instant and Niki let go of Dasha's leg. Drake dragged her down and mounted her, and Niki snapped and clawed, lashing out, wild to get out from under the big black wolf.

Niki, hold your wolf. Niki! Drake roared, pinning Niki down by her throat. *Stand down!*

Niki's senses filled with the power of the Prima, and the command echoed in her blood and her bones and her every cell—demanding she obey. She struggled to calm her wolf but she was too far gone, too wild for Sophia, too enraged by Dasha's challenge. She thrashed and bucked and her canines caught Drake's shoulder. Blood sprayed in her face and she tasted life. Rich, sweet, strong, and pure. Young. The Alpha's young.

Niki howled and gave up her throat, prepared to die.

CHAPTER SEVEN

Niki went limp, tilting her muzzle back to surrender her throat. Drake relaxed her jaws but continued to straddle her, her heart pounding wildly, her breath coming in sharp gasps. She wasn't certain she could trust Niki not to go after Dasha or someone else if she released her. She wasn't sure Niki was in control of her wolf, or even in control of her own mind. The scent of pheromones and sex frenzy and mating heat blanketed the clearing with a thick cloud of stimulants that would make any wolf in the vicinity lose control. Add to that *which* female was in heat, and she was surprised Niki had been able to bring her wolf to heel at all. From behind her a chorus of growls signaled the arrival of the *centuri*, racing from all corners of the Compound to coalesce in a snarling circle around her. If she didn't settle them down before they smelled her blood under all the blood spilled by Niki and Dasha, they would tear Niki apart. Beneath her, Niki panted, her stomach board-rigid, her sex, hot and full to bursting, pressed to Drake's belly.

Drake started to ease her weight away, hoping if Niki felt less threatened she'd recover her sanity. A rush of fevered power washed over her and she halted midstride, her body going rigid. Sylvan.

Sylvan was racing toward the clearing, broadcasting mindless fury. The crack of trees branches snapping as Sylvan forged a path straight to Drake ricocheted through the Compound like gunshots. Her roar split the air like thunder. Drake shuddered under the mental onslaught of her mate's wrath. She reached out to touch Sylvan's mind, to reassure her, but met only red-hot rage. Sylvan's wolf was in total control—no semblance of reason remained in Sylvan's consciousness. Niki was about to die, and Niki's blood spilled in the heart of their Pack land would destroy Sylvan. Beneath her, Niki lay on her back, neck extended, silent. Resigned. Next to her, Sophia inched closer—as if to put her body between Niki and the Alpha. Seconds, even less, and the Pack would be torn apart. Drake had no time. She lunged, caught Niki's throat in her jaws, and squeezed. She clamped down slowly, relentlessly, until Niki shuddered and lay still.

Sophia nosed Niki's still form and howled, a broken cry that shattered the sky.

An enormous silver wolf burst into the clearing and surged toward them, jaws wide, snarling viciously. Drake straddled Niki, keeping the defenseless wolf in the protective shadow of her body. She'd compressed the arteries in Niki's neck until she'd lost consciousness, but she wasn't sure how long Niki would remain unconscious. If Niki woke now, she would die.

Sylvan! I'm all right. It's done.

Sophia, so much smaller, vaulted into Sylvan's path and Sylvan swung her heavy head at her with a sharp growl, knocking her aside. Sophia landed ten feet away with a whimper. Sylvan gathered her powerful shoulders and went airborne, aiming for Niki's throat.

Sylvan! No! Drake lowered herself over Niki's motionless body. She couldn't challenge Sylvan in front of her Pack, nor would she if she could. Sylvan was driven by the prime instinct—to protect her mate and her young. Drake would do the same.

Mine, Sylvan. She is mine to kill.

Sylvan twisted in midlunge and landed facing Drake, her gaping jaws hovering over Niki's head. Saliva dripped from her canines, madness rode in her gold eyes. *You're bleeding. She dies.*

No. Drake nosed Sylvan's face. *It's nothing. A scratch. An accident.*

Beneath her, Niki twitched and whimpered. Sylvan snarled.

She submitted to me. I put her down. Let your wolves see I am truly Prima.

Niki shuddered and shifted to skin, and Drake eased forward, sidling up to Sylvan. She licked Sylvan's muzzle and rubbed her nose under Sylvan's jaw.

Rumbling, Sylvan rested her head on Drake's neck. *You're all right?*

Drake flicked her ears. *Fine. But our wolves need attention.*

Niki pushed up to her knees on the hard-packed earth, blood running between her clenched hands down her abdomen and onto her naked thighs. Head bowed, she waited for Sylvan to tear her throat out, and Drake was not going to let that happen. She would lose both of them then. She shifted to skin and Sylvan morphed instantly, catching Drake around the waist and pulling her roughly against her bare chest.

Sylvan sniffed her, licked her throat, kissed her bruisingly. Her canines scraped Drake's lip. "What happened?"

Drake kissed her. "I'm fine. It was an accident. I promise you."

"What happened? Why were you fighting? Where are your guards?" Sylvan threw her head back and howled in fury. "Who hurt you?"

"I did, Alpha," Niki said hollowly.

Sylvan grabbed her by the neck and pulled her to her feet, her face millimeters from Niki's. "I should kill you."

"I know."

Sylvan shuddered, her wolf coursing just below her skin. She panted, the muscles in her chest and abdomen rippling beneath a dusting of silver. She was still half-wolf and more than half-mad.

Drake ran a hand down her back. "Sylvan, she was fighting with Dasha. I put myself in the middle. Niki did not attack me. *And I put her down.*"

Sylvan growled continuously, struggling not to rip Niki's throat out. Her claws punctured Niki's neck. Crimson streaked Niki's throat.

The *centuri* crept closer, Jace and Jonathan snarling wildly. They were young dominants, less capable of controlling their wolves than the others, and they were both nearly frenzied from the scent of sex and blood and the Alpha's rage. In another minute they'd attack any wolf in their path.

"Sylvan," Drake murmured, caressing her chest. "We have injured. Dasha needs medical attention. So does Niki."

"So do you," Sylvan snapped.

"I'm all right, it's a scratch."

"You're *bleeding.*" Agony contorted Sylvan's face and Drake gripped her hair, pulled her head close.

"You came when I needed you. You always do." She kissed Sylvan hard, bit her lip, stroked the small puncture with her tongue. She rubbed against Sylvan, letting her essence mingle with Sylvan's. "I am not hurt."

Sylvan shuddered. "If you were—if the young…"

"We're fine." Drake kissed her again. "Calm your wolves, Alpha."

Sylvan breathed in Drake's scent and closed her eyes. Broadcasting her power, she settled her Pack. One by one the wolves in the clearing shimmered and took skin form. Dasha lay on the ground groaning softly, holding her twisted and bleeding right arm against her chest. Sophia got unsteadily to her feet, a purplish bruise on her jaw. Niki slumped to the ground, cradling her midsection. Blood seeped between her fingers.

"Max," Drake called. "Clothes."

Max bounded into the barracks and returned with an armful of T-shirts and pants. Sophia pulled on a navy blue T-shirt and jeans. Most of the others just took pants.

"Take Dasha to the infirmary," Drake said to Max, pulling on jeans.

"Yes, Prima."

Max lifted Dasha and carried her inside. Sophia crouched beside Niki, gripped her arm, and murmured, "Let me see your stomach."

"Leave me," Niki rasped.

"No." Sophia stroked Niki's blood-soaked hair. "I won't."

Sylvan stared down at Niki, her eyes flat arid plains. "Isolate her."

Sophia spun around on her knees, but her head was up and her eyes challenging. "No! She needs medical attention."

Sylvan towered over Sophia, her anger raising the hair on Drake's arms. "You challenge me?"

"I am a medic." Sophia took a shuddering breath. "She can't be left alone. I…This is my fault, Alpha."

Niki moaned and tried to rise. "No. I am at fault."

Sylvan paced. "Until I know what happened, Niki is confined to the infirmary." She signaled Andrew. "Guard the door. She does not leave the room."

Andrew's eyes widened but he nodded curtly. "Yes, Alpha."

Drake didn't object. Sylvan had no choice. She had to restore order, and she could not appear indecisive when surrounded by dominant wolves. If she wavered, she would be challenged, and although she would undoubtedly be victorious, the Pack would be unsettled. Now, with the threat of outside enemies, the Pack must stand strong.

"I want to go with her," Sophia said.

"You can tend to her injuries," Sylvan said.

"Thank you," Sophia said, running trembling fingers through Niki's hair, an unconscious movement Drake was certain she had no awareness of.

"I'll look in on her in a few minutes," Drake said to Sophia, "just to be sure you don't need help."

"Thank you, Prima," Sophia said softly. She wrapped her arm around Niki's shoulder. "I'm not sure she can walk."

Niki pushed to her knees. "I don't need help."

Drake leaned over and picked her up. "Your life is mine now, *Imperator*. Don't forget it."

"Yes, Prima," Niki murmured, her eyes closed.

Rest now. Drake carried her up the steps of the infirmary. *Let us help you.*

❖

Niki burned with the agony of failure. Drake had laid her down on the treatment table and left her with Sophia. "I don't need treatment. I'll heal."

"You need these wounds cleaned," Sophia said.

She didn't want Sophia to touch her. She didn't deserve her care. She had lost in battle, she had dishonored her rank, she had threatened the Prima. She didn't know why she was still alive.

"This is going to hurt," Sophia said, taking Niki's hands from her belly and placing them by her sides on the table, exposing her torn abdomen. Four jagged parallel lacerations stretched from just below her breastbone on the right side across her belly to her left hip, deep gouges that penetrated through the muscles and verged on opening her abdominal cavity. Ragged bits of flesh protruded from the wounds. Gently, Sophia rinsed the blood away with saline-soaked gauze. Then, because local anesthetics had no effect on Were physiology, she trimmed the damaged tissue without anesthetic. Even when she lifted the jagged flap on Niki's face to remove the grit from the tear beneath her eye, Niki lay still, a low rumble reverberating in her chest. Niki stared at the ceiling as if she were blind, but Sophia knew her gaze had turned inward where she was examining herself and finding only fault.

"What happened out there was my fault," Sophia said. "I'm so sorry."

"You're not to blame," Niki said, her voice echoing hollowly. "You're in heat. You have the right to say no when a Were answers your call and you don't want them."

Sophia's hands trembled and she set the instruments down. "You don't understand."

Finally, Niki looked at her, her eyes bleak. "I understand. You want Dasha. Not me. You've never wanted me."

"I don't want anyone," Sophia said.

"That's not what your wolf says. Your call is stronger every time. Don't you think I've felt it before, when you fought it and lost? When you finally tangled with someone else?" Niki gripped the table, her claws scoring the honed wood surface. "Why do you fight what's natural, deny what you need?"

Sophia placed a clean bandage over Niki's belly. "Once you've rested, you should shift. You'll heal these wounds faster. Right now, you've lost a lot of blood and your wolf will be weak if you shift. In the morning—"

"I am not weak." Niki grabbed Sophia's wrist, her strength astounding after all she'd been through. "And you are avoiding the answer. Why do you resist?"

Sophia licked her lips. She'd never told anyone. The only ones who knew were the Alpha and Elena, and they only knew because the Alpha knew everything that happened in the Pack, even the things that had happened before she assumed leadership. And Elena knew because Elena had saved her life. Holding so many secrets was so hard. "I don't want to mate. When I'm in heat—I can't control my wolf."

"Every wolf wants to mate."

"Really? You don't."

Niki looked away, the gesture so astounding Sophia caught her breath. She gripped Niki's hand. "Why is that, *Imperator*?"

Niki's head snapped around. "Don't call me that."

"Why? You think because the Alpha is angry that changes anything? You are who you are, Niki. While you breathe, there will never be another *imperator*."

"Sylvan will never trust me now."

Niki's desolation bruised Sophia's heart. "You don't know what the Alpha will do. The Prima is pregnant, you know that, don't you?"

Niki's eyes gleamed, pride and joy glowing in them. "Yes. I know."

"Then you know everything is changing. The Alpha will be unpredictable until after the young are born. She won't be able to control her wolf as easily. She needs us—you—now more than ever. She needs us to be strong."

Niki shuddered. "I don't know how to help her."

"Yes, you do. You need to do what you've always done—give her good counsel, protect her Pack."

"She doesn't need that from me now. She has the Prima."

"Niki, don't you see?" Sophia shook her head and skimmed her fingers through Niki's hair. "She needs to be free to protect her mate, and you can help her by uncovering our enemies, by ensuring we are all safe. She needs her general in command."

Niki couldn't let herself hope, and she was so weary. The soothing touch of Sophia's hand in her hair was the only thing keeping her from shifting and fighting her way out of the cage Sylvan had closed around her. She brushed her cheek over Sophia's palm. "Are you going to tell me why you don't want a mate?"

Sophia answered because Niki's need was too strong to deny. "I can't bear young."

Niki's eyes narrowed. "What? How do you know that?"

Sophia looked away. "I've always known. An injury—when I was very young. Before I came here."

Niki snarled. "Who hurt you?"

"It doesn't matter. My parents got me away before the other Alpha had me killed for being...defective. Sylvan's mother took us into this Pack."

"Killed you?" Niki tried to rise, her wolf in a fury. "Who—"

"Niki, Niki...don't." Sophia pulled Niki's head to her chest, stroking her face. "It's over—long ago."

Niki closed her eyes and pressed her face to Sophia's breast.

Sophia's scent was so pure, so clean and sharp. Niki's blood surged and her clitoris tightened. Someone had hurt Sophia, tried to destroy her. Niki growled.

"It's all right." Sophia kissed the top of her head, stroked her neck and her back, soothing her. "Don't rage for me. I'm alive, I have the Pack. I have my parents." She straightened her shoulders, took a deep breath. "But it's not fair to any other Were to risk a mate bond with me. When I'm in heat, when the frenzy is overpowering, I can't control my need. And if I lose control and bite, I might accidentally invite a bond."

"What if your mate doesn't care about not having young?"

Sophia's heart leapt. What was Niki saying? What was she offering? But there was more, more than she could ever reveal to anyone, even Niki. So she smiled and shook her head. "Why have a mate when you can't produce young? I would rather tangle without being tied to any one Were."

Niki looked up, searching her face. "That's what you want? To tangle with whoever happens to be available?"

Sophia forced herself to shrug, feigning nonchalance. "Why not, as long as they're not interested in mating? Isn't that what you do? With Anya and the others?"

"I don't want a mate either," Niki said. She didn't tangle with susceptible females in heat who might want a mate, and she was careful not to bite at critical moments and accidentally induce a bond. She wouldn't have answered Sophia's call while she was in heat if she'd been able to help herself, but she couldn't stop. Sophia's need was too great, and her wolf too set on answering. She wanted her still. Sophia's heat had waned from all the stress of the last few hours, but when it returned, Niki knew she would want her. She didn't care. She wasn't worried about a mate bond. She'd never been compelled to induce one, and Sophia's fear of not being able to have young meant nothing to her. She never planned on having young. She was a soldier, and she didn't plan on orphaning young the way she had been orphaned. Her only role was to guard the Alpha. Let others bear the responsibility of raising young.

"Then you understand."

Niki growled. She didn't want Sophia tangling with other Weres. "So you're going to tangle with Dasha?"

"No." Sophia sighed. "Dasha won't force herself on me, and I'm not going to tangle with her. She's too young, too dominant, and she's going to want more."

"She'll want you to carry her mark."

"I know." Sophia turned away and gathered up the instruments. "You should sleep. I'll bring you some food. Once you've eaten and rested, you can shift so your wolf will heal."

"Will she?"

Sophia looked over her shoulder, her heart aching. Niki was so pale, her eyes so devastated. "Your wolf is stronger than you know. So are you. Now is not the time to run and hide."

Niki stiffened and she snarled. "Be careful, Omega."

Sophia grinned. "You should listen to your wolf more often, Niki. She sees things more clearly than you do."

"I don't want a mate bond. I know how to avoid a bite, and I crave something else."

Sophia wrapped her arms around her middle, knowing Niki was trying to push her away even as she offered to tangle. "The Vampires, you mean."

"Yes."

"You aren't the only Were who craves a Vampire's bite. Are you trying to shock me?"

"I'm only trying to tell you that we're more alike than you think."

Sophia nodded. "Perhaps. Will you rest now?"

Niki was silent for a long moment. "Will you stay?"

Sophia's heart bled, but she forced a smile. "Yes. For a little while."

CHAPTER EIGHT

A lpha," Elena said quietly, "perhaps you should wait outside."

Sylvan stopped her furious pacing and took two rapid steps toward her *medicus*, her eyes flashing from deep blue to gold so quickly it seemed her wolf was more in control than she was. "Not while my mate is in here."

Drake sat up on the exam table and caught Sylvan's gaze. "It will just be a few more minutes. Elena will clean it and we'll be done."

"I can't leave," Sylvan said, a fine shiver coursing over her body. "Just hurry."

Drake glanced at Elena. "As soon as I shift, these will heal. I think I need to go now."

Elena rapidly cleansed the gouges on Drake's shoulder with an antiseptic, removing dirt and bits of stone from where Drake had crouched in pelt over Niki in the courtyard. "Go. She needs you."

Drake hopped down from the table and grasped Sylvan's arm. "Come with me."

Sylvan couldn't concentrate, couldn't think of anything except the panic that had overtaken her out in the forest when she'd sensed Drake in danger. Then her shoulder had burned as if she'd been shot, and she knew Drake was hurt. All reason had fled. All she knew was she needed to get to her, needed to protect her, needed to destroy whoever had threatened her family. She would have run a thousand miles, until her heart gave out, to reach her. And now, all that adrenaline, all those primal hormones, cascaded through her body and she needed Drake. She needed to feel her, smell her, taste her, claim her. She let Drake drag her down the hall and into an empty room before her restraint completely broke. She slammed the door, grasped Drake by the shoulders, and pushed her against the wall. And at last her mouth was on Drake's neck, her hands shredding Drake's jeans, her clitoris tight and ready. She panted, her pelt flowing down the center of her abdomen, her claws erupting. "I need you. I need you now."

"I know," Drake moaned, hooking the waistband of Sylvan's jeans and tearing them off. She kicked away what was left of her pants and straddled Sylvan's hips, opening herself. She grasped Sylvan's shoulders. "Now. Take me. Hurry."

Groaning, Sylvan grasped Drake's ass to hold her up and rubbed her clitoris over Drake's, feeling their heat and their hardness and their hormones blending. The shadow of her bite on Drake's shoulder pulsed and she pressed her mouth to it, letting her canines puncture the skin enough for their essences to meld. She drove into her, desperate to connect.

"More," Drake cried, gripping the back of Sylvan's neck. "Bite."

Drake's command, the heat of her sex closing around her, the need to drive away the terror, forced Sylvan deeper. Drake sank teeth into her and Sylvan came with a roar, the bright shining pain of Drake's bite on her breast pushing her over. She thrust, the muscles in her ass rippling with each surge of her release. She released until she was empty and dropped to her knees, Drake still wrapped around her, holding her inside.

"I need you," Sylvan gasped, her chest heaving.

"I'm yours," Drake murmured, stroking Sylvan's soaked hair, the harsh bones in her face, the sinful softness of her mouth. "I promise you, I will not leave you. I will protect our young. You don't have to fear."

Sylvan shuddered and buried her face in the curve of Drake's shoulder. "I never knew a need so great. I don't know how my father survived when my mother..." She raised her head, her eyes dark with loss. "I wouldn't live. Without you—"

Drake pressed her fingers to Sylvan's mouth, brushed her thumb over the point of her canine, and kissed her. "I'm so sorry you lost them. You won't lose me. I will always come home to you." Drake slid both hands into Sylvan's hair, holding her head, kissing her deeply, letting Sylvan taste her. She rubbed her breasts over Sylvan's chest, letting Sylvan feel her. Gliding her sex against Sylvan's belly, she coated Sylvan with her *victus*. Marking her. "You're mine. I'm yours. Do you hear?"

Holding Drake tightly, Sylvan stretched her out on the smooth plank floor. She rose above her, settling her hips between Drake's thighs. Gently this time, she let her clitoris stroke between the swollen folds of Drake's sex. Drake whimpered and lifted her hips for more. Sylvan kissed Drake's mouth, her throat, her chest. She sucked her nipples and licked her way down the valley between the ridges of muscles in Drake's belly. She took Drake's engorged clitoris into her mouth and sucked her slowly. Her mind was hers again and she wanted Drake to know she was cherished. Beyond need, beyond even passion, she was loved.

"Sylvan, you'll make me come." Drake twisted her fingers in Sylvan's hair and Sylvan licked her. "So soon. So good."

Sylvan closed her eyes and gripped Drake's hips, lifting her into her mouth. She sucked her, licked her, drank her. And when Drake hardened in her mouth, she entered her, claiming her everywhere. With a hoarse cry, Drake came in her mouth.

"I love you," Sylvan groaned, rising above her. Her heart holding Drake's, she came, surrendering all to her mate.

❖

Michel withdrew her incisors from the neck of the young Were and licked the puncture sites closed. The female shuddered against her, her wolf-slanted eyes ringed in gold and glazed from her release. Her canines glistened against her full lip. Her hips pumped languidly as she continued to empty, the stimulants Michel had injected into her bloodstream still exciting her. Michel groaned, the rush of vigor flooding her system as pleasurable as the orgasm that accompanied the rejuvenation.

Francesca ran her fingers down the center of Michel's abdomen, lightly grazing her clitoris. She ignored the Were host, a new and very eager volunteer. "I think you're developing more than a passing taste for them, darling."

Michel leaned up on her elbow and kissed Francesca. "I seem to remember your frequent visits with the Were Alpha."

Francesca smiled, her eyes glittering. "True, Were blood is potent, and that of an Alpha? Infinitely more satisfying than any human *or* Were."

"Speaking of the Alpha," Michel said carefully, "what do you plan to do about her if the Shadow Lords call for her death?"

Francesca slid from bed and poured champagne from the nearby ice bucket Daniela had left at sunfall while they enjoyed the host. She filled a second glass and handed it to Michel. "The Shadow Lords are short-sighted, I'm afraid. That's the problem when working with lessers. The humans' vision is so limited. The Fae really only care about protecting the secret locations of the Faerie gates. And the Weres?" She laughed. "Far too volatile—their instincts rule their brains far too often."

"Sylvan doesn't strike me as impulsive." Michel sat on the side of the bed and sipped champagne, enjoying Francesca's evening routine. The servants had filled the brass clawfoot tub with scented bathwater, and Francesca slid into the water, tilting her head back against the cushioned headrest with a languorous sigh. Her breasts rose above the layer of ivory bubbles, her rosy nipples flushed and firm.

"I think eliminating Sylvan would only introduce an unknown and potentially even more dangerous factor—a new Alpha, to begin with, and then almost certainly a power struggle between the various Were Packs. No one dares challenge her, but with her gone?" Francesca leisurely sponged her arms with the fragrant water, then let the sponge float away and cupped both breasts, running her fingertips over her nipples in slow, sensuous circles. "While chaos among the wolf Weres would definitely turn public opinion against any possibility of giving them legitimate civil status, we would likely feel the backlash as well."

"Better the enemy you know?" Michel pulled on a pair of pants and crossed to a velvet settee facing Francesca. Stretching out, she sipped champagne and enjoyed the rise of power that accompanied her feeding. A soft growl came from the young Were on the bed as she came to her senses. She'd been tasty. Her blood was rich, strong, and the heat of her blood filled Michel's belly. Her sex throbbed. She was potent now and would be for some hours. As her orgasm had pulsed with each swallow, she'd thought not of the Were whose blood she drank, but of the young female she'd had in the lab. Katya, just out of adolescence, was a dominant female whose taste lingered in her mind.

She brushed her fingertips over her chest and down her belly, imaging how Katya would taste as she came into her full power. Her clitoris throbbed. Francesca was right, as always. She was developing a taste for Weres—at least one female.

"Speaking of Sylvan," Francesca said casually, "the governor's fund-raising gala is this weekend, and all of the Coalition heads will be there."

"As will you, as Chancellor of the City."

"Yes." Francesca opened her legs and drew the sponge up her thighs. She raised one knee, exposing a long expanse of creamy flesh.

Michel's sex swelled, and she freed the top button of her pants, letting her fingers drift lower. Francesca's attention fixed on her movements, and a ripple of satisfaction heated Michel's chest. She enjoyed knowing she could still tease her mistress as much as her mistress teased her. "What about Nicholas? Will he be there?"

"Oh, I expect he will. He might privately want the Weres destroyed, but publicly he pretends to be neutral. Playing politics." Francesca's fingers slid higher between her legs and her mouth curved in pleasure. "Veronica Standish has requested our service again."

Michel sat up, the champagne flute dangling between her fingers. "Oh? More help with her studies?" Perhaps she had more Were subjects who required a Vampire's bite. The idea wasn't as appealing now that Katya had been freed.

"In a way. She'd like us to supply her with bodyguards."

Michel frowned. "Bodyguards? And does she intend to be open about having Vampires in her employ?"

"Apparently, yes. In addition to the work she does for our cause, she has a legitimate profession. She's a renowned researcher and heads a lab at the university."

"So appearing to embrace Praetern diversity would be good for her."

"Exactly. Actually, a very good cover."

"You're going to agree to her request?"

"Mmm, yes. This is an opportunity for us to have someone inside Nicholas's operation. We've never had that before. And of course, if we provide someone who is able to satisfy whatever else Dr. Standish requires, the good doctor will be grateful. Gratitude, darling, is the first step to allegiance."

Michel smiled. One of the many things she admired about Francesca was her ability to plan for the long game. After all, Vampires had nothing if not time. She'd also learned much from standing at Francesca's right hand for centuries—enough to know that what she admired most in her mistress was also something to be feared. Alliances and allegiances were as fluid as time itself in Francesca's dominion.

"You have someone in mind for the job?"

"Someone completely trustworthy, of course. I'd send you, darling, but I can't do without you."

Michel sipped champagne. "That's nice to know."

Francesca laughed. "Did you ever doubt it?"

Michel set the glass aside and strode to the tub. She picked up the sponge and pushed it beneath the water, skating the slightly rough surface down Francesca's abdomen and between her thighs. She drew it over Francesca's sex in slow circles, watching Francesca's eyes blaze scarlet as she teased her. When Francesca hissed a warning that she'd had enough toying, Michel knelt, let the sponge float to the surface, and slid her fingers deeper. Francesca arched, her lids nearly closed.

"I remain loyal to you," Michel said, "but how long will I be useful to you?"

"Always," Francesca gasped, pushing down on Michel's fingers. She grasped Michel's arm, her nails cutting crescents into the undersurface of Michel's wrist. "Always, darling."

Michel kissed her as Francesca came around her fingers. "Then I am yours to command."

❖

Sophia broke out into a sweat, sex hormones coating her skin. She pushed away from the treatment table and paced to the far side of the room. The Alpha was tangling, and the power of her call permeated the Compound. Sophia's heat returned with a vengeance, and she filled and ached and trembled. Niki was too close. Too close, too beautiful, too potent. And injured. "I have to go."

Niki turned her head. "Where?"

"Just…out." Sophia forced a smile. "You promised you'd rest."

"I smell you. I taste you on my tongue. Every breath you take, I scent your need." Niki pushed up on her elbows. The wounds in her stomach were starting to close, but blood still seeped from them. "I'm stronger than you think."

"I know how strong you are, *Imperator.* But you're not strong enough for what you're suggesting." Sophia smiled wanly. "If I stay… we're both going to frenzy."

"What are you going to do?" Niki grumbled ominously—the warning of a possessive Were not to threaten what was hers. "Who—"

"I'm going to feed Lara."

Niki's eyes darkened. "And end up craving mindless blood sex?"

"I don't think I will," Sophia said. "I'm stronger than you think too."

Niki's claws and canines erupted. "I don't want Lara fucking you."

"I said I was going to let her *feed,*" Sophia said quietly, choosing not to point out that Niki had no say in who she tangled with, or how. "That will be enough for my…needs."

"I don't trust her."

Sophia regarded her steadily. "Do you trust me?"

"With my life," Niki said quickly.

Sophia nodded. "Good. I feel the same. Trust is more important than anything else."

"If she hurts you—"

"She won't."

"You don't know that." Niki pushed to a sitting position, wincing, blood pooling at the base of her belly. "You don't know what she's like when the bloodlust takes her."

Sophia smiled and shook her head. "Niki, I'm a Were. Nothing is as wild as a Were in frenzy. If I could handle you, I can handle her."

Niki growled. "You challenge me again."

Sophia didn't want to challenge her, she wanted to calm her. She wanted to touch her, despite the risk. She crossed the room and brushed Niki's tangled auburn hair away from her haunted eyes. "Never. But I won't let you dominate me either. I'm not submissive."

Niki grasped Sophia's hips and jerked her between her legs. She kissed the base of Sophia's throat, letting her canines press into Sophia's neck. Sophia gasped. Niki licked her. "I know what you are, Omega. You might stand outside the hierarchy, but I know you burn."

Sophia grabbed Niki's hair and yanked her head away. She stared down at her, her blue eyes alight with power. "Don't try to seduce me now. I told you why I won't mate. I trusted you."

"And I told you I don't care." Niki rubbed her cheek against Sophia's breast. "You have to tangle with someone, why not me? I won't ask anything of you."

Sophia's heart lurched. So simple. She should be happy. She wasn't. "It doesn't matter. You're in no shape to tangle right now, whether you'll admit it or not."

"I know you can't wait," Niki said. "But there will be other times."

Sophia stepped away. "And you have more important duties, *Imperator*. You need to heal, and you need to make peace with the Alpha. The Pack needs you."

Niki gripped the table so hard the wood creaked. "And what about my needs?"

"The Alpha's needs are your needs. Have you forgotten that?"

Niki stared at the floor. She'd let herself think the Prima had taken her place, but maybe she was wrong. Maybe she'd been lying to herself her whole life, and she'd been waiting for the one time Sylvan didn't reject her offer to serve her need. But then Sylvan had mated and she didn't know where she belonged anymore. She looked at Sophia. "I thought everything changed when she mated."

"I know," Sophia said softly. "Everything *has* changed and will probably change again, but some things will always be. Sylvan is Alpha. And you are her second. She depends on you. She needs you. Stop being a coward."

Niki launched off the table and landed in front of Sophia with a snarl. She grasped Sophia's shoulders and lifted her up on her toes until they were nose to nose. "You test me."

Sophia's chin shot up. "You should be tested. Someone needs to."

Niki covered Sophia's mouth with hers and kissed her hard, sucking, biting, licking. Sophia's claws raked down her back, drawing blood, and Niki's clitoris stiffened. Before she forced Sophia against the wall and took her, she pushed Sophia away. "And someone needs to kiss you the way you should be kissed."

Sophia's breasts heaved and her eyes bored fire into Niki's. "Damn you."

"When Lara's teeth are in your throat and she makes you come, think of me."

I always think of you. Sophia wrenched away and raced from the room.

Niki slumped back against the treatment table and crawled up onto it. She curled on her side and clutched her burning stomach. If she thought about Lara making Sophia come, she'd want to kill Lara. She laughed bitterly. And Lara couldn't be killed. She was already dead.

CHAPTER NINE

Jody went from dreamless oblivion to total awareness the instant her eyes opened. She immediately scanned the surroundings for danger. Her guards were outside the door, an agitated Were paced farther down the hall, and distantly, the life force of the entire Pack beckoned as a single heart beating. Her incisors unsheathed and hunger as endless as eternity seethed inside her. The bed beside her was empty, but Becca was near. Becca's heartbeat, the steady pulse of blood flowing through her arteries and veins, her soft breaths, eclipsed everything in Jody's world. All but the need to feed.

Blood barely flowed in her body now, a protective mechanism to prevent complete depletion of the scarce oxygen-carrying compounds between feedings. After she fed, her heart would beat for a short time, her cells would activate, she would be sexually potent. In those moments, she would come as close to living as was possible while still being something other than alive. Her biological drive demanded she feed, and if she delayed, she risked a blood rampage. If hunger overpowered her control, she'd cut a deadly swath through every living creature in her path until she was sated or staked. Need gnawed at her guts, and she focused on the scent of the nearest host. Becca. So deliciously alive.

"Get out," Jody rasped.

"You're awake." Becca spun around from the desk where she had been typing up notes on the details she'd been given of the raid on the secret lab. She wasn't sure when she'd be able to go public with any of it—but she was used to spending months digging out facts on a story. And no story had ever been more important to her—or as personal. Across from her, Jody lay as she had all day, staring up at the ceiling, her arms by her sides, her sharply handsome face tense even at rest. But unlike when she had been somnolent, now her naked body vibrated with tension. "What do you need?"

"Go," Jody ordered. "I await a host. Go, Becca."

"You need my blood, though, don't you," Becca said. "Your transition isn't yet complete, and I am your bonded blood mate. You need the compatible blood I carry."

One second, Jody was on the bed; the next she was in front of Becca, stalking toward her so fiercely Becca almost took a step back. Jody's incisors were dangerous spikes glittering against her pale lips, her eyes as bright and hot as purest flame. Her face was knife-edged with need. Becca took a breath, steadied her voice. "Tell me I'm wrong, Vampire."

"Don't argue with me," Jody said slowly, as if each word was a terrible effort. She stopped with her body millimeters from Becca. "I will drain you."

"No, you won't. You didn't last night and you were practically insane then."

"I have a ready host. You are not needed." Jody turned her head to the closed door and though she made no sound, a second later it opened and Zahn stepped inside.

"You called, Liege?" Zahn wore a white silk shirt open between her breasts and tight, tapered black pants. She was barefoot. Her nipples were dusky circles beneath the sheer material, and her eyes, fixed on Jody's face, glistened with anticipation.

"She needs to feed," Becca said, grasping Jody's forearm. "And I'm staying."

Zahn's surprised gaze flickered between Becca and Jody, but she said nothing. Jody's arm was a steel band beneath Becca's fingers, the only outward sign of her struggle for control. Becca supposed if she was smart, she'd leave and let Jody feed from Zahn alone, but she wouldn't concede to Jody's fear of hurting her. If they were to have a true relationship, she needed to be part of Jody's life, including this part. She might not be as strong or resilient as a Were or as acclimated to giving blood as a human servant like Zahn, but she was Jody's blood mate. And she wasn't leaving Jody alone with another woman, blood servant or not. Jody was hers.

"You need this," Becca said, dropping her robe so she too was naked. She grasped Jody's arm. "Come back to bed."

"Becca," Jody said dangerously, her gaze caressing Becca's nipples until they hardened from the heat of her glance, "you play a dangerous game."

Becca shook her head, her heart hammering and her skin electric. "Oh no, I'm not playing at all."

"Always so stubborn." Jody lifted her so effortlessly Becca barely managed not to cry out in surprise.

Then they were on the bed, Jody hovering just above her, Zahn somehow beside her, their bodies lightly touching. Becca wrapped her arms around Jody's waist and slid her hands up and down Jody's back. Her skin was smooth and cold as marble. Oh God, she couldn't feel even a single heartbeat. She stroked Jody's face. So very cold. "Hurry, Jody."

"Zahn," Jody said without looking away from Becca, "are you ready?"

"Yes, Liege," Zahn whispered, turning on her side, pressing even closer to Becca.

Zahn's silk shirt brushed over Becca's breast like a gentle breeze. Zahn's voice had gotten slow and lethargic, as if she were drugged, and Becca realized she was. Thrall was very much like a drug. Zahn's hand drifted to Becca's hip and Becca didn't move away. Zahn was giving her lover life—she should not be alone.

"Do it, darling," Becca murmured, watching Jody's face, mesmerized by the intensity of her gaze, the hypnotic tone of her voice. "I want to be here with you completely. Don't enthrall me."

"You want to see me?" Jody's eyes became impossibly deep. "Watch."

Jody slid one arm around Becca's shoulders and lowered her head. Her lips caressed Becca's fleetingly before she took Zahn's throat in a single rapid plunge. Zahn gasped and her breath came out in a long, shuddering moan. Jody swallowed and her hips thrust between Becca's thighs.

"Oh," Becca whispered, her body igniting. She wrapped both legs around Jody's hips and fit her breasts to Jody's. She closed her eyes and pressed her cheek to Jody's shoulder, feeling Jody grow warm beneath her hands. This was Jody's life. Hers now. She had given Jody this existence with her own blood, freely and without regret. Jody's orgasm, Zahn's ecstatic groans, the life pulsating under her hands, pushed Becca close to climax. She groaned and pulled herself back. She wanted Jody. When Jody raised her head, Zahn fell away from them with a sharp cry.

"Oh God, Jody," Becca moaned. "I need you now." She turned her head to the side, exposing her neck. "I need you. I love you. Please."

The world exploded. Pleasure so exquisite she lost her breath, lost her voice, lost her sanity. Fire consumed her, burning her to ash from the inside out. Jody devoured her at the same time as she filled her. Power surged through every cell of Becca's body.

Becca came back to herself when she felt Jody moving away. She gripped Jody's hand. "Where are you going?"

Jody leaned down and kissed her. "To see that Zahn is protected while she recovers. I want to be alone with you."

"Don't go far."

"Never." Jody lifted Zahn, whose head lolled against Jody's shoulder in post-orgasmic languor. The door opened and a dark-haired Vampire dressed all in black stepped in.

"Liege."

"Rafaela." Jody passed Zahn to her guard. "See to her and keep watch on Lara's room. She is not yet awake. I'll be there soon."

"Yes, Liege."

"Have you all fed?"

"Yes, and well." Rafaela smiled. "The Weres are most accommodating."

Jody raised a brow. "And willing?"

"Quite."

Jody laughed and shut the door. She appeared by the side of the bed, cupped Becca's cheek, and kissed her again. Her lips were soft as silk and warm now. Her eyes had returned to the crimson darkness that was normal after she'd fed. "How do you feel?"

Becca laughed unsteadily. "A little like a phoenix—I feel like I've risen from the ashes. God, that was incredible. I was burning up and I never want it to stop."

"No pain?" Jody ran her thumb along the edge of Becca's jaw and over the fading punctures in her neck.

"God, no." Becca shivered as electricity streaked from the bite in her neck to her nipples and clit. "I love being with you anytime—any way—but that was…amazing."

Jody sat on the side of the bed and trailed her fingers down Becca's neck and over her breasts. "When I feed, some of my blood and hormones enter your body. The longer I feed from you, the more effect I'll have on you."

Becca pushed up against the pillows, grasping Jody's hand and molding it to her breast. She pressed Jody's fingers into her flesh, wanting nothing between them. She had a feeling these revelations were the things Jody feared would keep them apart. She wanted Jody to know she wasn't afraid of who Jody was or who they were together. "Is that why you don't have very many long-term blood servants?"

Jody smiled. "You understand more than most." She brushed her thumb over Becca's mouth and Becca caught the tip in her teeth, biting lightly. Jody hissed, her eyes darkening. "Absorbing a Vampire's essence, their power, imparts power to the host, but at a cost."

"What power?"

"Heightened immunity, for one thing. As a result, longevity and delayed aging."

Becca frowned. "How delayed?"

"It depends on the host," Jody said, "and the host's intrinsic potential for cell rejuvenation. Some families, like Zahn's, are genetically predisposed for compatibility with the Vampire species. Their bloodlines are rare, but long-lived."

"How old is Zahn?" Becca asked, thinking she didn't look more than thirty.

Jody smiled. "Not much older than me—but others in her line are much, much older. She is likely to live centuries."

"Are you saying, because we're bonded, the same thing will happen to me?"

"Possibly." Jody's expression became remote.

"What?" Becca grasped Jody's forearm. "What don't you want to tell me?"

Jody sighed. "Sometimes, while initially compatible, eventually the host will reject the Vampiric emissions. The host could become ill. Possibly very ill."

"Or addicted, like so many hosts after a while, right?"

"Yes, although you show no signs of that."

Becca sat forward to kiss Jody's throat, the center of her chest, her breasts. "Oh really? Then I don't think you've been paying enough attention."

"I speak of the blood addiction that leads to insanity." Jody caressed Becca's face. "Your need for me is an addiction I desire. As your power grows, so will the pleasure we share."

"In both directions?"

Jody smiled, her incisors still extended, flames sparking in her eyes. "Oh yes."

Becca's breath came faster and her stomach tightened. "I want you again."

"Are you tired? Dizzy?"

Becca reached up and grabbed Jody's head, tugging her down. "What I am is hungry. Feed me."

❖

"You've been pacing for half an hour," Drake said, sitting up in their bed. As soon as they'd left the infirmary, they'd come straight to their den and tangled again. Now Sylvan, naked, was wearing a path in the hard board floors. The silver line of pelt that transected her ridged abdomen signaled her wolf was close and restless, and Drake suspected that would be the case until the young were born. The Alpha wolf's ascendance probably also explained why Sylvan's sexual need was pretty much constant too. Sylvan was going to throw every susceptible female in the Pack into heat at this rate. Drake didn't find Sylvan's call a hardship in the least, since her pregnancy seemed to be heightening her need to tangle too, but an entire Pack in mating frenzy would leave them dangerously vulnerable. She had to settle Sylvan down. "What is worrying you?"

"I have to decide what to do about Niki."

"What are your thoughts?" Drake said carefully, reaching for a pair of loose scrub pants from a pile on a nearby chair. She didn't think it was her imagination that her jeans were tighter this afternoon than they had been in the morning.

"I can't allow an affront to you to go unpunished," Sylvan growled.

"Everyone there saw what happened, Sylvan. Niki did not attack me. She was frenzied, in the midst of a challenge from Dasha over a female in heat. Under the best of circumstances her control would have been uncertain. Add to that all she's been through lately—"

Sylvan spun around, snarling. "She is the leader of my warriors. She can't be undone by pain or frustration or the need to *tangle.*"

"What about the need to mate?"

Sylvan abruptly stopped and tilted her head, her wolf-gold eyes sharp. "Sophia?"

"I think so."

"Ah fuck." Sylvan resumed pacing. "This had to happen eventually, but why now?"

"Biology doesn't keep to a timetable." Drake pressed against Sylvan, forcing her to still. She rubbed over her, coating her with her pheromones. Sylvan rumbled and Drake smiled. "Do you object to your *centuri* mating? None of them are."

"There's no edict against them mating, although they often don't. Their first allegiance is to me, and that often supersedes their desire to mate."

"The blood bond?"

"Yes."

Drake nodded, aware of the near-sexual bond all the *centuri* shared with Sylvan. If that aided in their protection of her, Drake didn't mind. "Niki's bond with you is very strong."

Sylvan kissed her. "I've never tangled with her, with any of them. Although that would be natural."

"I know." Drake bit her chin. "Now you've lost your chance."

Sylvan grinned. "Even mated Alphas exercise that right."

"Not this one."

Sylvan laughed, then her face grew somber. "Sophia may not be open to mating."

Drake heard reservation in Sylvan's tone. "And it's not your place to tell me why? I consider Sophia a friend."

"I know." Sylvan sighed. "If I thought you needed to know—for your protection or the good of the Pack—I would tell you. I think Sophia could use a friend right now."

"I'll talk to her," Drake said. "But Niki is of more immediate concern. She needs you."

"And I need someone sound and strong in her position."

"I know." Drake smoothed her hands over Sylvan's chest and kissed her. "I know you do. And Niki is all of those things. Everyone in the Pack is a little unsettled. You've been attacked, you've taken a mate, our females have been victimized. It's a difficult time for everyone."

"All the more reason for discipline and order."

"Absolutely," Drake said. "Your wolves need to know they have a strong and responsible leader. Every single one of them looks to you to lead." Drake feathered her fingers through Sylvan's hair and kissed her again. "I know what that costs you. Niki is the strongest of your wolves. You need her. We all need her. Show your Pack that you lead with their welfare in mind."

"And what if Niki can't control her wolf?"

"Any Were who can't control their wolf is a risk to us all. Then, your path is clear."

Sylvan growled, the muscles in her jaw bulging. "I will put her down if she threatens you once."

"I understand. So will your Pack, if that becomes necessary." Drake did not intend to let that happen, but should Niki or any one of them, including her, threaten the well-being of the Pack, there would be no other choice.

Sylvan pulled her close. "I need to see her."

Drake kissed her mate bite on Sylvan's chest. "Good. I want to see Katya and Gray. Are they up to it?"

Sylvan nodded. "They're ready."

Drake glanced at their bed with a sigh. "I guess some things will have to wait."

❖

Becca's cell vibrated just after Jody left to see Lara. Private caller. She straightened in anticipation. "Becca Land."

"I talked to you before," a raspy male voice said. "There's more you need to know."

"I remember you," Becca said, switching on her recorder and plugging it in to the base of her phone. "Please tell me your name."

"My name doesn't matter. We have people watching the lab. Something's happening there. They're moving out all the expensive equipment and they've gone to a skeleton crew."

"What lab?"

"We think there are more."

Becca caught her breath. "More Weres? In the same facility? How—"

"The underground complex is extensive. Multiple holding cells in separate wings. There may not be much time."

"Tell me your name. How can I get a hold of you? Who are you?"

"Friends. Not what they think."

"Not what who thinks?"

"The females they held captive."

"You were with them."

"I'm sorry. I never meant to hurt them. The others may not have much time."

The line went dead and Becca stared at it for a second. More Weres in the lab? How could Sylvan and the others have missed them? She jumped up and ran to the door. She had to find Jody. And Sylvan.

CHAPTER TEN

Niki sat up as the door to the treatment room opened. When Sylvan walked in, she got to her feet and came to attention, ignoring the pain in her belly.

"Stand down, *centuri*," Sylvan said, closing the door behind her.

Niki didn't move, simply bowed her head once in salute. "Alpha."

Sylvan strode to her and stopped a foot away, her arms folded across her bare chest. She wore jeans and nothing else, but she couldn't have looked more formidable if she'd been in full body armor. Niki kept her chin up, but her gaze fixed midway to Sylvan's eyes. Sylvan's mouth was set in a straight hard line. Niki quivered inside, but she had learned long ago never to show fear, not even in front of her Alpha.

"Tell me why I shouldn't kill you," Sylvan said in a flat, neutral tone.

"I can't think of a reason," Niki said.

"Then we have a problem, because neither can I. You put hands on my mate."

"No, Alpha," Niki said quietly. "I didn't. Not intentionally."

"Do you think that matters to me? She carries my young. She carries the future of this Pack."

Sylvan's voice had dropped to a low growl, and Niki felt the presence of Sylvan's wolf bear down on her. She wanted to whimper. She wanted to fall to her knees, but she stood tall. She would die standing, for if she was nothing else, she was a warrior. "I know about the young." She hesitated. "Congratulations. I was wrong about her—about her being a worthy mate to you. I was wrong about many things."

Sylvan's expression didn't change. "What happened out there today?"

Niki was surprised at the opportunity to explain herself. She still didn't know why she was breathing. The rules of the Pack were clear, and everyone, from the youngest whelp to the most seasoned warrior, knew them. The Alpha's word was law. The Alpha's mate was sacrosanct. The duty of every Were in the Pack was to protect the Alpha pair and preserve the bloodlines of the Pack. She had failed on every level. She took a breath. "I'd just come from being with Lara. The Vampire bite clouds the mind, and I—"

"I know what happens," Sylvan said quietly. "That's no excuse. You aren't the only Were who services Vampires, or is serviced by them."

Niki flushed. She didn't like being referred to as no better than a blood addict. She raised her head, almost met Sylvan's eyes. "Lara might be a Vampire, but she is also a *centuri*. I did not service her. I protected her. As you ordered, Alpha."

Sylvan almost smiled at the show of defiance in her oldest friend and her most trusted warrior. But as much as she loved Niki, she loved her mate and her Pack more. She could not be wrong in this decision. "Regardless of how you define your need for the bite, if you cannot tangle with a Vampire and keep your head, you cannot be trusted."

"Sophia is in heat. I answered her call. I was about to…" Niki looked away. What had she been about to do? Take her, although Sophia had said she wasn't welcome? Seduce her, when Sophia could call any Were in the Pack she chose? Had she totally misread everything? "I was thinking only of Sophia, and then Dasha challenged. I…I lost control of my wolf."

"Mating frenzy will do that to a Were."

Niki jerked. "Sophia is in heat, but we're not mating."

"Drake thinks you are."

"No. That's not possible. Sophia does not want a mate and has not called for one."

Sylvan laughed. "And you think that makes any difference at all? You think I wanted a mate? You know better." Sylvan relaxed her stance and raked a hand through her hair. "Do you have any idea what it feels like to be truly afraid, Niki? Do you think I have the time or the luxury to be afraid? But I am."

Niki raised her eyes to Sylvan's. She'd seen her Alpha in frenzy, in fury, in battle—bloodied and blooded. But she had never seen the haunted shadows that swirled in her dark blue eyes now. The Alpha, afraid? She couldn't fathom it. "I don't understand."

"If something happens to her, I don't think I can survive, let alone lead."

Niki's jaw tightened and she growled. "No matter what you *think*, you will lead. You are the Alpha. We are here to ensure that nothing happens to her, or your young."

"Who would that be?" Sylvan asked softly. "Who can I trust with all I care about?"

"Your *centuri*," Niki answered instantly.

"And who leads them? Who can I trust above all others?"

Niki swallowed. "I have ever been and always will be loyal. My life for your life, for her life."

"I need you strong, Niki. No matter your personal needs. If it's a Vampire's bite you crave, satisfy yourself, but hold your wolf and keep your head."

"Yes, Alpha," Niki whispered, wondering if the oblivion of bloodlust was what she truly wanted. She was being given a second chance to find out what really mattered.

"And if you mate—" Sylvan shot Niki a hard stare when she started to protest. "If you mate, your mate will come first if threatened, but at all other times, your loyalty is to me and mine, above all others."

"Above all others." Niki pressed her palm to her heart in salute.

"How badly are you injured?"

Niki grinned crookedly. "I've had worse. I think you've given me worse."

Sylvan grasped the back of Niki's head and pulled her into her arms. She kissed her forehead. "We were younger then."

Niki rested her cheek on Sylvan's shoulder, breathed in the scent of Pack, absorbed the strength of her Alpha. She had been in the Compound for days, but this was the first time she'd felt as if she was home.

"We still have some fight left," Niki murmured.

Sylvan stroked Niki's hair and rested her chin on top of Niki's head. "Yes, and I'm afraid there are many fights to come."

❖

Lara woke snarling and jolted up on the narrow bed. She was naked, her skin burning, fiery blades slashing her to ribbons from the inside out. She took a breath, whipped her head around. Sophia stood at the foot of her bed. She was dressed in jeans and a T-shirt, her expression calm, unafraid. Lara searched for Jody in the shadows and didn't see her.

"She is just outside," Sophia said.

"Why are you here?" Lara asked, her voice thick with need.

"For you," Sophia murmured, walking closer. "Welcome back."

Lara gripped the mattress so hard she shredded it beneath her claws. Her canines were down, her clitoris rock hard. Her hunger painted the world in blood. "Are you sure? I can't wait—can't control it. If you're not sure, leave now."

Sophia came closer, sat on the edge of the bed facing her, cupped her jaw. "I'm sure. You're one of us. I'm here for you."

"I'm sorry," Lara whispered, twining her fingers through the hair at the back of Sophia's head to tilt her chin up and expose the thick, rich veins in her neck. "I hunger."

"I hunger too," Sophia murmured. "It's all right."

Beneath the lure of blood, Lara scented Sophia's need. Her wolf surged, a dominant Were driven to answer the chief imperative of a female in heat. "I want you."

Sophia shuddered, her heat an unbearable pressure pounding in her depths. Niki's words echoed in her mind. *When Lara makes you come, think of me.* She tightened her grip on Lara's shoulders. They were alike in their need—driven by instinct and nature to join—but she refused to surrender her will to the dictates of her biology. She would choose who touched her soul. Sophia framed Lara's face, stared into the eyes of her wolf. "Feed from me."

"Yes," Lara groaned, taking her swiftly, driving into her throat, swallowing ravenously. Sophia bowed in her arms, a sharp cry escaping as she pressed against Lara's chest. Sophia's nipples were hard, her breasts hot and full beneath the thin T-shirt. Lara tore the shirt down the middle, wanting skin on her skin, and pulled Sophia down to the bed. Still drinking, she rose over her, her tense clitoris riding over Sophia's thigh. The rush of Sophia's blood coursing through her forced her to release, but she wanted more. She wanted to be inside Sophia while she drank her. Her wolf circled, agitated and wild. Sophia smelled like the forest after a heavy rain—fertile and rich. Sophia was life, potent and powerful. Lara wanted to drink her, she wanted to fuck her. She slid her claws down Sophia's flank and over her thigh, barely aware of the vise-like grip on her wrist until she tried to part Sophia's thighs.

"Wait," Sophia whispered, and through the haze of bloodlust Lara heard the unmistakable command.

Lara stilled, her canines still buried in Sophia's throat, Sophia's blood flowing into her cells, her feeding hormones seeping into Sophia's system. Sophia should have been completely powerless, but she was still aware and she had said no. Lara would not take her against her will, but she needed more blood to blunt her hunger. She straddled Sophia's thighs, her release cresting as she drank. She thrust, groaning at the knifelike pleasure. Beneath her, Sophia stiffened, her claws stabbing into Lara's back as she spent in hot waves over Lara's belly. Sophia's call was powerful, unrelenting, but Lara pulled away. Any more and she would lose herself in the ecstasy of Sophia's blood and drink her dry.

"Oh!" Sophia gasped as Lara withdrew, instantly cast into aching loneliness. Feeding Lara had been intensely intimate. Severing the connection was physically painful, but through it all she had seen Niki's face, not Lara's, above her. When she'd tempered her heat with a gut-wrenching orgasm, she'd felt Niki's mouth at her throat. "Oh God."

Lara lay heavily on her, panting. "Are you all right?"

Sophia rubbed her cheek against Lara's, stroking the damp hair that clung to her neck. "Yes. Thank you."

Lara pushed up, her eyes scarlet pools, her face an elegant chimera of wolf and Vampire. "You thank me when you've just gifted me with life?"

Sophia smiled, determined not to let her sadness show. Lara was not to blame for Sophia's condition or for her own bloodlust. They were both trapped by need. "I came to you. I wanted to feed you—and I needed your bite. I'm sorry I could not give you more."

"I don't know how you stopped me."

"You are first and always a Were—I knew you would honor our code."

"Am I still Were?" Lara whispered, not seeking an answer where there could be none. She shuddered. "It's so lonely."

"I know." Sophia pulled Lara back down into her arms. She knew what it was to be thrust into an unknown world, to be an outsider, to struggle for a place in a new life, all the while consumed with powerful and foreign needs. "But you're not alone. I promise."

"You're in heat." Lara rubbed her cheek over Sophia's breast. "Why aren't you with a Were?"

"I am."

"Not one who can give you a mate bite." Bitterness flooded Lara's throat. She hadn't realized what she'd lost until she'd held Sophia in her arms and sensed the glory of her call. She was *centuri*. She hadn't planned on mating, at least not until the Pack was safe in the post-Exodus world, and hadn't thought it mattered. Until now, when she couldn't. How much of her was changed? How much of her was… dead?

"You don't know you can't mate," Sophia said. "When you're stronger, we'll find out."

Lara rested her forehead on Sophia's. "What kind of mate would I be—I couldn't even protect my mate during the day."

"You'd find a way. If you couldn't, another Were would stand for you. We are Pack. We protect our own."

"Our own." Lara shook her head and sat up, putting her back to the wall and her body between Sophia and the door. Another Vampire approached.

The door opened and Lara snarled a warning.

"Be careful who you threaten, newling." Jody stepped inside, her gaze passing over Sophia in the protective shadow of Lara's body. She'd agreed to let Sophia come in alone after Sophia had insisted she would be safe. Struck by a strong wave of psychic energy, Jody had probed Sophia's mind and found her inexplicably and powerfully shielded. Sophia was unlike any Were she'd ever encountered, with an extraordinarily strong path-signature. If she didn't know Sophia was a Were, she'd think she was Psi. All the same, she'd monitored Lara's feeding from close by, ready to intervene if Lara succumbed to bloodlust and threatened to drain the host. But Lara had surprised her too—she had a level of control to rival that of a seasoned Risen after only a few days. She shouldn't even be aware of what she was doing in the midst of feeding, let alone be able to stop herself from gorging.

Over the centuries, the Were and Vampire species had lost their interdependent connections, and it appeared that the Weres had acquired some very interesting powers. Now that she was in line to rule a Clan, she'd need to know what her allies—at least for now—were capable of.

"I'm not your newling any longer," Lara growled.

Jody laughed and materialized inches from Lara in the blink of an eye. She stroked Lara's cheek with one fingertip. "Oh, but you are." She glanced at Sophia. "Not many hosts are able to maintain awareness in the midst of a Vampire feeding. You're an empath."

"Yes."

"You could monitor her need while she fed?"

"Yes." Sophia regarded Jody steadily.

"And still keep your own consciousness separate."

Sophia nodded.

Jody regarded her contemplatively. Ability like that might make a host resistant to thrall—and if not enthralled, prey might refuse the bite altogether. "I'd keep that to myself if I were you."

Sophia smiled wanly. "I'm very good at keeping secrets."

"I imagine you are." Jody cocked her head. "Becca is coming. There's trouble."

CHAPTER ELEVEN

Jody left Lara and Sophia alone in Lara's room. Another risk, but Lara's unusual control needed to be tested. So did Sophia's unheard of ability to resist blood thrall. And something much more critical demanded her attention—Becca needed her.

Outside in the hall, Becca hurried toward her, radiating tension and distress. Searching for a threat, Jody extended her senses out over the Compound. Rafaela was only a few feet behind Becca, Zahn—resting but alert—was recovering in the second room down the hall, and two more of Jody's soldiers stood post on the porch at the front of the infirmary. She pulled Becca to her and slid her arm around Becca's shoulders. "Are you hurt?"

"No, no, I'm all right." Becca kissed her quickly. "I'm sorry, I forget how attuned you are to my moods now. I didn't mean to worry you."

Jody smiled faintly. "It's a new sensation for me. I don't mind." She sifted a lock of Becca's hair through her fingers, marveling at the silky softness and the twinge of desire that followed. Until Becca, only blood had stirred her. She had never expected the simple sight of a woman to awaken longing. "Something else is wrong, then."

"Yes, I think so. I just got another anonymous phone tip."

Jody's temper flared. "You have no idea who called?"

"A man. The same one who told me about the laboratory where Katya and Gray were imprisoned. That's why I believe him, and if what he said today is true—"

"What did he want?" Jody didn't like Becca being used as a conduit for cryptic messages from unknown contacts with questionable motives. Becca's job put her in the public eye. Her exposés on the Exodus, the Praetern battle for civil rights, and the sometimes violent opposition to granting Praeterns any protection under the law had earned her national coverage as well as acclaim. Jody could understand why individuals seeking a public forum for their views might contact her, but these anonymous callers were pulling Becca into a world of dangerous secrets. Becca could too easily become a target, and she didn't intend to allow Becca to be put in danger.

"I can sense your thoughts too, and we've had this discussion before, Vampire," Becca murmured as quietly as she could, knowing any Vampire and most of the Weres in the vicinity could hear them. "You can't protect me at the cost of me doing my job. And this is what I do. I've been doing it a long time with no backup and no guards."

"But you're not alone anymore," Jody said, her heavy tone filling the wide hall with her power. "You're mine."

Becca smiled. A wave of heat passed through her, making her knees tremble. She tightened her fist in Jody's black linen shirt. "Am I now?"

You need to ask?

"No," Becca said breathlessly. "I know."

"Then don't ask me not to protect you." Jody withdrew the slight thrall she'd cast. "Tell me what he said."

"He warned there are Weres left behind in the lab."

Jody's eyes narrowed. "My soldiers and Sylvan's warriors swept that wing. We left no one behind except the permanently dead."

"I'm sure you're right. But he said there are other underground wings. I wasn't able to get all the blueprints in the little time I had, and if there *is* more to that installation, there could be more captives."

"Why would anyone associated with that operation want us… you…to know?"

"I think this man was undercover in that lab. I think he's an ally."

"Undercover with whom?" Jody said. "No one has taken credit for what was going on there, and extremist groups are the first to claim responsibility for their destructive actions. It gives them credibility and power."

"I know the pattern of fanatics," Becca said, "which is why I think whoever is behind the abductions and experimentation is far more organized and probably much more politically savvy than the typical fringe group. Whoever is in charge is obviously well-funded and well-connected, and that makes them doubly dangerous."

"Point taken." Jody signaled Rafaela. "Call your soldiers. Put them on alert. We may need to assemble a strike force."

Rafaela saluted. "Yes, Liege."

Jody said to Becca, "Can you work on finding more detailed blueprints of that installation? We need to know what else is out there. I can get satellite imaging—"

"You can? How?"

Jody smiled. "Now that I am Risen, I can call on many resources that weren't available to me as a pre-an detective."

"Handy," Becca muttered.

"We'll set up surveillance—"

"I don't think there's time."

"Why not?" Jody asked. "If there are captives there, they've been there for months. A day or two more—"

Becca shook her head. "It's not that, although I hate to think of anyone being held there for a minute longer than necessary, but he said they're moving out a lot of the expensive equipment. And they've reduced personnel to only a skeleton staff."

"Getting ready to close it down or—"

"Destroy it."

Jody took Becca's hand. "I think it's time to find the Alpha."

"I want him," Sylvan growled. She leaned against the massive stone fireplace in the meeting room of her headquarters, the *centuri* and senior *sentries* flanking her and Drake. Jody and Becca, and Jody's guards, faced them, all looking coolly elegant and unperturbed by Becca's news. Sylvan signaled to Max. "Can you get a trace from Becca's cell?"

"Possibly." Max glanced at Becca. "Do you have any kind of blocker on your phone?"

Becca shook her head. "No, for exactly this reason."

"We might be able to trace the source through the cell network with the initiation time, length of the call, and a little help from some of our people in telecommunications. But it's going to mean calling in some favors and it won't be fast."

"Do it." Sylvan reined in her fury to keep her wolves calm in the presence of the Vampires. The Vampires might be allies, but they hadn't fought together in generations, and she was still wary of allowing any outsiders, including other Praeterns, to observe her inner circle. She knew the stories of the ancient allegiances, when in centuries past the Vampires had been greater in number and had held vast territories through merciless and brutal battles. The Weres, especially the wolves, had been their armies. The Weres had never been subservient to the Vampires, but the potent draw of the Vampire bite and the strength and powers bestowed through the blood exchange were payment enough for their mercenary services. As the Weres evolved, they claimed their own territory and created their own powerful society. As they did, their ties to the Vampires weakened and eventually disappeared. Still, Sylvan felt the echo of the primal connection in her blood—reason enough to be careful around Jody Gates, heir to an ancient Vampire Clan powerful enough to rival Francesca's.

Drake eased closer to Sylvan until their shoulders touched. Sylvan rumbled, appreciative of Drake's subtle support. Tempering her wolf was always difficult but almost impossible now, when she was constantly on alert to protect her mate. Drake's presence calmed her wolf, and Sylvan stroked Drake's arm in thanks. She turned to Becca. "How long will it take for you to get us a clearer picture of the extent of the underground complex?"

"An hour, perhaps less." Becca shook her head, upset. "I shouldn't have stopped last night, but when I knew you had them, and then Jody—"

"You had no reason to continue," Sylvan said, "once it seemed the mission was over."

"This could be a trap—another attempt on the Alpha," Niki said, standing at Sylvan's right hand. They'd been together when Andrew brought word that the Vampire needed to see the Alpha immediately. She'd thought Sylvan was going to leave her there, in the sickroom, even though it seemed Sylvan had forgiven her for her transgressions. She'd held her breath, hoping she wouldn't be relegated to some secondary role, despite everything that had happened. Sylvan had simply said,

"Come, *Imperator*," as she spun on her heel and vaulted out into the hall. Now Niki was present as Sylvan's general, and her role was to strategize and, above all, to ensure the Alpha was victorious in any encounter. "We would have sensed other Weres."

"Very possibly," Jody said coolly. "It's also possible whoever was once there is now dead."

The Weres in the room growled, and their anger and battle lust heated the air with clouds of pheromones. Jody appeared unfazed by the edgy Weres. "I brought this to your attention as it reportedly involves Weres. What you choose to do about it…" She shrugged.

"And if they were Vampires?" Sylvan asked.

Jody smiled faintly. "It would take more than silver in the air to imprison a Vampire."

Drake stiffened. "You know what they did to our adolescents. You witnessed how Gray and Katya fought back. You dishonor them."

Jody's eyes flashed and Becca casually gripped her arm and squeezed lightly.

"Maybe we should all settle down so we can make a plan," Becca said quietly. Jody's arm beneath her fingertips was immovable as stone. Her fury was a metallic taste on Becca's tongue. Since Jody had risen, the darkness Becca had once sensed only as a distant shadow cloaking Jody's heart was so much stronger. She thought of Francesca and her cold, heartless beauty. She would not lose Jody to that darkness. "Jody."

Jody shuddered so faintly, Becca knew no one could tell except her. Jody inclined her head infinitesimally to Drake. "You're right, Prima. Your adolescents are brave. Had their captors tried to hold a Vampire, they could only have succeeded with UV barriers. The effect would have been the same as the silver in creating a prison."

Drake's posture relaxed. Jody had offered an apology by revealing a potential weakness. She nodded. "Difficult to construct, but not impossible."

"No more sophisticated or expensive to build than the silver aerosol system we encountered in the lab," Jody said. "This time, we should be sure we haven't missed anything—or anyone."

"This time?" Sylvan said. "You plan on accompanying us?"

"You're going to search, aren't you?"

"We have to. I couldn't sense our own adolescents through the silver barriers, so it's possible there are others. Ours or someone else's. We can't take the chance of leaving them there to be tortured further or, if your informant is right, destroyed."

"Then we should go," Jody said. "Becca can relay anything she finds on the layout while we're en route."

Jace stood on Drake's left with her legs spread and her arms folded below her small tight breasts. Her eyes glittered with dislike as she took in Jody and her Vampire soldiers. "We don't need your help."

Sylvan cut her a glance but said nothing. The *centuri* were her strongest warriors and headstrong. The young blond twins, Jace and Jonathan, were her newest and not yet tempered, but they were brave. She gave them the respect they were due, as they had pledged her their blood.

"They'll have perimeter guards no matter how few they have inside," Jody said as if she were talking to a slightly slow student. "If you want to breach their outer defenses without losing half your numbers, you'll need someone faster than you to take them out of the equation."

"Possibly," Jace said, clearly not impressed. "Why do you care? You've just said there aren't likely to be any Vampires there."

"Now," Jody said softly. "There probably aren't any there *now*. But if whoever is behind this is interested in studying—controlling— Weres, then how long will it be before they turn their interest to us?"

Rafaela moved up behind Jody's left shoulder. Claude, apparently recovered from the gunshot wounds of the night before, flanked her on the right. They were all beautiful—dark hair, fathomless eyes, pale flawless skin. Rafaela's and Claude's deep blue eyes were as impenetrable as Jody's, but Jody's were Vampire red. Hers never lost the fire, the crimson a swirling backdrop to the midnight of her irises. Her expression was just short of bored, but she radiated power.

Sylvan had spent time with Francesca, intimate moments when she'd seen Francesca unguarded and unshielded, had felt the enormous press of her power. Jody was every bit as powerful as the Regent and somehow, Sylvan thought, even more lethal. "The wolf Weres welcome the Vampires in this fight."

Rafaela and Claude nodded. Jody smiled.

"You are an excellent politician, Sylvan. You make it seem as if you are bestowing a gift upon us by letting us risk our lives for you."

"I've offered you my trust. Is there more you want?"

"Yes." Jody took a step closer. "I want your pledge to fight for Clan *Chasseur de Nuit* in the days ahead—that our enemies will be your enemies."

"And our enemies yours?" Sylvan responded.

Jody nodded.

Sylvan cocked her head, listening for Drake's answer, for the opinion of her Pack. Drake growled. The room filled with the rumbles of Weres, muting the deadly hum of Vampire power.

Yes, Drake signaled.

Sylvan didn't move a muscle, but her skin shimmered with the force of her wolf rippling beneath the surface. Drake pressed tighter, her arm sliding around Sylvan's waist, her hand gliding up and down Sylvan's flank. Sylvan's canines shot out and her face morphed into sharp angles and hard planes. "The experiments we witnessed inside that facility require a lot of money, a lot of planning, and someone powerful and well-positioned to oversee them. This can't be the only installation. I doubt this is even the only project. If we don't stop them now, they'll hunt us. All of us."

"The war has already started," Jody said as Becca's hand slid down to grasp her fingers. "Shall we fight together once more?"

Sylvan extended her arm. "As equals, Liege Gates."

Jody clasped Sylvan's forearm. "As equals, Alpha Mir."

Chapter Twelve

A shaft of light cut through the gloom in the small cell. They were coming for them again! Gray jumped from her place against the wall and landed on the floor in a crouch, putting herself between Katya and the intruder. She growled a warning and prepared to spring. Her canines erupted, her claws extended, and she thrilled to the anticipation of blood. She would take her enemies down, tear them apart, and feast on their carcasses. She was powerful, the predator, never the prey. Never again. Her vision shimmered to shades of silver, her wolf taking command. She willingly relinquished control, reveling in the swell of strength that flowed through her on the tide of her pelt bursting free, her bones transforming, her senses and her sex surging with excitement. A rumble rose from deep in her chest, and behind her, Katya whimpered, caught in the wave of Gray's thirst to hunt. This was freedom, this was what she was born for.

"Gray, come here," Drake said quietly, closing the door behind her.

The Prima's voice was soft, gentle, but the command so clear, Gray could not suppress the need to obey. Still, she feared a trap closing on her leg, silver teeth biting into her flesh, crippling her wolf, killing her inch by inch. She whined and shuddered.

"Gray," Drake repeated, unmoving, waiting. "Come."

The edge of command was sharper now, impossible to ignore. Gray could run, or fight, or accept her Prima's dominance. Where would she run to? Whose body would curl against hers in the dark? Where would she find the comfort of another heart beating in time with her own? The utter, terrible isolation of the prison cell rose up to choke her, and she doubled over.

You're ours. You're not alone.

The Alpha's voice. The Prima's voice. A thousand voices of the Pack, calling her. Slowly, Gray straightened, finding her legs, quieting her wolf. She smelled Pack, felt the warmth and security of home wrap around her. Her wolf backed away, hunkered down, wary and watchful and waiting. Gray crossed the room and ducked her head. "Prima."

Drake stroked her face, clasped her neck. "It's good to have you home."

At the first touch, Gray stiffened—remembering other hands roaming her body, violating her. But this was no stranger, no enemy. This was a welcome. This was belonging. She relaxed into the caress, and Drake quickly kissed her forehead before releasing her.

"I need to speak with you and Katya about what happened to you," Drake said. "It won't be easy. Are you ready?"

"Yes," Gray said instantly, and from the shadows, Katya declared, "Yes, Prima, we are ready."

"Good. The Alpha and I, all of the Pack, need your help."

Gray's heart swelled with pride. She had wanted to be one of the Alpha's warriors one day. She had wanted to serve, and now, after this, she feared she might never be worthy. Drake opened the windows that had been shuttered since Gray and Katya had been brought into the room—a safety measure when they hadn't been able to control their wolves, to keep them in, to keep them safe. But a prison, all the same. Gray sniffed the air—smelled dew on the pines, the tang of prey, the crisp night breeze. The night sky was crystal clear, punctuated with bright stars and lit by a nearly full moon. Her wolf came to attention. The mountains called, the night seduced. The moon filled her with power. She panted and shivered.

"I know you want to run," Drake said, leaving the window open. "I know you both need to shift again. Let's talk, and then I'll find someone to take you out for a run."

Gray did not return to her bed but sat beside Katya, her hand finding Katya's. Any other time, they would have struggled for dominance, tussled for position in the presence of the Prima, the way all young dominants jockeyed to claim their places. Once, being of the same age and both dominant females, they had been friendly competitors.

She wasn't sure what she was to Katya now, but if they ever found their places in the Pack again, if they could, she would never challenge Katya for anything or anyone. She trembled and gripped Katya's hand harder. She did not want the Prima to know she was afraid.

Katya straightened and Gray felt strength flow into her.

"It's all right," Katya murmured, and Gray remembered the voice in the dark that had kept her sane and kept her safe inside her head for weeks.

Drake crouched in front of them, her arms resting loosely on her knees, her eyes level with theirs. She looked at them not as a dominant looks at submissives, but as a leader looks at warriors.

Gray swallowed. "Anything, Prima, anything you want to know."

"What do you remember about when you were captured?"

"Nothing," Gray and Katya said simultaneously.

"Go on," Drake said patiently. "Start with the last thing you can recall."

"I was on my way to a night class," Katya said. "I took a shortcut from the dorm across the parking lot, the way I always do, and the last thing I remember is walking between rows of cars. Then I woke up in a cell."

"Did you scent anything? Hear anything?"

"Nothing. If I had, they wouldn't have taken me so easily," Katya said bitterly.

"I know it's hard to relive this," Drake said, "but can you remember anything you saw or felt when you woke up?"

Katya shuddered and Gray slipped her arm around her shoulders.

"Take a minute," Drake said.

"I remember it was hard to breathe," Katya said softly. "The air was heavy, as if it was filled with smoke, but I couldn't see any. I couldn't see very far at all. My vision was blurry."

"Gray?" Drake asked, "Did you have the same experience?"

"Yes," Gray exclaimed, the memory flooding her senses as if it were still happening. "A bitter taste every time I breathed, and my arms and legs as heavy as if they had weights on them. They chained us—" She choked at the sensation of being helpless, spread out against the cold wall, blood running down her back.

"Easy," Drake said soothingly. "You're safe now."

Gray swallowed back the panic. "They chained us and we couldn't shift. My wolf was caught somewhere in a trap, held down—so weak. Couldn't fight back."

"It was silver," Drake said. "There was nothing either one of you could have done to escape. They poisoned you from the beginning, weakening your ability to think, to reason, to plan. You survived because you are both strong. Because you are both brave."

"I am not strong," Gray snarled. "I let myself be taken. I was hunting alone and I had just shifted back to skin after a kill. I was proud of myself, celebrating my hunt. I wasn't watching, I wasn't wary. I'd forgotten everything Callan taught us in *sentrie* training, forgot everything the Alpha taught us about hunting. It's my fault I was taken."

Drake shook her head. "No. There are reasons we hunt together besides capturing our prey quickly and cleanly, but there are reasons you need to run alone too. There is no prohibition against a solo hunt. You broke no rules. What happened to you could've happened to any of us—except the Alpha."

"A *centuri* would never have been captured."

Drake laughed, and the sound rippled through Gray like sunshine at dawn. When had she last heard laughter?

"Someday, you may be as strong as a *centuri*. But for now, you are both more than strong enough." Drake lightly gripped their legs. "Can you describe your captors?"

Katya's grip on Gray's hand tightened to the point Gray thought her bones would break, and she pushed closer, pressing her naked thigh to Katya's. Sharing her warmth, reminding Katya as Katya had reminded her so many times that she was not alone in the dark.

"I remember voices," Katya said slowly, "and hands touching me. Cold."

Katya shuddered and fur rippled beneath Gray's fingertips. Katya's wolf wanted out of the cage, wanted freedom. In another second she would break free and bolt out the window, and they would have to hunt her down and bring her back. Gray couldn't let her be a prisoner again.

Gray pulled Katya into her arms and tucked Katya's face in to the curve of her neck. "It's all right. No one will hurt you again."

Katya whimpered and licked Gray's neck, seeking comfort and security. Gray forced down a growl of fury at seeing her Packmate, so beautiful and strong, so terrified. She kept her voice soft, letting her wolf creep forward to nuzzle Katya's ear. "Let me tell her." She nipped Katya's jaw and Katya curled more tightly against her.

"I'm sorry," Katya whispered.

"No," Gray said, firmly, realizing now that as tormented as she had felt in that cell, Katya had been more abused. They had given Katya the hormones to stimulate her glands, siphoned off her blood, drained her sex, used Katya's body to excite Gray into ejaculating. Katya, a dominant Were, had been forced into submission over and over.

"They kept us drugged," Gray said. "Katya more than me. Still, it's hard to remember—they didn't give us food, tormented us, tried to force us to tangle."

"We couldn't stop them from making us...do things." Katya shivered. "I couldn't keep them from taking what they wanted."

Drake growled, her midnight eyes darker than the sky. "I saw the lab. I saw the restraining tables, the instruments, the drugs. They paid with their lives for what they did to you."

"We didn't tangle for them," Katya whispered. "They drained us, but we didn't give them everything. We never bit, we never completely emptied..."

"If you had," Drake said, "even if you'd *wanted* to, it wouldn't have been your fault. I suspect they gave you some kind of synthetic mating hormone. You couldn't have resisted that, but you both fought back. The Alpha and I are proud of you."

"Parts of it are like a dream—a bad dream you never wake up from," Gray said. "There were men who came for us, but now their faces are blurred, as if I was seeing them through a curtain of fog. I can't tell them apart anymore, can't remember what they were called."

"The aftereffects of the silver poisoning have altered your nervous system. Your memory has been distorted, but it may come back at any time. Don't try to force it. Whatever you can remember right now is fine. If more comes later, then tell me or the Alpha."

"There was a female—" Gray could see the shape of her body on the other side of the bars, smell her desire, feel the heat kindling in her belly at the sound of her voice. The face was a shadow, but Gray remembered the thrum of sex in her blood when the smooth voice caressed her. She remembered wanting to fuck her, and she remembered laughter. A shower of laughter that cut like shards of silver.

Gray growled, her thighs flexing restlessly, her clitoris tightening. Her glands pulsed and her hips jerked at the touch of rough hands on her sex, white-hot lightning streaking through her, the whip of pleasure snapping her control, forcing her to release. "She wanted us excited."

"Another Were?" Drake asked, her voice gravelly.

"Not a wolf," Gray said immediately.

"We think they might've been using cat Weres as guards," Drake said.

Gray had never seen a cat Were. She'd only been off the Compound a few times, once with Fala when she'd gone to the police station to see where Fala worked. She remembered not liking it there—too many bodies, too many foreign scents—gasoline, smoke, sweat. Too many humans. Her eyes flew open. "A human. A human female."

"One of the guards?"

Gray felt the press of power in her blood, thrilled to the command in the melodious voice. "No, not a guard. She was in charge."

"Would you know her again?"

"I think so," Gray murmured, aching with the need to be over her, inside her. She shuddered. She would kill her if she ever saw her again. Kill her because she still wanted her.

"What you're feeling," Drake said gently, "is because of everything that happened to you there. There is no shame in it."

Katya turned her head on Gray's shoulder, her eyes deep pools of misery. "They made us want things. Need things."

"I know."

"We didn't...They wanted us to tangle, so they could—" Katya jerked upright. "I remember! I remember at the end—I was chained, hanging, I think. She held me, she...took the pain away."

"Who? The human female?"

"No," Katya said, her voice wavering. "Not human."

Drake looked from Katya to Gray. "You're sure about the female? That she was human?"

"Yes." Even now, Gray's skin tingled with the memory of the female's pheromones coating her. Sweeter and subtler than Were, but still powerfully enticing. Her wolf bounded to her feet. The scent of sex coated Gray's tongue. She remembered tearing free from the restraints, leaping from the table, ready to take her. "She was there. In the lab. At the end."

Drake said to Katya, "But she's not the one you remember?"

"No," Katya said, her voice distant. "I felt her inside me, deep in my blood. She made them stop hurting me. She made me come." Katya pushed away from Gray. "She made me come, when she bit me."

"Vampire," Drake said flatly.

"Yes, yes." Katya rubbed her arms, pressed her hands down her thighs. "She was...beautiful."

❖

Drake found Sylvan at her desk at headquarters. She motioned Niki out of the room. "I need to speak to the Alpha alone."

"Yes, Prima." Niki spun on her heel and left quickly, closing the door quietly behind her.

Sylvan rose and leapt easily over the desk, landing in front of Drake to grasp her shoulders lightly. "What is it? I could feel your fury across the Compound. I would have come to you except I knew you were on your way here."

"I just finished speaking with Katya and Gray. When we find who is responsible, I want to leave their bodies on the steps of the state capitol building. I want everyone to know that no one touches our wolves and lives." Drake grasped Sylvan's hips and yanked her forward, kissing her hard. She needed the taste of her mate to settle her mind, to temper her wrath so she could think. All she wanted to do right now was kill.

"It shall be done," Sylvan whispered when Drake released her. She kept her arms around Drake and raked her canines down Drake's neck, running her tongue back up the faint crimson trail. "How are they?"

"Considering everything they've been through, amazingly well. But they're both traumatized. Their memories are fractured. Their wolves barely under control. They both need to tangle and I'm not sure who to trust them with. They're volatile and strong young wolves and they're going to be wild."

"I'll deal with that," Sylvan said. "Did they tell you anything to help us?"

"Right now, they can't remember enough to identify their captors."

"Something they said has made you furious. What is it?"

"Even by Were standards they're barely sexually mature. And both of them have been abused. By humans and at least one Vampire."

"A Vampire," Sylvan said softly, her body going as still as a predator crouched in the brush, stalking prey. "They're sure?"

"Katya still shows signs of being enthralled. Whoever fed from her was very powerful. I suspect Gray had more than one exposure to a human female. Judging by the extent of Gray's visceral response to the memory, she was sexually taunted and seduced."

"Weres are not usually susceptible to human pheromones," Sylvan said. She nuzzled Drake's neck. "Your effect on me was rare."

"But not unheard of. There are human and Were matings," Drake pointed out.

"Not true matings, but you're right, interspecies breeding is possible. Val's mother was Were, her father human."

"Probably some humans are more compatible with Weres than others, or," Drake said, "extreme deprivation over a long period of time may have increased Gray's susceptibility to human pheromones."

"We knew humans had to be behind this—they are the only group with the financial capability and organization to pull this off. But a human-Vampire alliance?" Sylvan snarled. "Let's see what our new ally has to say about that."

"Sylvan," Drake said reluctantly, "Jody may be an ally, but she is a Vampire first."

"As I am the Timberwolf Alpha before all else." Sylvan kissed Drake hard enough to bruise, and Drake welcomed the small bite of pain.

"What are you going to do?" Drake asked.

"Unless I'm greatly mistaken, no Vampire could be involved without the Viceregal knowing. We'll hear what Jody has to say, and after we've checked out the installation again, we'll pay the Viceregal a visit."

CHAPTER THIRTEEN

The buzzer rang just as Veronica finished pouring port into a crystal glass. She glanced at the antique walnut mantel clock above the marble fireplace. Seven p.m. precisely. She smiled. She valued precision, especially in those in her employ. Waiting a moment—sending a subtle reminder of who was in charge—she pressed the intercom. "Yes?"

"We have an appointment, Dr. Standish," a cool, husky voice replied.

"Yes, we do." Veronica smiled to herself. She recognized the voice. And how like that Vampire to respond with a subtle challenge of her own, not the slightest hint of respect or subservience in her voice. She liked that about the Vampires, although under certain circumstances their lack of appropriate deference could be problematic. All the same, she enjoyed the tingle in her clitoris at the sound of Michel's voice. A monitor, concealed in a bookcase next to the fireplace, revealed three individuals outside her door. Michel she recognized, lean and dark and lethal, even in apparent repose. The two Vampires with her were dressed similarly—black shirts open at the throat, tapered black pants, narrow belts around tight trim hips. No weapons that she could see. Of course, they *were* the weapons. "Take the stairs to the top floor. The door on the right."

"Thank you."

Veronica buzzed them in and crossed back to the open doors of the balcony and stepped outside. The night was clear and pleasantly cool. Light from the old-fashioned street lamps scattered throughout the park winked through the trees. She wondered briefly if the Vampires at her door had fed on any of the humans who ran along the paths below, going about their mundane and unexciting lives, unsuspecting of the monsters stalking them. She had never actually seen a Vampire feeding, other than the one brief time when she'd observed Michel feeding from a Were during her experiments—her *aborted* experiments, thanks to the treachery of one human guard and the persistence of Sylvan Mir. She'd been interrupted before she could gather the data she wanted—or share in the vicarious pleasure. Even now, anger at the memory of her lab being overrun with creatures coiled in her belly like a serpent, venomous and unrequited. Sooner or later, every one of them would pay. In the greater scheme of things, she wanted to biologically control the Were species, if not eradicate them altogether, for the good of humankind. On a personal level, she wanted to look into their eyes as they died, knowing she had triumphed. She wanted them to know that she, personally, had been responsible for their downfall. After all, behind every action, no matter how noble or ignoble, lay personal motivation. No one acted purely for the common good, no matter what they would have you believe. She at least admitted it. Fortunately, her goal to purify and protect the human genome was supported by any number of individuals and groups who wanted to exterminate the Praeterns. She merely took advantage of their resources.

A knock sounded on the living room door. Setting her glass aside, she smoothed her white silk shirt over her breasts, lingering just an instant on the tightness of her nipples, unburdened by a bra, beneath the sheer material. She squeezed lightly, sending the tingling into the pit of her stomach, and opened the door. The pair with Michel were as attractive as she expected—a female slightly shorter than Michel and reed-slender like so many of the Vampires, and a male, blond and handsome in an almost too-refined way. She thought briefly of Francesca, so very different from her minions. They'd only met in person once, but the Viceregal was a presence one couldn't forget. Voluptuous, sensual, radiating power with such casual disregard Veronica found herself so aroused she'd needed to masturbate as soon as she'd been alone. No hardship, but surprising, that a woman had incited such an uncontrollable response. Then she'd witnessed Michel feeding, and she'd understood. The Vampire thrall functioned beyond sexuality or gender—it struck at the primitive core of desire programmed into the DNA of every living being. Her clitoris tightened further. She was going to enjoy having these creatures around. "Come in."

Michel entered first, her dark gaze sliding down Veronica's body, fixing on the points of Veronica's nipples with arrogant disregard for decorum. Her eyes, when they rose to Veronica's, glinted scarlet. "Good evening."

Veronica backed away and indicated the seating area with the sweep of her arm. "Please, make yourselves comfortable. Can I get you anything? I was just having some port."

"No, thank you." Michel remained standing, as did the two guards with her, until Veronica retrieved her port and settled at the end of a butter-soft, cream-colored leather sofa. She crossed her legs, unobtrusively drawing the hem of her black silk skirt up her thigh. She watched Michel's eyes track her movements, thinking how very much Michel's hot gaze resembled that of a cat following the path of a mouse across the floor. Oh yes, they were predators. Beautiful, sensual predators. The idea of taming them made her wet.

At some signal from Michel she didn't see, the two guards sat on the matching sofa opposite her while Michel indolently leaned against the fireplace, her long, lean legs crossed at the ankles, her black boots gleaming. A bit of silver flashed at her wrist.

Veronica amended her first impression. She'd been wrong—they did have weapons, at least Michel did. A knife strapped on the inner aspect of her right arm. She remembered now, the slash of a blade releasing the Were female from the overhead restraint, allowing the captive to drop into Michel's arms, and the quick flash of Michel's incisors striking the Were's neck. Veronica's breathing quickened as she recalled the Were's frantic moans, her struggle to climax, and the flood of crimson followed by the shine of release coating her twitching thighs.

"Please tell your mistress I appreciate your assistance. But tell me, how will we manage daytime events?"

Michel smiled faintly. "Raymond is human. He will escort you during the day, and in the evening, Luce will be your primary guard, although Raymond will also be available. Should you for any reason need other assistance, we will see that you are well attended."

Veronica glanced briefly at her new bodyguards. Now that she saw them together, she detected the difference. Raymond was indeed beautiful by any standards, but his eyes did not carry the gleam of power that radiated from Luce's. He would no doubt be enjoyable in bed, and she looked forward to finding out, but Luce—she promised something more than an orgasm. She offered an experience beyond simple desire.

"I hope there comes a time when you might grace me with your presence, *Senechal*," Veronica said, showing Francesca's ambassador the appropriate respect in front of her underlings. "Your previous visit was disappointingly short."

Michel leaned back, her smile flickering over her exposed incisors. A wave of red heat flowed through Veronica's body, flushing her breasts, swelling her sex. If she tightened her thighs, she would orgasm where she sat. She laughed at the audacity of the beautiful Vampire. "I'll take that as a yes."

Michel inclined her head, her fiery gaze fixed on Veronica's throat. "With pleasure, Dr. Standish."

❖

"Stay with the Alpha," Niki said to Andrew and Max, who stood post outside the Alpha's office on the wide balcony overlooking the first floor meeting area. "I'll be outside."

"Yes, *Imperator*," Andrew said, and the restless churning in Niki's belly settled. Here, with the rhythm of the Pack thrumming through her blood, she knew who she was and what she had to do. She leapt over the railing and landed easily on the stone floor a story below, the muscles in her thighs tensing as the shock rippled through her. Her wolf stretched, awakening inside her skin again. Straightening, she pulled air deep into her lungs, searching for the one taste she craved. There. Undercutting the essence of all the Weres and wildlife, blunting even the seductive allure of the Vampires, the one single tantalizing scent that drew her like no other. Sophia.

She pushed through the enormous wooden doors and bounded down onto the hard-packed earth in the center of the complex. She knew where Sophia was, and she wanted her out of that room. Away from Lara.

She strode quickly across the yard and vaulted onto the porch, nodded to the Vampire's guards who flanked the door, and powered down the hall. She'd been where Sophia was now, and she was done pretending she didn't care. She'd had enough. She did not knock.

She shouldered into the dimly lit room and let the door swing closed behind her.

A growl filled the room. Lara, naked, held Sophia with an arm around Sophia's shoulders, a possessive gesture that brought Niki's wolf roaring to life. Her jaw elongated and her vocal cords thickened so she could barely speak around her snarl. "I've come for Sophia."

"Sophia is with me." Challenge in Lara's voice.

Niki had been challenged too many times for this female, and she ached to fight, but she remembered the Alpha's warning. If she could not control her wolf, she could not be trusted. Claws burst through her fingertips and pelt shot down her abdomen. Blood dripped onto the rough wood floor. She strode to the bed and held out her hand to Sophia, ignoring Lara's warning snarl. "Come with me."

"She is not yours to call," Lara rumbled.

Sophia sat up, slipping out from under Lara's shielding arm. "Nor yours," she said softly.

"You don't have to go with her," Lara said. "Your blood fills me—stay."

"Your Vampire rules you now," Sophia murmured gently, "or you'd know I can't."

"I feel your need," Lara said. "Come back when it grows too great."

Sophia kissed Lara's cheek. "I'm all right. Will you be all right?"

Lara pushed upright, her back against the wall. Her eyes shone more amber than crimson, more wolf than Vampire, but her scent was a mixture of both. She nodded curtly. "Go. And…thank you."

"You don't need to thank me," Sophia said, rising from the bed. She pulled on the T-shirt and jeans she'd shed earlier. "I told you, my need as well as yours."

Niki's chest tightened, knowing that Lara had given Sophia what she had not been able to, what Sophia would not accept from her—release and with it, pleasure. She didn't resent Sophia finding relief where she could, but she couldn't bear to see Sophia in Lara's arms. She gently closed her fingers around Sophia's hand. "Please."

Sophia followed Niki out into the hall. "What is it that you want, Niki?"

"I...I needed to see you." Niki entwined her fingers through Sophia's and drew her outside. The brush of Sophia's shoulder against hers warmed her. She could smell Lara on her, and knowing Lara had touched her blurred her mind with fury. She battled down the urge to go back and drag Lara to the floor and bloody her. Sophia had needed Lara, and there was no fault in any Were—or Vampire—she chose answering that need. Still, she couldn't help herself. "Did she fuck you?"

Sophia jerked Niki to a halt at the edge of the woods that ringed the Compound. "Stop it. Why torture us both?"

"Just tell me," Niki growled.

Sophia pulled her hand free and cupped Niki's jaw. "No."

Niki shuddered and rubbed her cheek against Sophia's palm. "I'm sorry."

"I know." Sophia kissed her. "I know."

Niki dropped her voice to a subvocal level, conscious of Jody's guards outside the infirmary. "There'll be a mission tonight. I wanted to see you before I went."

Sophia pressed against Niki's side, caressing down Niki's chest until her hand rested on Niki's bare abdomen. Her fingertips feathered the pelt along Niki's midline. "What is it? Can you tell me?"

"You need to know, so does Elena. You'll need to prepare. We've gotten word there are more Weres left in the installation where Katya and Gray were held captive. We're going to get them."

"More?" Sophia stiffened. "They can't be ours. We'd know."

"Maybe," Niki said. "But we always have a few adolescents who run solo until they decide how they fit in the Pack. We might not know anything was wrong if we didn't hear from them for a few weeks. Even a month or two. We can't be sure if we're missing anyone."

"Bring them home, Niki," Sophia said fervently. "What they did to them—bring them home."

Niki wrapped her arm around Sophia's shoulders and pulled her close. She rubbed her face in Sophia's hair, trembling at the touch of Sophia's breasts against her chest. "We will. We will, and you will heal them."

"I want you to come home too." Sophia rubbed against her and licked her neck.

Pheromones, Sophia's and hers, misted the air and Niki's sex readied. She let her hands roam over Sophia's back, tracing the delicate but strong muscles along her spine and the swell of her ass. She edged her thigh between Sophia's, aching to empty. Her clitoris distended, stiffened with urgency, and she growled low in her throat.

"I need your head clear tonight," Sophia murmured, edging her hand under the waistband of Niki's pants, pushing lower until her fingers slid on either side of Niki's clitoris. "I need you to be careful."

Niki's ass tightened and she pushed into Sophia's hand. "Sophia, what—"

"Shh," Sophia said. "You need this, so do I, before you go."

Her fingers worked magic, stroking the hard nodes of Niki's glands, caressing the length of her clitoris, sliding lower, deeper, until she cupped her inside and out. Niki's breath caught in her throat, her back arched, and she threw her head back. The stars revolved overhead, swirling faster and faster until all she saw was swaths of white light blinding her with unbearable pleasure. Sophia scraped her canines down Niki's throat, drawing blood, and Niki exploded so hard and fast her legs gave way. She dropped to her knees and found herself cushioned in Sophia's arms. So much stronger than she realized, so much more than she'd ever dreamed. Shuddering, she rested her head on Sophia's shoulder.

"Come back tonight, *Imperator*," Sophia whispered. "I'll be waiting."

CHAPTER FOURTEEN

The door opened and Lara jumped up, ready to fight. She'd been expecting Niki to return and challenge her for tangling with Sophia, to try to prevent her from feeding from Sophia again. She'd smelled the possessive fury coating Niki's skin. Sophia was in heat and Niki wanted to claim mating rights. A week ago, when she'd been Were and not part Vampire, she wouldn't have disputed Niki's claim, even if Sophia hadn't taken Niki as a mate. But she wasn't who she had been. She didn't burn to quench the fires of Sophia's heat, but she hungered for her just as strongly as Niki. Sophia's blood ran sweet and strong with the exhilarating pulse of life, giving her something she hadn't known she sought. Calm. No Were or human she'd fed from had given her that.

Feeding from Niki had been like opening herself to a forest fire. Niki's blood was a fury, boiling with power and undercut with rage. Niki's blood had filled her, driven her to mindless release, but left her restless and needing. Sophia had not only tamed her hunger, she'd silenced her need and given her an overwhelming sense of peace. She would have fed from her again if Niki hadn't arrived. If her hunger hadn't been so recently sated, she would not have allowed Niki to take Sophia without a fight. Sophia had come to her willingly, and a Vampire did not allow another predator to claim her host.

But she would not fight for peace tonight. The enemy who faced her was not Niki.

"Peace is not what you need," Jody said. "What you need burning in you is the thrill of the chase. We are, above all, hunters."

"What I need is freedom," Lara said. "I know how to hunt."

"Do you even know what freedom is now?" Jody said. "You once hunted prey who did not challenge you. Now you pursue the most intelligent prey on the planet—humans and other Praeterns. And you still have much to learn."

Lara hated the Vampire who'd made her what she was by destroying everything she had been, especially when she knew Jody was right. She wasn't born for peace. And she ached for the rush of blood in her throat. "What do you want?"

"You will pledge to me now," Jody said quietly, "or you will never leave this room."

"Do I have a choice?" Lara looked at the window behind her—at the night outside. Once she had run beneath the stars, strong and fast and sure. She could feel the distant longing of her wolf to leap free, to find the Pack, to hunt. If she turned her back on Jody, took her chances at surviving without Jody's protection, would she find herself alone in the night? She was no longer *centuri*. She was no longer Were. She'd rather keep her wolf in chains than find she had no longer had a home. She wanted to kill the Vampire whose power filled the room with such force she ached to kneel and offer up her throat. She struggled to bury the foreign desire to submit. "Why don't you kill me now? I will never bend to you."

"I did not ask you to bend."

Jody was suddenly in front of her, her warm, long fingers clamped around Lara's throat. Jody had fed recently, and her strength took Lara's breath away. The crimson flare in Jody's eyes flamed through to Lara's core. The part of her that was Were readied for the release promised in Jody's bite, her glands filling so sharply she gasped. She shuddered with need. Her heart might beat with Sophia's blood coursing through her veins, but her body burned for Jody, the master she craved and loathed. "What is it you want?"

"You are so much stronger than you should be," Jody murmured, her mouth brushing along the edge of Lara's jaw. "You were so completely empty when I animated you, only my blood flows in you. I was wrong about what you are."

Lara's stomach iced. "I don't understand."

Jody released Lara's throat and stroked her fingers over Lara's cheek, tracing the curve of her cheek with her thumb. "You are not a newling—not a living Vampire. You are Risen, a full-blooded member of my line. Your powers are already stronger than a youngling Risen Vampire's. I suspect you'll be able to stay awake during the day before long."

"Like you?"

"Yes."

"And if I want to be free from your Dominion?"

Jody smiled. "Do you seek to challenge?"

Lara didn't think she could defeat Jody in battle, but she would not surrender, she would not submit without a fight, and she would die before she would kneel. "You haven't told me what you want."

"I need a warlord—a Vampire to lead my soldiers, to enforce my word, and to protect my consort. Pledge to me, and you will live."

"And if you go to war with the Weres?"

Jody's alabaster face was as unyielding as stone, her crimson eyes volcanic. "You pledge to me for life, with your life. Break your pledge and you will die."

Lara thought back to the moments with Sophia. Lara's wolf had longed for the touch of another Were, but Sophia had not wanted a mate. If she had, Lara would have failed her. She could never mate with a Were—never provide a mate with young, never be part of the Pack the way she had been. She was *other* now, Vampire, and the Weres could never be more to her than hosts. She had no place in Sylvan's army, no place in the Pack. But she was and always would be a warrior. She was Praetern, Were or Vampire, and the Praetern struggle was hers, as it always had been. Jody, her lord but never master, was offering her honor and purpose. She went down on one knee.

"I pledge my service to you, Liege."

Jody drew Lara to her feet with the force of her thrall. Lara shuddered but held her position, even though her wolf trembled on the verge of release. Jody kissed her and a wave of heat passed through her, igniting her, empowering her. She bit back a moan as *victus* flooded her thighs.

Jody kissed her. "Welcome to my Clan, Warlord."

❖

"I have to go," Niki murmured, her cheek against Sophia's breast. She knelt at the edge of the forest, spent and defenseless in Sophia's arms.

"I know you do." Sophia threaded her fingers through Niki's hair, feeling as if she might shatter inside. She couldn't let Niki feel her terror. From her first consciousness of being Were, she'd known she was different. She'd never felt the same drive to find her place as the young dominants who tussled endlessly in search of their position in the Pack. She didn't burn with the need to nurture and protect like the non-dominants who became the teachers, the caretakers, and the soldiers. She'd always been other, even while being part of the whole, and Elena had helped her find her place as a healer. As an adolescent she'd watched the hunters foray into the mountains for weeks at a time to bring back food for the Pack, seen the young non-dominants—male and female alike—find mates, care for the young, and create the fabric that held the Pack together. Since the Exodus, she'd seen the warriors leave for battle. Some of those warriors had come back injured and dying. Niki, standing at the Alpha's side, was at greater risk to die in battle than any in the Pack. Niki would give her life for the Alpha's, as was her duty, and Sophia could never let Niki know that if Niki did not return, she might not survive. "Go, *Imperator*. We both have duties. I need to find Elena so we can be prepared if you find captive Weres."

"I would not leave you if I didn't have to."

Sophia smiled and stroked Niki's cheek. "You don't need to tell me that."

Niki's green eyes were wolf-shot, hot and possessive. "Your heat is not over. You'll be in need again soon."

"This is far from the first heat I've been through. I'll be all right."

"I would not have you suffer," Niki grumbled, "but Lara—"

"I'm not going to her again," Sophia said gently.

"There are others who—"

"Perhaps you would like to choose someone for me to tangle with while you're gone."

Niki snarled and Sophia pulled her up until they were face-to-face. "Then stop pushing me to tangle with someone else." She caught Niki's lip between her teeth and tugged it. "I'm all right."

Niki cradled Sophia's face and kissed her softly. "When I return, let me answer your need."

"I told you I would be waiting." Sophia grasped Niki's wrists and kissed first one palm, then the other. "When you leave tonight, your duty is only to the Alpha. That will always and ever be the case."

Niki rested her forehead against Sophia's. "Then you know why I can't mate."

"I already told you, that's not what I want." Sophia forced a laugh. "I'd forgotten why I didn't want to tangle with you. Your head is like a rock."

"I might not be what you want," Niki said, "but I can give you what you need."

"Go, Niki," Sophia said, her heart bleeding, her wolf in a rage. She'd had this power struggle with her wolf in every heat. What she knew she couldn't have and what her wolf demanded were forever at war. The struggle tore her in two every time, and letting Niki close made it worse. Tangling with her and not biting her, not giving herself totally, made the pain unbearable. She wanted her, needed her, ached for her—but her wolf wanted a mate. A true mate, with a union of blood and hormones and *victus*. She couldn't risk that, and avoiding the mate bond was endless agony.

"Your wolf is restless," Niki murmured, skating her hands over Sophia's breasts. "Your heat is already rising and your wolf wants a joining. How long can you fight her?"

"As long as I have to." Sophia pressed against Niki's hot, hard body. She needed the feel of Niki's heart beating against hers to carry her through the long hours of waiting. "You're needed with the Alpha, Niki."

Niki kissed her swiftly, a hard, deep, claiming kiss. The scrape of Niki's canines over Sophia's lip made her sex clench and she readied instantly. She quivered in Niki's arms. "Niki, stop."

"Sorry," Niki murmured, sucking the bite she'd made in Sophia's lip. "I had to taste you."

Sophia couldn't hold her wolf back any longer. In another second she would need to taste Niki too, and she wouldn't stop with a nip. She'd bite and her mating hormones would surge into Niki's blood. No, God no. Sophia pushed at Niki, her claws scoring down Niki's chest. "Go. Hurry."

Niki didn't budge. She pulled Sophia's mouth to her chest. "Taste me."

Whining deep in her throat, Sophia licked.

Niki growled at the soft rasp of Sophia's tongue over the marks Sophia's claws had made. "Remember my taste in your blood if you let anyone else take you."

"If you care about me," Sophia gasped, "you'll go."

Niki vaulted away and landed on the wide porch of the Alpha's headquarters. Panting, Sophia watched her disappear through eyes slanting to ice blue. Snow-white pelt shimmered over her as her wolf broke free, and she raised her head and cried to the sky before streaking off alone into the dark.

❖

"Friday night," Veronica said, swirling the burgundy liquid in the glass cradled in her palms, "I'll be attending the governor's gala." She smiled at Luce. "You'll be available?"

"Of course," the Vampire replied. "What time would you like to leave?"

"Would nine p.m. suit?"

Luce's mouth curved and the tip of a gleaming incisor dimpled her full lower lip. "Your pleasure always suits, Dr. Standish."

Veronica's breath hitched at the sensation of warm fingers brushing over her breasts, though no one touched her. Her clitoris pulsed between her thighs, engorged and insistent, as soft lips closed around her. The tug of a silken mouth had her on the edge of climaxing. Veronica was an expert at schooling her expression so nothing showed, but Luce's smile widened and her eyes flashed scarlet. The Vampire knew her thrall had excited her. Veronica gritted her teeth. What arrogance! But so intriguing.

"Is it in your control?" Veronica asked, sipping her port to hide the tremor in her hands. Luce was testing her, but she discounted Veronica's strength. Veronica knew how to gain the upper hand—she'd had plenty of practice with the men she worked with. She hadn't gotten as far in her life as she had by letting the bluster and physicality of others overpower her. The one thing men couldn't seem to process, or ignore, was sexual aggression from a woman. They'd go anywhere their cocks led them. Perhaps the promise of her blood would work the same way. "The seduction? Is it selective or will anyone do?"

"Oh," Luce replied, her voice husky and her eyes glinting, "my interest is quite voluntary. You're a beautiful woman."

Veronica glanced at Michel, whose elegant features were ever-so-slightly amused. "You've no problem with your—employee—attempting to seduce me?"

"Did you expect us to behave like humans?" Michel asked quietly, brushing her fingers over Raymond's neck. The human servant drew a sharp breath, his hands tightening on his thighs. An erection swelled beneath his black trousers, pushing along his inner thigh.

"I see," Veronica said, taking in the display of dominance. The Vampires survived by enthralling their hosts, and sex was the currency of their power. Seduction was as natural to them as breathing. Rising, she circled behind the sofa where her new bodyguards sat and leaned over Luce from behind. She brushed her lips over Luce's ear. "I don't want you distracted while you're working."

Luce tilted her head back, her mouth skimming Veronica's neck. "I'll be sure to come to you well-fed. Unless you prefer to feed me."

Veronica ran her tongue over Luce's lower lip, so close to orgasm she barely held back a moan. "I'll expect you at sundown tomorrow."

"And Raymond?"

"He can watch."

Chapter Fifteen

I want you to stay here tonight," Sylvan said, tucking a tight black T-shirt into black BDUs. She bent to lace up her black combat boots.

Drake crossed her arms and leaned against the bedroom door. "What should I do while you're leading your warriors on a night mission, Alpha? I think we've got plenty of cooks in the mess hall. As far as I know, there aren't any household chores that need doing."

Sylvan cut her a glance, strapped on a thigh sheath, and slipped in a twelve-inch double-sided KA-BAR. "You're a medic. Katya and Gray need you."

"They do," Drake said reasonably. She'd been expecting this, wondering how long Sylvan would wait. "Katya and Gray need you too. As far as their medical and psychological condition, Elena and Sophia are more qualified than me to take care of them."

"Then stay here and take care of the young in your belly." Sylvan straightened and stalked toward her, a new dark dangerous glint in her eyes.

"Are we going to have this struggle for the next two months?" Drake stopped Sylvan's march with a palm pressed to the center of Sylvan's chest. Hard muscles bunched beneath her fingers and her body heated. She could never touch Sylvan without wanting her. "Before you growl," Drake said, "listen."

Sylvan's lip curled into a snarl, but she held her peace. Her mate was stubborn and she wouldn't yield to dominance, not even from her Alpha. "I don't have much time. The *centuri* are waiting."

"They'll wait for you as long as they need to." Drake slid both hands down Sylvan's torso and hooked her fingers around the waistband of Sylvan's tight pants. She yanked her forward until Sylvan's body was pressed against hers. They were eye to eye, Sylvan's deep blue eyes shimmering with shards of gold. Sylvan's wolf was always at the surface these days, riding her hard, driving her with all the primal instincts of a Were with a pregnant mate. Add to that the enhanced aggression inherent to the Alpha and she was close to being beyond reason. Drake kissed her softly. "I love you."

Sylvan frowned. "I don't understand."

"I know." Drake grinned. "You aggravate me ninety percent of the time just the same."

Sylvan's brows shot up, the rumble that reverberated through her striking the center of Drake's chest like a thunderbolt. If she didn't concentrate, she'd forget the point she was trying to make and simply let Sylvan have her way, let Sylvan take her the way her wolf wanted right this minute. Drake felt herself opening, readying, responding to the call of her mate, and something more. She ached with the need to answer Sylvan's need. Sylvan's need for her, and only her, made every challenge attainable, every hurdle surmountable. She caressed Sylvan's face with one hand and slid the other arm around Sylvan's hips, holding her close. "I need to be where you are. I can't stay here and wait."

"I can't let you put yourself in danger," Sylvan said, her husky voice strained. "I have to protect you and our young for the sake of the Pack." She closed her eyes and rested her forehead against Drake's. "And for my sanity. Please, understand that."

Drake curved her fingers around Sylvan's neck and rubbed her cheek against Sylvan's. She kissed her eyes, her mouth, her throat. The Alpha, the strength of hundreds, trembled in her arms, and she felt power beyond any she had ever known. That power humbled her, making her hands even more gentle. "And I need to be close to you, for my sanity. I'll drive the Rover. I'll stay with the vehicles, and if you want, you can leave a guard."

Sylvan broke away and strode to the window. When she grasped the rough wood frame, the boards creaked, threatening to splinter. From behind, Drake could see Sylvan's wolf straining to emerge. Sylvan's shoulders hunched and flexed, her arms shook, her ass tensed. Drake didn't want her mate to struggle, didn't want Sylvan at odds with her wolf, but Drake's wolf paced and growled and gnawed at her insides too. *Her* need to protect her mate was every bit as strong as Sylvan's. Drake went to her, laid her cheek between Sylvan's shoulder blades, and wrapped her arms around her waist. Pressing close, she whispered, "Trust me, mate. Trust me to care for our young and you."

"What you're asking goes against every instinct I have." Sylvan spun around and gripped Drake's shoulders, her eyes completely gold, her face sharp and heavy, her canines lethal blades. "I can't have any harm come to you or our young. I can't lose you. I can't."

"You won't." Drake grabbed a fistful of Sylvan's hair and kissed her hard. Her canines caught the corner of Sylvan's mouth and drew blood. She sucked on the scrape and Sylvan, growling, lifted her and carried her in three long strides to the bed. Sylvan dropped her on the blanket and fell on top of her, caging her between her arms and her legs. Drake swelled inside her jeans as Sylvan's thigh clamped hard between hers. She was too ready to wait. Her claws shredded the back of Sylvan's shirt. Sylvan's tongue was in her mouth, hot and demanding, filling her. Sylvan's hands were on her breasts, tormenting her nipples, and Sylvan's hot hard heat was everywhere over her. Drake thrust and dug her claws into Sylvan's back. Sylvan reached between them, ripped away clothing, and suddenly she was all Drake knew. Drake covered the bite on Sylvan's chest with her mouth and came with a fierceness that purged her mind of every thought.

When the haze cleared, she tightened her hold on Sylvan, who lay spent and panting. Sylvan's face was pressed into the curve of her neck, and Drake was so overcome by the need to protect her, she could barely breathe. She stroked Sylvan's back, caressing the small wounds she'd left. "Just because I can't resist you doesn't mean you can always have your way."

"You're supposed to want to give me anything I ask for." Sylvan nipped Drake's neck hard enough for Drake to feel her clitoris tighten in anticipation.

Drake laughed. "I bet your mother didn't tell you those stories."

Sylvan propped herself on an elbow and nibbled Drake's lower lip. "No one had to tell me. It's in my genes."

"Your genes are a few centuries behind, Alpha." Drake ran her fingers through Sylvan's hair. She was so beautiful—so strong, so brave, and still so vulnerable. Not immortal. Drake remembered the bullet wounds in Sylvan's chest, the silver burrowing into her lungs and her liver, nearly destroying her. She remembered the feral silver wolf who almost hadn't come back to her. "You're my heart. Don't ask me to let you go."

Muscles bunched in Sylvan's jaw. A grumble rolled through her throat. "You'll stay in the Rover. Dasha will stay with you. No matter what you hear, what you see, you stay there until I return."

"Agreed, except—"

"No exceptions."

Drake shook her head. "If I feel you're injured, I will come to you."

"No."

"Not negotiable."

Sylvan threw her head back, her roar loud enough to bring footsteps to their door.

"You can roar all you like." Drake turned her head at a knock on the bedroom door. "We're fine."

"Yes, Prima," Jace said from the other side.

Drake kissed the mate bite on Sylvan's chest. "You can't ask me to do less than you would do. I won't be less to you than you are to me."

"I can't give the Pack what you can," Sylvan said. "You give them the next Alpha."

"You could," Drake said softly, "if you bore the young, or bred them on some other—"

"No," Sylvan roared.

Drake caressed Sylvan's cheek. "Your wolf is getting everyone agitated. You need to settle down before this mission."

Sylvan had never felt so unsettled. She'd never had so much trouble controlling her wolf before, not even when she'd been an adolescent and so much more powerful than all her Packmates. She'd tussled with Niki and even then had had to be careful not to hurt her, but she'd managed. She'd always had control, and now it was gone. Now her wolf raged, constantly in a red-hot fury. She was ready to fight or fuck every second she was awake. She panted, struggling for balance. "I don't know how my father put up with this."

Drake laughed shakily. "Just think. His mate was a pregnant Alpha—and I'm sure your mother didn't sit in the den for months."

"My father was stronger than me."

"I'm sure he was incredible," Drake said softly, "but there is no one stronger than you, Sylvan. We'll be all right. Trust me."

Sylvan rolled over, settled her back against the wall, and pulled Drake into her lap. She cradled her in her arms and rested her chin on top of Drake's head. "I never wanted this. I never wanted to need so deeply. I need you more than I need the Pack."

Her last words were whispered, heavy with remorse and regret. Drake's heart tightened, feeling her mate's struggle. She twisted until she could look into Sylvan's face. "You'd give your life for any member of the Pack, from the youngest to the oldest, from the weakest to the strongest. We all know that. You have no reason to fault yourself. Your need is between us. I won't let that need hurt you or our Pack."

Sylvan swallowed, nodding slowly as her wolf curled up with a weary huff. "As you wish, Prima." She kissed Drake gently. "Let's gather our warriors."

Becca slid her laptop into her briefcase and handed Jody the printout of the building plans she'd cobbled together from a series of permits she'd pulled from the archives of the municipal offices nearest the installation. "They aren't complete, but they're more extensive than what I was able to find earlier. There are at least three additional underground wings."

"Good. This will help." Jody buttoned her black silk shirt, zipped her tailored blended-silk trousers, and slipped a slim black leather belt around her waist. "I've asked Zahn to take you back to the town house when we leave here. It may be late when we return, and the soldiers will need to feed. You'll be safe in our quarters."

"You'll need to feed too. I'll be there."

"You've hosted three times in less than twenty-four hours. I'll feed before I return."

"Where?"

Jody regarded her impassively. "Nocturne if there's time, elsewhere if there isn't."

"Elsewhere," Becca said slowly. "A random host—on the street?"

"They don't suffer, Becca."

"Oh, I know what they feel." Becca's face heated. She was not going to be jealous of orgasms that meant nothing to Jody, but she still had a hard time thinking of anyone else touching what was hers. "Bring them home."

Jody went still. "It means nothing to me, Becca."

"Maybe so—but you mean everything to me."

Jody sighed. "I'll instruct Zahn to call my blood servants."

"No Nocturne?"

"Not without you."

Becca's breath hitched at the swift arrow of arousal that lanced through her. She had an image of reclining on one of those velvet sofas, Jody at her neck, other hands, other mouths on her breasts, her belly, her... "Jody—stop."

Jody smiled. "Would you mind?"

"You're trying to distract me."

"I have to go." Jody kissed her. "Stay with Zahn."

Becca grasped Jody's hand. "Why do you have to go with them? Can't one of your soldiers lead the strike force?"

"I am a newly Risen heir. I have to show my strength immediately or my claim may be challenged." Jody brushed her lips over the pulse in Becca's throat. "Besides, Lara is my new warlord. My soldiers must see she has my support—and she needs to show her allegiance to me publicly."

"Lara." Becca sat on the edge of the bed. "You've taken a Were, one of Sylvan's *centuri*, to lead your soldiers?"

Jody smiled thinly. "Lara is a Vampire. A very powerful Vampire, and she's one of mine. I need her in a position where I can control her, and I need the strength she will bring to my Clan."

Becca nodded. "Sylvan's not going to be happy."

Jody lifted a shoulder. "How the Alpha feels about it is not my concern."

"You know, you've developed tunnel vision since you've risen."

"You disapprove?"

"You've always been a bit arrogant," Becca said casually. "But I used to have the feeling that you were a little more diplomatic. You seem to have lost that skill."

"Diplomacy is generally the province of the weak."

"As I was saying, arrogant." Becca rose and wrapped her arms around Jody's shoulders, leaning into her. "These Weres are our friends. And your allies. I want to know when you go out to fight with them that you go as a united force."

"Centuries past, Vampires ruled the armies of the Weres."

"I know there's a lot I need to learn about your history, and correct me if I'm wrong, but it is history, isn't it?"

"It's also true what is said about history repeating," Jody said. "The old alliances are being resurrected."

"Yes, but the balance of power between Weres and Vampires has changed. If the Vampires aren't flexible enough to deal with the current reality, you'll all be in danger, no matter how strong you are individually."

"That's what my father said, when he supported the Exodus." Jody considered Becca contemplatively. "You'd make a good *conseiller*."

Becca smiled. "I make a good consort. And your father was right."

"The Viceregal didn't think so."

"The Viceregal is protected by an army of guards and who knows how many secret alliances." She kissed Jody. "At least let your warlord lead the strike. I really can't take you coming home full of holes again."

"I'm Risen now. Much harder to kill."

"But not impossible." Becca shuddered. "I know you need to do this—we all need to know who's behind these experiments. The story needs to be told, and I've been sitting on it long enough."

"Why does it have to be you who tells it?"

Becca searched Jody's eyes. Opaque crimson, ringed in black. Endless night. "Because this is what I do."

"It's dangerous."

"Excuse me? Newly Risen, just-dead Vampire?" Becca poked a finger in Jody's chest. "Don't even go there. Just do this thing and get your pale ass home. Then we'll talk about when and how I break the story."

"And if I refuse?"

"If you don't tell me what you find when you return, I'll have to look for another way to get the information."

Jody grew completely still. "And what would that be?"

"I'll have to ask whoever might know." Becca drew a slow breath. "I'm a reporter, and I'm human and always will be. I have a responsibility."

"To humans first?"

"I don't put humans above Vampires, or Vampires above humans. I won't make that choice."

"Even considering who I am?" Jody asked so softly her voice was a razor in the air.

"Especially considering who you are." Becca kissed her. "I'm not losing you to your biology or xenophobia or anything else. I love you too much."

"I remember now why I fell in love with you," Jody whispered, pulling her close.

"Why is that?"

"You force me to feel."

"No, darling—I just make it safe for you to acknowledge what's already there." The kernel of fear that had been slowly growing in Becca's heart since Jody had risen fractured and blew away on the wind of Jody's tenderness. Jody had changed, grown stronger, harder, more lethal. But her heart had survived. Becca kissed her again.

Jody stroked her cheek and stepped away. "It's time for me to go. The Alpha is on her way." Jody laughed. "And you're right as always. She's not happy."

CHAPTER SIXTEEN

W e have a problem," Niki said, intercepting Sylvan outside her headquarters.

"Tell me." Sylvan stopped midstride. If Niki wanted to speak to her without the other *centuri* present, the problem was highly sensitive. Or highly dangerous. "We don't have much time. Drake went to get the Rover. She'll drive tonight."

"Of course." Niki looked surprised but didn't argue. "Lara is awake and was conferring with Jody's soldiers."

"She's better?"

"She must be." Niki's voice grew harsh. "She's Gates's new warlord."

"I take it that's the problem."

"Yes. Alph—"

Sylvan spun around and bounded across the yard onto the porch of the infirmary. She landed in a crouch just as the door opened and Jody Gates walked out.

"You were looking for me?" Jody said as her guards moved in behind her, their expressions blank, their eyes kindling with nascent flames.

"You've overstepped for the last time, Vampire." Sylvan straightened, the full length of her claws exploding through her fingertips so sharply blood dripped onto the rough-hewn logs at her feet. The Vampire guards grew as still as the water in a frozen lake, their hunger so rabid Sylvan's wolf set to spring.

Jody, appearing unaffected by the richest blood in the Northern Hemisphere being wasted without a care, slid her hands into the pockets of her trousers and regarded Sylvan calmly. "I could play games with you, Alpha, but we don't have time for it. My Vampires are mine to do with as I will. We have nothing to discuss."

"Lara is not yours." Sylvan's wolf was in midshift, and Sylvan had no urge to rein her in. She'd been reining her in all day, and right now, she welcomed a fight. She almost wished the Vampires would try feeding from her. She'd had to compromise with Drake about her participation in the upcoming mission because her mate demanded it, and above all else, she honored her mate's independence. She did not have to honor anything with a Vampire. They were no longer her masters and never would be.

"Nor is Lara yours. We share her in some ways, perhaps," Jody said quietly, "but she is my warlord now. Since we're allies, you should welcome a friend to the Pack at my back."

"Friend," Sylvan growled. "Then perhaps, *friend*, you can explain why Katya shows signs of having been fed from while in captivity. What do you know about Vampire involvement in the assault on my young?"

"Nothing."

Sylvan cocked her head at the swift answer that said little. Vampires were master negotiators as well as master manipulators. They were nearly as hard to negotiate with as the Fae, who were so clever a wrong word could put you in their debt for a century. "And what do you suspect?"

"What I know," Jody said, "is that conclusions based on appearances alone are often wrong. Limited facts can be dangerous."

Sylvan turned to Niki, who had followed her. "Give us space."

Niki curled her lip, staring at the Vampires at Jody's back. "I'm not leaving you outnumbered with them."

Jody signaled her guards to back up. "Your Alpha is safe with me, little Wolf."

"*Imperator*," Niki said, locking eyes with Jody.

"Of course," Jody said.

Niki stepped away and Sylvan said, "What else do you know?"

"One of Francesca's Vampires was at the installation. She carried your young to me."

"A rescuer or a jailor?" Sylvan snarled. The idea of Katya and

Gray being at the mercy of humans *and* Vampires drove her wolf into a frenzy.

Jody paused. "I don't know."

"If Vampires are in league with the humans at the expense of the Weres, where do you stand?" Sylvan felt Niki move back to her right shoulder, a protective stance and a signal to the Vampire soldiers not to make any aggressive moves.

"You show little respect for your allies," Jody murmured.

"Maybe because Vampires interpret the word differently." Sylvan wanted to trust Jody, welcomed her solidarity in a world that suddenly wanted her and her Pack gone, but she couldn't afford to be wrong. The welfare of her *centuri* was at stake in the coming fight. The future of her whole Pack could be at risk. "Funny that Francesca—your Viceregal—had someone there the very night we raided the place. I don't like coincidences."

"Are you accusing me of something?" Jody asked icily. "I've been patient with your insinuations and your insults, but I'm done defending myself to someone who claims to be my ally."

"And I wonder why I'm just hearing about Francesca's minion now," Sylvan growled.

The door behind Jody opened and Becca stepped out with Lara and one of Jody's guards—a human. Jody didn't move, but her eyes glowed hot.

"Zahn," Jody said, her focus still on Sylvan, "take Becca to the vehicle."

"Yes, Lie—"

"What's going on?" Becca asked, avoiding Zahn's grasp and sliding up next to Jody.

"I believe the Alpha is spoiling for a fight," Jody said.

Niki growled a warning.

"Stand easy, *Imperator*," Sylvan murmured. She would not fight, with Jody's mate in danger of injury.

"I don't take my alliances lightly, Alpha," Jody said, turning slightly so her body shielded Becca. "I assume you don't either."

"I stand ready to support you and your Clan." Sylvan tested Jody's resolve, adding, "We will need to confront Francesca about what you witnessed."

Jody's brows rose ever so slightly. "The Viceregal is a formidable opponent."

"So are we." Sylvan caught Lara's gaze. "Where do you stand?"

Lara, dressed in a black shirt and jeans, her chestnut hair wilding around her shoulders and her amber eyes ringed with crimson, took a position opposite Niki on Jody's left. "Your orders, Liege?"

"Warlord," Jody said, her gaze never leaving Sylvan's, "see my consort to the limo."

"Yes, Liege."

Sylvan snarled. "Lara."

"Alpha Mir," Lara said. She did not lower her gaze.

"You traitor," Niki snapped.

Becca stepped into the gap between the Vampires and the Weres. "Well, now that we've all said our hellos, maybe we can get down to business. Remember the captives we're trying to find?"

"*Centuri*," Sylvan said to Lara, ignoring everyone else, "you swore a blood oath to me and to the Timberwolf *centuri*. Your bond is immutable."

"If I may speak," Lara said, directing her statement to Jody.

Sylvan's wolf raged and she dragged her back. This was not the place to fight. "You ask permission of a Vampire?"

"I am a Vampire," Lara said, her chin tilting upward in defiance.

"You are Were."

"Warlord," Jody said, "make your statement. We have work this night."

"As of this night, I pledge my service to Liege Jody Gates and the Night Hunters Clan. I seek the wolf Alpha's permission to be released from my oath," Lara said, her voice emotionless, her face without expression. "I ask that I may be allowed to leave honorably, without challenge."

"And if I refuse?" Sylvan said. Beside her, Niki trembled, fury coating the air with a haze of pheromones and adrenaline.

"Then I seek challenge," Lara said.

Before Sylvan could answer, Niki said, "I will accept the challenge in the Alpha's stead."

Sylvan glanced at Niki, saw her pelt flare and her wolf surge. The blood addiction—or attraction—between Lara and Niki made the whole situation more volatile, but there was something else fueling

Niki's fury. She pulled air deep into her lungs. Sophia. All over both of them. No wonder they were half-crazy and spoiling to fight. Sylvan searched for Sophia, but she was not in the Compound. Just as well. "My *centuri* cannot rescind their oaths."

"I am not *centuri* any longer," Lara argued. "I ceased being *centuri* when I died. I choose to serve as I must live. I choose to fight as a Vampire."

Sylvan raked a hand through her hair. "You don't know *how* you can live."

"I know for now, Alpha," Lara said. The mask fell away and torment rode through her eyes. "Please, Alpha."

"I do not release you from your oath," Sylvan said. Beside her, Niki tensed, her claws erupting, her canines dropping. "But there will be no challenge. You are free to serve Jody, until such time as you relinquish the oath to her and return to the Pack."

"Thank you," Lara said.

"Don't thank me. I've done you no favors." Sylvan spun on her heel and vaulted from the porch. Over her shoulder she called to the Weres and the Vampires. "Let's hunt this night as one."

❖

"Come." Niki motioned to Jace, Jonathan, and Andrew to fall in behind her and Sylvan.

Leading her *centuri* across the Compound, Niki drew up short when she saw Drake waiting with another Were by the Rover just inside the fortified gate. Dasha Baran. Niki growled. Dasha straightened and snarled.

"The Prima will drive," Sylvan said, pulling open the rear compartment of the Rover. "Dasha is with her tonight. The rest of you, with me." She glanced at Niki. "*Imperator*, are your warriors ready?"

Niki stared at Dasha for another long second, waiting for Dasha to drop her gaze. When Dasha finally did cast her eyes aside, Niki said curtly, "Yes, Alpha," and climbed into the back of the Rover. Inside, she settled on one of the long benches next to Sylvan, across from Jace and Jonathan. Andrew sprawled on the floor with his back against the front seats. Drake slid behind the wheel and turned to look back.

"What about the Vampires?" Drake asked.

"They have their own vehicles," Sylvan said. "They'll follow."

"Good, then let's go." Drake eased the Rover through the partially open gates and stopped far enough away for the limos to exit. Two cars filled with Vampires and their guards and servants pulled in behind her. She waited until the gate swung closed, securing the Compound, before she set off into the forest. "Same approach as last time?"

"Yes," Sylvan said. "There'd be no reason to guard that access road now."

"Unless they know we're coming," Niki said.

Sylvan grumbled, reminding Niki of her place. "We'll have Max run a satellite sweep of the area before we get there. If they have vehicles hidden along the way, he'll find them." Sylvan smiled thinly. "And if they've posted sentries, we'll smell them."

Satisfied, Niki settled back against the wall, closing her eyes as the Rover bounced over the narrow forest trail toward the highway. She could smell Dasha in the front seat, scent the aggression rolling off her. She slid her hand under her T-shirt and traced her fingers over the healing scratches on her chest. The scratches Sophia had made. Her clitoris tightened as she remembered Sophia's mouth against her skin, recalling the sweet torture of Sophia's fingers stroking her to release. She wanted more. She wanted to know that no one else tasted Sophia, satisfied her. She rumbled and twitched, scraping her claws over tight nipples.

Sylvan said, "Now is not the time to be thinking about breeding."

"That wasn't what I was thinking," Niki said without opening her eyes.

"Wasn't it? Whatever you're thinking, it's loud enough for everyone to feel."

"My apologies, Alpha," Niki said, straightening.

"I need you focused."

"I am."

"Good. I need Dasha tonight—the Prima needs her."

Niki couldn't hold back the growl. "Sophia refused her. She should learn her place."

"Niki," Sylvan said quietly, "Sophia is not just any Were."

Niki swung her head slowly until her eyes glanced over Sylvan's face, as close as she would come to warning her Alpha not to come between her and this female. "I know what she is."

"No, Niki," Sylvan said, "you don't. Listen to her. Trust her. She knows what she needs."

Niki gritted her teeth. Now was not the time to challenge. Sylvan couldn't know what she felt. She glanced into the front seat, saw the Prima at the wheel, where she had no business being when she carried the Alpha's young. Drake should be back in the Compound, where she would be safe and protected. Maybe the Alpha did understand that one female could change everything, even instincts borne over centuries. It made no matter to her what the Alpha thought. She would not watch Sophia satisfy her needs with others. When she returned, she would make sure Sophia understood that.

❖

Drake sniffed the air and turned to Sylvan. "I don't scent anyone in the woods." The last time they'd stood on the ridge overlooking the experimental installation, they'd discovered cat Weres posted throughout the forest, mercenaries hired to guard the far perimeter. Tonight, all she smelled were deer, fox, opossum, and smaller prey.

Sylvan surveyed the labyrinth of buildings through night binoculars. "I don't see any guards along the fence."

The sprawling complex was illuminated sporadically by halogen lights suspended on poles in uneven intervals along the expanse of concrete that extended fifty yards in all directions from the building. A huge parking lot, eerily empty, stretched from one end of the complex nearly to the tree line at the foot of the mountain. Surveillance cameras were mounted along the fence line and on the eaves of the building. Anyone approaching the building would be exposed long enough for the cameras to capture them, unless they were Vampire-fast.

"The surveillance cameras aren't moving," Sylvan noted.

Drake rested her hand at the base of Sylvan's spine. Anytime she wasn't touching her, an ominous sense of foreboding spread through her. As soon as she felt the heat of Sylvan's skin beneath her fingertips, the disquieting sensations disappeared. She'd always needed contact with her, but now the physical need was acute. "It looks deserted, but that doesn't make sense. I wonder if that's not just a lure."

"No one knows we're coming," Sylvan said.

"Not necessarily. I agree with Niki—the anonymous caller

could be trying to trap you. Anyone who knows you knows you will come if there's any chance at all there are Weres held prisoner in that building."

Sylvan glanced at her, moonlight dancing over the surface of her golden eyes. "That would seem a very elaborate ruse. It's not as if I'm not exposed at other times."

"Yes," Drake said, the muscles in her jaws tightening painfully. She was well aware of how vulnerable her mate was whenever she walked into the capitol building, when she appeared on television, when she was interviewed by friend and foe alike. Just as Sylvan wanted to keep her safe in the den until the young were born, she wanted Sylvan to do all her business from the headquarters building, secure in the heart of the Compound. Neither was possible. "But out here we're isolated. This is the place for a clandestine attack—I doubt whoever built this place wants publicity. You'll be a huge target until you're inside, and then you'll be a potential captive."

"Then we'll have to be very careful." Sylvan stroked Drake's face. "I promise."

"I think I should bring the Rover down to the edge of that parking lot over there," Drake said, pointing to the vacant expanse. "We can stay under cover right at the tree line but be nearby in case you need to evacuate injured."

Sylvan rumbled. "I don't like you being that close to the building."

"We'll have a clear view of anyone who might be coming," Drake said. "We'll have plenty of time to evacuate if we have to."

"All right, but you don't break cover for any reason."

Drake remained silent. If Sylvan was in danger, she was not going to stand by waiting. "We send the Vampires in first?"

"With their speed, they'll be able to reach the installation without being seen—if anyone inside is monitoring the perimeter."

"You'll go in skin?"

"Unless there's some need to shift. Easier to handle the mechanics of the building with hands."

"Just be careful."

Sylvan kissed her. "I will."

Drake and Sylvan walked back to the vehicles. Jody leaned against the front fender of her fortified limo with Lara and three of her soldiers.

The second vehicle had continued on to Albany with Zahn, Becca, and several soldiers.

Sylvan said, "We don't see any guards. We'll follow you down. As soon as you clear the side entrance, we'll come in behind you."

"Something is off," Jody said. "An installation this size should have at least a skeleton security crew at night. There are always people working—maintenance, engineering, if nothing else. This looks like a trap."

"It might be," Sylvan said. "But if it is, we need to know who set it. Without getting inside, we can't be certain who—or what—we're facing."

"How much damage are you willing to accept to find out?" Jody asked.

Drake's stomach tightened at Sylvan's slow, dangerous smile.

"These bastards took my young. Now they may be holding more Weres. Damage is not an issue."

"These might not even be your Weres," Jody said.

"That's going to change," Sylvan said.

"Then I can see I've chosen the right ally." Jody motioned to Lara. "Take point. If there are cat Were guards down there, you may scent them sooner than we do. Kill any you find."

"Yes, Liege." Lara didn't look at Sylvan as she turned, signaled to the soldiers, and misted into the trees.

Sylvan turned to Niki and Jace. "You'll take the front with me. Jonathan and Andrew, guard our flanks."

"Yes, Alpha," the *centuri* answered in unison.

And then they were gone and Drake was left alone with Dasha, wanting nothing more than to follow. A stirring in her belly, warm and strong, reminded her of why she had let Sylvan go alone.

Chapter Seventeen

Sylvan crouched at the edge of the tree line with Niki beside her. Jace had circled through the forest to watch the main access road, and Andrew and Jonathan guarded their flanks. The Vampires had been gone almost a minute—more than enough time for them to cross the five-hundred-yard expanse to the loading dock entrance in the rear. She hadn't seen anything happening at the installation that suggested Jody and her soldiers had been observed or intercepted. "Let's go."

They broke from the underbrush and streaked across the open expanse of concrete, sticking to the shadowed areas beyond the floodlights. On their last foray, the entire place had been brightly lit, but now half the lights were out around the perimeter, providing them plenty of cover. They vaulted up onto the loading platform, keeping close to the wall and away from the immobile security cameras. Sylvan tried the handle below the big red sign declaring "Security Alarm Will Sound—No Entrance." The handle turned. She pushed on the windowless metal door, and she and Niki slipped into the wide, empty hallway. The door swished closed behind them and Sylvan lifted her head, scented. Her nose wrinkled. Industrial waste—acrid and sour, cleaning fluids, recirculated air that was flat and stale. She growled, thinking of Katya and Gray trapped in this lifeless place for weeks. "If we find them, show no mercy to whoever is holding them."

"Yes, Alpha," Niki said swiftly. "Let me search this wing. You should stay—"

"Let's not waste time," Sylvan said and strode down the dimly lit corridor. A few doors stood open on darkened rooms. Most were closed. The blank faces of the motionless security cameras turned blind eyes on their passage. They reached the far end of the wing that ended at the central elevator shaft. "Clear."

"And empty." Niki slid the Glock she carried in her right hand into the waistband of her BDUs. "We could search faster in pelt."

"Yes," Sylvan agreed. "And stamp our signatures on any dead we leave behind. Bullets and blades carry no names." Sylvan halted, sensing a disturbance in the air.

Jody appeared from around the corner. "Did you see anyone outside?"

"No. Anything in here?" Sylvan asked.

Jody shook her head, frowning. "Nothing. All the upper levels appear to be empty. They're mostly engineering and maintenance. The few labs seem to be very basic and mostly unused."

"For show, maybe," Sylvan said. "We know the real experiments were going on underground."

"If we go down, our escape routes will be vulnerable."

"I'll go down. Niki will stay here to guard our rear."

Niki's eyes sparked, but she knew better than to question Sylvan's orders in the field.

Jody nodded. "Lara and I will go with you. Rafe can stay with your *imperator*."

"Agreed. According to Becca's drawings," Sylvan said, "several wings extend from the central tower with fire stairs adjacent to the elevators. This is the wing we were in last night, where we found our young below us. There are more we haven't searched."

"Let's go down the stairs by the elevator and work our way around the core," Jody said. "Someone must know the perimeter has been breached by now, even if they're monitoring remotely. We don't have much time."

"They've clearly abandoned this installation. Maybe they expected us to return," Niki said.

"Or *hoped* we would," Sylvan growled. She couldn't believe Katya and Gray had been mere pawns in some elaborate trap to draw her out, but she couldn't discount the possibility.

"Ten minutes," Jody said, "and then we need to abort. Becca thinks there are three more wings mirroring the ones we know about."

"Then we need to hurry," Sylvan said as Lara and Rafaela came around the corner and joined Jody.

Lara tapped her fist to her chest in salute. "The stairwells are clear, Liege, as are the other wings on this level."

"We're going down to search the underground labs," Jody said to Lara. "You're with me. Post Rafe and Louis to secure the exits."

"Yes, Liege." Lara turned to Rafe, her gaze passing over Niki without a pause. "Post Louis outside. You coordinate interior coverage with the Were."

"Yes, Warlord," Rafe said, spinning to face Niki. She grinned. "Try to stay out of the way of any bullets, Wolf."

"Don't worry about me, Vampire," Niki rumbled. "Just watch your back. I'll worry about my Alpha." She pointed to the fire door to the right of the elevators. "Last night their forces set up cross fire from in there. Be careful."

Rafe nodded, her amused expression growing sharp and hard. "We will. One-minute security checks?"

"Roger," Niki said, pulling the two-way from her pants pocket.

"If we're not back in ten minutes," Sylvan said to Niki, "take Drake back to the Compound. We'll make our own way home."

"Yes, Alpha."

Sylvan and Jody started down the stairwell and Jody glanced at Sylvan. "Do you still think this is a trap?"

"I know it is. Even if this installation is marked for deactivation, someone should be here."

"Why bother looking, then?"

"I think you were the one who mentioned earlier that it's a bad idea to base decisions on appearances. We won't get another chance to search this place." Sylvan paused at the door to the lower level and listened. Nothing. She pushed through and surveyed another long, dim, empty corridor. "I'm not even sure who the target is here. After all, it was your consort who received the call. Maybe you're the one they're interested in luring out."

"With the threat of imprisoned Weres?" Jody smiled grimly. "A convoluted plan at best."

Sylvan said, "You don't need to stay, Vampire. You made the initial pass and cleared the way for us. No need to risk yourself or your soldiers."

Jody's mouth lifted slightly. "As one, remember, Alpha?"

"Then let's get this done. I want to get back outside. This place is like a tomb."

Jody laughed. "I was thinking I rather liked it."

❖

"Prima," Dasha said, pointing to the woods behind them, "the wind shifted. I scent someone."

"What do you think it is?" Drake asked, her attention riveted on the building. Sylvan had been gone almost ten minutes. With every passing minute, the foreboding pressure in her chest grew. She expected to see a caravan of Humvees filled with armed mercenaries converging on the installation any second.

"At least one human, on that ridge above us," Dasha said.

"Find them, bring them back."

"The Alpha said I was not to leave you."

"The Alpha isn't here right now," Drake said sharply. She understood the ingrained, immutable instinct to act upon the Alpha's commands, but she needed the Weres to obey her in Sylvan's absence. They could not question or hesitate. Lives might depend upon it. "You have your orders. Find him."

"Yes, Prima." Dasha's smile in the moonlight was feral.

"Alive, Dasha…and able to talk."

Dasha growled. "They tortured Katya and Gray."

"I know. That's why I want to know the names of everyone involved. One death will not be enough."

Dasha glanced toward the building and back to Drake. "The Alpha will be upset if I don't stay here."

"The Alpha is my concern." Drake softened her words. The wolves would adjust to the new order in the Pack in time, but time was something they didn't have with Sylvan in the field, in possible danger. "Go now, before we lose him."

"I won't be long."

"Do what you have to do, and, Dasha—"

"Yes, Prima?"

"Be careful."

Dasha shifted, and her sleek brown wolf bounded soundlessly into the forest. Drake scanned the road leading down from the mountain on the far side of the installation. She might have been looking out over a ghost town. She checked her watch. She'd give Sylvan another three minutes and then she was going in after her.

❖

"Lara," Jody said, "clear this wing."

"Yes, Liege."

Lara disappeared so quickly Sylvan almost blinked in surprise. She'd gotten so used to Lara being at her side—as she'd grown up, as she'd assumed the mantle of power, as she'd faced her enemies, public and private. Lara had been with her, as Niki had been with her, unchanging, unchangeable. And now she was gone. Not just from sight, with the uncanny speed of the Vampires, but gone from Sylvan's life, leaving aching loss.

"She needs this," Jody said, as if reading her mind. "Without purpose, she would be dangerous. I cannot allow Vampires to exist who might threaten all of us."

"I could have given her purpose," Sylvan said.

"But not control her—not now."

Sylvan couldn't disagree, and it rankled that she had to concede power to anyone. But if she had to entrust one of her wolves to someone outside her Pack, she'd choose this Vampire. "Just take care of her."

Jody laughed. "Always so concerned."

Sylvan growled, checking the rooms they passed. Laboratory benches, most of them still holding equipment, with obvious gaps where some had been removed. Desks with books still on them. Trash bins waiting to be emptied. It was as if the people who populated this building simply got up and walked out in the middle of whatever they were doing. Maybe they had. Maybe there'd been a biological breach or a chemical spill. Maybe there'd been a viral contamination. If that were the case, the safety gates recessed in the ceiling at regular intervals should have come down, isolating the areas at risk. Some of these labs had to be Level 3 and 4 labs. They would have been the first to be locked down if there'd been an industrial catastrophe, but all of the pressurized portals appeared to be functional. None were locked.

"It's as if everyone was ordered to evacuate, but nothing seems to be wrong."

Lara appeared beside them. "This wing is clear, but I think there's another area beyond this one." She pointed to a solid metal barrier that blocked the far end of the corridor. A retinal sensor on the wall next to it appeared dark—inactive. "Behind there, I scent Were."

Sylvan charged to the door, pressed her hand against it. Sniffed the air. She sensed nothing. She stretched her awareness, felt Niki floors above her, Andrew, Jace, and Jonathan outside. In the distance, Drake and Dasha. But nothing inside. Nothing beyond the cold metal. "I don't scent anyone."

"They're there," Lara said. "The spoor is clear."

"How can you tell if I can't?"

"I don't know," Lara said, "but somewhere beyond that barricade, there are other Weres."

Jody said, "There may be silver residual in the air or the walls. Lara's Vampire blood may give her resistance to it."

Sylvan nodded. Another unexpected change in Lara's abilities. No time to consider what that meant. "We need to get in there."

"There might be a way to trigger the sensor if we can activate it," Lara said.

"We don't have time." Sylvan drove her clawed fist into the metal. The barricade buckled but did not give. With a roar, she struck again and again until a rent appeared big enough for her hand. She tore the door from its frame, the metal peeling down like the lid of a tin can. Beyond the shredded gateway, darkness beckoned.

❖

A faint ripple in the air alerted Drake to movement in the underbrush behind her. Dasha returning—with a human. She smelled blood and fear and watched Dasha drag a human male in camo fatigues and dark boots from the forest. Dasha pushed him down on his knees in front of Drake. About thirty, big, but not fat. Nothing remarkable about his shaggy brown hair. The skin above his unshaven chin was faintly pock-marked and smudged with dirt and sweat. Blood seeped from scrapes on his left cheek and jawline. He appeared to be otherwise undamaged. *Well done, Lieutenant.*

"He says he has information," Dasha said, her wolf still ascendant. Her long canines and heavy jaw made her words thick and gravelly. "So I didn't kill him right away."

"Who are you?" Drake asked. "Tell me now why I shouldn't let my wolf finish what she started."

"My name is Martin. I'm the reason you're here."

❖

"Wait," Lara said before Sylvan could step through into the murky hallway. "Let me go first."

"No," Sylvan said. "If there are Weres here, they are my responsibility now."

"And if it's warded with silver, you'll be useless to them."

Sylvan snarled.

"Stop!" Jody tilted her head, listening. "Rafe has found something. She's on her way down."

Rafe appeared behind Jody, her face tense. "I searched the elevator shafts to be sure no one could circle behind you. This entire complex is cantilevered off that central core, like spokes on a wheel, and the core is packed with explosives."

"Did you find detonators?" Sylvan asked.

"No. They're probably set for remote detonation."

Sylvan glanced over her shoulder into the catacomb on the other side of the opening. "Two minutes." She vaulted over the door, telegraphing Niki, *Find Drake, get her back over the mountain. Do it now.*

Lara followed. Together, they loped down a narrow passageway. The only light filtered in from behind them, but Sylvan had no trouble seeing in the dark. "How many?"

Lara frowned. "I can't tell. There's something off. Their signatures are all wrong."

"Maybe they're not Weres."

"No, they are. But—not."

"Dead?"

"No," Lara said. "Not all of them."

At the end of the tunnel, they found another barrier like the one they'd just come through. Lara ripped it free, wrenching it so far off its hinges the door clattered against the opposite wall and spun away like a discarded hubcap.

Sylvan growled at the miasma of scents that accosted them from the dank space. Blood, disease, death. Rows of beds surrounded by monitors along the opposite wall. Most were empty, but not all. She held back a howl of rage and fury and strode across the room. The female in the first bed was dead, her body bloated, her features unrecognizable. The two in the beds beside her still lived. Sylvan leaned over them, sniffed. Not Weres. Humans, infected humans.

"Were fever," Lara said flatly. "We should kill them."

"Please," one of the young girls moaned, her face glistening with sweat, her feverish eyes wolf-tinged. "Please help us."

Sylvan thought of Gray and Katya, chained, tortured, abandoned. Already these girls were part Were, but their chance of surviving was zero. She owed them justice. And mercy.

Niki stiffened, struck by a wave of wrath and urgency. Danger. The Alpha was in danger. She raced toward the fire stairs, stumbling when the command rifled into her consciousness.

Find Drake, get her back over the mountain. Do it now.

She took one step toward the stairwell, driven to find Sylvan, to protect her. *Find Drake. Get her back over the mountain. Do it now.* She whined deep in her chest, torn by loyalty and love. Abandoning Sylvan went against everything she was. But obeying Sylvan, especially in this, defined everything she believed in. She spun around and charged toward the exit. As she reached for the door, it opened and Drake barged inside.

"What's happening? I felt Sylvan. She's in trouble."

"We need to leave." Niki grasped Drake's arm and pushed her toward the exit.

"I'm not leaving her." Drake pulled away. "Where is she?"

"The Alpha ordered—"

Drake grabbed Niki by the shirtfront. "Don't make me repeat this. *Where is she?*"

"Downstairs. I don't know what's happening, but there's danger. Prima—the Alpha can take care of herself. You have another duty."

"She's my mate." Drake twisted her fist in Niki's shirt, her face morphing, her dark eyes splintering with golden shards. "Show me the way."

A tremendous explosion rocked the floor beneath Niki's feet and she fell to her knees. Drake dropped beside her. The elevator shaft exploded into a fountain of flame, littering the hallway with burning shards of glass and metal. Her ears rang as thunder rolled down the hallway, battering her senses. She shielded Drake as best she could from the flames lapping along the walls. Rafe staggered out of the stairwell, her shirt on fire. She tore off the flaming material. Her face was scorched, the skin on her chest bubbling and crusting even where the shirt hadn't burned. She gasped, "UV radiation."

Niki staggered to her feet as Drake pulled herself up along the wall.

"Where?" Drake coughed. "Where are they?"

Rafe shook her head. "Somewhere behind me—underneath us. If these floors collapse—"

Drake started forward and Niki gripped her arm. "No, Prima."

"Let me go," Drake snarled.

Niki yelled, "Help me get her outside!"

Rafe grabbed Drake's free arm, and together, they dragged Drake snarling and thrashing from the inferno.

CHAPTER EIGHTEEN

The building shuddered and the floor heaved under Sylvan's feet. Chunks of tile, shards of metal, and flaming wood rained down. Sylvan pulled the girl from the bed, sheltered her against her chest, and yelled to Lara, "Get the other one."

Without waiting to see if her order was followed, she sprinted toward the jagged opening Lara had made in the security barrier and leapt through. The hallway glowed red and a rush of heat struck her in the face. At the far end of the corridor tongues of fire lashed out of the stairwell, licking at the walls and floors. Portions of the ceiling had collapsed, and the piles of rubble formed a partial firewall, probably saving them from instant immolation. Jody slumped on the floor, her face and hands charred.

Sylvan knelt beside her. "Jody. Jody, how bad?"

"Feels like a walk in the sun. Weak. Burning inside." Jody coughed and pushed herself up.

Lara said from behind Sylvan, "The explosives were either laced with UV emittors or the blast triggered a radiation surge from somewhere in the building. I'll carry her—I'm not affected."

Sylvan glanced up at her. Lara's bronzed skin was smooth and whole, unburned. Jody's flesh blistered more with each passing second. "Give me that one," Sylvan said, indicating the unconscious human in Lara's arms. "You take your Liege."

"No," Jody said. "We can't get out the way we came in, but if you shift, your wolf might be able to."

"I'm not leaving you down here." Sylvan tightened her hold on the girl in her arms. "Or them. There has to be another way out. They would need to bring in supplies, equipment, and these girls without coming through the main complex. We need to find it."

"Then I'll walk," Jody said. "Rafe was in the stairwell when it collapsed. She might have made it out."

"So will we," Sylvan said. She wasn't dying down here, far from Drake, from her young. Her Pack needed her, and so did these half-Weres left behind to be incinerated. She'd find who did this. "Let's get out of this corridor. The walls of that lab may shield you from the radiation. Lara, go ahead of us and search for an exit."

Lara picked up the human, her attention on Jody. "Liege?"

"Go," Jody said.

"Can you make it?" Sylvan asked. Blood streaked down Jody's neck and soaked her shirt.

"I'll make it."

"You can heal this, can't you?"

"Not as long as I'm still in the radiation field."

"What if you feed now?"

"Are you offering?"

Sylvan grinned. "One-time deal."

Jody sucked in a shuddering breath. "I might take you up on it, but we need to get out of here first."

Sylvan led the way back into the cavernous room, following Lara's scent deeper into the underground labyrinth. The lights had gone out with the explosion, and the air was thick with smoke and particulate debris. Visibility was almost zero. Behind her, she heard Jody stumble through the piles of wreckage. From what she knew, UV radiation exposure to a Vampire was equivalent to walking into the sun, and since Jody was newly Risen, her system was especially sensitive. The burns on the outside were just a reflection of the internal damage. Her cells were leeching oxygen, she was suffocating, and her tissues were dying. She needed healthy blood soon.

"Jody—just take a minute to—"

"No," Jody rasped. "I'm not going to be locked for eternity down here with you. Keep going."

"Good point," Sylvan muttered. Her respect for the stubborn Vampire tripled. Her lungs burned and her legs trembled. Silver in the air. "I'm not feeding you for the next millennium."

The girl in Sylvan's arms moaned. "Who are you?" she whispered brokenly against Sylvan's throat.

"I'm your Alpha," Sylvan murmured.

"Don't let them hurt me anymore."

"I won't. That's a promise."

"There's another passageway just ahead," Lara reported, appearing like a specter out of the clouds of floating wreckage. "It's partially collapsed and sounds like it's about to cave in completely. There's not much time."

Jody rasped, "Shift, Sylvan, and leave the girls with us. If we don't make it out in time, you can bring help back."

"And what if you get trapped down here without blood?"

"We'll manage."

"These girls can't host for you," Sylvan said. "They're both infected."

"Despite what you might think," Jody said, "we don't prey on the weak."

"Then you should let me feed you." Sylvan snarled and thrust her face close to Jody's. The Vampire smelled sick. No way was she facing Becca Land and telling her she'd led Jody to her death. "I'm not weak."

"Not yet." Jody grinned through cracked lips. "That's a pleasure I intend to reserve until I don't have to rush."

"Then we shouldn't waste time now. We came down together, we leave together." Sylvan turned to Lara. "Lead the way, Warlord."

❖

Drake didn't want to hurt them, but they didn't leave her any choice. Once she let Niki and Rafe drag her far enough away from the building that they weren't in danger of being immolated, she jerked her arms free and let her wolf have her way. Her skin stretched, her bones thickened, and wrath to match the blaze behind her poured out. She stopped her shift in half-form. She'd need both the strength and maneuverability of her wolf soon, but first she needed to see to her Pack. "The Rover is across the parking lot. Dasha is there. Evacuate this area. Everyone—back to the Compound."

"You need to come with us," Niki said.

"You know I can't." Drake blocked Niki's arm when she tried to grab her and took her to the ground. She held her down with a hand on her neck, but she did not break skin. She needed Niki to listen, not submit. "A strike force may be on the way to the Compound, and they need to be alerted. *You* need to be there to secure the Pack until the Alpha and I return."

Niki's eyes blazed with the ferocity of a dominant wolf, but she nodded. "Yes, Prima."

Drake lunged to her feet and spun on Rafe. The Vampire was bleeding, her chest and shoulder crusted and cracked with third-degree burns. She swayed, weakened, but her eyes were clear, and she gave no sign of the agony she must be suffering. "Where are they?"

"The Liege was behind me when I started back," Rafe said. "The others were in an adjoining room—farther underground I think. If they haven't come out of the stairwell by now, it must have been too dangerous. They'll be looking for another way out."

Drake fought down the blind urge to rush back into the building, to race through fire, to find Sylvan. Panic tore at her throat. She had to think. Her mate was inside, in danger, hurt, possibly dying. She couldn't leave her any more than she could stop breathing.

"Get Becca on the phone," Drake said to Niki as another section of the building collapsed and a geyser of flames shot into the sky. Drake swallowed back bile. No one could have survived that conflagration.

"I've got her," Niki said a few seconds later, extending the phone.

"Becca," Drake snapped. "I need you to study the plans. I need alternate exit routes, something not connected to the central core. I need it now, Becca."

"Everything I have is sketchy, especially concerning the underground areas. There could be corridors, entrances I can't see." Becca's voice rose, tight with anxiety. "Why, what's happening?"

"There's been an explosion. Some of our team are trapped inside and the main stairs are impassable. I need another way in. Can you see anything that looks like a direct route to the underground portion of the complex?"

"Oh God," Becca said, "let me pull up the aerials again."

"Hurry. Scan the terrain for signs of other roads. Something undeveloped—tractor paths, ATV trails, firebreaks."

"There's just the one road coming down from the mountain. There's nothing else developed in this whole area. I don't see…Wait, there's a fairly linear break in the trees just north of the complex."

"A road?"

"Maybe," Becca said. "Some kind of unpaved artery branching off from the main road about a half mile from the installation. It just goes off into the forest—doesn't look like it goes anywhere."

"That's because it probably ends at the entrance to the underground complex. Give me coordinates."

"These satellite images might be old. This could be nothing."

"It's all we've got." Drake looked at Niki. "Give me your GPS." Niki pulled the locator from her belt. "Go ahead."

"Wait, wait," Becca said frantically. "All right. I've got it."

Drake punched in the GPS coordinates that Becca read off the computer. "Keep looking. If you find anything else, call Niki."

"Should we send backup?" Becca said.

"No," Drake said instantly. They needed to retreat, care for their injured, and regroup. "Where are you, exactly?"

"In Albany. At Jody's town house."

"Who's with you?"

"Right now, no one. But Zahn is here somewhere. Claude, I think."

"Stay there and advise your security we've been attacked. It may be dawn before your people return. Make sure you have hosts available."

"Drake—who—"

"We'll get them out, Becca."

"It's Jody, isn't it?"

"Not just Jody," Drake said grimly.

❖

Tears flooded Sylvan's eyes, smoke charred her throat. Her lungs burned. The girl in her arms had gone limp and quiet, but her heart beat, faint but steady against Sylvan's chest. The girl smelled sick, but she smelled like Were too. Sylvan would not let her die.

"Jody, are you all right?"

"I've lost a lot of blood," Jody said, her voice ringing hollowly. "The radiation poisoning is spreading, affecting my senses. Sylvan, if I don't—"

"You will," Sylvan growled. "If we aren't out in another minute, I'll feed you."

"I thank you," Jody said, "but this close to rising, this damaged, I need bonded blood."

"Then I'll get you to Becca." Sylvan pushed through air so heavy she felt as if she was slogging through mud. Impotence clawed at her insides. Maybe Jody was right—maybe she should let her wolf lead the way out. But Jody couldn't carry one of these sick girls, and Lara might need to carry Jody. If she left them, she might lose them all. Her wolf raged, caught in a trap and determined to escape. Drake was outside somewhere—maybe under attack. Pain lanced through Sylvan's belly as she battled the imperative to protect her mate at any cost.

"Alpha." Lara appeared out of the murk. "Stairs leading up, just ahead. They're blocked with debris, but this must be a way out."

"Leave the girl here with Jody and come with me." Sylvan gently placed the unconscious human on the floor next to the one Lara had been carrying and bounded over the jumble of twisted concrete and steel to the stairs. Halfway up, a steel girder encased in rubble blocked the staircase.

"We'll have to clear this." She clawed a chunk of concrete loose and let it tumble down behind her. Lara squeezed in next to her, and they put their shoulders under the girder and heaved. It moved a few inches. Already, the stairwell was flooded with heat and smoke seeping up from below.

Jody called up, "The tunnel behind us is burning. It's up or nowhere."

"We are not dying down here," Sylvan said. "I need your strength, Lara. Help me move this."

"Yes, Alpha."

❖

Drake ran along the overgrown track through the forest, the uneven ground lit by a flickering glow that painted the sky the colors of a bloody dawn. Fingers of gray smoke signaled she was close to the burning complex. Abruptly, she burst from the trees into a small clearing. An empty clearing. No sentry shack, no loading dock, no shed or storage unit. She'd gambled and she'd been wrong. Sylvan was still trapped somewhere and she had failed her. She howled and dropped to her knees. Panting, she called her wolf and opened herself to the night. If Sylvan lived, she would find her.

The panicked rush of creatures fleeing from the flames struck her first, and her skin tingled with the urge to run with them, to protect the young in her womb. The pelt thickened on her torso as her wolf fought to ascend. She shut her mind to the cries of the injured animals and the raging growls of her wolf and focused on Sylvan, on her wild pine scent, her sharp earthy taste, the force of her essence flooding inside her. A ripple of connection pulled at her consciousness and she turned to her left. Drake raced across the clearing and ripped the bushes and debris aside. There—hidden in the brush. A portal built into the side of the mountain, large enough to accommodate a small truck.

Two huge metal doors were set into the hillside, secured by a heavy chain and padlock. She grasped the chain and jerked, snapping the links. The metal seared crevices across her palms. Whatever lay below was burning. Anyone inside might already be dead.

She yanked the doors open and bounded inside.

CHAPTER NINETEEN

Francesca leaned back in her leather-upholstered eighteenth-century desk chair, listening to the excuses of her *capitaine* in New Orleans flow from the phone, and gazed at the gilded ceiling above her. Delicate flowers with maroon centers that resembled drops of blood bordered the ivory coffered panels. Strands of pure gold ran through the lacy pattern along the hand-carved crown moldings. After so many centuries, ordinary beauty rarely moved her anymore, and finding artists capable of providing her with pleasure, aesthetic or otherwise, had become increasingly difficult. When she'd relocated the last time and created her new lair beneath Nocturne, she'd expected to be here for three or four decades until she was forced to move on and reestablish herself with a new social identity in another city. All the same, she'd vowed long ago that she would not live like a transient for eternity. She would surround herself with splendor and immerse herself in pleasure. Now that the Exodus had made it unnecessary for Vampires to hide the signs of their immortality, she would no longer have to move periodically. She could devote herself to preserving her true passion—power.

When she'd allowed her underling to talk himself into an untenable position, she finally interrupted. "The thing is, darling, you are running a casino protected by my soldiers, financed by my money and resources, and you owe me tithe. You've missed two payments."

She waited to see if he would offer another excuse. He didn't know if he did, he'd be signing his death warrant. Immortality was relative, and a Vampire without his head would never see another moonrise. When he wisely allowed he did indeed owe everything to her, she added, "And the proper amount would be sixty-five percent of your quarterly intake. I'm sure you don't want me to send someone to review the terms with you."

His rapid, anxious agreement made her smile. Engendering fear was every bit as satisfying as precipitating pleasure. Perhaps more so, as the climax was so sweet. "I'm sure you'll take care of it promptly. I'll let you get back to work."

She rang off and made a note for Michel to pay him a little visit. A drop by from the Viceregal's enforcer usually ensured she would not have to make a repeat phone call. A gratifying warmth spread through her belly. Doing business satisfied her. Clean, ruthless, violent—but unsentimental and practical. Much like sex.

The phone rang and she answered it herself rather than letting it go through to voicemail or waiting for Daniela to pick up.

"Yes?"

"Are you free?" Nicholas asked abruptly.

"Not exactly. This is the middle of my workday." She disliked his attitude—he seemed to feel that he was the leader of their small cadre, when in fact, of all the Shadow Lords the Vampires had the most at risk. When their loose alliance of humans and Praeterns had decided to thwart the mission of Sylvan Mir and the Praetern Coalition by any means possible, they'd all accepted the chance of life-threatening repercussions. She had no doubt Sylvan would go to war with her if Sylvan discovered she had allied with enemies of the Pack. The most Nicholas might suffer if his involvement was exposed would be social sanction and perhaps loss of some of his business associations. A great proportion of the human population might be opposed to Praetern sovereignty, but humans wouldn't go on record as supporting genocide, and their trappings of civility usually prevented them from killing each other over ideological differences. At least openly. The Fae were largely untouchable—no one had successfully gone to battle with them in millennia. As to Bernardo and his Weres, Sylvan would crush him—and good riddance. He was a pathetic pretender next to a true Alpha like Sylvan. Nicholas was far from the leader of this group, but she still needed to cultivate his confidence. His money, his control over HUFSI, his many contacts in Albany and Washington had made him the architect of their plans. His obsession with destroying the Weres was only a breath away from extending to exterminating all Praeterns, and she didn't intend to allow him to take her by surprise. Hiding her annoyance, she asked, "What is it you need?"

"To speak with you for a few moments."

"All right."

"In person."

"Can't this wait?"

"I don't think you want it to."

Francesca sighed. As Viceregal and Chancellor, she oversaw one of the largest territories in the world—and controlling half a country full of ruthless, independent predators was not easy. Unlike the Weres, the Vampires felt very little sense of community or loyalty that wasn't imposed by force. Some Vampires, the young or the aged, welcomed the protection of a more powerful Vampire and congregated in seethes controlled by a dominant leader, but in general the Clans segregated along bloodlines and functioned as feudal states. All six North American Clan leaders were aggressive, dominant Vampires—and each of them had an eye on her position. She did not want a war, not until she'd had a chance to build an army, and considering that Vampires rarely died and just as rarely produced offspring, recruiting soldiers from the limited ranks of those who might be qualified was a challenge.

If Nicholas ever succeeded in creating his hybrid Weres or found a way to control born Weres, she would have access to the perfect soldier. The genetic link that bound Weres and Vampires centuries ago was broken, but science might possibly forge a new one, and with unlimited ranks of fierce fighters, she would not need to worry about securing her sovereignty. With her power base unassailable, she could look to Europe and even greater influence. To accomplish that, she needed to know what Nicholas had planned. Then she could protect herself and her Vampires from fallout should the plans fail.

"Of course I'll make time, then, for you," Francesca said. "Where would you like to meet?"

"I'm outside in the parking lot."

She laughed. "Really. Are you sure you wouldn't like to come inside? I can promise you an enjoyable experience."

"I'm quite sure you could," he said, his tone warming. "Regrettably, I have to decline."

"Some other time, then."

"Yes," Nicholas said. "I know you're busy. Ten minutes should be plenty of time."

"I'll see you in two. And you can have all the time you need."

She disconnected and mentally called for Michel. A moment later the door to her office opened.

"You have need of something, mistress?" Michel asked.

"Yes," Francesca said, rising to cross the room. "Nicholas is outside. I need to see him."

"You don't intend to meet with him alone?"

"Darling, I can take care of myself."

"I'm quite sure you can. But there's no reason to put yourself in danger just to prove it. I'll go with you."

Laughing, Francesca slid her arm through Michel's and leaned in to kiss her. "Mmm. Where have you been?"

Michel frowned, leading the way through the underground hallways to an exit only she and Francesca used. "I was in the club. I didn't think you'd need me tonight."

"So you've been fucking Weres. Anyone I know?"

"No," Michel said abruptly, keying in the code to release the locks on the security door. She ascended the stairs first, checked the outside for any sign of danger, then reached down for Francesca's hand. "No one important."

"You're restless," Francesca murmured, stroking her nails down the side of Michel's neck. "I think we'll have to find someone for you to kill."

❖

Jody leaned against the wall as chunks of rock and twisted metal rained down from the stairwell a few feet away. She remembered dying the first time, the burning pain, the dulling of her senses, the agonizing grief at leaving Becca. She hadn't fought it. She hadn't wanted Becca to try to save her. This time she struggled to stay alive. Becca had made the ultimate sacrifice—risking her own life for Jody's, and Jody couldn't let it end like this. She'd opened herself to Becca and let Becca be vulnerable to her. And now, without her bite, without her blood, Becca could end up the victim of mindless blood craving, and she could not let that happen. She would not let that happen. The smoke-filled air didn't bother her. She didn't get most of her oxygen from the air she breathed but from the blood she ingested, rich with ferrous carriers. She was better equipped than the others to withstand the flames that even now consumed the tunnel behind her, but the radiation had already done its damage. Her organs were shutting down, her systems failing. She wasn't sure she could stand.

From nearby, a weak moan took her attention away from her own dying body. One of the captives was awake.

"Please," a faint voice came to her out of the darkness. The girl coughed, her voice cracking. "Please, who are you?"

A hand found her thigh and feeble fingers plucked at her pants. Jody covered the girl's hand with hers. The girl was hot, burning from the inside, like her. A different kind of fever, but dying all the same.

"A friend," Jody said, her voice sounding empty as a well that had gone dry.

"Are we going to die?"

"No," Jody said. "Help is coming."

"Please don't leave me."

Before Becca, she'd cared little for humans. Like all Vampires, she saw them only as prey. Becca had taught her that humans might be physically fragile, but they could be valorous and foolishly brave. She squeezed the girl's hand. "I won't."

She only hoped she could keep her word.

In the dim space carved out of the mountainside, Drake searched for some indication of a way inside. The loading area was the size of a football field, complete with winches, hoists, and pneumatic lifts. Three new-looking all-terrain vehicles were parked against one wall. Clearly, items were off-loaded here and then taken deeper into the complex. The entire place was dark, dark and empty. She tilted her chin, smelled smoke. The mountain was burning.

An ominous rumble rose from all around her, and the concrete beneath her feet shifted. The moment's instability reminded her of the time she'd been on the West Coast during an earthquake. This entire place was about to collapse.

She caught the scent of someone approaching from behind and whirled around. Rafe vaulted through the open bay doors.

"Most of the aboveground complex is fully involved," Rafe shouted. "The underground must be too. You need to go."

"Where's Niki?"

"She took the Rover back to the Compound, as you ordered."

"What are you doing here?"

"I've come to look for my Liege. Go," Rafe said. "If they're here, I'll find them."

"We'll find them. There must be a stairwell or an elevator shaft," Drake said. "You go right, I'll go left."

A huge crack appeared in the center of the concrete floor, and a roar like an avalanche cascading down a mountainside preceded the creak and groan of rock and metal shifting. The structure was folding in on itself, much the way the towers in Manhattan had accordioned when the temperature at their cores had reached a critical level, destroying the infrastructure of the steel and literally melting the buildings from the inside out.

"There," Drake shouted, hope cresting in her chest. She pointed to a door with a sign, nearly obliterated by soot, warning an alarm would sound if opened. Beside it, an elevator, no doubt inoperable now. Drake shoved against the bar holding the door closed and it moved an inch. Gathering all her strength, she shouldered it again and felt some obstacle on the other side preventing it from opening further.

"Let me help," Rafe said, crowding in next to Drake.

"Not with those burns on your shoulders," Drake said. "You'll strip the flesh right off your bones."

Rafe grinned. "If I don't return with my Liege, it won't matter. If she dies, her personal guard will all be sacrificed. Our allegiance to her is for life. Her life."

"Then use your hip," Drake said, "because if we find them, you might need to carry them."

"Good thought," Rafe said, and together they shoved again.

Finally, they wedged the door open enough to slide through, but when Drake started to inch her way inside, Rafe stopped her.

"Smoke," Rafe said, wheezing. Blood streamed down her arms and chest. She pointed to the gray plumes wafting through the crevices in the walls and spaces between the rubble that blocked the stairwell. "If they came this way, they would have been trapped in the burning tunnel."

"They came this way," Drake said, grabbing a chunk of metal and stone and throwing it out into the room behind them. "Sylvan is down there. And so is your Liege. If you can walk, you should get out of here."

Rafe's face set with determination. "I've already carried her dead body once. I'm not doing it again."

"Then we have to get down the stairwell. This has to be the only way out."

"If Jody was alive, she would sense me," Rafe said, helping Drake shove a section of broken wall aside. "She would reach me with her mind, and I don't feel her."

"Maybe she can't." Drake nearly choked on the words. Except for that very brief whisper of connection outside in the clearing, she couldn't feel Sylvan either. Even before they were mated, she'd been able to sense her on some deep level. Since their mating, Sylvan always filled her mind and body and consciousness. If she thought about what might have severed their connection now, she would suffocate with despair. So she did the only thing she could do. She blanked her mind and dug down toward the flames.

Sophia rushed out of the barracks when the general alarm sounded. Weres streamed out behind her, hurrying to take up positions on the ramparts at the top of the stockade. She headed across the Compound to the infirmary but stopped when the gates crashed open and the Rover barreled inside. *Sentries* jumped aside as the vehicle careened across the yard up to the headquarters building. The doors flew open and Niki leapt out, followed by the other *centuri*. They pulled someone out of the back of the Rover and dragged whoever it was into the building. Sophia reversed course and ran to catch up to them. Niki stopped her headlong rush on the porch.

"We need to prepare for an attack," Niki said. "You should stay in the infirmary in case we have wounded."

"You're hurt," Sophia said. Niki's entire left side was scorched.

Large patches of skin on her shoulder and hip were burned and encrusted with debris. "You need attention."

"Later," Niki growled, turning away.

Sophia caught her undamaged arm. "Niki, where is the Alpha? And the Prima?"

Niki spun around, her teeth bared, her eyes glazed with pain and fury. "Missing."

The breath stuttered to a stop in Sophia's chest, but she forced the swell of panic aside. She slid her fingers down Niki's arm and clasped her fingers, letting Niki feel how much she trusted her, how much she believed in her. "What can I do?"

For a second, Niki swayed and Sophia moved closer, shielding her from anyone who might be looking. Niki was in command now, and the Pack needed a strong leader. She could not appear weak.

"We have to be ready for anything," Niki said. "The Alpha may be injured. Possibly the Prima too."

"Oh God," Sophia murmured. "Niki, what happened?"

"An explosion." Niki shook her head as if trying to clear her thoughts. "We have a prisoner—a human. I need to interrogate him now. He may know what we're facing."

"At least let me clean your wounds."

"No." Niki cupped Sophia's cheek. "If we're attacked, Callan has orders to evacuate the Compound. I want you to go with the others."

Sophia stiffened. "I'm a medic, Niki. I can't leave the fight. You know that."

Niki growled, her wolf in control. Red pelt streaked down her chest, over her abdomen. Her canines jutted out. She growled.

"Niki, I'll be careful," Sophia said soothingly, stroking Niki's face until she settled and her wolf relaxed. "Don't worry about me."

"I had to leave her," Niki said hollowly. "I had to leave the Alpha behind."

"You wouldn't have if there had been any other choice." Sophia kissed her. "I know that. She would have wanted you to protect us."

"I don't want to leave you."

"You're not." Sophia smiled though it took every ounce of willpower she had. "I'll be across the Compound in the infirmary. I expect you to report to me so I can take care of those wounds the minute you're free."

Niki nodded. "I might need you to bring Katya and Gray over here. Are they well enough?"

"Misha took them for a run. They were much better when they came back. Why?"

"This prisoner. He says he knows them."

CHAPTER TWENTY

Michel opened the rear of the Town Car, and Francesca slipped inside. Nicholas sat on the far side of the plush leather seat exuding the air of confidence and entitlement of a man used to occupying the central chair in the boardroom of a Fortune 500 company. His charcoal pinstripe suit, monochrome silk shirt, and matching tie with subtle stripes complemented his silver mane. His hair was carefully styled, and his tight jawline and wrinkle-free brow hinted at surgical enhancement. Nicholas Gregory, secret leader of Humans United for Species Integrity, was vain. Francesca smiled to herself. Narcissism was a weakness to be exploited.

Michel closed the car door behind her and Francesca slid to the center of the seat. The night was warm and she hadn't bothered with any kind of wrap. Nicholas struggled, and failed, not to stare at her breasts, barely contained in a loosely laced red satin bustier, before his gaze traveled down to her low-cut black pants and exposed abdomen. She'd fed well upon rising, but the presence of such vulnerable prey stirred her desire to hunt. She rested a fingertip on the top of his hand. "I know you didn't come all this way just to talk to me." She laughed. "Of course, I could always hope."

"I'm afraid tonight is about business," Nicholas said, sounding almost as if he really regretted it. She knew he loathed Praeterns, but like so many humans, he seemed fascinated by what he hated.

"Well then, I suppose we'll have to put pleasure aside." Francesca slid her entire hand onto his thigh and enveloped him in a subtle thrall. His heart rate kicked up instantly. His blood rushed faster through his arteries, pulsing hot and thick beneath her fingers. His cock stiffened, and by the rigid set of his jaw, he wasn't used to his body responding without his permission. "At least for now."

Nicholas cleared his throat and pushed back in his seat, casually folding the front of his suit jacket over the mound in his crotch. "We had a break-in at one of our installations last night. Sylvan Mir led the raid."

"Really." Francesca waited, wondering just how much of the truth he intended to tell her. Thus far, he'd kept the specific details of what his experiments entailed from the other Shadow Lords. She hadn't minded, because the less she knew, the less culpable she would be if they were exposed. On the other hand, knowledge was power, and she wanted as much of both as she could get. "Sylvan doesn't seem the type to flout the law without good reason. She is, after all, a public figure and the representative of all the Praetern species in Washington. How do you know it was her?"

"We have…witnesses."

Francesca nodded, uncertain if he knew Michel had been there when Sylvan's forces arrived, and if he did, whether he would acknowledge it. Veronica Standish was aware of Michel's involvement, of course, but Francesca doubted Veronica shared everything she knew with Nicholas—or anyone else. In this elaborate game, everyone had secrets. "I see. What was she after?"

"We can't be sure, of course, but we believe she was acting on misinformation. She was under the false impression that we had somehow detained some of her…Pack."

"Why would anyone want her to think that? As if you would be that foolish." Francesca knew of Nicholas's experiments with human females aimed at producing a synthetic toxin that would cause the nearly universally fatal Were fever in humans. Unleashing such a virulent substance among the human population would induce worldwide panic and turn humans against the Weres. Even Sylvan would abandon her attempt to work with the humans if the autonomy of the Were species was in danger. Michel had reported that several Were females had been imprisoned and were the subject of experimentation. Nicholas and Veronica Standish had not shared that information with anyone.

If she kept Nicholas talking, perhaps she'd find out why. "What possible use would Weres be to you?"

"None, of course," Nicholas lied.

"Unless, of course, you were hoping to find some way to control them?"

Nicholas grimaced. "As if that was possible. The only way to control a Were is with silver bullets."

"And what could Sylvan hope to accomplish by such an obvious maneuver as attacking one of your laboratories?"

"Who can know what motivates irrational creatures like these Weres?" Nicholas shrugged. "The point is, she's dangerous, and she needs to be stopped."

"I agree," Francesca said, slowly tracing her fingertips along the sharp crease in his trousers. "Sylvan Mir is a formidable and unpredictable opponent. But she's highly visible, and any assault on her is very likely to bring a public outcry and intense scrutiny. We had agreed we would try to dissuade her from pursuing the Coalition goals and convince her to our agenda before resorting to more...forceful means."

"True," Nicholas said smoothly. "But that was before this open act of aggression. We don't know what she might do next."

"How much does Sylvan know?" Francesca doubted Nicholas had any idea exactly how aggressive Sylvan could be. Michel had said there were young Were females in that lab—and whether they were Sylvan's or not made no difference. Sylvan would never rest until she discovered who was responsible. Nicholas was putting them all at great risk—his usefulness was rapidly drawing to an end. "Does she know who was behind the work there?"

"There's no way she could," Nicholas said. "We've gone to great lengths to shield the identities of the investigators from the guar—employees. None of the scientists know the exact nature of our experiments. Even the location of the labs is camouflaged."

"Someone must be providing her with information, or why would she have broken in?"

"As I said"—Nicholas said slowly, adjusting his cuffs. Diamond links glinted on his sleeves—"misinformation. All the same, we have to assume that particular site is no longer viable. We also have to assume that Mir will start looking for other labs."

"I imagine your security is very vigorous."

"Oh, it is. Everyone who works on sensitive projects is constantly monitored, their access to the labs is limited to work-specific areas, and any kind of data transmission—on- or off-site—is screened."

"Then she isn't likely to discover anything."

"Unlikely, but not impossible."

Francesca grew tired of his game playing. "You, of course, have a plan."

He smiled and glanced at his platinum Rolex. "We've had to abandon the installation. Unfortunate, but necessary. My concern now is preventing further interference from Sylvan Mir."

At last, he was getting to the reason for his visit. Francesca moved closer until her thigh rested against his and her breasts brushed his sleeve. She enthralled him just enough to cloud his thinking but not enough that he would notice and try to resist. She could overpower him mentally, but she didn't want to arouse his suspicions. She just wanted him to be disinhibited enough to reveal his intentions. "How?"

"We either have to kill her or neutralize her…" Nicholas said, his attention slowly shifting from her face to her breasts, his words slowing. "If we kill her…If we kill her, she becomes a martyr. But if we discredit her, have her removed from the Coalition…"

"What, darling?" Francesca murmured, brushing her lips along the underside of his jaw. "What will you need to do?"

"Everyone saw that picture of her when she lost control."

Nicholas seemed to lose his train of thought, and Francesca found his hand and guided it into her top. "What about the picture, Nicholas?"

"Animals. They're just animals."

"I know." Francesca nearly smiled. Humans were so terribly easy and ultimately so terribly boring. She'd never been able to capture Sylvan's mind and would have been disappointed if she'd been able to. Sylvan had come closer to dominating her than any being she'd ever known, and after an age of enthralling others, she'd been thrilled to be enraptured. Right now, however, she welcomed her ability to manipulate her prey. She grazed her incisors over the bounding pulse in his throat and he gasped. "What is it you want to do, Nicholas darling?"

"Force her to show the world what she really is."

"How?"

"Kill everyone she loves."

"Why are you telling me?" Francesca punctured the skin in his neck and allowed a slow infusion of her feeding hormones to enter his bloodstream. If she fed from him fully he would orgasm, and she didn't want him to remember being enthralled. His blood trickled into her mouth and she swallowed. So much thinner than a Were's, but blood was always pleasurable. Her clitoris tightened with the first surge of blood. He gasped and his cock swelled against her hip. Only a moment more and she would need to stop. "What is it you want?"

"Your help."

"Tell me."

❖

"One more time," Sylvan said. "We've almost got it. Push again, Lara."

Lara rumbled, and Sylvan felt the presence of another Alpha wolf crowd into the space beside her. Her own wolf charging at the invasion, Sylvan growled a warning. Lara's body grew larger, heavier, a hulking form in the smoky, dust-filled air. Even in the dim light, Sylvan could see Lara's transformation, a transformation Lara should not be able to make. She was not shifting—she was arrested in half-Were form, a fully functional hybrid wolf Were, a throwback to millennia past when the progenitors of the species walked on two legs while partially transformed. Now only the strongest Alphas and their mates retained that ability. Until Lara. But even in her half-form, Lara was unlike any Were Sylvan had ever seen. Lara's Were characteristics were absent— her pelt hidden, her claws and fangs sheathed. Except for her size, her features were more Vampire than wolf. Sylvan had never seen anyone, not even another Alpha, free her wolf while still in skin. Lara's wolf snarled, her amber eyes flashing gold.

Sylvan roared in challenge and clamped a fully formed claw around Lara's neck. She squeezed until the breath stopped in Lara's throat and pulled Lara to her until they were eye to eye. She unleashed her wolf and let Lara see the power of a full-blooded Alpha. "Hold your wolf or I'll tear your throat out."

Lara shuddered, her eyes flashing crimson and slowly fading to wolf-amber. Sylvan loosened her grasp and Lara panted and shook. Slowly, her body settled into its normal shape. "What happened? I don't remember—Alpha?"

"Your wolf wants out of here. So do I," Sylvan said, letting her go. She'd worry later about what she'd just witnessed. "Now help me push this damn hunk of steel out of our way."

Sylvan gathered all her strength, and this time when they shouldered upward, the girder shifted another inch. The murky darkness seemed to lighten. Sylvan caught a scent of fresh air, the first smoke-free breath she'd had in what felt like hours. The gray veil that had fallen over her since the explosion began to lift. The effect of the silver that had weakened her and dulled her senses was dissipating. She heard the breeze rustling through the trees, scented life coursing through the forest. Her skin tingled and every sense sharpened. Her wolf sprang up, alert and searching. Drake! Drake was nearby. Sylvan's wolf tore at her insides in a frenzy.

"Drake," Sylvan roared. "No! Go back."

"Sylvan? Sylvan!" Drake's voice rose in triumph and joy. "Sylvan, we're almost to you. Are you hurt? Sylvan!"

"Go back," Sylvan shouted furiously. "We'll get out. You're not safe here."

"I'll leave as soon as you're free."

"They're only a few feet away," Lara said. "Drake and Rafe."

Sylvan said, "You feel them both?"

Lara nodded. "Yes."

"Just above us?"

"Yes."

"Drake," Sylvan called, "wait where you are until we move this last obstacle. The stairwell might collapse. You need to be clear."

"Go slowly," Drake said. "We've braced the walls above you as best we can. We'll keep bracing from our side."

"Damn it, Drake—"

"Don't waste time, Sylvan. I'm not leaving you."

"Just be careful." Sylvan glanced at Lara. "This may all come down on our heads when we shift this last beam out of the way."

Lara grinned. "Then I guess we'll find out which one of us can jump the farthest. Are you up for a challenge, Alpha?"

Sylvan growled and peered at the specks of sky showing through the chinks in the barrier above her. She scented Drake, felt the heartbeats of her young echo in her chest. She pressed her bruised and bleeding shoulders against the jagged steel and called upon the will and strength of her wolf. "Be careful what you ask for, Warlord. Now let me see how strong you really are."

Her breath turned to fire in her chest, her muscles stretched and tore from her bones, her consciousness narrowed until all she knew was pain and fury and the mad need to reach her mate. Metal screamed, stone cracked and shattered, and a torrent of rock rained down on them.

CHAPTER TWENTY-ONE

Sophia knocked softly on the door to Gray and Katya's room. They were physically well enough to return to the barracks, but neither seemed eager to leave the infirmary, and that worried her. It wasn't natural for any Were to choose to be separate from the rest of the Pack, but particularly not the adolescents. Very young Weres slept together in the nursery in a jumble, often four or six in a bed, many shifting involuntarily in their sleep. The presence of warm, familiar bodies and comforting scents helped dispel the sometimes disorienting effect of waking as a wolf. As they grew older and learned to control their shifts, adolescents were consumed with defining their places in the Pack hierarchy, forming intense friendships with Weres of both sexes—tussling, tangling, assessing potential mates. Katya and Gray had both spent time in *sentrie* training, where they'd lived, eaten, worked, and slept with their Packmates in the barracks. For them to want to stay alone now wasn't healthy.

Sophia knocked again. They would know it was her by her scent, but she wouldn't intrude without permission. They'd had too much of that in the last weeks.

Gray rumbled, "Come in."

"Have a good run?" Sophia asked. The room was lit by silvery moonlight streaming through the open window, and Gray, naked except for a pair of jeans, seemed wary and distrustful. She occupied her usual position with her back against the wall, watching the door, putting herself between Katya and any potential threat. Katya, in a black T-shirt and camo BDUs, lay curled up on top of her cot, her arms wrapped around the pillow and her knees drawn up to her midsection. She looked small and wounded, and Sophia's heart wept.

"Callan called us back before we got very far." Gray's eyes glimmered gold, her wolf prowling, restless. "Then we heard the alarm. We can fight. We're ready."

"There's no fight yet," Sophia said, considering how much to tell them. She ached to protect them, but that time had passed. "Niki has a captive—a human. We don't know very much about him, but he says that he knows you. From the lab."

Katya gasped and Gray leapt to her feet, snarling.

"The Alpha isn't here right now, but it's possible she'll want you to see him." Sophia spoke calmly, ignoring that Gray was on the verge of shifting. Gray was volatile, barely in control, but she had to be given the chance to control herself. Gray had to know that she and her wolf were one, as they always had been, and the Pack trusted her. "I know you don't remember much about the humans who held you, and that's okay."

"Only broken memories," Katya murmured. She sat up, her arms tightly folded around her middle, and glanced at Gray. "What does the Alpha need us to do?"

"Niki is talking to him now. If you see him, you may remember more." Sophia saw no point in saying the Alpha was missing. The Alpha would return. Any other possibility was unthinkable. "How do you feel about that?"

"We'll do whatever the Alpha needs," Gray said.

"I know you will." Sophia smiled softly. "But I want to know how you *feel* about doing it."

"What does it matter how we feel?" Gray growled. "We're warriors. We follow the Alpha's command."

"Do you think she doesn't care how you feel? That I don't care?"

"We don't care about feelings," Katya said flatly, sounding bitter but stronger than she had before.

"They hurt you," Sophia said to Katya. "We know that. We all hurt for you."

"Don't," Katya said. "We don't want you to pity us."

"Pity is not the same as love." Sophia wanted to gather them both up—to soothe them, heal them. Their shame and sorrow and guilt choked her, and they were so wrong. They were so heartbreakingly brave. But they did not need her tears. "The Alpha will decide what to do with him. And I know you will do what she asks."

"Where did she go?" Katya asked.

The Pack had few secrets, living as they did in intense community, aware of each other's impulses and desires and needs. Sophia didn't ordinarily discuss battle plans with adolescents, but these weren't just any adolescents. These were two young wolves who were no longer young in anything except years, already seasoned in the worst kind of battle. They needed honesty and respect. "The Alpha went back to the installation where you were held. There may be other captives."

Katya whined, an anguished cry caught in her throat. "No. The Alpha wouldn't have left anyone."

"We can't be sure. They could be hidden in some other part of the installation. Your captors found a way to prevent the Alpha from sensing you."

Gray shuddered and her eyes glazed. "I couldn't feel the Alpha—couldn't feel the Pack. The air was...wrong. Stinging, bitter."

"They poisoned you."

"I should've gone back with them tonight," Gray said. "I remember...some things. Places they took us. I might have helped."

"Do you remember a human—a big man with long brown hair and dark eyes?"

Gray shook her head, pacing back and forth in front of her narrow bed. "Faces. I can't see the faces."

"You will, you're doing fine."

"I killed one. I remember his blood in my mouth." Gray looked at Sophia, questions in her tormented eyes.

"Yes, you did," Sophia said. "Any one of us would have done the same. There's no shame in that."

"I still want to kill them."

"Of course you do. So do we. All of them." Sophia cupped Gray's face. Gray went very still, but did not pull away. Sophia stroked her thumb over the sharp edge of Gray's cheekbone, brushed the hair from her eyes. "What you feel *is* important. What you do about what you feel is what defines you. That's up to you, Gray. I trust you. We all do."

"I remember scents, touches. Pain, I remember pain, and—" Gray abruptly snarled so violently, Sophia nearly growled a warning. She wasn't dominant, but her wolf instinctively responded to the threat.

Sophia calmed her wolf, waiting for Gray to settle. She'd sensed a surge of rage and, unexpectedly, excitement. Whatever Gray remembered had aroused her.

"I want to see him," Gray said, a low heavy, rumble in her voice. Her eyes shimmered gold again and her canines jutted from behind her full upper lip. Pheromones clouded the air. Gray was a mature young dominant, and Sophia was in heat.

Sophia backed up a step. "No, Gray. Not now."

Gray snarled. Her face grew sharper, her skin shimmering with sex-sheen.

"Listen to me," Sophia said gently, "I don't want you to answer my call."

"I don't care." Gray stepped closer, her pelt line flaring. She was fiercely beautiful, potent and primed. Sophia walked a fine line between continuing to stimulate her if she stayed, encouraging her by her very presence, and risking further injury to Gray's self-esteem by denying her the opportunity to restrain her wolf. She wasn't even certain Gray *could* contain her urges, but she needed to give her the chance. Softly, she said, "You know the rules. My choice who answers my call."

Gray shuddered and panted.

Sophia suddenly heated, skin tingling as if she'd been electrified, and her body quickened. Her need surged, fed by the flood of neurostimulants set off by the Were bearing down on them. Niki was coming. Sophia sensed her from across the courtyard. Niki stormed closer, possessive and aggressive. If she burst in on them now, Gray would attack and Niki would probably kill her. Sophia reached inside herself, projected her thoughts, never questioning if she could reach Niki.

I'm all right. Don't hurt her.

She challenges.

No. No, she doesn't. Niki, don't hurt her.

The door behind her banged open and Sophia spun around. Niki stood framed by the golden glow of the lights in the hall behind her. Her hair shimmered like fire and her green eyes glowed as hot as embers. Her chest was bare, breasts tight-nippled, her heavy pelt line bisecting her rigid abdomen. Her claws were down, her canines extruded. She dripped sex and adrenaline.

"Mine," Niki growled.

Gray's head snapped up and a rumble rose from her throat. *Niki, wait. Please.*

Behind her, Niki growled again, a tone so dangerous and so primal Sophia wanted to be under her, her teeth buried in Niki's throat, Niki buried inside her. She fought for control, fought to project calm. Her wolf howled for release, to mate.

"Gray," Sophia murmured, holding her place between the two of them. "Gray, I choose Niki."

Gray's pelt rolled beneath her skin, her jaw elongated, her eyes angled. She shimmered and started to shift.

"*Gray,*" Niki snapped. "Hold your wolf. We need you here."

Sophia held her breath, watching Gray struggle to obey the Pack *imperator.*

Gray sucked in a shuddering breath and her wolf receded. Softly, she whispered, "Yes, *Imperator.*"

"Next time, mind your place, whelp." Niki came up behind Sophia and wrapped an arm around Sophia's waist, pulling Sophia back against her chest. Heat poured from Niki's bare torso through Sophia's body as if they were skin to skin.

Thank you. Sophia arched her back, exposing her neck, and Niki grazed her throat with her canines.

I won't be so generous again.

Sophia knew Gray was watching, knew she needed to be reminded of one of the most basic rules of the Pack—a female always chose who answered her call. Her mind assessed her patient's welfare, but her body surrendered to the overwhelming pleasure of Niki's hands on her. Her breasts tingled, her belly rolled with need, and her clitoris expanded. She rocked her hips into Niki's crotch, inviting her to take more. Try as she might, she could not resist the need roaring through her.

"Sophia is mine," Niki said to Gray, running both hands up and down Sophia's body. She pulled Sophia's shirt from the waistband of her pants and slid her hand underneath. "Remember that."

"Yes, *Imperator.*" Gray backed up until her legs hit the bed, and she sat, her hands between her knees, her eyes lowered focus somewhere between them.

Sophia reached behind Niki's head and ran her fingers through Niki's hair, turning her head to bite her on the jaw. "She didn't touch me."

Niki kissed her. "If she had, she'd be bleeding on the floor under me right now."

"You claim rights you don't have."

"Then give them to me." Niki spread her hand over Sophia's lower abdomen, her claws pressing into Sophia's belly. Her teeth penetrated Sophia's shoulder as quick as lightning, and Sophia's sex readied.

She couldn't fight her wolf and her instincts and her heart all at the same time. "Yes," Sophia whispered. "Yes."

❖

Drake coughed the dust from her lungs, her heart pounding furiously. "Sylvan!"

The rumbling of stone and screeching of shifting metal finally stopped, and she listened, willing Sylvan to answer with every ounce of her being. The silence was suffocating. Even the crackling roar of the fire ravaging the surrounding forest and the cries of terrified animals had disappeared. Wiping grit from her eyes with the back of her arm, she started down what remained of the stairs.

"Wait," Rafe yelled, grabbing her arm. "Let me go first."

"No." Drake jerked her arm free. She'd waited long enough. Sylvan was near and nothing would stand between them now. She jumped over a gap in the cracked and canted stairwell, landing on a narrow ledge of stone that overlooked an abyss. She peered down. "Sylvan?"

Only darkness awaited her.

Despair, black and heavy, seeped through her like poison. The only thing keeping her from leaping into the yawning cavern in search of Sylvan was the ever-growing presence of the young she carried. She cared nothing for herself, but for them, for Sylvan's heirs and hers, she would not take the last step. A howl rose from her chest, haunted with grief and fury. Only an echo, lonely and desolate, filled her battered soul.

"I'm going down." Rafe paused on the brink of the impenetrable. "If I don't return—there's something you should know. When we broke into the lab last night, the Vampire who was there before us was the Viceregal's *senechal*. Michel."

Drake nodded. "Thank you. When you find them, call me."

"Of course."

"Hurry."

Rafe disappeared and time stopped. Drake called out again, "Sylvan?"

She couldn't sense her, couldn't feel her. Every breath was a blade piercing her heart.

"Drake," Rafe called. "There's a landing fifteen feet below you." Instantly, Drake jumped. The blackness was absolute. Even her wolf eyes could not see what surrounded her. She extended a hand and felt rock, spikes of steel, burning wood. Her shoulder touched Rafe's. "Do you feel—"

"Rafe? Drake?" a disembodied voice croaked.

"Liege!" Rafe shouted and disappeared in the direction of Jody's voice.

Another crack like thunder, and clouds of stone dust rose up around Drake's feet. Rocks rolled down what must have been the remains of a hallway.

Someone moaned. Someone close by.

"Sylvan!" Drake dropped to her knees and ran her hands over the uneven surface of the mounds of rubble. She touched warm flesh. Sylvan's flesh. Drake heaved rocks aside, felt Sylvan move, and then Sylvan was kneeling in front of her, warm, alive. Drake gripped Sylvan's shoulders and kissed her, desperate for the taste of her, the scent of her, the press of her flesh. Drake's breath came in jagged rasps. Her face was wet with tears she didn't bother to hide. Sylvan gripped her hair, kissed her with a hot, fast plunge of her tongue, bruising her mouth, drinking her. Drake opened, absorbing the ferocious power of the Alpha, her mate. Her life.

"I thought…" Drake couldn't touch her enough. Couldn't form words. All she needed was Sylvan under her hands. She ran her hands over Sylvan's face, down her neck, her shoulders. "I couldn't feel you. Why couldn't I—"

"Didn't I tell you to go?" Sylvan muttered against Drake's mouth, unable to stop kissing her. "Will you never listen?"

"Are you hurt?" Drake rasped her claws down Sylvan's back. Hers again. "Sylvan, are you hurt?"

"Nothing serious."

"You're bleeding."

"Just cuts and scrapes. We have injured—humans."

"What? Why?"

"They have fever," Sylvan said. "They're both in midtransition."

"God. What were they doing here? Where's Lara?"

"Here," Lara grunted. "My arm was broken but it's healed now. I'll get the Liege."

Drake said, "The air down here is toxic. We need to get out of here."

Rafe and Lara crowded next to them, each with a girl in her arms.

"These two are still alive," Lara said. "Do you still want to take them out?"

"Yes," Sylvan said. "Where's Jody?"

"She's…injured," Rafe said. "I'll go back for her."

"No," Sylvan said. "Drake, go back to the surface. Lara, Rafe, take the humans up with you. Jody and I will be behind you."

"No," Lara said. "I will take my Liege. You take this human."

Sylvan snarled. "You disobey my orders?"

"Warlord," Jody said in a toneless, flat voice. "Take the humans, go up first. Clear the way for all of us."

"Yes, Liege."

Drake waited until Rafe and Lara disappeared up the precipitous stairwell. "What's wrong?"

"Jody has severe UV exposure," Sylvan said. "She needs blood."

"I can wait," Jody said.

"You can't even stand." Sylvan gripped Drake's shoulder. "I need to feed her, or she won't survive to get bonded blood."

"Then do it." Drake circled her hand over the center of Sylvan's back. "We don't have much time."

Sylvan took Drake's hand and they eased over portions of a collapsed wall to where Jody lay. Together they lifted Jody until she was cradled against Sylvan's chest.

Drake guided Jody's head to Sylvan's neck. "Jody, you must stop before you weaken her."

Jody was beyond hearing. Her mouth was already against Sylvan's neck, her teeth in Sylvan's throat. Sylvan gasped and reached for Drake.

"Come here, mate," Drake murmured, cupping Sylvan's cheek. She kissed her, and Sylvan groaned against her mouth. Drake tasted her power, the heat of her, and her body stirred. She kissed her and kept kissing her until Jody pulled away with a gasp.

"Thank you," Jody said. "I am in your debt."

Sylvan shuddered, her hands trembling on Drake's shoulders.

Drake stroked her face. "We need to go now."

"Yes," Sylvan said hoarsely.

Lara called down, "The forest is burning. Hurry."

Jody disappeared into the stairwell above them.

"Drake," Sylvan said. "That was not—"

"I know." Drake kissed her. "Let's go home."

Chapter Twenty-two

"Niki, wait," Sophia said urgently as Niki dragged her out of Gray's room and slammed the door closed. "What's happening outside? You don't need to stay—everything is fine. I'm fi—"

"Callan is in charge. And you're not fine." Niki, her shoulders tight and her eyes flashing brighter than any fire, grasped Sophia's wrist and pulled her down the hall toward one of the empty rooms. "If you were fine, I wouldn't have found you with a young wolf about to jump you."

"She wasn't. I could have handled—"

Without breaking stride, Niki silenced her with a hard, ferocious kiss.

Sophia knew her legs were moving but she had no sense of her feet touching the floor. All she knew was the thick, heady force of Niki's desire flooding her—her head whirled, sound faded to nothing but the roar of her blood and the drumbeat of her heart, her sight was blind to everything but the dense green of Niki's eyes. A green deeper than any forest, hotter than any flame. She braced her hands on Niki's chest and pulled free of the kiss. Instantly she wanted Niki's mouth on her again. "Niki, oh God—Niki, wait. We can't—not now."

Niki yanked her into the darkened room, shoved the door closed, and pushed Sophia against it. She caged her with an arm on either side of Sophia's shoulders, pinning her with her body. "Yes now. I'm done watching other Weres try to claim you."

Sophia struggled for reason, but Niki's mouth was on her neck, kissing her, nipping at her skin, scraping along the muscles with her teeth. Niki was hot and heavy and hard, and Sophia wrapped her arms around her neck as naturally as she lifted her face to the moonlight when she ran under the stars. Niki was the key that opened every need she'd worked so hard to lock away. "Niki, they might need you outside. I—I can wait."

"I can't...Not anymore. I need you," Niki said, her mouth on Sophia's throat. "I need you now, just for a minute."

Sophia caressed Niki's back, played her fingers over the massive muscles in her shoulders, traced the smooth slope of her waist. She spread her fingers through Niki's hair and pressed Niki's face harder to her neck. "I love the way you feel. You're so beautiful."

"Don't stop touching me," Niki growled, her teeth grazing Sophia's shoulder. She pushed Sophia's shirt up and lowered her head, sliding her mouth along the curve of Sophia's breast, sucking, teasing, tormenting.

"I want your skin," Sophia gasped, hooking her fingers in the waistband of Niki's jeans and tearing them open. She shoved the pants down over the curve of Niki's muscular ass, scoring her with her claws, so ready for her she could only whimper. "Niki. I need you."

Niki panted, wanting her like she wanted prey on a hunt—with a single-minded ferocity that blinded her to everything else. She'd waited so long, wanted so madly, she was afraid she would lose herself, take her too hard, too fast. Hurt her. Breath burned in her lungs, her stomach knotted. Another second and she'd mount her and take her, and she wanted so much more. She went to her knees and forced herself to go slowly. Niki pressed her cheek to Sophia's abdomen and rubbed her face over the soft dusting of silver pelt low on her belly. "I'll hurt you."

"You won't." Sophia dug her fingers into Niki's broad shoulders. "I'm a Were. I'm not fragile."

"You make me wild," Niki muttered.

"Good."

Niki opened Sophia's pants, guided them down her long sleek thighs, kissed the quivering muscles she exposed. She ran her palms up and down Sophia's legs, careful not to press too hard, careful not to draw blood. Yet. If she bit her, tasted her, her wolf would rule, and she wouldn't stop until she'd come inside her.

"I *want* you inside me," Sophia gasped.

Sophia raked her claws over Niki's shoulders, and the lightning strokes of pain set Niki ablaze. Her clitoris stiffened, beating rapidly in time with her furious heart. Niki groaned when Sophia's fingers came into her hair, pressing her face lower. A cloud of pheromones and sex engulfed her. She was blind with the beauty of her, wild with the scent of her. She was so ready to be inside her she could think of nothing else. Niki pressed her lips to Sophia's belly, ran her mouth over the silky skin, dragged her teeth down to the junction of her thighs.

Sophia cradled Niki's neck. "Please, oh please. Now."

Sophia's gasps of pleasure, her small cries of need, drew a possessive snarl from Niki's throat. "Mine."

"Yes, yes." Sophia lifted her hips to Niki's mouth. "Taste me."

Niki's wolf surged and Niki strained to hold her back. She stroked the insides of Sophia's thighs and pressed her legs open, following the path of her fingers with her mouth. She licked lightly, teasingly, until Sophia jerked her head forward with a low warning growl.

"Now, Wolf. Now."

Claws pierced Niki's neck, another shock of bright, shining pain shot through her, and Niki shuddered on the edge of exploding. She closed her mouth around Sophia, taking her full, firm clitoris between her lips, sucking her deep. Sophia's legs quivered as she tasted her.

"Niki, Niki, take me. Please, please."

Niki held Sophia in her mouth, licking, sucking, teasing until she felt Sophia swell, felt the deep glands tense, and knew she was ready. She surged to her feet, pushed her hips tight between Sophia's thighs, and pulled Sophia's legs up around her hips. Holding Sophia against the door with her body, she pressed her tense clitoris beneath Sophia's, joining them.

Sophia's head fell back against the door. "Oh yes. Yes. I love you over me, inside me."

Niki pushed deeper, and Sophia closed around her. The pressure was unbearable, agonizingly sweet—shatteringly perfect. Niki's ass tightened and she thrust, forcing Sophia to coat her in pheromones and sex. Sophia's wolf was hungry to mate, and Niki wanted her.

"Bite me," Niki growled in Sophia's ear. "Do it. I want your teeth in me when I come."

Sophia quivered, her body, her mind unleashed, but no matter how badly she needed, she would not risk Niki. Panting, sobbing, wild with hunger, she clung to reason. She'd always managed to avoid the final union, but she'd never wanted it so fiercely. Sliding her hands down Niki's sweat-slick back, she cupped her ass, burying her claws in the hard, tight muscles. Tightening her legs around Niki's hips, she rode her harder, faster, mercilessly.

Roaring, Niki jerked and her clitoris tensed.

"Now, Niki." Sophia dragged Niki's mouth to her shoulder. "Taste me."

Niki was lost. She buried her canines in Sophia's shoulder and thrust wildly, releasing a flood of victus over Sophia's sex.

"*Yes*," Sophia cried, releasing violently, devastatingly. But she held on, held back. She did not, would not, bite.

Niki buried her face in Sophia's neck and emptied helplessly, over and over. Her legs gave way and she crumpled. Sophia cushioned her slide to the floor and held Niki's damp face to her breast.

"Say it," Niki gasped. "Please, say it."

Sophia closed her eyes and rubbed her tear-streaked cheek over Niki's hair. "I'm yours, Niki." *In every way I can be.*

When Sylvan scrambled out of the hole in the side of the mountain behind Drake, she found Rafe waiting for them with one of the girls in her arms and the other on the ground at Jody's feet. Sylvan got a good look at the two Vampires for the first time since the explosion. They were both more badly injured than she'd realized—their clothing smoldering, their flesh blistering, huge areas blackened and charred. She'd never seen a Vampire walk into the sun, but she thought these two might have come close to that final immolation. She had to get her mate and her friends out of this death trap. She lifted the unconscious girl into her arms. "Where's Lara?"

"She went to get our vehicle," Rafe said. "The limos are designed to resist fire."

Around them, the forest burned, flames leaping from treetop to treetop, huge pines exploding like matchsticks, the sky swallowed by black clouds of smoke. Even the wind had been silenced by the roar of the fire.

"She'll have to run through flame to find it," Sylvan said.

"She said her wolf can outrun it," Rafe said.

Sylvan glanced at Drake. The conflagration was closing in on them. She couldn't risk her mate and her young, and she doubted she could get Drake to leave without her. *Shall we wait? The fire is close and we might have to carry Jody.*

Give Lara five minutes. The Vampires will be safer inside the car.

"All right," Sylvan said. "We'll wait."

Jody turned to Sylvan. "You and Drake should shift and get out before that road disappears. Rafe and I will stay here with the humans."

"We're not splitting up," Sylvan said. "Lara is strong and fast."

"There's no reason we should all die," Jody said.

"No," Sylvan said, "there isn't. And we won't." She pointed. "Look."

A hazy light shone through the torrent of burning embers, growing brighter with every second. A vehicle burst into the clearing and skidded to a stop. The doors flew open, and Sylvan pushed Drake toward the rear compartment. "Hurry. Everyone inside."

As the doors slammed shut, Sylvan called to Lara behind the wheel. "Can you get us out?"

"Yes," Lara said calmly. "Everyone hang on."

Drake knelt on the floor next to the two humans and checked their vital signs. "Is there anything to cover them with? They're both in shock."

"There's a pull-out compartment under the seat," Jody said. "We have a few medical supplies."

"IV fluid?" Drake asked hopefully, bracing a hand against the door as the vehicle jounced and careened over rocks and other obstacles.

Jody grinned thinly. "Synthetic blood."

"It will do." Drake sorted through the supplies and found intravenous needles and plastic bags of fluid. She managed to get lines into both the girls, despite their dehydrated state, and connected the bags to delivery tubes. That was all she could do for them now.

"Come here." Sylvan pulled Drake onto the seat and sheltered her against her side. "Are you all right? You should have left when I—"

Drake kissed her. "I'm fine. You're the one who's injured."

Sylvan grumbled. "You shouldn't take risks. I told—"

"I love you," Drake whispered. "Now shut up."

Sylvan's lip curled, but she rested her forehead against Drake's and contented herself with holding her.

Lara said, "We're approaching the junction with the main road. Where do you want me to go?"

"Head to Jody's town house," Sylvan said. "As soon as we can get a cell signal, we'll call the Compound and have them send a vehicle to intercept us. You need to get Jody home."

"Yes, Alpha," Lara said, flooring the accelerator as burning trees crashed around them. Branches and bushes like flaming torches scraped and slapped at the car, but she maneuvered through the last obstacles and bounced out onto a paved surface. She followed the road around the perimeter of the burning complex and up into the mountains.

Sylvan caught sight of flickering lights in the sky. "Helicopters. Probably news and police."

"We can't afford to be detained—not with these girls in the car," Drake said. "If they're infected, we don't want them in a human hospital."

"We don't want to be associated with this sabotage either," Jody said.

"They'll block these roads before long," Sylvan said.

"Call Becca," Jody said. "She has an emergency scanner. She'll be able to track which highways are open."

"Give me the car phone," Sylvan said, reaching into the front seat. "And activate the vehicle's GPS."

Lara handed the phone to Sylvan, and Sylvan punched in Becca's number.

"Yes?" Becca answered instantly.

"Becca," Sylvan said. "Jody's with me. We're in the middle of a forest fire, and we need to get out of here quickly before the police close the roads."

"Give me your location."

Sylvan checked the GPS reading on the dashboard and told her.

"One minute. Is Jody all right?"

"She's injured. She'll need bonded blood as soon as she arrives home."

Jody snarled and tried to grab the phone.

"She's not happy I told you that," Sylvan said.

"No, I imagine she isn't," Becca said, her voice steady but crackling with urgency. "Thank you."

"None needed."

"If you take 22 through the mountains south, you'll be clear."

"Rafe and Lara will see she gets home soon."

"Tell them to be careful."

Sylvan disconnected, ignoring the look of cold fury on Jody's sheet-white face, and called the Compound. Callan answered. "Is everything secure?"

"Yes, Alpha."

"Good. Have Dasha fix on our vehicle and meet us with the Rover en route. We have injured."

"Yes, Alpha."

Jody snarled, "You forget yourself, Wolf."

Sylvan tossed the phone into the front seat and shrugged. "You told me that's what you needed. She has a right to know."

"She doesn't have to worry—"

"She has that right too."

Jody's eyes ignited.

"Enough," Drake muttered. "The both of you."

Sylvan grinned, glad to see Jody's fire returning. "If you were a little quicker and managed to stay out of trouble, Vampire, I wouldn't have to interfere."

"I should have drained you."

Sylvan leaned back and pulled Drake closer. Her back and shoulders were torn and bleeding, her legs and abdomen bruised from the rockfall, but she was alive, and Drake was next to her. The life force of her young beat through her blood, steady and strong. Her allies—her friends—had survived.

She glanced at the emaciated, feverish young girls stretched out on the floor of the car and frowned. She felt them, the way she felt her wolves, but they were not Weres. They weren't human anymore either. Until she knew what they were, they were hers.

Drake circled her palm over Sylvan's abdomen, her claws lightly scoring her skin. She kissed Sylvan's neck. "I love you."

Sylvan kissed her. "I love you too."

"You need healing when we return."

"That's not what I need."

Drake smiled and kissed the shadow of the mate bite on Sylvan's chest. "I know. That too."

Chapter Twenty-three

Niki rolled over and propped her back against the door, pulling Sophia against her side. They were still on the floor, and when Sophia made a soft rumbling sound in the back of her throat and draped herself over Niki's torso, Niki wanted to take her again. Sophia's skin was damp with a coating of the blended pheromones that enveloped them both. She smelled rich and powerful, like a hidden glade deep in the forest filled with ancient trees and untouched earth. Niki wanted to roll with her in soft fragrant leaves beneath towering pines and mate in the hot summer sun. She kissed her, stroked her bare shoulder and down her arm. She feared if she left her, Sophia would disappear. "I need to check with Callan on the status of our defenses."

"I know. You also need to see Gray," Sophia said, circling her fingertips over Niki's chest. "She needs guidance right now, from someone like you."

"Like me?"

Sophia kissed her neck, scraped her teeth along the thick muscle that ran down to Niki's shoulder. "Someone she looks up to. A dominant, aggressive wolf—like she will be one day very soon."

"There are plenty of those around."

"But none who just put her down for encroaching on their territory." Sophia smiled and rubbed her cheek on Niki's breast. "She needs to understand that what she was doing—what she was feeling—wasn't wrong. They're confused, both of them, by what was done to them and how they responded. Heightened emotions—anger, fear, pain—often produce a sexual response. You and I know it, but the young have a hard time sorting it all out. Let her know she's not the only one who's felt that way."

"I'm not a very good example," Niki said bitterly. "You forget I was very nearly blood addicted."

"What I remember," Sophia said, running her tongue over Niki's lower lip and nipping her hard enough to make Niki wince, "is that you saved an ally's life. You risked your own to save Jody's. I have nothing but respect for you."

"You're not—" Niki broke off, embarrassed by her weakness, not only her weakness for the euphoria of a Vampire's bite, but her need to know she wasn't just any Were in Sophia's bed.

"Threatened by your hunger?" Sophia said softly. "Jealous of what a Vampire can give you?"

"No! That's not what I meant." Niki tightened her hold on Sophia. She was being foolish for expecting, for hoping, Sophia would feel things she'd already made very clear she wasn't interested in feeling. Sophia didn't want a mate. What she wanted was what Niki had just given her, relief from her heat, sexual release. "Never mind."

Sophia gripped Niki's shoulders and straddled her, her thighs clasping Niki's hips. Her breasts nearly brushed Niki's mouth and Niki snarled.

Smiling, Sophia leaned down and kissed her. "To answer your question, *Imperator*, yes, it bothers me that you might find more satisfaction than I can give you with someone else."

"I don't. I never have," Niki said, rubbing her cheek over Sophia's breast. "What I find with the Vampires is oblivion, and that's not what I want with you." She stroked Sophia's back, loving the softness of her skin and the strength in her lithe muscles. Pulling Sophia close, she kissed her, sliding her tongue deep into her mouth, letting Sophia taste the surge of hormones in her mouth, smell them on her skin. "I want the sweetness of you everywhere inside me."

Moaning softly, Sophia rubbed her breasts over Niki's and entwined their legs. The hot wetness between her legs coated Niki's thigh. "We can't. You need to go."

"I still want you again."

Sophia pushed away, her hands shaking. "Good. You can have me again, when you're sure we're all secure. Go now. Before I don't let you."

Niki rose, lifting Sophia in her arms. She held her tight to her chest and kissed her until Sophia moaned and writhed in her arms. The sound filled Niki with power even as her heart trembled. "Don't forget me."

"I won't," Sophia breathed unevenly. "I can't."

Niki carried her to the bed and gently laid her down. She stroked her fingertips over Sophia's breast and traced a line up to the bite marks she'd made in Sophia's shoulder. She didn't carry a matching mark. She'd never wanted another Were to mark her, to claim her, but she wanted it now. "I'll be back soon."

Sophia caught her hand and kissed her knuckles. "Be careful."

Niki turned abruptly and strode out before she wasn't able to go, duty or not. Sophia hadn't bitten her. Sophia didn't want a mate, and she wouldn't bite. Niki had always been the one to avoid the possibility of a mate bite, but when Sophia refused her, she ached. She wanted her. Wanted her for her own, completely. But Sophia had been clear, and she would honor Sophia's desires. What she had was already far more than she ever thought she would.

She passed Elena and her mate, Roger, carrying supplies into one of the treatment rooms.

"Sophia?" Elena said, concern darkening her elegant features.

"Down the hall. She's fine."

"And the Alpha?"

Niki ground her teeth. "She's been delayed."

Elena's eyes widened, and Niki slowed to touch her cheek. "Don't worry. Drake is with her. You know how careful she'll be with the Prima with her."

"It's good the Alpha has her," Elena said, her eyes on her mate. "Good for all of us."

"Yes," Niki said, meaning it without reservation. She'd always known Sylvan would mate, but the eventuality had always seemed far off in the future, something that would not alter their intimate bond. And then Sylvan had chosen a turned Were, a *mutia*, someone far beneath her and hardly worthy to be Pack, let alone Prima. But Niki had been wrong about Drake—Drake was everything Sylvan needed in a mate and every bit as much a Were as a *regii*. "Very good for us."

When Niki reached Gray and Katya's room she rapped sharply and stepped inside. Katya was on her bed as she had been before, curled up with her eyes open, unblinking, endlessly sad.

"Where's Gray?"

"She shifted," Katya said bleakly. "Gone. Out the window."

Niki cursed. They'd had no sign of attack teams anywhere near their territory, but the Timberwolf holdings were vast, and small strike forces could easily cross their borders and approach the Compound without being detected. If Gray was running alone, she was vulnerable.

"Stay here," Niki leapt from the room and vaulted down the hall. Callan stood in the center of the Compound, conferring with one of his lieutenants.

"Where's Dasha?" Niki called.

Callan looked over. "She went to get the Alpha."

Niki's breath exploded in relief. The Alpha was returning. She was all right. "Did you see Gray?"

Callan shook his head.

"Is everything quiet?"

"Yes. I've doubled the border patrols and we have spotters on the barricades. Everything is secure."

"Good." Niki crossed to the barracks where the *sentries* and the trainees bunked. She knocked on Misha's partially open door. The young brunette jumped to attention.

"*Imperator!*"

"I need you."

Misha straightened even more. "Yes, *Imperator.*"

"Gray is running alone. Do you know where she usually hunts?"

"Yes, *Imperator.*"

"She hasn't been gone long—probably hasn't gone far. I need you to find her and bring her back." Niki saw the barest hint of hesitation in Misha's eyes. "She trusts you."

"I'm not sure she trusts anyone anymore."

"All the more reason to bring her home. I need you both to be careful. There may be enemies in the woods. If her wolf is in control, don't fight her. Leave her."

"She's my friend."

"I know." Misha and Gray were very nearly equal in their level of dominance, but Misha was the more mature. Levelheaded, in control of her wolf. Niki was asking a lot of her, but she thought Gray would respond better to her than one of the older wolves. "I don't want either of you injured."

"I understand."

"Report to me when you return." Niki turned for the door. She wanted to see the Alpha. She needed to know Sylvan was all right. And she couldn't tolerate being so far from Sophia. Her wolf paced, agitated and angry. She ignored the clawing need in her belly. She had duties.

"*Imperator?*"

Niki glanced back over her shoulder. "Yes?"

"Thank you for trusting me to bring her back."

"You probably won't thank me when you find her. Go now."

Misha shimmered, and a sturdy gray and white wolf bounded onto the bed and out the open window.

Niki found Callan at headquarters, conferring by sat phone with one of his soldiers. She waited until he'd finished and asked, "Why didn't you come and get me when the Alpha called?"

"She requested a vehicle—the call was brief. There wasn't time for anything else."

"Where are they?"

"Just crossing into New York. Dasha should intercept them at any moment. They'll be back here soon."

"What's the status of the injured?"

Callan shook his head. "I don't know. The Alpha didn't tell us anything else."

"All right. Keep up the surveillance and the extra soldiers on patrol. I'll be with the prisoner."

❖

Sophia started at the knock on the door. She didn't feel Niki. She felt her absence—a longing deep inside, a restless, anxious need to be close to her. She drew a breath and all she could scent was Niki, covering her, filling her.

"Who is it?"

"Elena."

Sighing, Sophia sat up on the side of the bed and reached for her pants. She wasn't embarrassed by her nudity, no wolf ever was, but she needed distance, and even this false shield helped bolster her courage. She stepped into her khaki cargo pants. "Come in."

Elena entered, flipped the switch that lit a muted bulb in the ceiling, and leaned back against the closed door. "Are you all right?"

Sophia laughed shortly. "I think so. Yes." She raised her eyes to Elena's, found sympathy and understanding. "Wonderful. Frightened."

"She wants you, you know that."

Sophia spun around and walked to the window, searching above the treetops for the moon. The luminous warmth always calmed her, but not tonight. Her blood was still raging for Niki. "I know."

"And you want her."

Sophia pressed her forehead to the rough wood frame and closed her eyes. She couldn't lie to Elena. She could barely lie to herself anymore. How would she face Niki and keep the truth from her? "Yes, I want her."

"You don't have to suffer like this."

Fury displaced the despair and Sophia spun around. "How can you of all people say that. You know—"

"I *don't* know. I know what the tests showed years ago. Years ago. When you were an adolescent. But you're not any longer. When is the last time you let your parents study you?"

"So I can see their sadness and disappointment again?" Sophia shook her head. "Not for years."

"I know how terrible it is for you, how frightening—"

"You can't know. You can't know what it feels like to never totally belong. To fear what you feel and what you want."

Elena crossed the room in one graceful leap and pulled Sophia into her arms. "I do know. I do." She stroked her hair. "But you can't be sure. You deserve to know, and Niki deserves the truth."

"She'll hate me."

"No," Elena murmured, kissing Sophia's temple. "She loves you."

Sophia shuddered and clung to Elena. "She won't, not if she knows. You know how she feels. You know how proud she is."

"You need to trust her."

Sophia tilted her head back and searched Elena's face. "Trust? Trust she won't break my heart? Or worse?"

"She would never do that."

"I would never force her to make that choice." Sophia wrenched herself from the comfort of Elena's embrace. Comfort and sympathy only made her weak. "There's work to do. I'll help you get ready in case we have casualties."

"What are you going to do?"

"I don't know." Sophia wrapped her arms around herself. "I should stay away from her. But I don't know if I can."

Becca heard the security door in the main chamber beneath Jody's town house open and close. She took a breath and, steeling herself to be calm, crossed their bedroom and opened the door into the common area. Her heart thudded madly, and when she saw Jody, she choked back a cry. Jody and Rafe were covered with burns, horrible charred patches of skin oozing blood and sluggish, sickly fluid. She'd never seen Jody stumble, but she could barely walk now.

Keeping her head up, her voice steady, Becca walked to meet them and slid her arm around Jody's waist. "I told you not to get shot. I obviously need to be more inclusive next time." She glanced at Rafe. "What do you need?"

"Just to feed," Rafe said, her voice rusty and weak.

"Zahn has arranged for hosts. Thank you for bringing Jody home."

"I'm honored," Rafe said, disappearing through a door leading to the inner rooms.

Becca turned to Lara, who looked clear-eyed and healthy. Her skin glowed a deep bronze and her hair shone brilliantly. She'd never looked stronger or more beautiful. "Are you hurt?"

"No," Lara said.

"It's not long till dawn. You'll need to feed."

Lara shuddered. Her eyes ignited. "Yes."

Becca glanced at Zahn, not certain if Lara could be trusted with one of Jody's blood hosts. Lara seemed in control of her hunger, but she was still a newly turned Vampire.

"I'll feed you," Zahn said.

Lara snarled. "You're human. I prefer Weres."

"I am a blood servant," Zahn said archly, "not some rabble you picked up in a blood club. Whatever you need, I can provide."

"Then you'll have to do."

Wordlessly, Zahn opened the door to the hall and Lara followed, leaving Becca and Jody alone.

"Come with me, darling," Becca said, leading her toward their bedroom. "Let me take care of you."

"Becca," Jody said hoarsely, holding back. "You can't be alone with me now. We need—"

Becca's frayed temper snapped. "Don't you dare tell me what *we* need. I know what you need. *I'm* going to feed you. *I'm* going to give you whatever you need. Don't argue."

"I'm sorry."

"I'm not." Becca led her to the bed and helped her to lie down. She undressed herself, undressed Jody, fighting back tears at the devastation of her lover's beautiful body. She slid under the silken sheets and wrapped her arms around Jody, drawing their bodies together, guiding Jody's mouth to her throat. "You never need to be sorry for needing me."

Jody gave a desperate snarl and struck swiftly, sharply. Becca arched, gasping at the rush of heat that surged through her. She cried out, climaxing instantly. Shivering as the orgasm flowed through her, building again immediately, cresting again, the cycle repeating over and over as she fisted her hand in Jody's hair.

She lost herself in pleasure and only slowly returned to awareness. When she opened her eyes, Jody was leaning over her, worry etched in her striking face. Becca traced the arch of her cheekbones, the line of her jaw. Her skin was flawless, her eyes clear. Becca smiled lazily. "Are you better?"

"Yes." Jody kissed her. "Are you all right? I took more than I should have."

"You took what you needed." Becca stretched, contentment making her muscles soft and her mind just a little bit mushy. "I feel wonderful."

Jody's frown deepened. "You should feel weak, dizzy. A headache?"

Becca shook her head. "No. None of those things." She pulled Jody down beside her. "I want you to tell me everything that happened tonight, but first, I need you again. While I'm not consumed with bloodlust, when you can come with me. Make me come again."

Jody cupped her breast, grazed her mouth over Becca's flesh, raising goose bumps of pleasure. "I want you."

Becca arched over her and slid her hand between Jody's thighs. Jody was wet and hard for her. "Anytime, Vampire mine. Anytime."

❖

"A vehicle approaches," one of the soldiers on the stockade called down.

"The Rover?" Niki asked, bounding the steps from headquarters. The prisoner had refused to speak to anyone but the Alpha, and she feared if she stayed with him much longer, she might tear his throat out. Every time she looked at him she saw Gray's wild eyes and Katya's sad ones.

"No, it's civilian. A limousine."

Niki looked at Callan, who'd come out behind her. "Were you notified?"

"No. It may be a trap."

"Keep the gates closed," Niki shouted to the soldier on the fence. She held out a hand to Callan. "Give me your weapon and alert the *sentries*."

She shouldered the assault rifle and leapt up onto the rampart at the top of the twelve-foot barricade. Headlights cut through the trees less than a hundred yards away. She dropped down into the brush and raced to intercept the vehicle as it emerged from the forest. When the limousine slowed, she leapt into the road and aimed her rifle at the driver. The sleek black car slammed to a halt a foot from her. Armed Were *sentries* converged on either side. A pale, indistinguishable face peered out through the smoked glass windshield.

"Turn off the engine and step out of the vehicle."

The window rolled down and a male called out, "We seek audience with the Alpha."

"Step out of the vehicle," Niki called, "or we will open fire."

Nothing happened for a second, and she signaled to the *sentries* to prepare to fire. Then both back doors opened. Francesca and Michel stepped out.

"I'm so sorry we arrived unannounced." Francesca smiled, and Niki quivered under the crush of her thrall. "But I think the Alpha will want to hear what I have to say."

CHAPTER TWENTY-FOUR

The stockade gates parted, and Dasha drove the Rover into the center of the Compound, veering around a stretch limo parked in front of headquarters.

Sylvan turned to Drake. "It appears we have visitors."

"Tonight of all nights," Drake grumbled, "I trust no one."

"We can trust Niki and Callan—they would not have allowed anyone to enter if there was the slightest possibility of a threat."

"Still, I don't like it."

"Will you be all right with them?" Sylvan gestured to the two unconscious humans.

"Yes. I'll get them settled in the infirmary, but we may not be able to take care of them here long-term."

"If they survive, we may not have any choice."

Drake touched the nearest girl's forehead. "They're consumed with fever."

"And if they turn, even if they carry only some Were traits, we have to protect them."

"Is everyone yours to protect?" Drake shot back. "No matter the cost to you, the risk? Wasn't tonight enough to prove you're in danger?"

"I'm fine," Sylvan said softly, stroking Drake's cheek.

Drake grabbed her hand, kissed her palm. "You're *not* fine. You're torn and bleeding, and the blood you didn't lose in the blast you gave to Jody."

"She needed it—and I heal quickly." Sylvan kissed her. Drake was agitated and wary, her wolf driven to protect her mate even more now that she was carrying their young. "Go take care of the injured. I'll probably be at headquarters for a while."

Drake frowned. "I should be with you."

"You always are. But right now, these two need you more."

"Elena can monitor them after we stabilize them. I'll be over as soon as I can." Drake gripped Sylvan's neck. "You need attention too. Those burns are serious, and they'll heal faster if I clean them up."

"I'll see to them as soon as I can." Sylvan bounded from the Rover and vaulted onto the porch. Jace and Jonathan, standing post by the door, jumped to attention and followed as she strode inside and up the heavy rough-hewn log stairs. Niki stood guard outside her office. "What's happening?"

Niki took in her appearance. "You're wounded."

"It's nothing," Sylvan snarled. She was battered and bruised, and still hyped physically from the explosion and her worry about Drake, Jody, and the injured girls. What she really wanted was to drag Drake off to some private corner and bury herself in her. But before she could do that, she needed answers. Who had alerted them that the installation was being abandoned—and were they hoping the prisoners inside would be rescued, or was their plan to trap the rescue party in the explosion? Who was behind the experiments on these human girls, and what was their intention? Why wasn't Lara susceptible to the same radiation damage Jody and Rafe had suffered in the explosion, and why had she been able to sense the injured girls through the silver barrier when Sylvan couldn't? "What do you have to report?"

Niki grasped the door handle before Sylvan could push through into her office. "You may not want to go in there covered in blood."

Sylvan raised a brow.

"The Viceregal and her *senechal* have paid us a visit."

"Really?" Sylvan considered that. Francesca rarely held any meetings outside of her own territory. Part of her power was in making others come to her. An impromptu visit in the middle of the night was completely unlike her. "Did she bring soldiers?"

"Only Michel and her driver."

"Search for other vehicles. She wouldn't allow herself to be vulnerable."

"We have teams out looking."

"Good." Sylvan rolled her shoulders. The wounds were already healing but wouldn't heal completely until she shifted. Even then, they'd heal better if they were cleansed of silver-contaminated debris first. She had time for neither. "Get me a shirt."

"Yes, Alpha." Niki paused. "It's good to see you back, Alpha."

Sylvan snaked an arm around Niki's neck and pulled her close. She rubbed her cheek on Niki's hair. "It's good to be back. And it's good to have you by my side."

Niki nuzzled Sylvan's neck. "There's nowhere else I'd rather be."

"That's because this is where you belong. My shirt?"

Niki broke free, loped down the hall, and pulled a plain black long-sleeved shirt from the closet. Returning, she handed it to Sylvan.

"Thanks." Sylvan shrugged on the shirt, ignoring the burning pain in her back and arms. She shoved the shirttail into her dusty, tattered pants. "This is as formal as I get in my own den."

"They're Vampires," Niki said dismissively. "They deserve nothing from you."

Sylvan grinned. "Leave Jace and Jon here. Check on the wounded I brought in—and make sure Elena and Sophia are all right."

Niki tensed, a vicious growl erupting from between her bared teeth. "Why wouldn't they be all right?"

"They should be fine—but the captives are…sick. It looks like Were fever."

"And you brought them here? To Sophia?" Niki roared.

Sylvan scanned Niki's chest. She didn't see a mate bite, but Niki was acting mated. Mated Weres had no sense of their own safety and would challenge even her when they thought their mates threatened. She decided to let Niki's insubordination pass. "Just follow orders, *Imperator*."

Still growling, Niki vaulted over the railing to the floor below. A few seconds later, the front doors crashed open and slammed closed.

Turning, Sylvan pushed open the tall carved wooden doors and stalked inside. Francesca, dressed formally in tapered black silk pants and a matching fitted jacket buttoned over her obviously bare breasts, sat in a wide brown leather library chair in front of Sylvan's desk. Michel, looking like a black flame in tight black leather pants and shirt, stood by her right side. Andrew, bare chested in threadbare jeans, lounged casually against the fireplace opposite Michel, his alert gaze fixed on Francesca's enforcer.

"Francesca," Sylvan said, crossing to stand in front of her desk. "This is an unexpected pleasure."

Francesca rose and kissed Sylvan on the mouth. "Any time I see you is a pleasure, Alpha."

Sylvan edged a hip onto the front of her desk. "What can I do for you?"

"I think, darling," Francesca said, gliding closer and running her fingers lightly down Sylvan's chest, "it's what I can do for you."

From behind them, Drake said, "You'll want to stop touching her, Viceregal. I'm not feeling in a generous mood."

Francesca glanced over her shoulder, her full red lips tilting upward in what appeared to be real pleasure. "Hello, Prima. You must be used to having others admire Sylvan by now."

"Admire, yes." Drake crossed to Sylvan's side and wrapped her arm around Sylvan's waist. "Touching, I'm afraid not."

"How could I forget how territorial you Weres can be." Francesca's tone was lightly teasing, but her eyes smoldered.

"It's been a long night," Sylvan said, "and I'm sure with dawn not that far away you'll want to be leaving soon."

Francesca laughed. "Subtlety never was your greatest skill, Sylvan darling." She settled back into the leather chair and crossed her legs. Her jacket was cut low, and she indolently traced her fingertips along the inner curve of her right breast. Her nipples tightened beneath the silk, and Drake rumbled a warning.

"I'm certain you don't intend to be disrespectful to my mate, particularly not in her own territory." Sylvan clasped the back of Drake's neck, running her thumb up and down the tight muscles in her neck. Drake was furious, her wolf snapping and growling, eager to fight. Generally Drake was the calmer of the two, no less aggressive, no less territorial, but a diplomat by nature whereas Sylvan was a warrior. Right now, though, her mate didn't want to talk, she wanted to fight.

"I think your mate will appreciate my visit, darling." Francesca lowered her lashes as she smiled seductively at Drake. "Last night, I was invited to participate in an assault on your Pack."

❖

Don't fight. Don't fight.

Nose to the ground, Misha pounded through the woods, bounding over logs, swerving along nearly invisible trails that snaked between brush and trees, following Gray's scent. The *imperator* had ordered her not to fight, but she hadn't told her wolf not to tussle. She and Gray had grown up together, had hunted together, and tussled more than once. They hadn't tangled—they were so close in dominance they usually picked other Packmates, even though Misha had been with other Weres more dominant than her. They'd just fallen into the role of friends and sometimes rivals. Gray was close now, crashing through the undergrowth, not even bothering with stealth. She wasn't hunting—she was fleeing. Misha wasn't going to let her run away.

Misha picked up her speed, and when Gray shot into the clearing where the two trails met, Misha hit Gray broadside, clamping her jaws on Gray's ruff when she struck. They tumbled over and over, a tangle of legs and snapping jaws and slashing claws. Fire streaked down Misha's hip where Gray's claws caught her. She growled and grabbed Gray's ear in her jaws. Gray howled in indignation and pain and, rearing back, flipped Misha onto her back. Gray was fast, and furious, and pinned Misha with her heavy weight bearing down on her. Misha was vulnerable, her belly exposed and her throat bared to Gray's snapping jaws. Her adrenaline surged—Gray might kill her if she totally lost control. Misha gathered her hind legs and thrust against Gray's belly, raking through her fur and slashing skin. Gray arched to avoid the deadly claws, and Misha dislodged her. Gray landed on her back, and Misha immediately mounted her. Gray was strong and angry. Misha felt her pain and confusion, but she didn't let up, she didn't relent. She circled and charged, snapped and bit, until they were both torn and bloody and exhausted.

Enough?

Enough, Gray panted.

Misha collapsed and shifted back to skin. She rolled onto her side and looked into Gray's dark eyes. "Where were you going?"

"I don't know."

"Why are you so angry?" Misha edged closer until their bodies nearly touched and their faces were only an inch apart. She draped her arm over Gray's shoulders, and Gray tensed. Gray wouldn't have mistrusted Misha's touch, not before. Carefully, Misha stroked the hard muscles in Gray's back and traced the ridges in her spine down to the curve of her ass. Gray whined softly in her throat, her hips rocking forward, and Misha's fingertips dampened with Gray's pheromones.

"I don't want you to go anywhere," Misha whispered, her mouth grazing Gray's.

Gray's eyes caught fire and her canines pressed down beneath her lip. She clasped Misha's hip, her claws scraping lightly. "I was just running. I—I made the *imperator* angry."

"She sent me to bring you home. She wants you to come home—we all do."

Gray nipped at her neck. "I don't want to go anywhere right now."

Misha's heart thudded and her sex tightened. Belly jumping, she clasped Gray's ass and kissed her. Gray growled, a low, ominous, exciting sound in her chest that made Misha's nipples ache. She rubbed her breasts over Gray's and tugged Gray's leg until Gray's thigh came over her hip. Gray was wet, her clitoris hard and swollen against her leg. She nipped Gray's lip and slid her tongue over Gray's. She wanted to roll over onto her and come. She wanted to rub her clitoris over Gray's until they both released.

Gray's claws dug into her hip and Gray's growl turned into a snarl. Gray pushed away. "I can't."

Misha stared, panting, breathless. "Why not?"

"I can't." Gray jumped to her feet. "Leave me alone."

Misha rose and faced her. "No."

Gray shoved her. "It's easy for you."

"What is?"

"Tangling." Gray swept her hand toward the ground where they had just been. "You feel the call, you do it. I can't."

"Why not?" Misha repeated.

"Because I want...something else."

"Someone less dominant?" Misha shrugged. "I know that—me too. Most times. But I felt you. You're ready. So am I." Gray was still coated with sex-sheen. Her clitoris was swollen, her naked body trembling. "So why not?"

"I want to hurt," Gray whispered.

Misha didn't think Gray was just talking about physical pain. "You need to be hurt?"

"Yes," Gray said, her voice tortured and her eyes desolate.

"We're Weres," Misha said calmly. "We're warriors. Pain is part of our life. You have nothing to be ashamed of."

"You don't know what you're talking—"

Misha tackled her and dragged her to the ground. Caught off guard, Gray's inaction gave Misha a momentary advantage, enough for her to flip Gray onto her belly and mount her back. She snaked one arm under Gray's throat and the other under her hips. She pressed her clitoris against the cleft of Gray's ass and nipped her earlobe. "I've been wanting to do this for a long time."

Gray thrashed, and Misha tightened her hold around her neck. She worked her fingers between Gray's thighs and around her clitoris. Gray's hips bucked and she gasped.

"You better not come yet." Misha rubbed her clitoris over Gray's ass and stroked Gray hard, tugging and squeezing.

"More," Gray groaned, clutching Misha's wrist as Misha stroked her. Her claws dug into Misha's skin. "Harder."

Misha felt herself getting ready to release and tried to wait, but Gray felt so good, smelled so good, she couldn't hold back. She buried her face in Gray's neck, and when her clitoris contracted and her glands exploded, she bit her just hard enough to break the skin. She came, her fingers tightening on Gray's clitoris, twisting as Gray thrashed. She heard a howl, felt Gray come on her hand, and held on. Held on. She wasn't letting Gray leave.

Chapter Twenty-five

Sophia placed the cap on the tube of blood and carefully placed it into the rack on the bench. Her hands shook as she extracted the next tube and carefully labeled it: *Unknown female number two.*

"Their temperatures are bouncing between one-oh-four and one-oh-six," Elena murmured.

"That's usually fatal for humans after a few hours," Sophia said, pleased that her voice was steady. "They should be seizing." She leaned against the counter to steady herself. "We need to do something to get their fevers down. Ice?"

"We can try. At least they'll be more comfortable." Elena placed a damp cloth on the forehead of a blonde whose skin was so thin and pale she looked more like a mannequin than a living being. A moment later the door to the treatment room opened and her mate leaned in. "Can you bring us ice?"

Roger nodded, and the door closed.

"But you know," Elena said tentatively, "the normal temperature for a Were is several degrees higher than that of a human. Maybe... maybe what we're seeing is just an effect of the transition."

"But we don't get sick, or almost never, and even when we do, our temperatures remain steady." Sophia adjusted the intravenous line carrying fluids and nutrients to the dehydrated, emaciated young female. She wondered if she'd looked like this when her parents had brought her to Elena that first night. "Maybe you should check your records—check my history."

"These girls aren't like you," Elena said.

"We don't really know that, do we?"

Elena lifted the eyelid of the unconscious girl and flicked a penlight back and forth. "You always responded to stimuli. Their central nervous systems are so depressed, even their brainstem functions are nonreactive. I don't think—"

The door swung open and Sophia glanced over, expecting Roger. She froze when Niki strode in. She'd been aching for and dreading this moment. They'd only been apart a little while, but the longer they were separated, the more anxious and agitated she became. Her wolf clawed at her until she was certain her skin must be bleeding. Holding Niki at bay was exhausting, and she was already running on empty. She'd been fighting her heat for the better part of two weeks, and now she was faced with two patients who embodied everything she feared.

Niki took in the two girls on the table with a hot, hard glance. "The Alpha said they had the fever. Is that true?"

Elena slipped between Niki and the end of the treatment table, partially shielding the first girl. "We're not sure yet what they have—or what was done to them. We've just begun running tests."

"They're human," Niki said, her growl filled with disdain and distrust. "I can smell it."

"Yes, they are," Elena said. "But they smell like Weres too."

"They smell like sick animals, not wolf Weres. Sick animals ought to be put down." Niki snarled, her wolf demanding action. These humans, these sick, dangerous humans, could harm Sophia, and she could not allow that. "They're going to die, you know that. Why risk yourselves or anyone here when it's pointless?"

Elena shook her head. "We don't know that. We don't even know what's happening to them yet."

"You know what happens to infected humans," Niki said. "If they don't die, they're feral, or they end up spreading the disease. Either way, they're a danger to us all."

"That's not what happened with Drake," Sophia said quietly. She wasn't afraid of what Niki might do to her—she'd lived with the possibility of what might have to be done all her life. But severing the connection to Niki was going to destroy her as surely as an execution.

"Drake is different," Niki said, her wolf close to breaking through her control. Her face elongated, her claws ripped free, and pelt thickened over her belly. "Drake had the Alpha's blood, her pheromones, her essence to counteract whatever destruction the virus was doing. These girls—we don't even know what kind of mutants they will become."

Sophia shuddered. Mutant, *mutia*, mongrel, mutt. She knew the terms, and she knew how a proud, dominant Were like Niki viewed anyone who was non-Pack. "If we feel they're contagious or capable of infecting any of the Pack, we'll recommend extermination. But the decision is not up to us. The Alpha will decide."

Niki closed the gap between them in one explosive leap, gripping Sophia's shoulders. "They're not worth it. They're not worth one wolf in this Pack. I'm not going to risk losing you."

"Niki, you have to go." Sophia shuddered. Every fiber of her being yearned for Niki, to join with her.

Niki's eyes flashed wolf-green and her canines plunged outward. Her voice turned to gravel. "No."

Sophia braced her hands against Niki's chest. "Drake is normal, she bears the Alpha's young. She may have been infected by a similar virus, and she lived. These girls may survive, and if they do, they may help us learn how to protect ourselves and all our young in the future."

"They won't survive." Niki drew a breath, dragging her wolf back, holding her down.

"There's no evidence they've ever been bitten. Whatever was done to them, it was some kind of medical experiment. They've been tortured, Niki."

"That's not my problem—they're dangerous," Niki said. "They're a risk to others in the Compound. They should be caged."

"They're too weak to be of any harm," Sophia said quietly. "They're patients, not enemies."

"You don't know that. Elena just said you don't know *what* they are. We don't know what they're capable of, what they might transmit. We have young in the Compound." Niki gripped Sophia's arm. All she could see was danger to Sophia. "At least restrain them."

"The nursery is not accessible from this area," Sophia said reasonably, nearly dizzy with the rush of pheromones released by Niki's touch. "When we know something, we'll let the Alpha know."

"The Alpha depends on me to protect the Pack," Niki said, her voice and her eyes hard and unyielding. "You reminded me of that just today. I say they ought to be behind bars. Move them to the prison block."

"We can't right now. They're too unstable. They're unconscious—they can't harm anyone." Sophia ignored the tendrils of fear snaking through her depths. She had known this day would come, but she'd let herself forget. She'd let herself believe, for a few hours, that she and Niki could share what other Weres shared. She'd always known that wasn't possible for her, but for Niki, she'd ignored her own defenses, and now, she was defenseless. But she would not abandon these girls, even if it cost her everything. "You should leave, *Imperator*. This is our job."

"And mine is to protect the Pack." Niki couldn't think beyond the raging of her wolf and the rush of adrenaline warning her of a threat to all she loved. "Mutants do not belong here—how many times do we need to see them turn into mindless beasts before we learn that?"

Elena growled. "Niki, mind your—"

"Drake didn't turn into a beast," Sophia said calmly, beyond worry and fear now. The time for truth was long past. "And neither did I."

Niki jerked. "What?"

"Neither did I, Niki," Sophia repeated, her heart shattering at the flare of wrath rising in Niki's eyes. "I was human once too."

"No," Niki roared. She rounded on Elena. "I remember when the Alpha brought her here with her parents. The Revniks are Weres."

Elena shot Sophia a helpless glance.

"My adoptive parents," Sophia said. "They rescued me when the Pack *imperator* wanted me killed. They sought sanctuary here, and Sylvan's mother granted us asylum."

"All this time?" Niki asked, dazed. "All this time and you've never—" She stiffened, fury burning through her disbelief. "Sylvan knows, doesn't she?"

"Yes. Niki—" Sophia reached for her and Niki jerked away.

"You don't want to touch me right now," Niki said with deadly emphasis. She pointed at the sick girls. "If I see one of them outside this room, they die."

Niki whipped around and wrenched the door open, nearly tearing it from its hinges.

Sophia pressed a hand to her stomach, wondering how she could still be alive when everything inside her was dying.

❖

"What kind of assault on the Pack?" Sylvan asked Francesca, tightening her grip on the back of Drake's neck. Her mate was on the verge of losing control. "When and where?"

Drake snarled. "Who? Who is planning to attack us?"

"Well, that's the problem," Francesca said quietly, crossing one leg over the other. She extended her arm and stroked the length of Michel's outer thigh. Her *senechal* stood as if carved from marble, never taking her eyes off Drake. "I don't know the details, only that something is planned and my assistance was requested."

"To do what?"

"I'm afraid I don't know that either."

"What do you know?" Drake snapped, breaking away from Sylvan and striding over to Francesca. She towered over the seated Vampire, staring down at her as anger hardened the planes of her face. "You enjoy playing games, and I'm not in the mood tonight."

"Step back," Michel murmured, her body still as stone.

Sylvan rumbled a warning.

Francesca merely smiled, tilting her head ever so slightly to glance at Drake. "I know Sylvan has acquired some very powerful enemies in some very high places. Her intention to form an alliance with the human governments is seen as a betrayal of Praeterns."

Sylvan said, "That's certainly not the opinion of the other councilors on the Coalition or the Praeterns they rule. Zachary Gates is the leader of one of your most powerful Clans, and he supports both the Praetern union and the goals of the Coalition."

"Zachary is a businessman before all else," Francesca said with a shrug. "His primary investments are in the military-industrial complex, so of course he will ally himself with the human governments that provide so much of his business."

"Why are you telling me this?" Sylvan asked. Francesca never did anything that didn't ultimately benefit her. "Why ally with me if you don't agree with me?"

"Sylvan," Francesca said, sounding hurt. "You know I've always supported the Timberwolf Pack, and I'm so very fond of you."

Drake snarled.

Michel slid in front of Francesca, nearly touching Drake. "You would do well not to threaten the Viceregal."

Sylvan bounded forward, landing between them, forcing Michel to back up. "Threaten her again and I'll tear you apart."

Michel smiled. "I welcome your attempt."

"It's all right, darling." Francesca gripped Michel's hand. "Ordinarily I love a fight—especially when it's over me—but now might not be the time. Drake—forgive me, the Prima—is just marking her territory."

Sylvan sent Michel another warning glare and slung an arm around Drake's waist. She wasn't about to let her mate fight, but she wouldn't stop her from stating her claim either.

"You still haven't answered my question," Sylvan said. "Why are you telling us?"

"I was hoping if you realized how unpopular your position has become, you'd rethink it."

"And if I change my mind, what exactly would you and your... allies like me to do?"

"Ultimately, we'd like to see the Coalition disbanded," Francesca said. "We believe the cost of civil integration is too high and unnecessary. What we seek is sovereignty, the right to govern ourselves, separate from human law."

"You want to live among humans but not be subject to human law?"

"We already are, darling—we have been for millennia."

"The humans are not likely to accept that," Sylvan said. "And until human law recognizes us, humans will not be dissuaded from attempting to exterminate us."

"If we have our own army," Francesca said softly, "they won't dare."

"You would go to war rather than negotiate?"

Francesca lifted a shoulder. "Some very powerful individuals would prefer just that."

"Who?" Drake demanded. "Who came to you?"

"I hear a great many things from a great many sources," Francesca said. "What matters is Praetern unity—together we are strongest."

"Unity," Drake said coldly. "Is that what you call sending your enforcer to help human monsters torture Weres in a secret lab?"

Francesca shook her head. "And this is why we need to work together. Michel wasn't in that lab to harm anyone. When we heard rumors of its existence, naturally we wanted to learn more. If you hadn't freed them, we would of course have notified you."

"Of course," Drake said.

Francesca rose and Michel stepped to her side. "I've come out of respect for our ancient alliances and to affirm our new ones. Please consider where your true loyalty lies, Sylvan, before it's too late."

Drake wrapped her arm around Sylvan's waist and watched the Viceregal sweep from the room. "The next time she touches you, I'm going to tear her arm off."

Sylvan caressed Drake's neck. "She is very old and very powerful."

"I don't care. She might have enjoyed you once, but now you're mine."

"Yes," Sylvan whispered, backing Drake against the desk. She scraped her canines down Drake's throat, then licked her way back up until she reached her mouth. She kissed her, sucking the sweet tang of Drake's pheromones from her tongue. She'd been waiting since they'd escaped the burning forest to taste her. "I'm your—"

The doors banged open and Niki lunged into the room, her eyes wild. "You knew! You knew and you let her live like that! What kind of Alpha are you?"

Sylvan leapt before Niki could issue challenge. She caught Niki by the throat and took her down, clamping her thighs around Niki's hips and her hand on Niki's throat. "Another word and I'll kill you."

CHAPTER TWENTY-SIX

S ophia stared at the closed door, unable to feel the connection
she'd had with Niki only moments before. Their nascent bond
had snapped under the weight of Niki's anger and loathing, leaving
a cold void darker than her loneliest nights. She forced her gaze to
the monitors next to her patient's bed. The girl's temperature was still
elevated, but there was nothing more she could do. Waiting was all that
remained. The fever would burn itself out or destroy her. "You don't
need me here right now. I'm going to go for a run."

"She doesn't mean it, you know," Elena said quietly, her hand
on the blonde's wrist, her expression so tender Sophia ached to be in
her arms, ached for the comfort of Pack. She had been Pack as long as
she could remember—she'd awakened with Elena leaning over her and
her mother and father crowding close to the small bed, touching her,
soothing her. She'd awakened to warmth and love and belonging, and
that hadn't changed even when her parents had told her right before
her first heat why she was different. They'd admitted they didn't know
what would happen if she consummated a mate bond, but they were
scientists and they loved her. They told her the truth—her blood tested
positive for Were fever antigens, even though she had no symptoms.
Her blood profile was that of a carrier—but they couldn't be sure if the
disease was dormant, neutralized, or waiting for a new host. She still
didn't know, but she couldn't take a chance. She'd rather leave the Pack
than risk infecting a single Were.

"I won't go far," Sophia said, already halfway to the door.

Elena finished a note on the chart and hung the clipboard on the side of the bed. "They haven't sounded the all clear yet. You shouldn't—"

"The Alpha is back. The forest is filled with our *sentries*. I'll be fine."

"She doesn't mean what you think," Elena called after her.

"Of course she does. She's always meant it." Sophia slipped outside the sickroom and carefully closed the door behind her. By the time she reached the end of the hall and launched herself out the open window, she was in full pelt. She soared into the dark, welcoming the night as it closed around her. She landed lightly, silently, and streaked into the forest, alone as she had always been and would forever be.

❖

Sylvan crouched over Niki, prepared for a fight. Niki smelled of fear and pain and fury. She hadn't been this out of control when she'd mindlessly hungered for a Vampire's bite. Instead of thrashing, Niki went limp beneath her, as if she were already dead. She didn't submit, she simply surrendered. Frowning, Sylvan sat back on her haunches and released her grip on Niki's throat. "What the hell are you doing?"

Niki's chest heaved as if she had just finished a vigorous hunt. She was half-wolf already, her torso shimmering with red-gray pelt, her eyes elongated, her face sharp and dangerous. "You knew Sophia was *mutia*."

Sylvan blew out a breath. "Yes."

"You never said anything, even when you knew I wanted her. Even when she refused me over and over."

"Sophia's past is her own business."

Niki shuddered under Sylvan's weight, her canines gleaming. "No, it isn't, not when it affects the Pack's safety. Then it's my business too. Or am I only your *imperator* when it suits you, to serve on my belly and accept your decisions even when you're wrong?"

"Careful," Sylvan growled. "I've already given you more leeway than you deserve."

Niki lay completely still, offering no challenge. "I've always loved you."

Sylvan glanced at Drake, expecting her mate to object, but Drake's face was composed, her dark eyes concerned but calm.

"I know," Sylvan said, easing over until she knelt by Niki's side. Niki had no fight left. Drake crouched on Niki's other side, resting one hand on Niki's shoulder. "As I've loved you."

Niki's gaze was riveted to Sylvan. "You didn't trust me. Sophia didn't trust me. Everything I am means nothing without that."

"This was never about you, Niki." Sylvan gently cupped Niki's cheek and stroked her fingertips over the sharp ridge of bone. "You are my friend, my general, my second. But every wolf in the Pack is mine to protect, including Sophia. Her secrets are her own."

"Why didn't she tell me?" Niki asked, her voice raw with pain and bewilderment.

Sylvan imagined how she'd feel if Drake kept something so important from her. She'd be furious and heartbroken, just like Niki. She would rage as Niki raged. "Sophia was just a child—four years old—when she was found wandering in the mountains in northern New Hampshire. She'd been attacked by a Were."

Niki snarled. "In Blackpaw territory?"

"Yes. Her parents were presumed killed and Sophia left for dead. Their bodies were never found—her identity never discovered. She'd survived alone, racked with fever, until a scout team happened upon her. When she was brought before their Alpha, she was sentenced to death."

"I would have recommended the same." Niki's gaze turned inward, agony slashing across her face. "I would have been wrong. She must have suffered so much and I—"

"Niki." Drake stroked Niki's hair. "You're not responsible for what was done to her. Only what happens to her now."

Niki growled and jerked away, refusing comfort and absolution. "I would've killed you too. I advised the Alpha to execute you. But she—she loved you too much."

"Would you have me execute Sophia now?" Sylvan asked mildly.

Niki came off the floor with a savage growl and only Sylvan's quick reflexes prevented Niki from burying her claws in Sylvan's chest. Sylvan caught her from behind and clamped Niki's arms to her side. She yanked Niki back against her. Niki thrashed, wild with fury, and Sylvan pressed her mouth to Niki's ear. "You're more important to me—to the Pack—than you know, *Imperator*. And what you feel for Sophia is more than you'll admit. I value her as much as any wolf in my Pack. I would protect her with my life. Would you say the same?"

Niki panted, a tormented howl tearing from her chest. Sylvan relaxed her hold and Niki crumbled, barely catching herself on her outstretched hands. Head down, back bowed, she whispered, "I would die before I let anyone hurt her. Anyone, even you."

"That's as it should be with your mate."

Niki jerked. "We're not mated."

Drake caressed her gently. "Aren't you?"

Niki pushed up until she was kneeling, her hands limp at her sides. "She doesn't want a mate. She—she doesn't want me."

"You know now why she fears the mating. We've never been sure how to interpret the tests, and Sophia cares more for you than her own needs."

Niki frowned. "What are you talking about?"

Sylvan glanced at Drake. "She didn't tell you everything, then."

"Tell me now," Niki's growled. "As your friend, as the Were who loves her—tell me now."

Sylvan glanced at Drake again, who nodded. "When the Revniks sought asylum with us, Sophia was close to death. She survived, and no one knew how or why. Her parents tested her repeatedly for the first few years after she appeared to have recovered, and every single time the tests indicated that she had Were fever."

"But she was never sick again?" Niki asked.

Sylvan shook her head. "No. In fact, after the acute illness passed, she developed like any other young. Her adolescence progressed normally."

"I don't understand, then."

"The Revniks' interpretation is that Sophia is a carrier of Were fever."

Niki jerked. "A carrier. Her bite is contagious?"

"We don't know. It's possible, although the scientific conclusion is far from certain. Sophia won't take that chance."

"That's why she won't mate. That's why she won't bite," Niki said hollowly.

"Yes."

Niki stared at Sylvan. "You've allowed her to live among your Pack, knowing she might spread the fever."

Sylvan held Niki's gaze, watching the excruciating battle play out across her face. "She is one of mine. I don't execute my wolves because of needs or desires they cannot control. I judge my wolves by their actions. You should know that."

Niki pushed to her feet, her eyes dull and empty. "I ask to be relieved of my duties as your—"

"No." Sylvan bounded to her feet and gripped Niki's nape. Drake was instantly by her side, a hand in the small of Sylvan's back, centering her. "The Viceregal says there's a campaign under way to weaken the Pack—we don't know when or what form the attack will take, but we have to expect an assault at any time. I need you."

"You have others who can serve you—others you trust."

"I trust *you*," Sylvan said. "I trust you to be more than you think you are. You have until dawn, then I need you by my side. Go and prove my faith in you."

Niki shuddered, then ducked her head once, about-faced, and strode from the room.

"What do you think she'll do?" Drake rubbed the knots of tension in Sylvan's back.

"If she listens to her wolf, she'll be fine. If she doesn't, we could lose them both."

❖

In the rear of the limo, Michel stretched her arm out along the back of the soft leather seat and caressed Francesca's shoulder. "What did you hope to accomplish tonight?"

Francesca slid closer and curled her fingers around the inside of Michel's leg, the edge of her hand resting against the vee between her thighs. "I'm not certain that Nicholas's scheming will be successful, and if he fails and Sylvan prevails, we do not want her as an enemy."

"And if Nicholas is successful in weakening her, even forcing her to change her platform?"

"Well then, we will have won, won't we?" Francesca kissed Michel's throat, teasing her tongue along the undersurface of Michel's jaw. "This is one of those circumstances, darling, where we need to be on the side of the winner, no matter who that might b—"

The car skidded and screeched to a halt. Michel grasped Francesca and pushed her down on the seat, covering her with her body. She shouted to the driver, "What is it?"

"There's a…a wolf out there."

Michel hissed. "We're in the middle of Were territory. Of course there are wolves."

"This one just jumped onto the hood of the limo."

Michel released her grip on Francesca and swung around to stare out through the windshield. A white and brown wolf stared in at her, legs spread, lips pulled back in a warning snarl. Something in the fiery gold gaze made her breath catch. Despite the heavy fortification of the limo, she smelled her. Her focus narrowed until all she sensed was her prey—*her* prey. She opened the door and stepped out. Holding the door ajar, shielding Francesca, she said to the driver, "Keep driving. The backup car is waiting at the entrance to the Pack land. They'll escort you home." She glanced at Francesca. "I won't be far behind."

"Do be careful, darling," Francesca murmured. "These are dangerous hunting grounds."

Michel grinned. "That's what makes them interesting."

The limo pulled away and the wolf disappeared into the dark. As Michel drifted to the edge of the forest, the wolf jumped from the brush and padded after her. Michel stopped beneath a tall pine, moonlight filtering through its branches like the bars of a prison. She leaned back against the tree and stared at the wolf. "You were looking for me."

The wolf shimmered, flickering in the moonlight like an ethereal dream, and then Katya rose from a kneeling position and stood inches from her. "I felt you in the Compound."

She was naked as she had been when Michel had first seen her, strung up in the lab and helpless. She'd been gorgeous even then, but now she was far from helpless. She was glorious in the moonlight—tight-bodied, full-breasted, and exquisitely beautiful.

"I've been looking for you." Michel slid her fingers into Katya's hair and drew her forward, covering her mouth with her own. She kissed her, slowly, letting her teeth glance over the inner surface of Katya's lip, exploring the hot, firm slope of her tongue, the sharp points of her canines. She didn't enthrall her. She didn't have to. She'd drunk from her, and some of Katya's blood still flowed in her veins. She'd filled Katya with her hormones, and they would share a connection until the feeding bond disappeared or she fed from her again, renewing their connection.

"I need you." Katya pressed Michel back against the tree, rubbing against her, her hands in Michel's hair, her mouth hot and hungry.

"You remember," Michel murmured.

"Only you." Katya pulled at the buttons on Michel's shirt. "I remember you. I remember you holding me. I remember you being inside me. I remember you saved me."

Michel gripped Katya's wrist, stopping her before she opened her shirt completely. "What are you doing out here?"

Katya shuddered. "I don't know. I felt you. I needed..." She shivered uncontrollably. "I need you."

"No," Michel said roughly, recognizing the sex frenzy. "You don't need me." She gripped Katya's hair and tilted her head back. "You need this." She sank into Katya's throat and Katya came with a strangled, exultant cry. Michel drank and pretended Katya's blood was all she wanted.

CHAPTER TWENTY-SEVEN

Sylvan stepped into the small holding room in the far corner of her headquarters, closed the door, and folded her arms across her chest. She said nothing, surveying the man who sat shackled to a plain, straight-backed wooden chair ten feet away. The window behind him, unlike every other window in the Compound, was shut. The moon, nearly full, glided just above the treetops, cutting a silver swath across the black sky. Its clarion call was a sweet, sharp pull in her blood. He didn't look at her.

She didn't know him, could never remember having seen him anywhere before. He was big by human standards. His thick brown hair covered the collar of the khaki camo shirt that matched his BDUs. His eyes were a flat, even blue, the color of the sky at midday—unbroken by the slightest fleck of gold or green. His cheeks were windburned, dusted with dark stubble, his skin above the beard-line ruddy and faintly pebbled. A purplish bruise covered his left cheek, underscored by a single claw mark.

Dasha Baran had shown admirable restraint in taking him down. He was undamaged, other than the bruise. Dasha had reported he'd carried no weapons, only binoculars and a radio. Unusual for a mercenary to be without weapons.

Sylvan rumbled softly and he blanched.

"Who are you?" Sylvan asked.

"My name—" He broke off, coughing, his voice sounding rusty and unused. He straightened. "My name is Martin Hoffstetter."

"All right," Sylvan said. "Now I know your name. Tell me who you are and make it quick. I have little patience for those who torture my wolves. If I didn't think you had information I wanted, you'd already be dead. If I find that you have nothing to tell me, then you will be."

He wisely dropped his gaze to her shoulder, pressing his trembling hands flat against his thighs. His breath came quickly, shallow breaths, anxious and fearful. His Adam's apple bobbed in his thick neck as he swallowed several times. "I didn't torture them."

"What *did* you do?" A cold fist centered in Sylvan's chest. He had been there. He knew what had been done to Katya and Gray. Her wolf wanted retribution, wanted his blood, wanted his guts spilling out onto the floor, steaming and red—the color of her rage. She held back the wild wolf, even though she wanted the same.

"I tried to protect them—when I could."

"But not free them."

"I couldn't!" He looked up into her face, then quickly away. "I tried to get information to you. I called the reporter."

Sylvan studied him. No one except a trusted few knew Becca had received an anonymous call about the captive young. "Why not call me or the police?"

"The police?" He grimaced. "No thanks—some of the security guards were off-duty cops. And I figured if you didn't find them, a reporter might dig out the truth, eventually. This goes beyond those prisoners—it's bigger than that."

She knew that now—the human females added another layer to the conspiracy. "Who do you work for?"

"I'm not sure," he said. "The name on my check was Biotech Research Center. I don't know who owns it."

"Who do you report to?"

"We got our assignments by e-mail, usually only twenty-four hours in advance. We moved around a lot. I wasn't in any one installation for more than a few days at a time, then I'd be transferred somewhere else and cycled back again. I don't know who is in charge."

"Someone on-site must have been giving you orders." Sylvan took a step closer, and he flinched. She could feel the bones in her face shifting and her pelt slicking down her torso and abdomen. She couldn't keep her wolf at bay, not now, not thinking about the enemies who had taken and tortured her young.

"Please," he whispered. "I did as much as I could."

"I hope you're right," Sylvan murmured, stopping a foot in front of him. "Otherwise, you're dead."

"I was a guard," Hoffstetter said. "I got my orders by radio while I was in the installation. I worked with the same team of guards most shifts, so I don't know how many are involved. I rarely saw anyone else, except a few lab technicians when we delivered the"—sweat broke out on his forehead—"the subjects."

Sylvan growled, and he squirmed in his chair. "You know their names."

He shook his head. "They wouldn't tell us. The bigger one, the one with the dark hair, she was subject number one. The other one, the blonde—subject number two."

"Gray and Katya," Sylvan said. "Those are their names. Those are the ones you tortured."

"I'm not one of them."

"You kept them prisoner. That makes you one of—"

"No." His voice was stronger. "I was trying to help stop it. I'm not one of them. I don't want to hurt any of you. But if we don't know who they are, we can't stop them."

"Who's we?"

His gaze shifted away from her shoulder to the far corner of the room.

"Now is not the time to keep secrets," Sylvan said with lethal softness.

His shoulders sagged, as if he'd decided his fate was already sealed. "I belong to a group that supports your goals. We believe that all the Praetern species should be given equal rights and protection under the law. That the sovereignty of your territories and governance should be preserved. We're on your side. We know there's strong, organized public opposition, but we also have proof now that there's an even more dangerous covert opposition. We're trying to find out who they are—just like you."

"You want me to believe that you were there to help us?"

"When I went undercover, we didn't know what was happening—not for sure. We'd heard rumors of experiments, of secret labs, and some of us used contacts we had to get jobs inside. I didn't know enough at first to stop them from taking your…your Weres. I tried to protect the subje—Gray and Katya. I swear to you I tried to help. Ask them."

"Oh, I will." Sylvan considered that her public persona might have prevented her from learning about this group—and the secret labs. Perhaps she had distanced herself too much from the needs of the Pack while playing politics with humans. Guilt burned in her belly. "How long were you undercover?"

"Seven months." He sounded bitter. "The longest and ugliest seven months of my life. It made me sick to go there every day, but I was afraid if I stopped going, they'd all be dead."

Sylvan turned abruptly and paced to the far wall. She gripped the windowsill so tightly her claws made dents in the wood. Her wolf's solution was simple—protect, fight, kill. She had to think. She pushed the window up so hard the glass rattled in its frame. Breathing deeply, she let the scent of mountain air and wildlife soothe her wrath. She watched the moon slide across the sky, flirting in and out behind banks of clouds, and ached to feel pine needles under her paws and the night breeze rustling her pelt. She breathed again and thought of all Gray and Katya had suffered, of how they had fought to survive, and her desire to escape disappeared. She sensed Drake across the Compound with Elena, felt the heartbeats of her Pack—even the thin, distant pulse of life in the infected girls. She couldn't run from the pain, or turn away from the ugliness of hatred and prejudice. She was the center, born to duty—the duty she willingly embraced. Leaving the window open, she turned back to the prisoner.

"How big is their operation?"

"Big, I think. I was in at least four different labs."

"And all of them held captive subjects?"

"I only had direct interaction with prisoners in two." Martin winced. "But that doesn't mean they weren't there. Just that I didn't see them."

"Were they all wolf Weres?"

Martin nodded, as if he was afraid to speak.

Sylvan growled. "Can you tell me where the other labs are?"

He shook his head. "No, we were transported by bus from a central loading area each night. The windows were blacked out, and we weren't allowed to have any kind of electronic devices. There was no way to track our location or even compute the distance. I do know we were usually riding about an hour."

Sylvan believed him. She smelled fear, but also outrage, when he spoke of the torture. He did not smell like the enemy. "I want to meet your leaders."

"I think my cover is compromised, and if I'm seen with any of them, I'll endanger them." His jaw tensed. "I won't do that."

Brave man, and Sylvan was in his debt. "Will your organization provide sanctuary?"

"If they can."

"What were you doing in the woods tonight?"

"I escaped when you raided the place the first time and kept watch today. When I saw the trucks moving heavy equipment out all day long, I realized they were evacuating the place and called the reporter again. I wasn't certain, but I thought there were others still in there. Then when all the employees, including the guards, left at sundown, I knew something was going down."

"Were you in communication with anyone?"

Martin shook his head. "No one, then. I'm supposed to report in tomorrow at seven."

"If we can corroborate your story, then perhaps you'll still be able to." Sylvan left the room. She needed her mate before she lost the last of her control.

Sophia followed the moon, running without destination, surrendering to the primal call. Leaves danced above her on silver threads, the ground shimmered with shifting shadows, the air bit and teased at her nose. Breath burst from her lungs in ragged pants, her shoulders strained, and her hindquarters stretched and thrust as she drove her body hard and fast, slicing between trees, leaping over rocks and fallen branches, skating down mossy slopes. Surrounded by beauty, she ran until her heart hurt with every pace, but she could not outrun her sorrow.

A scream shattered the steady thrum of blood in her ears, and she skidded to a stop, chest heaving. Shaking her head from side to side, she lifted her muzzle and searched the wind for the scent of danger. A keening cry cut through the night, and she caught the scent of Were from the forest to her left. One of the Pack was in trouble. She smelled blood and her wolf raced toward the source.

She broke into a clearing and saw Katya at the edge of the forest, naked, bleeding, in the grip of a Vampire. *Protect. Defend. Kill.*

Snarling, every fiber set to kill, she streaked toward the enemy. She launched herself to strike at the throat, but an unseen blow struck her while she was still in the air, bludgeoning her body, blasting awareness from her mind. She yelped, an explosion of pain detonating inside her head.

❖

Niki had plenty of practice tracking enemies through the dark, dense forest. Following Sophia's trail was easy. Her blood surged in time to Sophia's, her heart beat in synchrony. She felt her, knew her in her deepest reaches, as clearly as she knew her duty to the Pack and her place at Sylvan's side. Chest heaving, lungs screaming, she raced to find her. Her wolf couldn't remember what she had done to drive Sophia away, but she knew she had to bring her home. She couldn't leave Sophia alone. She needed Sophia. She couldn't be alone anymore.

Blinding pain struck the back of her head and she stumbled, rolling over and over on the ground. Staggering to her feet, she whined and searched in vain for an enemy. She was alone. Gait faltering, senses dulled, she lost the trail. She dropped to the ground on her belly, whimpering, scrabbling in useless circles, unable to escape the horrible assault.

Sophia. Sophia was hurt. Niki forced herself to her feet and pushed forward into the wall of agony. She had to find her. Someone, something, was hurting her mate, and she would make it stop or die trying.

CHAPTER TWENTY-EIGHT

Drake let herself into Gray and Katya's room and took in the two Weres on the bed. Misha sat facing the door with Gray reclining between her spread legs, her back to Misha's chest. Misha loosely clasped Gray's waist and rested her chin on Gray's shoulder, at once protective and possessive. Gray was as relaxed as Drake had seen her since the rescue, despite a fading bruise on her jaw and a cluster of scratches on her chest that might have been from a tussle or a tangle—probably both, from the way the two of them were wrapped around each other. "Are you two going to stay put for the rest of the night?"

"Yes, Prima," Gray said. Misha nodded.

"Where's Katya?"

Gray hesitated, and Misha murmured something in Gray's ear. Gray took a deep breath. "I don't know. She was restless, like she needed to tangle, and then she shifted and disappeared."

"She didn't say anything? Is there someone she'd been tangling with she might have gone to meet?"

Gray shook her head. "No one I know about—but she acted as if she'd been called."

Drake kept her worry out of her eyes—the Compound was still on alert, and if Gray sensed Katya was in trouble, she'd go looking for her, and Misha would likely go along. Bad enough one of them was roaming around—she didn't need a whole passel of hot-headed, hot-blooded adolescents roving the woods.

She'd find Katya as soon as she'd seen to her mate. "You two get some sleep."

"What about Katya?" Gray said. "I should look for her."

"The Alpha and I will take care of her. I want you both to stay here. That's an order."

"Yes, Prima," Misha said instantly, and Drake had a feeling she would see that Gray complied.

Drake left them and headed for headquarters. Sylvan was on her way, and she was agitated. Sylvan had insisted on interrogating the captive before anything else, even though she needed to shift to heal the burns, and she needed to tangle to blunt the adrenaline and stress. As soon as Drake found out what was driving Sylvan's wolf to a near frenzy, she would make her run.

"What is it?" Drake asked, pushing open the wide front door and intercepting Sylvan as Sylvan jumped up onto the porch. Sylvan grabbed her shoulders and pulled her into the shadows. She pressed Drake's back to the wall and took her mouth, kissing her hard, probing deep, covering her with hot, hard flesh. Drake grazed her claws lightly up and down Sylvan's back, slicing the back of her shirt to stroke flesh. She lifted her chin and let Sylvan feast on her throat. "Tell me. No one can hear."

"When I was trapped in the building," Sylvan muttered, gripping Drake's shirt and pulling it from her jeans, "I was afraid you'd be caught in the blast, injured, that the young would suffer." She licked the bite on Drake's shoulder and scored the skin with her teeth. "I was going crazy trying to get to you, and then the fire—"

Drake gripped Sylvan's hair and pressed Sylvan's mouth harder into her skin. "I'm fine. You were the one in danger, not me." She cradled Sylvan's ass and pulled her tight between her thighs, needing the press of Sylvan's heat against her own. "I called, and you didn't answer—I couldn't feel you. The world stopped, Sylvan. Everything ended for me."

Sylvan raised her head, her gold eyes boring into Drake's. "No. You have everything to live for." She pressed her hand to Drake's belly. "You have them. They're everything now."

Drake covered Sylvan's hand. "You are everything. They are everything. You're all my world."

"I need you so much," Sylvan murmured, wrapping her arms around Drake's waist, dragging her closer until the planes of their bodies met and molded. "You give me strength."

"Sylvan," Drake whispered, stroking her hair, drawing Sylvan's mouth back to her throat. "I love you. You are our touchstone—you give every Were in the Pack strength and courage."

Sylvan buried her face in Drake's neck, drawing deeply of her scent, absorbing her heat, replenishing herself in the power and certainty of Drake's caress. Her wolf slowed her relentless pacing and dropped, exhausted, into the background, releasing her ferocious hold on Sylvan's mind and instincts. Sylvan trembled. "I need you."

Drake held Sylvan's hips and slid her thigh between Sylvan's. "I'm here. I'm always here. I'm yours."

Sylvan braced both arms on either side of Drake's shoulders and kissed her. "Touch me."

Drake shuddered with a rush of desire so powerful her throat ached. Sylvan so rarely let her need surface. Only now, in these private moments, did she let herself be comforted. Drake opened Sylvan's pants and slid her hand inside, cupping Sylvan's wet, swollen flesh. Sylvan's clitoris, firm and thick, rubbed her palm, and she squeezed.

Sylvan threw her head back, growling deeply as Drake stroked her, massaging her clitoris, milking her, filling her. Sylvan's arms trembled and her thighs shook. She let herself come, and when her legs gave out, Drake was there.

❖

Sophia's scent was stronger, closer now, and Niki's wolf crashed through the underbrush, heedless of the thorns and branches tearing at her. She smelled blood. Sophia's blood.

Crazed, wild with fear and fury, she broke into a small clearing, growling, challenging, searching for the enemy. A snow-white wolf lay crumpled in the center of the leaf-strewn ground. Sophia. On the opposite side of the glen, Katya slumped at the base of a tree, naked.

Niki raced to Sophia and threw herself down beside her. Whining, trembling, she nosed her. When Sophia didn't answer, she howled and licked her muzzle and neck. Still Sophia didn't answer. Katya whimpered, and Niki shed her pelt and staggered to her feet. "Katya! What happened?"

"I don't know," Katya said, sounding confused. She wrapped her arms around her bare chest and pushed up until her back was supported by the tree. "I don't remember how I got here. What happened? Is that

Sophia? Is she—" Katya pressed her fingertips to her neck. "I don't remember."

"Are you hurt?"

"No, I don't think so. I…I feel…" She shook her head. "I feel fine—nothing like what happened…before. I just don't remember."

Niki knelt beside Sophia and pushed her fingers into Sophia's thick ruff. A bounding pulse beat beneath her fingertips, strong and steady. Relief so sweet and strong enveloped her that she shuddered. "Sophia. Baby, can you hear me?"

She gathered the white wolf into her arms and sat on the ground, supporting Sophia's weight against her body, shielding her in the circle of her arms. She stroked her muzzle and chest. "Sophia. I'm here. Baby, I'm here." She turned to Katya, who stood uncertainly a few feet away. "Go back to the Compound, get Elena. Bring the Rover. Can you do that?"

"Yes." Katya nodded once, her expression determined. She shifted, and her wolf disappeared as silent as the night.

Niki buried her face in Sophia's pelt and breathed her in. At first she didn't recognize the dampness glazing her cheeks. She hadn't cried in so long, the sensation was foreign. She didn't bother to brush the tears away, but held Sophia tightly, pouring all her strength and devotion into her. If she could have given her the essence of her life, she would have.

❖

The Pack had always been home. Home was shelter, belonging, freedom. The Pack had given her refuge, community, purpose, but she had still always been alone. Even when she'd been held and loved, she'd always been apart. She drew in the scent of the night, of the forest, of her mate. As always, she felt the connection to all the Pack, but now she was not alone—she was united, joined, one. Joy, bright and sweet, shot through her and she opened her eyes.

Overhead, the moon was starting its downward journey and the stars were sliding away, softly making way for the dawn. The faintest touch of red glowed above the mountaintops. Niki was holding her, and she was crying.

Sophia's wolf retreated and Sophia shifted. "Niki." Wrapping her arms around Niki's shoulders, she pressed her face against Niki's breast. "What is it? Are you hurt?"

"Sophia," Niki gasped, her voice breaking. She crushed Sophia to her chest, caressing her everywhere she could reach her face, her neck, her body. Cupping her face, she kissed her. "I thought—I was afraid—"

Sophia curled her fingers in Niki's hair. "Where are we?"

"In the forest. Your wolf was hurt."

Sophia jerked. "Katya!"

"She went for help. She's all right. What happened?"

Sophia tried to sit up, but Niki held her tight. "Don't try to get up yet. You were unconscious, but I don't see any signs of a struggle."

"I don't remember how I got here."

"It's all right. We'll figure it out. Where are you hurt?" Niki's hands were so gentle, her embrace so strong, Sophia never wanted to move.

"My head—I remember the pain." Sophia touched Niki's cheek. "Why are you crying?"

"Am I?" Niki laughed bitterly. "Any other time I would have been ashamed to admit that in front of you, but not now. I was afraid I might lose you."

"You couldn't, don't you know that? Even if you don't want me." Suddenly Sophia remembered running—running away. Niki had turned away from her—left her. Pain lanced through her and she tried to pull free.

"I'm sorry," Niki whispered. "So sorry. I know I hurt you, but I want you more than I can say."

"I should have told you a long time ago." Sophia rested her cheek on Niki's breast. If she only had these few minutes with her, she wanted nothing between them. "I should have trusted you."

"You were probably right not to tell me," Niki said, her voice jagged with regret. "I said stupid things, and I was wrong. I know you might not be able to forgive me right away—"

Sophia pressed her fingers to Niki's mouth. "Stop. I don't want your apologies."

Niki grasped Sophia's wrist and gently tugged her hand down. "I need to apologize, for that and so much more. You are one of the strongest, bravest in the Pack, and everyone needs you. You take care of us, not just by being a medic, but by understanding our pain and taking it away. None of us deserves that, but you give it to us over and over again."

Niki was breaking her heart. Sophia never wanted her to feel the anguish and remorse that was pouring out of her now. "Listen to me," Sophia said firmly. "Your job is to act for the benefit of all. We all trust you to put the Pack first—to take care of the Pack first, and individuals second. Everyone understands that. I know that's why you said the things you said about the humans."

"That was my excuse," Niki said darkly, "but it doesn't excuse me. I was wrong about Drake and I was wrong about you. Maybe I'm wrong about those two humans back there in the infirmary too. The Alpha declared you Pack when she took you and your parents in, and nothing from that point on matters. Nothing can change that. Not where you came from, not what is in your blood. You're Pack." Niki kissed her, a hard, demanding, claiming kiss. "And you're my mate."

Sophia jerked. "Niki—if you know—"

"I know. I know what you're afraid of—of what might happen if you bite me. I don't care—I'm not afraid. You're healthy and strong, but if you don't want to bite me, we can wait until you have more tests. And no matter what they show, it won't matter. You're my mate. Bite or no bite."

"It's not fair to you." Sophia shuddered. "Without the bite you'll never completely release—you'll never have the final joining."

"I've tangled all my life and avoided any chance of a bite," Niki growled. "I'll tell you what's not fair. Being without you—that would be worse than death. Please don't make me go. Please." Niki kissed her again. "I love you."

"Oh, Niki." Elated and terrified, Sophia kissed her. She couldn't bear to hear Niki plead. Not her strong, valiant, brave lover. Her heart ached as if it might burst. "I love you."

Niki sighed as if she had just finished a long hunt and closed her eyes. "You're sure you're not hurt?"

"Not now."

"The Rover's coming," Niki said, rubbing her cheek on Sophia's hair. "We'll be back at the Compound in a few minutes. Elena will make sure everything is all right."

"Don't leave me," Sophia said, unable to help herself. She

shouldn't, she knew that, she should try to find the strength to send her away, but she couldn't. Not yet.

Niki shook her head. "That won't work."

"What?" Sophia said softly, tucking her face into the curve of Niki's neck. She loved the way she smelled, the slight roughness of her warrior's skin, the sweet taste of her kisses. "What won't work?"

"You can't send me away. I won't go."

Tears filled Sophia's eyes. She kissed her, uncertain of what another day would bring, only knowing she could not deny her. She needed her, loved her, too much.

CHAPTER TWENTY-NINE

Luce knelt beside Veronica, stroking Veronica's hair and lifting the long strands away from her throat as Veronica straddled Raymond on the wide, silk-covered bed. Veronica rode the cock buried inside her as automatically as she checked her reflection in a mirror for imperfections—reflexively, without even really thinking about it. She was thinking about Luce, though—Luce was all she could think about. "Bite me again—for God's sake, hurry. I want to come."

She grasped the Vampire's hand and pulled her closer, molding Luce's hand to her bare breast. "Again. Bite me again."

Luce cupped Veronica's breast and teased her nipple into a hard, aching point. "Three times already tonight," Luce murmured. "You'll be weak tomorrow if I take more."

"I know what I want," Veronica snarled, gripping Luce's chin. Just the sight of the Vampire's incisors pressing against her lower lip made her want to come. "I want your essence inside me again. So good, so powerful. You want my blood—make me come."

Luce's eyes darkened to a violent magenta, and she was at Veronica's throat before Veronica had even sensed her move. Fire scorched through her, immolating her with more pleasure than she'd imagined possible. She came in a hot flood, drenching Raymond, not caring what became of him. She dug her fingers into Luce's shoulders and rubbed her breasts over the Vampire's firm, sculpted chest. Luce's small, perfect breasts were faintly cool, like exquisite glass. She came and came and came, crying out as her control shattered and flew apart.

Veronica heard voices, but her mind was too hazy to make out words. She willed herself back to awareness. She couldn't allow her pleasures to interfere with her objectives. Raymond sprawled beside her, his face lax, the evidence of his satisfaction glistening on his washboard stomach. She barely spared him a glance—he'd served his purpose. Luce stood by the French doors overlooking the park, splendidly nude, every inch of her gleaming skin enticing. She held a cell phone in her hand. Veronica's phone.

"Who is it?" Veronica asked, holding out her hand as she crossed barefoot on the thick Persian carpet.

"The Viceregal," Luce said, her pupils vast pools of inky black as her gaze slid over Veronica.

Veronica smiled and stroked a fingertip down her cheek. "Still hungry, darling? You'll have to wait."

Luce hissed and Veronica laughed. She took the phone. "Yes?"

"Teasing her is inadvisable," Francesca said mildly.

"You needn't worry. I know how to handle a lover."

"Perhaps—under ordinary circumstances. But these are not ordinary circumstances, are they?"

Veronica heated inside at the razor-sharp memory of the crystal pain lancing her neck and the explosion of sensation in her mouth and her throat, driving into her stomach, lower, exploding outward in an orgasm so devastating she was reduced to helplessness. She'd always used physical pleasure to dull the edge of her mental aggression, the intensity of which sometimes made her feel as if she were in the center of a hurricane. But she'd always been aware, always maintained control, always tempered relief with her need to be in charge. Tonight, all that had changed. Still, she'd handled the powerful exchange without any mishaps. Her only concern now was when she could repeat the activities. "Is there something I can do for you, Viceregal?"

"It's almost sunrise," Francesca said. "Luce will be leaving soon. I'm sending another guard to replace her. Raymond will remain with you during the day."

"I thought there'd be only Raymond by day, except in the case of a threat. Is there some reason you feel I need added protection?"

"I was about to ask you," Francesca said, her voice as thick and rich as honey, "if you knew anything about the explosion at the laboratory."

Veronica cursed Nicholas silently for having failed to keep her informed of the timetable for his plans. She assumed whatever had happened was his doing, but she couldn't be sure, and now she was placed in an awkward position. This was exactly the reason why she didn't like to become involved with the agendas of others. If she wasn't making the critical decisions, she couldn't control the outcomes or plan for contingencies. "I'm afraid I don't."

"I suspected that was the case," Francesca said. "After all, why would you want to destroy your own work?"

"Exactly," Veronica said, realizing that Francesca had just provided her with the perfect defense should anyone ever question her. On the surface, she had nothing to gain by destroying the facility. "You obviously know more than I, but if I learn anything, I will of course pass it on to you as soon as possible."

"Of course," Francesca said. "By the way, are you happy with the arrangements we've made for your protection?"

Veronica's gaze flitted over the exhausted man on the bed and the smoldering gaze of the Vampire leaning against the wall with her arms crossed beneath her flawless breasts. Luce looked hungry, and Veronica wanted nothing more than to feed her. "Quite satisfactory."

"Be careful, my dear," Francesca said softly. "Accidents like the one tonight have a way of recurring."

"I'll remember that, thank you." Veronica wondered if Francesca had just delivered a warning or a threat. She also wondered if Nicholas wasn't becoming more of a liability than he was worth.

"What do you think?" Michel asked, propped up against the satin-sheathed pillows on Francesca's bed. She lifted a glass of champagne and sipped it.

Francesca tossed her cell phone onto her dressing table and leaned back against it, her fingers curled over the ornately carved edge, her attention on the beautiful androgynous form of her longtime lover and second in command. "She's lying. She wasn't surprised or upset by the news of the laboratory being destroyed. She and Nicholas must be working more closely than I realized. Placing Luce with her was a very good idea. Hopefully, we'll learn something of their plans in enough time to decide if we want to support them or stop them."

"And if Sylvan discovers you're playing both sides of the street?"

Laughing, Francesca slid the straps of her sheer negligee over the slopes of her shoulders and let the filmy material fall to the floor. Naked, she reclined on the bed and faced Michel. "Sylvan is enough of a politician to understand that those in our position must make decisions to benefit those we serve." She kissed Michel lightly. "Or perhaps, in our case, those who serve us."

"Why not just ally with Sylvan openly now?"

"For all the reasons I've resisted doing that so far," Francesca said quite seriously. "Sylvan's stance of cooperative coexistence with the humans is not popular among our kind nor among many of the other Praeterns. And I'm not at all convinced it's to our advantage. Now that we are visible to the humans, we have almost more prey coming to us than we can handle. Why change the balance of power, particularly when that means giving up some of ours?"

"It's possible after these attacks on her Weres, Sylvan may rethink her position on the Coalition and change her mind about working with the humans. After all, they were the ones experimenting on her females."

"Yes," Francesca said. "And the more information we can provide her about humans working against us, the better. We just need to keep our association with the humans from becoming known." She tapped Michel's cheek playfully. "And you should stay away from Sylvan's Weres unless they come to us at Nocturne. Poaching on her territory is a challengeable offense."

"Sylvan should be the last one to complain about a Were consorting with a Vampire," Michel said.

"Well, darling, what the Alpha does is one thing. What she wants her wolves to do is quite another."

"I haven't trespassed. And I haven't taken anyone against their will."

Francesca's eyes narrowed. "You don't want to give this one up, do you?"

"She interests me."

"Really. Who is it?"

Michel lifted a shoulder. "What does it matter? After all these centuries, a momentary interest is nothing."

"Just remember," Francesca said, her smile not reaching her eyes, "who you fuck and who you feed from is of no concern to me. Who you confide in—now, that's entirely different."

"You have nothing to be concerned about, then." Michel kissed her, her blood surging with the strength and power of the Were she'd fed from not an hour before. Katya. Katya more than interested her, and she had no intention of letting the Viceregal know just how much.

❖

The headlights of the Rover cut through the trees, but before the vehicle emerged, two huge wolves burst from the forest, one black as midnight, the other a slice of gleaming silver as bright as a shard of the moon fallen to earth.

Niki straightened, holding Sophia close. "Alpha! Prima!"

Sylvan and Drake shed pelt so quickly Niki couldn't even see the shift.

Sylvan's eyes blazed gold. "What happened?" She cupped Sophia's chin. "Are you hurt?"

Behind them, Dasha angled the Rover into the clearing, and Elena jumped out. Katya, dressed in jeans and a T-shirt, followed.

"Katya said you were injured," Elena said, hurrying to Sophia. "What happened?"

Sophia wrapped her arms around Niki's waist and pressed against her side. "I don't know. I remember running, and sensing danger." She shook her head. "I sensed Katya in trouble, and then..." She shuddered and Niki growled, pulling her even closer. "A pain, a blinding pain in my head and then—nothing."

Sylvan said to Niki, "What did you sense?"

"Only her pain."

Sylvan looked over her shoulder at Katya as Elena handed the clothes she'd brought to Sophia. "And you can't remember anything either?"

Katya looked away. "I don't remember coming out here. I remember—I'm not sure. I don't know what is now and what is from... before."

Drake slid her arm around Katya's shoulders. "It's all right. You haven't done anything wrong. Just tell us whatever you can recall."

"I remember need," Katya whispered, "and pleasure. I needed something, someone. A terrible aching emptiness and then…then heat, and belonging. Pleasure. And then—everything was all right. I remember feeling as if I were running in pelt, strong and free and happy."

Sylvan glanced at Niki again. "Does that sound like thrall to you?"

Niki's canines shot down and she growled savagely. "They're both describing thrall. Katya was probably bitten…and the stimulants blocked out every other sensation and memory. But Sophia—someone forced a thrall on Sophia, against her will, damaging her. If I find out who it is, I'll kill them."

Sophia murmured, "Niki, I'm not hurt." She rubbed Niki's chest and belly to calm her. "I'm all right."

"You're not." Niki covered Sophia's hand with hers. "Someone struck you…psychically. They'll die for that."

"Stop. I'm here. I'm not damaged." Sophia licked Niki's neck, bit her softly. "But I love you for wanting to protect me."

"Katya?" Sylvan said. "Let me see your neck."

Katya came forward, her eyes lowered. Sylvan cupped her chin gently and turned her head from side to side. She frowned. "I don't see any bites."

"A master Vampire probably would make only the barest puncture, and the growth factors in their bite would heal the wounds almost instantaneously," Niki said.

"We had Vampires in the Compound tonight," Sylvan said. "Francesca, her *senechal*, her soldiers. If one of them took advantage of our Weres, our treaty is void."

"I'm sorry, Alpha." Katya spoke quietly, but she straightened to attention. "I don't think anyone took advantage of me. I think I would feel differently if they had."

"Sylvan," Drake said quietly, drawing her aside. "Michel is the one who was with Katya in the lab. Maybe she was with her tonight too."

Sylvan rubbed her thumb along the edge of Drake's jaw. "You think Katya's involvement was voluntary?"

"Maybe. Or maybe it was a thrall." Drake sighed. "The first we need to respect, especially if Katya sought her out. She did go out running, according to Gray. But if she was bitten against her will, we cannot let that stand."

"Niki will want retribution. If Michel enthralled Sophia, and Niki challenges her, we'll likely have a war."

"Right now, we can't afford to lose our alliance with the Vampires, no matter how shaky it is."

"I know." Sylvan watched Niki nuzzle Sophia, rumbling and fretting. "They're newly mated. She's not going to be reasonable."

"We can't be sure it was Michel," Drake pointed out. "And when is Niki ever reasonable? She'll do what is best for the Pack." Drake rubbed Sylvan's back. "Let's get everyone back to the Compound where they'll be secure. I'll check Sophia over with Elena, just to be sure she's all right. You can talk to Niki."

Sylvan glanced at Drake. "How is it you get the easy jobs?"

Drake kissed her. "Because you're the Alpha."

Chapter Thirty

Drake slid the stethoscope from around her neck and placed it on the tray beside the treatment table. "Not that I expected anything different, but you seem a hundred percent fine. How's that headache?"

Sophia pushed her hair back from her face with both hands, grimacing slightly. "Just a dull throb in the back of my head. I don't think I've ever had a headache before."

"I don't imagine you have. Weres aren't subject to that sort of malady." Drake leaned her hip against the table a few feet away from Sophia, careful not to touch her. Sophia was still in heat, and with the new mate bond, she would be hypersensitive to any physical contact from a Were. As careful as she had been during the exam, she'd felt Sophia's discomfort every time she'd touched her. Sophia was better than most Weres at hiding her physical and emotional states, but her shields were shaky after her injury. The only thing preventing Niki from charging in was Sylvan's order that Drake examine Sophia while Elena checked Katya. Nothing short of the Alpha's command could have convinced Niki to let Sophia out of her sight, and Drake doubted even that would hold her back much longer. Still, she and Sophia needed to talk. "Your atypical physical reaction to whatever happened out there points even more strongly to a thrall. Unless you were hit by lightning, or shot, stabbed, or poisoned with silver, I don't see any other explanation."

"But why? Whoever is responsible must have known we would figure it out."

Drake had been asking herself the same thing. "Maybe they didn't have any choice. You were in pelt when you sensed Katya in danger, weren't you?"

Sophia nodded.

"Do you think what your wolf sensed might have been Katya in bloodlust? The scent of pain and blood might have overpowered your wolf's ability to recognize Katya's involvement. Or her pleasure."

"It's possible my wolf misunderstood." Sophia snarled softly. "I've sensed Niki's response with a Vampire when she fed Lara. I...felt her pain...and her pleasure." Her canines flashed. "But I was in skin."

"And able to reason." Drake shrugged. "I'm not excusing what was done to you. You were assaulted, and that cannot stand. But it's not exactly easy to reason with a charging wolf bent on protecting one of the Pack."

Sophia's expression changed and she frowned. "But it would be easy to kill one."

"Yes. A very strong Vampire could have submitted your wolf and drained her. Maybe the thrall seemed like a better choice."

"If the only way to avoid doing greater harm was to subdue me with a thrall, I hold no quarrel with the Vampire as long as Katya was not taken against her will," Sophia said. "Do you think Niki will accept that?"

"Right now, Niki's not going to be very rational. In fact, she probably won't be able to control her aggression or her possessiveness until she is sure that everyone recognizes the mating."

Sophia rubbed her arms, pulled her T-shirt from the pile of clothing next to her, and slipped it on. "We aren't mated."

"The Alpha senses you are," Drake said softly. "Sylvan recognizes the physical and chemical signs of your mating. If she says you're mated, I think you can trust her."

"But how? I didn't bite Niki."

"You know that physiology is not always one hundred percent predictable. The mate bond is a chemical fusion, yes, but also a physical and psychic connection. Maybe what the two of you share is strong enough, intense enough, to induce the chemical blending without the bite. Or maybe your mate bond is expressed slightly differently than the usual one."

Sophia stared at the floor. "It's not fair to her. To take less."

"I don't think Niki would agree that anything about you is less. Do you love her?"

Sophia's head jerked up, her eyes flashing wolf for a second. Her voice came out a growl. "Of course."

Drake smiled. "Do you want her as your mate?"

"Always."

"I think it's safe to say that Niki feels the same way. Would you consider yourself mated if the Alpha and the Pack looked at you that way?"

"Without a mate bite?" Sophia shuddered. "I want to bite her. I want that final claiming. I want everyone to see my mark on her."

"Niki has already claimed you."

Sophia brushed her shoulder. "I carry her mark. She doesn't carry mine."

"It's time for you to have the immunologic studies repeated. Another tissue biopsy. A bone marrow biopsy." Drake glanced toward the door, feeling Niki pacing restlessly in the hallway. "We'll run the same tests on me too. Maybe something we discover will help our new patients."

"You're pregnant," Sophia said. "The Alpha will never allow testing now."

Drake grinned. "Let me talk to her."

Niki prowled furiously up and down the center hall in the infirmary, rumbling steadily, staring at the closed door to the treatment room. Her skin glistened with sex-sheen, her muscles rippled with tension. She wanted Sophia, and she wanted everyone else to get away from her. Sophia was hers.

The main door behind her opened and she spun around snarling, warning the intruder away. There were already too many dominant Weres in the building for her comfort.

Sylvan strode toward her. "Sophia still with Drake?"

"Yes," Niki growled. "They've been in there almost thirty minutes."

Sylvan gripped the nape of Niki's neck and drew her away from the door. "Sophia is safe with Drake. The Prima will respect your claim, you know that."

"I want to see Sophia."

"I'm sure they won't be much longer." Sylvan shook Niki hard enough to bring fire snapping into her eyes. "Can you hear me through your need?"

Niki shivered, her skin tightening over her bones. "Yes, Alpha."

"I know what you're feeling. I know your rage…and your fear. When your mate is in danger, there's nothing else that matters. But she's all right now."

"Someone hurt her," Niki rasped, her voice so thick with fury her words were barely intelligible.

"I know. But we don't know why—sometimes, accidents happen."

Niki whipped her head around and glared at Sylvan, so close to shifting her muscles screamed to make the final change. "Someone *hurt* her."

"If we find out the attack was willful and malicious, I promise you blood."

"I want retribution."

"You shall have it. But I'm asking you to wait until we know the circumstances." Sylvan slid her arm around Niki's shoulders and pulled her close. "You didn't intend to injure Drake—you didn't deserve to die. But believe me, I wanted your blood in my mouth."

"I'm sorry," Niki rasped.

"You're forgiven." Sylvan rested her forehead against Niki's. "Sophia needs you right now. She needs to feel safe, and she needs not to be frightened by what you might do. Don't let your need to protect her hurt her even more."

Niki dragged in a breath, visibly settling her wolf. "I feel like I'm burning."

Sylvan laughed. "That's because you are. As soon as Drake finishes, take Sophia somewhere, make her understand that she belongs to you, to the Pack, and always will."

"She won't claim me."

"She already has. Long before today." Sylvan rubbed Niki's back. "Your Alpha declares you mated. The rest will come."

❖

The instant Sophia opened the door, Niki grabbed her and yanked her close. "Are you all right? Did she hurt you?"

"Of course not," Sophia murmured, stroking Niki's face. "The Prima was very careful. I'm fine. Are you all right?"

"No," Niki growled. She grasped Sophia's wrist and tugged her toward the outer door. "I want to see for myself that you are all right."

Sophia's stomach tightened and need raced along her nerves. She wanted Niki over her, inside her, quenching her fires, drowning her thirst. She hesitated, unable to pull away, unable to deny her, but frightened. So frightened. She couldn't hold back any longer. Her need was too great. "Niki, wait. Please."

Niki rammed the door with her shoulder, not even bothering to flip the latch. The door banged open, revealing a sky already aflame with the first rays of dawn. The Compound would be waking any minute—Weres would be rising to run, to eat, to train. Sophia would be surrounded by other dominants who would sense her heat, respond to her call. Niki wanted to cover Sophia in her scent, fill her with her essence, so no one would mistake who she belonged to. "I want you now."

"Niki," Sophia whispered. She grasped Niki's shoulders, catching her off guard, and pushed her against the post before Niki could drag her across the Compound to the barracks. She kissed her, rubbing against her. Niki was naked except for jeans, her nipples stone-hard, her abdominals as wooden as the railing Sophia gripped on either side of Niki's hips. She sucked Niki's lip and thrust her tongue deep into Niki's mouth, piercing Niki's lip with her canines. Niki's hips lurched, and Sophia felt claws shredding her shirt, scraping along her spine. She slicked her tongue over Niki's mouth. "I want everyone to know you're mine too. I'm tired of holding back. I've wanted you for so long."

Niki arched against the post and threw her head back, giving her throat, a position she would never give to another. "Please, bite me."

Sophia pressed her face to Niki's throat, licking her, scoring her skin with the tips of her canines, fighting her instincts with every ounce of her reason. "I can't. Not yet. I'd rather die than hurt you."

"You could never hurt me," Niki snarled, thrusting her hands into

Sophia's hair. She pulled Sophia's mouth tight against her skin. "I need you. I'm lost without you."

"You're mine," Sophia cried, raking her claws down Niki's abdomen, raising welts in the lush line of her pelt. "Say it."

"I'm yours." Niki pulled Sophia's thigh between her legs, groaning at the pressure against her swollen sex. "I've always been yours."

"Then trust me, please," Sophia whispered. "Wait for me."

Niki jerked, her grip on Sophia's hips tightening. "What are you saying? You're not going anywhere."

Sophia braced her hands on Niki's shoulders and pushed away, the distance between them chilling her like death itself. "I have to go. Please, this time, you have to wait for me."

Niki grabbed for her, but Sophia shifted and bolted up onto the railing and down onto the ground. As she raced for the trees, she heard Niki shouting her name. She pushed on until she couldn't hear Niki's voice. All she could feel was Niki's call in her heart. Niki's pain echoed inside her like a thousand silver bullets shredding her soul.

Dasha saw a glimmer of snow flickering through the trees off to her right. She shouldered her rifle and sighted on the ghostly form. Callan's orders were to shoot any intruder without giving a warning. She scented the wind, searching for a foreign Were, and her finger stilled on the trigger. She smelled Pack. A wolf vaulted out of the underbrush a few feet away, and Sophia shimmered into skin.

"What the hell do you think you're doing?" Dasha snarled. "I almost shot you."

"I knew you wouldn't. You're too good to fire without being sure."

"What are you doing out here?" Dasha eased the butt of her automatic off her shoulder. "We're still on general alert. That means no one leaves the inner Compound."

"I know that. I need the keys to one of the vehicles."

"What for?"

"I need to leave."

Dasha shook her head. "I can't let you do that."

"If you care about me, you'll let me go."

"You know I do."

Sophia reached out but stopped when her fingers were a few inches from Dasha's face. She couldn't touch her—something inside her prevented her from making contact. The sensation was almost painful. "I'm sorry. I'm not free."

Dasha raised her head, breathed in sharply. "You're mated. I didn't realize. My apologies."

"I owe you an apology too. I shouldn't have let you close yesterday—you and Niki would not have fought."

"We would have anyway," Dasha said, laughing wryly. "The *imperator* and I needed to sort out our places." She studied Sophia narrowly. "Where is she? Why did she let you come out here alone?"

"She won't be far behind. That's why I need the keys. It's important, Dasha. Just trust me."

"If Niki doesn't flay me alive, Callan will."

"I'll call them both as soon as I'm on the road. I'll explain."

"And the Alpha?"

"She'll understand."

Dasha heaved a sigh and dug the keys out of her jeans. "It's fifty yards down the fire road. You ought to hurry. Niki's not likely to let her mate get far away."

Sophia grabbed the keys and ran.

Chapter Thirty-one

Just after dawn, Sophia drove down a single-lane, unpaved road that climbed through the Adirondacks overlooking Lake George. The farther she traveled from the Compound, from Niki, the more her chest ached. She pushed on—she couldn't wait any longer to face the truth. The road ended in a small grassy clearing where tall firs shielded a rustic two-story log cabin. Just as she pulled up in front of the wide front porch, the door opened and her mother came out.

"Sophia! What are you doing here?" Nadia frowned. "The Alpha transmitted an all-Pack general alert last night, and we still haven't received an all clear. We've been waiting to go into the lab until then."

Sophia climbed the rough stone steps and hugged her mother. "I have to talk to you."

Nadia gripped her shoulders and held Sophia at arm's length, appraising her critically. Her eyes flared. "You're mated."

"I don't know for sure," Sophia said. "The Alpha says yes, but we haven't…I haven't bitten her. The bond isn't complete."

Nadia gently lifted the pale blond strands from Sophia's neck. A smile touched the corners of her mouth. "She has bitten *you*." She raised an eyebrow. "She must be persuasive if she's gotten this far. A dominant, or am I wrong there?"

Sophia laughed. "You're not wrong. It's Niki."

Nadia caught her breath. "You've chosen the *imperator*?"

"I think I've always known."

Nadia nodded. "Sometimes the bond is there before we even realize. It was that way for me with your father." Nadia stroked Sophia's cheek. "She will be a formidable mate. Her duties—and the price—will become yours."

"I know. I don't care. I'm proud of her. And I love her."

"Of course you do." Nadia wrapped her arm around Sophia's waist and hugged her as the door opened and Sophia's father came out. He looked from one to the other, his eyes questioning. Both her parents, lithe and blond and blue-eyed, looked young enough to be her siblings, and would for many decades. Her heart swelled when she looked at them. "I'm sorry I didn't call."

Her father waved her words away. "Something has happened?"

"Sophia is mated to the *imperator*," Nadia said.

Sophia's father grunted. "She's almost worthy of you."

Sophia laughed despite her fears and uncertainty. Her parents had always made her feel as if she was the most special Were in the world. "She is brave and strong and tender. She's good to me. Good for me."

"She'd better be," her father grumbled.

"She is willing to accept me as her mate without a bite, but I want to give her that." Sophia looked from her mother to her father. "I need to give her that. I need to understand…everything."

Nadia glanced at Leo.

He nodded almost imperceptibly.

Her mother pulled her closer. "We've always told you what we thought you needed to know to deal with whatever arose in your life. We weren't certain this day would come."

A cold hand squeezed Sophia's heart. "But there's more you haven't told me, isn't there?"

Her father came to stand beside her mother, sliding his fingers around Nadia's nape. Her mother leaned into his chest as he said, "We've never been certain that anything we could tell you would change your situation. And there's nothing we can tell you that would make you less our daughter, less a Were, less a valuable member of the Pack."

"Whatever it is, I want to…" A wave of heat brushed over her, as if the sun had suddenly fallen to earth. Her mother and father stiffened, their attention jolting to the woods. Sophia spun around just as a red-gray wolf charged from the woods and launched itself toward the porch. Her father growled and started to shift.

"No," Sophia cried. "It's Niki."

Niki landed in the center of the porch, shedding pelt almost instantaneously. She crouched, naked, quivering with aggression that clouded the air. A rumble rose from her chest when Leo put himself between her and Sophia.

"You trespass in my territory," Leo snarled, "and dare to challenge me when my mate and daughter are vulnerable?"

"I've come for my mate." Niki bolted to her feet and brushed Sophia's father aside with a twist of her shoulder, stalking Sophia.

"How did you find me?" Sophia backed up rapidly to give herself a chance to think. Her skin tingled in response to the pheromones pouring off Niki's body. Another second and she'd want Niki over her, Niki's teeth in her neck. The mate bond tugged at her heart, stirred her body. She could think of nothing but Niki, feel nothing but Niki.

"You think I can't scent you—feel you?" Niki growled, her eyes glowing lakes of hunter green. Her canines lanced down from beneath her upper lip, sparkling like blades in the dawn sunlight. "You think you can run away from me—leave me behind and face whatever hurts you without me?"

"Niki," Sophia whispered, clasping Niki's shoulders, stroking the rigid muscles in her neck. "I can't be with you until I know."

"You are mine. I'm yours. Nothing else matters."

"It does," Sophia cried. "I have to know. I can't be with you and not know—"

Snarling, Niki grasped both Sophia's wrists and jerked her forward until their bodies clashed. She kissed her, bruising her mouth, claiming her with a slash of canines and a soothing stroke of her tongue. "I don't care what some tests show. I'm in your blood now. You're in mine. Nothing else matters."

Sophia clenched fistfuls of Niki's hair, unable to get close enough to her. She twined her leg around the back of Niki's thigh, cleaving to her, losing breath even as warmth and sunlight filled her. "Oh God, Niki. I love you."

Niki finally released her mouth and drew back, keeping one arm possessively around Sophia's shoulders. "You're my mate. Don't ever run away from me again. I will always follow you. Whatever needs to be faced, we will face together. I love you."

Sophia rubbed her cheek against Niki's shoulder, tears dampening Niki's skin. "I'm sorry. I love you so much. I want to give you everything."

"You already do." Niki looked at Sophia's mother and father. "Whatever you have to say, I want to hear it with her."

"My daughter has chosen well," Leo said. "Come inside, *Imperator*."

Veronica stepped out of the steaming shower and wrapped a white bath sheet around her body, tucking it absently under one arm as she crossed to her bedroom. She was tired, pleasantly so. She couldn't remember the last time she'd felt so relaxed. She ran her fingers over the side of her neck and turned her head in front of the mirror on her dressing table to study the faint bruises on her throat. The punctures were gone; just a faint blush of the skin and tenderness remained. She rubbed her fingertip over the spot and imagined she could feel the scorching heat streaking through her again. Her nipples hardened underneath the plush cotton towel and her clitoris quickened deliciously.

How strange, that a creature like Luce could feed in such a primitive fashion and still induce such incredible pleasure at the same time. The evolutionary advantage for Luce's kind was astounding. Every other predator provoked fear and dread in their prey, but the Vampire bite incited such a rush of endorphins and erotostimulants the prey actually sought out the predator. She ought to take a sample of her own blood before the chemicals Luce injected were metabolized. She might be able to isolate the kinins and neurotransmitters that were producing this remarkable reaction. To know was to control, and control was the ultimate power.

Veronica dropped the towel and studied her form in the ornately carved antique mirror. She was paler than usual, but her eyes gleamed as if she had a fever. Maybe she did. Her skin rippled with galvanic tension and her heart raced. And she was restless. She was never restless. Luce had left before dawn and wouldn't return until after sundown. The day stretched before her with an odd sense of emptiness she'd never experienced before. Usually, her work was the siren call that enchanted and satisfied her. Now she felt herself longing for something else. *Someone* else.

Veronica shook her head. These reactions had to be a side effect of whatever hormones Luce had transferred into her blood during the bite. Fascinating. She cupped her breasts, imagining the hands on her breasts in the reflection in the mirror were Luce's. Her nipples were hypersensitive, and when she brushed her thumbs over them, she tightened inside. She was wet. Her clitoris throbbed. She considered her options. Raymond was here along with another guard sent to replace Luce. Jean-Paul. She supposed she could try fucking them to see if that would still the simmering urgency in her loins, but she really couldn't be bothered. She knew they wouldn't satisfy. She wanted Luce's mouth, her bite, her essence streaming through her blood.

She needed to work. Work would help her forget her needs.

With a sigh, she walked to her bedside table and picked up her cell phone. She speed-dialed Nicholas and idly watched the sunrise while the phone rang. She rarely noticed the dawn colors, though she was usually awake. Today she wondered when Luce had last seen the morning sky.

"Yes?" Nicholas said brusquely.

Veronica glanced at the bedside clock and smiled. Just after five. She'd probably awakened him. She hadn't slept at all.

"What is it?" Nicholas injected into the silence. "Veronica?"

"You didn't tell me you intended to move forward so quickly, darling. I heard about the…incident."

"That sort of undertaking needs to be completed without delay. We'd been compromised—I needed to sterilize the site as soon as possible. Fortunately, we'd already prepared for the possibility of abandoning the facility on short notice."

"It would have been nice to know even after the fact," Veronica said. "The point is, I am publicly associated with your enterprises, and I don't want to be kept in the dark. Not knowing all the details puts me in an awkward position."

"Then I apologize for the oversight."

"Well, as long as we understand each other now," Veronica said, opening her closet door and riffling through the row of silk shirts with one hand. "I assume there's been some public acknowledgment?"

"The local news has our story—corporate terrorism perpetrated by persons unknown."

"Hmm, I suppose that works, although it might lead to speculation as to what about our work warranted such extreme opposition."

"That's been covered also." Nicholas murmured something she

couldn't hear—perhaps he was speaking to his wife. He said more clearly, "Within the hour, an animal rights group will take credit for the destruction of our lab."

"That's a good idea. It might be an even better idea if another facility was also targeted—one not associated with you or me."

Nicholas laughed. "We think alike. I believe you'll be pleased with this morning's scheduled events."

"The animal rights group is about to strike again?"

"Those types do tend to use multiple targets to make a statement."

"And we will of course have plausible deniability." Veronica slipped a blood-red silk shirt off a hanger.

"My dear," Nicholas said, an undercurrent of self-satisfaction in his tone, "we can hardly be accused of having anything to do with an installation run by an entirely different species."

"Ah," Veronica said, thinking of the only other major lab doing any kind of research that rivaled theirs in scope, "and you'll eliminate the competition while reinforcing the domestic terrorism angle."

"I take it you approve?"

"Oh, very much so. You'll have my new facilities operational by tomorrow?"

"It may take a little longer—we've had some major equipment losses."

"Don't take too long, darling. There are other labs, you know." She rang off before he could comment, not convinced that Nicholas's plan was really to her advantage. After a moment, she dialed another number.

CHAPTER THIRTY-TWO

Sylvan entered the holding cell where Martin Hoffstetter sat, still shackled to the wooden chair. She walked over and released his hands. "You need something to drink or eat?"

He brushed a hand over his mouth. "What time is it?"

"About six in the morning."

"If I don't report in by seven a.m., my contact will alert our cell and people will start looking for me."

"Where would they search?"

Martin looked confused, then chagrined. "Probably in the woods around the installation."

"I doubt anyone will be able to get close to that place for weeks. If they try, they'll run into the police barricades and a whole lot of questions they may not want to answer." Sylvan rumbled, remembering the explosion and the fierce fire that killed so many animals and almost claimed her mate, all to destroy evidence of experimentation. She needed to find the humans behind the projects—and she didn't doubt the leaders were human. Humans seemed to be the species most bothered by the discovery that not everyone was exactly like them, and their immediate reaction was fear and hatred. Those experiments might not be exclusively perpetrated by humans, but they were designed to annihilate those who were different. "Your people are likely to think you dead or captured."

"I didn't see what happened after your soldier caught me," Martin said. "I heard the explosions. Did you find any others?"

"Why did you think we would?"

Martin raked his hand through his hair and shook his head. "I wasn't sure, but I knew the place was bigger than the wing where I guarded your Weres. It didn't make sense to me that there *wouldn't* be others, and when I saw what was happening—that they were preparing to abandon the installation so precipitously, I was afraid they might be trying to hide evidence of more captives."

"Do you know how long it's been going on?"

He shook his head. "Months, maybe longer. At least one of the installations where I rotated had clearly been in operation for years. But the experimental wings were usually attached to legitimate research labs, so that other work provided a public cover."

"Everything you've told us makes sense," Sylvan said, "except why you care."

He stared at her, meeting her eyes for the first time before something he saw there made him look away. "I don't know if I can explain it except to say that what they're doing is wrong, and trying to destroy the Praeterns for being non-human is evil. Whoever is behind these experiments—human or otherwise—needs to be stopped. I don't want to live in a world where these things happen. I don't want my children to inherit that world."

"Katya and Gray can't remember what happened to them. I can't confirm what you tell me unless I know who you work with." Sylvan walked back to the door. "I want to meet with your leaders before I release you."

Martin straightened in his chair. "I don't think they'll agree to that. Some of them—most of them—I don't even know. Many are high-profile public figures and don't want to disclose their identities. Our goals are unpopular with some powerful—and dangerous—people."

Sylvan shrugged. "Then you should plan on a prolonged stay."

Niki pulled on the clothes Sophia's mother brought her and joined Sophia on the sofa adjacent to a huge stone fireplace in the main room of the cabin. The ceiling climbed two stories above a stone floor covered by thick area rugs in the colors of the forest. The walls were board and batten, the heavy-paned windows oversized—designed to accommodate wolves leaving and entering. Under other circumstances, she would have found the space comfortable, but not today. Sophia was upset, and so Niki's wolf was unhappy.

Leo and Nadia sat on a facing sofa, Nadia's hand resting on Leo's thigh. Niki put her arm around Sophia and pulled her close. Sophia trembled and a surge of protectiveness filled Niki's chest. She rubbed Sophia's arm. "It'll be okay."

Sophia wrapped her arm around Niki's waist and leaned her cheek against Niki's shoulder. "I love you."

Niki kissed Sophia's temple. "I love you too. Don't worry."

"Niki," Sophia said softly, "some of the things you might learn about me…"

"It doesn't matter," Niki growled.

Sophia kissed her neck. "Thank you." She straightened and faced her parents. "We're ready."

Nadia glanced at Leo. He brushed his lips over her hair and murmured, "Go ahead."

Nadia took a breath and looked from Sophia to Niki and back to Sophia. "What we need to tell you, even the Alpha doesn't know."

Niki stiffened. "I am the Alpha's *imperator*. You must know that my duty is to protect her and the Pack. I can't keep anything from her."

"We know," Leo said, "and we wouldn't have either, except to protect Sophia. Our first duty is to our family. Then the Pack."

Niki nodded. She would protect her mate first above all, and the Alpha would expect nothing less. "I understand. But anything you tell me—"

"We know you will have to tell the Alpha. We accept that," Nadia said quietly. "It's time."

Sophia jumped to her feet. "No. I don't want to endanger you. I don't need to know." She faced Niki. "I love you. But I can't put my parents in danger, not even to be with you."

Niki rose, holding back her wolf, who wanted to grab Sophia and drag her to safety. She wouldn't let her run away, but she wouldn't frighten her either. She loved her too much. "I don't need to know anything more than what I know about you right now. I've loved you for a long time. My wolf chose you. Your wolf chose me. Do you choose me too?"

Sophia's eyes filled with tears. "You know I do. I've loved you for so long."

Niki held out her hand. "Then we can leave right now. There's nothing more I need to know."

Sophia went into her arms and kissed her throat, her mouth, her eyes. Her hands went into Niki's hair, gentle but demanding. "I would give you everything. You should have offspring. Your place in the Pack—"

"You forget, the *centuri* often do not mate. My duty is to you first and then the Alpha. That's enough."

Sophia turned in Niki's arms, pressing her back to Niki's chest, drawing Niki's arms around her waist. She said to her parents, "I won't have anything you say put you at risk. If there is something I need to know to protect Niki from harm, I want you to tell me. I don't need to know anything else."

Leo slipped his arm around Nadia's shoulders. "We would have told you everything before this, but we weren't certain you would take a mate. You always insisted you wouldn't."

Nadia grasped Leo's hand, threading her fingers through his. "I'm so glad you have. And your mate is all she should be, and because of who she is and everything that has happened, we think you should know this."

"You're sure?" Sophia asked. "I love you both so much."

Leo rumbled, a protective, possessive rumble that Niki recognized well. Whenever she thought of Sophia, she felt the same desire to shelter her, to prevent her from ever being hurt. She wrapped her arms more tightly around Sophia's waist, kissed the side of her neck, and pulled her back to the sofa. She met Leo Revnik's gaze. "I will never let anything harm her. The Alpha is fair and she loves every wolf in the Pack. You can trust her with your secrets."

"We do," Leo said. "It's others we don't always trust—there are others outside our Pack who might be dangerous if they knew."

"Weres," Nadia said quietly, "and humans."

Niki's gut tightened. "All the more reason we should know who our enemies are. We cannot fight shadows."

"You're right," Nadia said. "You need to understand who we were before we had Sophia—long before the Exodus changed how we lived."

"You can trust me," Niki repeated.

"Before the Exodus," Nadia said, "we hid our true natures, like all of our kind. Leo and I were Blackpaw, and we mated young." A small smile crossed her face. "We shared a love of research and science and, like most Were scientists, wanted to find a cure for Were fever. Mir Industries existed then, but we were not Timberwolves, so we went to work for another large research institute. Of course, we passed as humans."

A chill spread through Niki's belly. "What did you study?"

"We're virologists," Leo said, "and we worked with a team studying human diseases with mechanisms similar to those of Were fever—hoping to extrapolate what we discovered about transmission into a way to counteract the effect in Weres."

Niki said, "That's not so different than the way Praeterns have always secretly integrated into the military, government, and medicine."

Nadia nodded. "We were young and a little naïve. As you know, the Were fever virus is capable of interspecies transmission from infected Weres to humans, although most infected Weres die so quickly the risk is small. That's why the human population doesn't know about it."

"At least not publicly," Leo growled.

Sophia gripped Niki's hand tightly. "What do you mean?"

Her mother's expression darkened. "We thought at the time those in charge of the project were unaware of Weres. We didn't realize some scientists were secretly experimenting with a mutant strain of a virus extracted from infected Weres."

"Did they know the original hosts were Weres?" Niki asked, her wolf clawing at her insides.

"We don't know," Nadia said, "but in retrospect, we think so. We suspect they kept quiet because they had no real proof, and because they wanted to hide the true goal of their research."

"The real focus of the research wasn't medical at all, was it?" Sophia whispered. "The Were virus is almost uniformly fatal in humans. They were developing a biologic weapon."

"Yes," Leo said. "We thought we were searching for a suppressor gene to counteract the virus, but we only had access to a small part of the project."

"What happened?" Niki asked.

"We worked closely with another research team—another husband-and-wife team."

Nadia shuddered and pulled Leo's hand into her lap, wrapping both of hers around his. "We think now, reconstructing everything that happened, that they were aware of the origins of the Were virus and might have suspected us of being Were. We think that's why we were chosen to work with them."

"And their goal?" Sophia asked.

Leo said, "They were trying to extend the viable latency period of the virus."

Sophia caught her breath. "The Were virus has a very short latency period, which is why we have never seen an epidemic. A high kill index in a virus that can exist for days or weeks could destroy millions."

Leo said, "That was part of the project that we didn't work on and didn't know about until it was too late. We would have tried to sabotage it, even if it meant exposure, but we never had the chance."

When Leo and Nadia fell silent, Niki said, "This is the part you kept from the Alpha."

Leo snarled. "We had to. There was nothing we could do, and we had Sophia to protect."

"Tell us the rest," Sophia said, her claws digging into Niki's arm.

"The other team managed to manufacture a potent virus capable of replicating Were fever symptoms, but in the process, the research team became exposed," Leo said.

Tears glistened on Nadia's lashes. "The husband and wife we worked with contracted Were fever, and so did their child."

"No," Sophia whispered.

"By the time we found out what they were doing, it was too late. They came to us late one night, already too sick for us to help. They begged us to take their child, to do anything we could to save her."

"I wasn't bitten by an infected Were, was I?" Sophia asked, her voice tight but strong.

"No," Nadia said. "That's the story we told the Blackpaw Alpha when we took you and ran. We hoped if you survived, you would be accepted as a turned Were."

"But I'm not," Sophia said. "I'm not really Were at all. Not even *mutia*. I'm—I'm some kind of—"

"No," Niki growled, her mouth close to Sophia's ear. "You are

Were. I scent you. I've tasted your skin. The Alpha recognizes you as Were. We all do. What are we, any of us, except what we believe and how we behave? We are more than what is inside our cells. We are what lives in our heart." She pressed her hand to Sophia's chest, covering her wildly beating heart. "In here, you are every bit Were. I don't care whether you were born Were or turned or something else. You are Were, and you are mine."

"We've always been afraid," Nadia said, "that if Sophia's identity was known and those in charge of the experiments knew of her, she could be at risk. We hid the truth to protect you. We're so sorry."

"No," Sophia said. "You saved me. I love you both."

"Who are these people? Who runs this laboratory?" Niki needed to know her enemy.

"We don't know who formed this project," Leo said, "but we believe the work probably continues. We think that these human girls are part of the same project."

Sophia tensed in Niki's arms. "And one of those girls bit Drake. That's why Drake and I are different. We're similar because we were both turned from the same manufactured virus. That's it, isn't it?"

"We think so," Nadia said. "Unlike the natural viral strain that can infect Weres, the strain infecting both you and the Prima is a much more potent manufactured strain."

"What happened to the infected humans?" Niki asked.

"We took them to the mountains, kept them comfortable to the end, and after their deaths, staged a car accident. The Blackpaws thought we were destroying evidence that they'd died as a result of a rogue Were attack."

"Who were they?" Sophia asked. "The scientists…my biologic parents?"

Nadia and Leo spoke together. "Carol and David Gregory."

Chapter Thirty-three

Michel eased the redhead from her lap onto the sofa beside her, positioning the girl's head on one of Francesca's brocade pillows. The girl was a novice, having only hosted once before, and Michel had barely begun to feed before the girl had orgasmed loudly and repeatedly until she'd collapsed and fallen into a dense slumber. In centuries gone by, Michel had appreciated prey who were so willing and so unlikely to reveal her identity to others. Usually it took very little effort to enthrall them, to erase their memories and leave them with only the faintest sensation of having had a very exciting dream. When it had been necessary for Vampires to hide, to feed in secrecy, she had deliberately sought out passive prey who were easy to ensnare and even easier to forget. Feeding became nothing more than a biological urge, a driving force that ruled her waking moments but gave her no pleasure. When she and Francesca had shared their prey, she'd at least experienced the excitement of Francesca's dominance. When Francesca's thrall washed over the host, the backlash often incited Michel to orgasm, and for a short time she was carried outside herself on the waves of Francesca's power. When the thrall ebbed, however, she was still alone.

Since the Exodus, her tastes had changed. Now that she could feed openly, she chose hosts who would give her more than nourishment. Weres were always desirable, their iron-rich blood so potent she was empowered for days after feeding, their strength emboldening her body and her mind and her sex. But even so satisfied, she still never felt filled in her deepest reaches. She was always hungry, always searching. Until Katya.

When she'd held Katya the very first time, she had sought only to taste her blood, and then Katya had reached for her, asking for something more than pleasure. She couldn't remember the last time anyone had wanted anything other than the thrill of bloodlust from her. Katya had wanted freedom, something no one ever expected from a Vampire. Katya had touched her in a way no one had, before or after her turning.

She wouldn't have taken the memory of their last joining if she hadn't needed to hide her identity from the wolf who'd wanted her throat. She'd had time to do nothing else. She could have killed the wolf, but Sylvan would have wanted blood in return. She might be able to take Sylvan in a fight if she was very lucky, and she didn't fear death. But she hadn't wanted to kill the wolf that was bent on protecting Katya. She respected the wolf, and Katya would never have forgiven her if she'd killed it. So she'd done the only thing she could, she'd enthralled the wolf and taken the memory of her presence from both of them.

"You look bothered, darling." Francesca reclined on the sofa across from Michel, indolently stroking the shoulder of the naked human male sprawled beside her. Francesca's dressing gown was open, her bare breasts flushed with the blood she had just taken, her eyes sparkling with the aftereffects of her orgasm. Her blood-red nails trailed along the pulse beating sluggishly in her host's throat. "Was she not to your liking?"

For a second, Michel didn't understand the question, her thoughts going immediately to Katya, who had been so much more than simply satisfying. Then the redhead beside her moaned softly in her sleep, and Michel took in her surroundings with brutal clarity. The rich tapestries, priceless antiques, finest wines and works of art. Francesca lived surrounded by beauty, feasting on the blood of the young and lovely and vital, all to camouflage the barrenness of her existence. Of their existence.

"She was perfectly satisfying," Michel said carefully, knowing Francesca would hear a lie.

"I think we've gone too long without a war," Francesca mused, angling the edge of her nail to open the skin over her host's jugular and paint a streak of crimson down his throat. "You need to burn for something other than blood, my darling. The Exodus has made life easy, perhaps too easy."

Michel cupped the redhead's breast. The ruby nipple hardened under her touch and she felt nothing. She met Francesca's probing gaze, hiding the ennui threatening to suffocate her. "You would risk all of this," Michel asked with a sweep of her arm over the opulent surroundings, "for excitement?"

Francesca laughed. "Darling, what else is there?"

As if invigorated, Francesca slipped out from underneath her host, letting him sleep on without her. She tied her dressing gown and smoothed it over her breasts and down her belly, lingering over her nipples before striding to the priceless side table, where an ornate, ivory phone was connected to a landline. She picked up the gilded handset, pausing to study Michel. "I hope you're still as good as you used to be, darling, because I really don't want this to be our last battle."

"I take it the call earlier was from someone interesting?"

"Our dear friend Dr. Standish appears to be switching allegiances. At least, she's considering it and very helpfully shared some interesting information with me as to Nicholas's plans."

Francesca held out her hand and Michel got to her feet. Francesca pulled her close, and Michel pressed against her, kissing her slowly and thoroughly. The swell of Francesca's breasts and belly was as familiar to Michel as the taste of blood. "And you're going to use it how?"

"I rather like the idea of having a Were Alpha in my debt," Francesca said.

"Even if it means making enemies of one of the Shadow Lords?"

"Who would you rather fight? The Weres or the humans?"

Michel laughed. "Can you be certain the others won't side with Gregory? I don't mind fighting humans, but I'd rather not have to take on the Fae and other Vampires at the same time."

Francesca ran her nails down the center of Michel's chest, making her nipples tighten and her belly roll. Filled with blood, Michel's sex beat steadily and she was ready to orgasm again. She caught Francesca's wrist and guided her hand inside her open trousers, pressing Francesca's fingertips firmly to her clitoris. Francesca hissed and let her incisors tease at Michel's throat.

"When the time comes, darling," Francesca murmured, "I promise you'll have all the power you need at your disposal."

Michel wanted Sylvan as her ally. She intended to see Katya again, and she'd rather avoid a fight that would put Katya in the middle. She cupped Francesca's breasts and rubbed her thumbs over her nipples. "Then by all means, make the call."

❖

"The Alpha needs to know everything you've told me," Niki said. "The humans we liberated from the laboratory yesterday and the one who infected the Prima have a form of Were fever, but there's no evidence they were ever exposed to a rabid Were. This can't be a coincidence. These experiments have been going on for much longer than we imagined."

"We thought there might be a connection when the Prima was infected," Leo said, "and we've been trying to isolate the antigen from her tissue specimens." He looked at Sophia. "We've also been comparing them to samples of your blood and tissue we've had banked since the last time we tested you. So far they look identical, but we can't find any evidence of an immune response in her specimens."

"You'll need new specimens from me," Sophia said, her voice strong and clear. "The last ones were taken when I was still an adolescent. There may be important changes now." She squeezed Niki's hand. "And I need to know whether or not I'm infectious."

"Your last test results showed circulating antigen," her mother said, "but we've never been able to induce symptoms in laboratory animals using derivatives of those agents."

"No," Sophia said, smiling wryly, "but then you've never tested them on Weres or humans. This may be very species specific."

"It's always been our hypothesis," Nadia said, "that the manufactured virus only infected humans, but until the sick humans showed up in the ER and then the Prima was turned, we never had any indication that the project was ongoing."

"I know that," Sophia said. "The Alpha will understand that too." She kissed Niki. "I need to go to the laboratory with my parents right away. If there's any possibility that something in my blood might help those two females you rescued, we have to find out now. They probably won't survive much longer."

"I need to speak with the Alpha," Niki said, pulling Sophia against her side. "But I want to go with you." A rumble resonated in her chest and gold streaked through the green in her eyes. "I don't want you so far away."

Sophia rubbed her cheek against Niki's throat and kissed the side of her jaw. "I don't want to be away from you either, but the Alpha may need you back at the Compound. I want to look at the specimens with my parents. You have duties elsewhere. I ought to be back by nightfall."

"I'll report to the Alpha, but then I'm coming to get you."

Sophia nodded and kissed her again. "All right. Take the SUV back. I'll ride to the lab with my parents."

Nadia grasped Niki's arm. "Please tell the Alpha if there's anyone to blame, it's me. I trust her as I trusted her mother, but my daughter's life was at stake. I couldn't risk exposing her to harm."

"You don't have to worry," Niki said. "We are not the Blackpaws. We do not kill innocents, and our Alpha is just."

Leo said, "I must speak to the Alpha also. It's important that we monitor the Prima carefully during her pregnancy. We haven't been able to find any evidence of circulating antigen in her blood, probably because she was turned as an adult while Sophia was still young enough that her immune system tolerated the foreign particles. Nevertheless, we have to ensure that the offspring are not exposed."

"I'll tell her to call you." Niki kissed Sophia and smoothed her hand over the bite she had made in Sophia's shoulder. "I won't be long, mate."

The caress heated Sophia deep inside and she trembled at Niki's words, knowing the truth of them in her deepest self. "I love you, Niki...my mate."

❖

Niki headed back to the Compound on a little-used fire trail. In another ten minutes she'd be able to make her report and rejoin Sophia. She didn't want her mate going through any more of this alone. She didn't blame Sophia's parents for keeping the whole story from her, for if Sophia had known the entire truth, she might never have let herself tangle at all. Niki's wolf snarled at the idea of being kept from Sophia, even by Sophia's fears. But all that was behind them now. She didn't understand everything Sophia's parents had revealed, but what she did understand was that Sophia and the Prima might share the same origin, and the Prima was fine. Drake was healthy and able to bear young. Sophia might not be able to have offspring, but Niki knew she was healthy. She'd felt her strength, tasted her essence. Sophia was wrong to fear biting her, but she could be patient. She had waited all this time, and she would wait for as long as it took for Sophia to believe.

The radio receiver on the dash crackled and she grabbed the microphone. "Kroff."

"Where are you?" Sylvan said.

"About five miles from the Compound. Alpha, there's something important I need to tell—"

"Is Sophia with you?"

"No, Alpha. She's with her parents."

"At their cabin?"

Niki's wolf stilled her relentless pacing and growled. A hand squeezed Niki's heart. "No. They went to the lab—"

"Turn around," Sylvan said, "and go after them. Keep them away from the lab. We're sending word to evacuate it now. I'm on my way, but you're closer."

"Why?" Niki's throat went dry, and her wolf threatened to climb through her skin to race after Sophia. She held her down despite the claws flaying at her insides.

"Someone is planning to blow it up, and we think the bombs are already planted."

Chapter Thirty-four

Niki screeched to a halt and jerked the wheel around, flooring the accelerator and tearing back through the woods toward the cabin. She'd only been gone a few minutes, but the lean-to where the Revniks' vehicle had been parked was empty. Sophia and her parents were gone. A black curtain of panic clouded her vision, and she gathered her strength to push through it. She'd fought by the Alpha's side in battle, she'd faced death without fear. Now more than ever, she needed to stand strong. Facing her own death had been easy. Contemplating losing Sophia threatened to destroy her.

She careened around the cabin and accelerated down the mountainside, navigating the twisting turns in the narrow dirt road so fast the vehicle skated around turns on two wheels. Once she hit the highway, she slowed, weaving her way through the early-morning southbound traffic as quickly as she dared. She couldn't afford to be stopped by the authorities—she would not be able to explain the urgency of her mission. The Timberwolves did not reveal Pack matters to humans. Gripping the wheel so hard her knuckles threatened to tear through the tops of her hands, she fought for calm while every instinct screamed for her to go faster. Sophia was somewhere ahead of her, in danger, and she wasn't there to keep her safe.

Failure was unthinkable. Her only purpose was to protect. She wasn't the Pack enforcer by accident. She was born for that role—the need was programmed into her DNA. Now that she was mated, the drive was even more acute. Her wolf was so close to taking over, her pelt shimmered beneath her skin, and her muscles tightened over bones growing heavy and hard. She could sense her mate's urgency and stress, but she registered no fear. Sophia was not afraid. Pride displaced the last of Niki's trepidation. Her mate was as brave as any warrior she had ever known.

She exited onto the drive leading to Mir Industries and picked up speed. Cars streamed past her, going the other way. The evacuation was well under way. Security vehicles blocked the main entrance to the vast parking lot surrounding the sprawling complex, and officers in black BDUs ringed the building, some guiding employees on foot toward safe zones while others directed the fleeing traffic. Niki barreled around the circular drive that marked the inner perimeter until she reached the entrance to the north research wing. That's where Sophia and her parents would have gone. A command station had been set up, and wooden barricades blocked the road. She screeched to a halt abreast of a guard with an automatic rifle slanted across his chest.

She rolled down her window as the dark-haired Were shouted, "Turn around and proceed—"

"Have you seen the Revniks?" Niki growled.

The security officer came to sharp attention. "Sorry, *Imperator*. I didn't recognize your vehicle. The Revniks passed here several minutes ago."

"Why did you let them in?"

His face went white. "They insisted, *Imperator*. Dr. Revnik said they had to secure the lab. He assured me they'd only be a few mi—"

Niki didn't wait to hear anything else. She slammed the SUV into gear and bounced up over the curb onto a grassy strip and veered around the barricades. Once past the obstacles, she gunned the engine, careening around security vehicles with rotating light bars, squads of guards setting up more barriers, and clumps of employees rushing from the building. She left the road and shot up a walkway toward the entrance. The Revniks' lab occupied the entire top floor of this wing. Another guard stepped through the double glass doors as she sprinted forward.

"Stand aside," Niki shouted.

"*Imperator!*" Chris, a blond Were lieutenant and head of security, pushed the door open to let Niki by. "The Alpha sent orders—"

"I know." Niki slowed. She needed to find Sophia, but she also needed to secure the safety of all the Pack members at risk. "Who's left inside?"

"Not many—the evacuation is almost complete. I have containment teams searching every wing with radar and infrared explosive detectors. So far nothing."

"Where are the Revniks?"

"In their lab. They insisted they needed to safeguard data vital to the security of the Pack. I sent a team up with them to search the floor and ordered a guard to stay with them." Chris pulled her radio from her belt and keyed her mic. "Status update?"

A voice crackled over the radio. "They need five more minutes, Lieutenant."

Niki grabbed Chris's mic. "This is Niki Kroff. Get those civilians out of there now."

"I'm sorry, *Imperator*," the guard said, "they refuse to leave until their data downloads are complete."

"I'm on my way." Niki tossed the mic back to Chris. Nothing was worth their lives. "Radio?"

"There's one at the security station." Chris pointed to the counter with a bank of monitors just inside the door. "Comm channel three."

Niki grabbed a radio on the run. "Make sure all civilians are out of the building. Alert me if the search teams find anything."

"Yes, *Imperator*."

Niki glanced at her watch—0657. At 0700 the night shift would be clocking out and the day shift clocking in. A perfect time to effect maximum damage.

Three minutes.

"Andrew, pull over here," Sylvan ordered, surveying the barricades and the line of cars filling the drive to the complex. She kissed Drake as Andrew stopped the Rover. "I'll go on foot from here. I'll be back as soon as we have an all clear."

"I'm going with you," Drake said.

Sylvan held back a snarl. She understood Drake's need, she just couldn't accept it. Not this time. "If we have injured, you'll need to triage. You're the best one for it, and you'll have to be clear of the danger zone to do it." She pushed the rear doors open and was about to jump down when Drake grabbed her arm. She spun back. "We don't have time to argue, Prima. Don't make me order you to stay."

"I'm not going to fight you on this, but don't think I don't know what you're doing, Alpha. You can try to manage me all you like—but don't imagine I won't know." Drake cupped Sylvan's face, her dark eyes pools of molten gold. "I happen to agree with you this time. Just be careful."

"I will." Sylvan kissed Drake and pressed her hand to Drake's belly. "I'll see you all soon."

She raced for the buildings, Jace and Max right behind her. "You two be sure the main wing is clear. I'll take research."

"Yes, Alpha," the *centuri* called and loped away.

Sylvan checked her watch—0658.

Niki didn't bother with the elevator but pushed into the stairwell and raced up the stairs. Even on two legs, she was faster than the elevator. Halfway to the top floor she met a security team coming down. Several officers carried handheld bomb detectors and infrared heat detectors.

"Anything?" she called.

"Nothing, *Imperator*," the team leader, a redheaded female, reported smartly.

Niki remembered the explosion in the human lab and the near-instantaneous collapse that ensued. "Have you searched the underground loading facilities?"

"Not yet. We started in the labs."

"Check the support columns on the lower levels. If they want to bring down the building, that's where they'll set the charges." She didn't bother to see that her orders were followed. She knew they would be. She shoved through the fire doors into the main corridor of the high-security Level 4 lab and ran toward the air lock leading to the Revniks' lab. As she keyed in the code to the decontamination chamber, she scanned the lab through the glass window in the inner door. A security officer stood just inside. Leo and Nadia were bent over computer monitors where data streamed in complex, indecipherable rows. She couldn't see Sophia, but the stirring in her core signaled her mate was near. She passed through the air lock, not bothering with protocol, and burst into the lab. "Everyone out now."

She signaled the guard, who had jerked to rigid attention. "See to it."

"Yes, *Imperator*."

Following the scent of her mate, Niki turned down an aisle bordered by lab benches laden with electronics and other equipment. At the far end, Sophia stood before an open cold case transferring specimen containers and test tubes into a large insulated transport container. Wisps of smoke-like frost poured over the edges of the box, enveloping Sophia in cold mist. Niki grasped her arm. "You need to get out of here."

"I'm almost done," Sophia said, continuing to transfer labeled vials into racks sitting on dry ice in the chest.

"There may not be—" Niki's radio buzzed and she grabbed it. "Kroff."

"We found them, *Imperator*," Chris said brusquely. "Multiple C-4 packs dispersed throughout the infrastructure."

"Can you deactivate?"

"Not enough time. They're set for zero-seven hundred."

"Evacuate your teams." Niki jammed her radio back under her belt and shouted, "We're out of time. Clear this area. Exit the building now!"

Sophia scooped up another handful of test tubes and put them in her case. She snapped the cover closed and grab the handle. "I have to help my parents. We have raw data—"

Growling, Niki raced back up the aisle. "I thought I told you to evacuate!"

"We need another sixty seconds," Leo said calmly, continuing to key in instructions on his computer. Next to him, Nadia pushed in another jump drive. She said, "Ninety seconds and I'll have all the latest figures."

Niki wanted to smash every computer in the lab. She could carry Sophia out bodily, but if she left Sophia's parents behind and they perished, Sophia would never forgive her.

"You." She pointed to the security guard. He was young, but solid, his eyes calm and clear. "I want you to escort the Revniks down the north stairwell and across the parking lot to the woods."

"Yes, *Imperator*," he said, his eyes flicking to Leo and Nadia, who ignored him. The clock above their workbench read 0659.

"Leo—take your family to safety. That's an order."

Leo spun around but Nadia continued to work, saying, "We can't lose this. This work is vital to the Pack."

"Then I'll wait for it," Niki said. "Officer—remove these three from the lab."

"No," Sophia said.

Niki growled and grabbed her by the shoulders, pushing her toward her parents. "Don't argue. I'm ordering you to go. Leo?"

Leo met her eyes. He was dominant, but she was second only to Sylvan in power. He looked away and nodded. "Yes, *Imperator*." He grabbed Nadia's wrist and wrapped his arm around Sophia's shoulders, pulling them toward the air lock. "Let's go. Hurry."

Sophia tried to pull away, but the guard blocked her from turning back.

"Niki?" Sophia cried.

"I'll be there," Niki called as Leo shepherded Sophia and Nadia into the chamber. The air lock swished closed, locking her mate away from her, leaving her with a gaping void in her chest. "I promise."

CHAPTER THIRTY-FIVE

Sylvan loped up the sidewalk to where Chris guarded the entrance. "Any word?"

Chris came to attention. "Yes, Alpha. Multiple explosive charges are deployed throughout the lower levels, set to detonate at zero-seven hundred."

Sylvan led Chris into the building and mentally reached out through her Pack to locate the life signatures of her wolves. Only a few remained inside the complex, but losing even a single life was unthinkable. "Instruct your teams to withdraw immediately. Escort the remaining civilians to the safe zones."

"Yes, Alpha." Chris keyed her microphone and barked out orders while Sylvan paced. She had ordered the evacuation based on Francesca's information alone because she hadn't any choice—she couldn't risk several thousand lives while she verified what the Viceregal called a credible rumor. Francesca had maintained power through centuries of internecine wars and held the Clans together during an era when Vampires had been hunted nearly to extinction by secret cabals of humans who knew of their existence and vowed to annihilate them. Francesca protected her reign through labyrinthine alliances and by erecting complex intelligence networks. She was always one step ahead of her enemies, and today, she had put Sylvan in her debt.

The fire door just beyond the security station banged open, and Nadia Revnik burst out, followed by Leo and a security officer. The males escorted a struggling Sophia between them.

Sylvan signaled the officer. "Get them outside."

"I'm not leaving," Sophia said, ripping her arm free of the security officer's grip with surprising strength. "Niki is still upstairs."

"I know," Sylvan said. "I can feel her. She sent you out with good reason. Do as she asked."

"Please." Sophia shivered, her eyes huge and wild. "Please, tell her to leave."

"I intend to," Sylvan said. "But I want all of you outside on the far side of the safety perimeter. Go now."

The force of her command crashed over the four of them so sharply a low whine escaped Nadia's throat. They didn't argue, and even Sophia stopped resisting.

Sylvan turned to Chris. "Time?"

"Thirty seconds, Alpha."

Sylvan calculated the distance to the lab. Not enough time for her to reach Niki and physically remove her, but she could still reach her. Her connection with Niki was stronger than with any other Pack member except Drake. They were bonded by history, by blood, and by love. She sent her call with all her force. *Get out now.*

Ten seconds.

Sylvan spun around and saw Chris by the open glass doors. At that instant, sunlight broke over the complex, clear and bright. Beyond the perimeter cordons, civilians and security officers crowded around, waiting. She sensed no one inside except Niki.

Five seconds.

Niki had not yet moved.

Sylvan thought about her mate and her offspring and her Pack, and the war that would surely come. Her responsibility to all of them outweighed her love for the one. The decision tore her heart in two. She raced outside, shifting as she ran and pulling Chris into pelt with her. *Follow me.*

Two seconds.

❖

Sophia quivered, her heart racing and her throat tight with dread. The Alpha and the security chief raced toward them. Frantically she searched the ground beside the great silver wolf for Niki. She wasn't there. Icy terror rushed through her, and she braced her hands on the barricade. She had to get back inside, had to find her mate. Arms gripped her around the waist and prevented her from leaping over the barrier.

"Let me go," Sophia cried.

"I'm sorry," her father murmured. "I can't let you go."

"You have to," Sophia screamed. "She's my mate. I can't leave—"

As the Alpha leapt over the barricades, Chris close behind, the earth seemed to shake and heave. Vehicles rattled and jumped, as if trying to take off by themselves. Pack members lost their balance and crashed into one another. And then the north wing of the complex exploded outward, windows shattering and sections of roof blowing up into the air. Shards of metal and glass rained down on the parking lot and beyond like glittering confetti edged in razor blades.

Sophia dropped to her knees, pain lancing through her heart so sharply she thought it might have burst. *Niki.*

She threw back her head and howled.

Sylvan landed on the far side of the barricade and shifted into skin. Chris dropped beside her, blood staining her brown and white pelt. Sylvan gripped Chris's ruff and pulled her against her side. *Good work, Lieutenant. Get that shoulder looked at. You did well today.*

Chris rubbed her muzzle against Sylvan's thigh and whined softly. A few seconds later she shifted into skin. "I'm all right, Alpha. I have to organize my teams. We'll need to transport wounded—a lot of debris fell in the crowd—and we need to secure the building."

"There may be other charges set to go off when the first responders are inside," Sylvan said, fury boiling in her chest. Someone had tried to destroy her Pack. And to set those charges inside her research facility without being detected—that required intimate knowledge of the layout as well as access. The saboteurs had inside help. One hundred percent of the civilian employees at Mir Industries were her wolves. She refused to believe one of her Pack had betrayed her. The pain of contemplating such treachery cut deep into her heart. "Organize search teams, but only bomb-detecting units enter—make a quadrant search, and be careful."

"Yes, Alpha," Chris said, signaling to officers nearby. "We'll set up a command center here and I'll report to you myself. I'll send another detail to establish a field hospital for the injured."

"Good. The Prima will be in charge there," Sylvan said. Chris saluted and disappeared, and Sylvan turned to Sophia. Her eyes were bleak and dazed. Sylvan cupped Sophia's face and kissed her forehead. "I need you to search inside yourself. If she's alive, you might be the only one who can sense her. Your connection to her is even stronger than mine."

Sophia's expression blanked and then her eyes grew wide. She shimmered into pelt, leapt over the barricade, and raced toward the smoking destruction. Sylvan bounded after her, closing the distance in long, powerful strides.

Instead of heading for the area where the entrance had been, now identifiable only by the skeletal remains of the elevator shaft pointing skyward like an accusing finger, Sophia swerved around a pile of rubble and pounded through the detritus-covered parking lot until she reached a heap of smoking debris near the far end of what had once been the research wing. Whining, she paced and circled the heap of twisted beams and broken glass.

Sylvan shed pelt and stood, growling in her chest as she surveyed the damage. She sniffed, felt a twinge in her chest, and sniffed again. Packmate—somewhere close—

Sophia burst into skin and pointed. "There!" Sophia began clawing at chunks of rubble and flinging them aside until she uncovered a red-gray wolf lying motionless amidst hunks of concrete and smoldering wood. "Oh no, oh no, *nonono. Niki!*"

Sylvan scooped up her injured wolf and pulled her tight to her chest. "I have her. Let's get out of here."

Sophia's eyes blazed. "I'll take her."

"You can have her as soon as you're both somewhere safe." Sylvan understood a mate's need to protect, but she had to protect them both. "She needs your strength to survive, Sophia."

"Then hurry, Alpha. I'm not losing her now."

Chapter Thirty-six

Sophia curled up around the red-gray wolf and wrapped her arms around the powerful shoulders. She rested her cheek against Niki's neck and ran her fingers through the thick ruff, absorbing the heat of Niki's body and sending all her strength and healing force into her mate. She drifted, feeling the spirit of the Pack close in around them, knowing the Alpha was near. She was frightened, but she felt safe too. She was home.

She hadn't meant to sleep, but she must have, for when she opened her eyes, twilight silvered the sky outside the open window. She blinked and focused on the green-gold eyes studying hers. Niki was awake.

"Hi," Sophia said softly, stroking the soft muzzle.

The wolf blinked and nosed her neck. Sophia laughed.

"How are you feeling?"

Better. Are you all right?

Sophia caught her breath, never having realized how intimate, how very special the silent communion between mates could be. "I'm all right. I wasn't hurt. Everyone is fine."

Niki's ears flickered.

"Really. Quite a few had cuts and bruises and a broken bone or two. Nothing that didn't heal with the first shift. You were the one who was hurt the most."

Niki rumbled and stretched against Sophia.

"I know you think you're indestructible, but you're really not. And since you've decided to be mated, you're going to have to be more careful from now on."

Niki drew back her lips in a half smile, looking as supremely contented as a wolf ever could.

Sophia rested her forehead against Niki's neck. "I was really scared. I don't know what I would do if I lost you now. I've waited so long—" She stopped, feeling the powerful body in her arms shudder, shift, and change until suddenly she was holding a very naked, very warm Niki. Niki's lips moved over her temple and down her cheek to her mouth. The kiss was soft, almost apologetic. Sophia eased away and searched Niki's face. Her forest-green eyes were clear and bright. And so beautiful.

"Hi. Welcome back."

"Hi," Niki said. "Sorry I scared you."

"I know why you did it, I know that you had to, but next time, try not to leave things until the last second."

"Did you find the jump drive?" Niki asked.

Sophia laughed. "Drake was examining you and you sneezed it out at her."

"Well I couldn't think of any place else to put it when I got ready to shift, except in my mouth," Niki said. "I thought my wolf would have a better chance of jumping clear."

Sophia's heart trip-hammered. "She did, although not completely clear. Don't ever do that again."

"Hey," Niki said, kissing her again. "It's just a little bump on the head. I'm fine. The Alpha? The Prima? Everyone is okay?"

"Really. Everyone is fine."

"How long have I been asleep?"

"Just about ten hours."

"Does the Alpha have any idea who was behind this?"

"I don't know. I know she and the Prima have been sequestered at headquarters all day. I'm sure she'll fill you in soon."

Niki rolled onto her back and pulled Sophia into the curve of her arms. "I'll find her soon. Right now, I just want to hold you. You scared me too."

"I'm sorry. I wanted my parents to test me again." Sophia smoothed her hand down the valley between Niki's breasts. "I want to be a complete mate for you."

Niki squeezed her. "You already are. I've already told you that. There isn't a single thing I want you haven't given me."

"You know that's not true," Sophia said softly. "Without the mate bite, we'll never be completely connected. You deserve that."

Niki cradled Sophia's face. "Deserve? I don't even deserve you at all. But I love you, and I want you. You. You've already given me everything I want and need. If the rest comes, I'll welcome it. But I don't need it. Will you believe me?"

Sophia looked deep into Niki's eyes and found only truth. She sighed. "I do believe you." She laughed shakily. "But *I* want more—everything. I want to bite you, mark you, join our scents, our bodies."

"That time will come, I know it," Niki said firmly.

Sophia stroked Niki's face. "As much as I want to be able to give you everything, I won't take a chance on harming you. Until we can reestablish my parents' lab and complete the testing, I won't bite you."

"Do you accept me as your mate?" Niki asked.

"Yes—with all my being."

"As I accept you—with all my being." Niki caught Sophia's hand and held it to her breast. "Will you promise me right now that you will never leave me?"

"I love you," Sophia whispered, kissing her long and deep. "I will never leave you."

"Then I am yours."

With a low, fierce growl, Sophia pushed Niki onto her back and climbed atop her. She entwined her legs with Niki's, coating her with her essence, marking her with her scent. "Yes," she said, her canines just grazing Niki's neck, making her arch and moan. "You are mine."

Niki pulled the sheet up over Sophia. "The Alpha is coming."

Sophia laughed softly. "You don't want her to see me naked?"

"I don't want anyone to see you naked," Niki grumbled.

"We're Weres, sweetheart. Plenty of Pack members are going to see me naked."

Growling, Niki pulled Sophia close, wrapping her arms around her waist from behind, resting her chin in the curve of Sophia's shoulder. She kissed the side of her jaw. "That may be so, but not when you're still in heat."

"I'm mated, remember," Sophia whispered. "Everyone will respect that."

"I'm not taking any chances," Niki muttered.

The door swung open and Sylvan strode in. "Don't look for fights where there are none, *Imperator*. You'll have plenty of chances to do battle before long."

Niki pushed up on one elbow. "Have you found out anything about the orchestrators of the explosion?"

"Not yet. How are you feeling?"

"I'm fine. I healed while I was sleeping."

"It looked to me as if your wolf had broken a foreleg. Is your shoulder all right?"

Niki rolled her arm forward and back. "No pain. I'm fit for duty."

"Good, because I need you."

Niki kissed Sophia and slid out from under the covers. "There's something I need to tell you first."

Sophia sat up, letting the sheet drop to her waist, and grasped Niki's hand. "There's something *we* need to tell you."

Sylvan folded her arms across her chest and waited.

Sophia took a deep breath. "My parents explained something to me about my birth that they didn't tell your mother, or you."

"Something they kept from the Pack?" Sylvan's voice was even and calm. Dangerously calm. Her eyes were stormy.

Niki rumbled low in her chest, and Sylvan shot her a look that warned her to stand down. Niki tensed, unwilling to have her mate upset. She did not want Sophia to be afraid or anxious, not even at the hands of the Alpha.

A smile flickered across Sylvan's face. "For a Were who never wanted a mate, *Imperator*, you've assumed the mantle without reservation."

"Sophia deserves nothing less."

"And I deserve nothing less than your respect, so hold your temper and let your mate talk."

Niki dipped her head a fraction. "Yes, Alpha."

"Go ahead, Sophia."

"It's about my turning." Sophia lifted her chin and focused on Sylvan's face, meeting her eyes for a second so the Alpha could read the pride in hers. "My parents love the Pack and you, as they loved your mother. But they love me more."

"As they should. But when the love for an individual endangers the Pack, it's my job to decide the proper course. They know that. You all know that."

"Yes, Alpha," Sophia said softly. "And I hope that you will be generous in your decision when you hear all the facts."

"What do I need to know?"

"I wasn't turned by a rabid Were—I was infected with a synthetic virus manufactured to induce Were fever. Like the girls you rescued."

Sylvan's eyes narrowed and her lips pulled back, revealing lethal canines. "Girls like the human who infected the Prima?"

Sophia nodded. "We believe the early experiments were carried out in a human laboratory where my parents worked with a team of human researchers—my biologic parents. Leo and Nadia didn't know about the secret experiments until it was far too late to do anything except save me."

"And they made up the story that you were turned by a bite?"

"Yes."

"And all this time they've kept it a secret?"

"To protect me," Sophia said anxiously. "They've been working all this time to discover what was done to me and to find a cure."

"And whatever was done to you possibly also affects the Prima?"

Sophia nodded.

"Your parents had a difficult decision to make," Sylvan said, "but to protect the Pack, I cannot allow Weres to live among us who willingly endanger—"

Sophia gasped and Niki jumped to her feet.

"If you banish the Revniks," Niki said, "I go with them."

Sylvan moved so quickly, Niki didn't have time to flinch. The Alpha's hand was around her throat, claws just puncturing her skin, before she could raise a hand to defend herself, not that she would have. One did not raise a hand to the Alpha and live. Sylvan's face so close to hers she could smell the power rolling off her. Niki whimpered and tried to lick Sylvan's hand, but Sylvan's grip was iron.

"I recognize your responsibility to your mate, but my duty is to the Pack, and your duty is to serve me. Until I make a decision on this matter, you will hold your tongue."

"Please, Alpha," Sophia said, "I do not want her hurt because of my situation. I would not have her banished from the Pack even if I am to lea—"

Sylvan whipped her head around, her hand still on Niki's throat, and silenced Sophia with a glare. "You trust me so little, Sophia, that you think I would destroy four lives so easily? I will speak to your parents when the more critical issues facing us have been settled. Until then, I need my *imperator*'s loyalties to be undivided. We have business this night."

"Yes, Alpha," Sophia said, resting her hand on Niki's bare shoulder. "We are your wolves and will do our duty."

Sylvan released her hold. "Well, Niki?"

"I have ever been and will always be yours to command," Niki said solemnly.

"Then meet me outside in ten minutes. Arm the *centuri* for this mission and instruct Callan to order all free-living wolves back to the Compound."

"Yes, Alpha."

"Where are you going?" Sophia asked, looking from Sylvan to Niki.

"To visit the Viceregal," Sylvan said. "I suspect the rumor she heard was a little more than that. I want to know who is behind this, and tonight I am not asking."

Sophia grabbed her pants from the floor and pulled them on. Niki handed her a shirt, and she dropped it over her head. "I want to go with you."

"No," Niki said instantly.

Sophia's eyes flashed. "Whenever the Pack goes to war, the Alpha always travels with a medic. The Prima is pregnant. If something happens to either one of them—"

"You're right," Sylvan said to Sophia. "We're stopping to pick up Liege Gates and her warlord on the way to Nocturne. Tonight will gauge the true strength of our alliances. You'd better gather your gear, *Medicus*."

"Alpha," Niki protested.

"We're at war, *Imperator*. Your mate is one of our two medics. She travels with the *centuri* from now on."

"The Viceregal may consider our appearance in her territory with a war party an act of aggression," Niki said. "We could be in a fight before the night is out."

"We didn't start the war," Sylvan said, "but tonight everyone—Praetern and human—will know we show no mercy to those who threaten the Pack."

"Yes, Alpha," Niki said.

Sylvan clasped Niki behind the head and shook her lightly. "Your mate will be fine. She knows her duty. Trust her."

As soon as Sylvan strode out the door, Niki grabbed Sophia and buried her face in the curve of Sophia's neck. "I do trust you. I just don't want anything to happen to you. I love you so much."

"Nothing is going to happen to me." Sophia stroked Niki's hair. "I love you too—and whatever comes, I'll be with you. I can't imagine a safer place to be."

About the Author

Radclyffe has written over thirty-five romance and romantic intrigue novels, dozens of short stories, and, writing as L.L. Raand, has authored a paranormal romance series, The Midnight Hunters.

She is an eight-time Lambda Literary Award finalist in romance, mystery, and erotica—winning in both romance (*Distant Shores, Silent Thunder*) and erotica (*Erotic Interludes 2: Stolen Moments* edited with Stacia Seaman and *In Deep Waters 2: Cruising the Strip* written with Karin Kallmaker). A member of the Saints and Sinners Literary Hall of Fame, she is also a 2010 RWA/FF&P Prism award winner for *Secrets in the Stone*. Her 2010 titles were finalists for the Benjamin Franklin award (*Desire by Starlight*), the ForeWord Review Book of the Year award (*Trauma Alert* and writing as LL Raand, *The Midnight Hunt*), and the RWA Passionate Plume award (*The Midnight Hunt*). She is also the president of Bold Strokes Books, one of the world's largest independent LGBT publishing companies.

Books Available From Bold Strokes Books

Night Hunt by L.L. Raand. When dormant powers ignite, the wolf Were pack is thrown into violent upheaval, and Sylvan's pregnant mate is at the center of the turmoil. A Midnight Hunters novel. (978-1-60282-647-2)

Demons are Forever by Kim Baldwin and Xenia Alexiou. Elite Operative Landis "Chase" Coolidge enlists the help of high-class call girl Heather Snyder to track down a kidnapped colleague embroiled in a global black market organ-harvesting ring. (978-1-60282-648-9)

Runaway by Anne Laughlin. When Jan Roberts is hired to find a teenager who has run away to live with a group of antigovernment survivalists, she's forced to return to the life she escaped when she was a teenager herself. (978-1-60282-649-6)

Street Dreams by Tama Wise. Tyson Rua has more than his fair share of problems growing up in New Zealand—he's gay, he's falling in love, and he's run afoul of the local hip-hop crew leader just as he's trying to make it as a graffiti artist. (978-1-60282-650-2)

Women of the Dark Streets: Lesbian Paranormal by Radclyffe and Stacia Seaman, eds. Erotic tales of the supernatural—a world of vampires, werewolves, witches, ghosts, and demons—by the authors of Bold Strokes Books. (978-1-60282-651-9)

Words to Die By by William Holden. Sixteen answers to the question: What causes a mind to curdle? (978-1-60282-653-3)

Tyger, Tyger, Burning Bright by Justine Saracen. Love does not conquer all, but when all of Europe is on fire, it's better than going to hell alone. (978-1-60282-652-6)

Wholehearted by Ronica Black. When therapist Madison Clark and attorney Grace Hollings are forced together to help Grace's troubled nephew at Madison's healing ranch, worlds and hearts collide. (978-1-60282-594-9)

Haunting Whispers by VK Powell. Detective Rae Butler faces two challenges: a serial attacker who targets attractive women, and Audrey Everhart, a compelling woman who knows too much about the case and offers too little—professionally and personally. (978-1-60282-593-2)

Fugitives of Love by Lisa Girolami. Artist Sinclair Grady has an unspeakable secret, but the only chance she has for love with gallery owner Brenna Wright is to reveal the secret and face the potentially devastating consequences. (978-1-60282-595-6)

Derrick Steele: Private Dick—The Case of the Hollywood Hustlers by Zavo. Derrick Steele, a hard-drinking, lusty private detective, is being framed for the murder of a hustler in downtown Los Angeles. When his brother's friend Daniel McAllister joins the investigation, their growing attraction might prove to be more explosive than the case. (978-1-60282-596-3)

Nice Butt: Gay Anal Eroticism edited by Shane Allison. From toys to teasing, spanking to sporting, some of the best gay erotic scribes celebrate the hottest and most creative in new erotica. (978-1-60282-635-9)

Initiation by Desire by MJ Williamz. Jaded Sue and innocent Tulley find forbidden love and passion within the inhibiting confines of a sorority house filled with nosy sisters. (978-1-60282-590-1)

Toughskins by William Masswa. John and Bret are two twenty-something athletes who find that love can begin in the most unlikely of places, including a "mom-and-pop shop" wrestling league. (978-1-60282-591-8)

me@you.com by KE Payne. Is it possible to fall in love with someone you've never met? Imogen Summers thinks so because it's happened to her. (978-1-60282-592-5)

Awake Unto Me by Kathleen Knowles. In turn of the century San Francisco, two young women fight for love in a world where women are often invisible and passion is the privilege of the powerful. (978-1-60282-589-5)

Bloody Claws by Winter Pennington. In the midst of aiding the police, Preternatural Private Investigator Kassandra Lyall finally finds herself at serious odds with Sheila Morris, the local werewolf pack's Alpha female, when Sheila abuses someone Kassandra has sworn to protect. (978-1-60282-588-8)

Franky Gets Real by Mel Bossa. A four-day getaway. Five childhood friends. Five shattering confessions…and a forgotten love unearthed. (978-1-60282-585-7)

Riding the Rails: Locomotive Lust and Carnal Cabooses, edited by Jerry Wheeler. Some of the hottest writers of gay erotica spin tales of *Riding the Rails*. (978-1-60282-586-4)

Rescue Me by Julie Cannon. Tyler Logan reluctantly agrees to pose as the girlfriend of her in-the-closet gay BFF at his company's annual retreat, but she didn't count on falling for Kristin, the boss's wife. (978-1-60282-582-6)

Snowbound by Cari Hunter. *"The policewoman got shot and she's bleeding everywhere. Get someone here in one hour or I'm going to put her out of her misery."* It's an ultimatum that will forever change the lives of police officer Sam Lucas and Dr. Kate Myles. (978-1-60282-581-9)

High Impact by Kim Baldwin. Thrill seeker Emery Lawson and Adventure Outfitter Pasha Dunn learn you can never truly appreciate what's important and what you're capable of until faced with a sudden and stark reminder of your own mortality. (978-1-60282-580-2)

Murder in the Irish Channel by Greg Herren. Chanse MacLeod investigates the disappearance of a female activist fighting the Archdiocese of New Orleans and a powerful real estate syndicate. (978-1-60282-584-0)

Sheltering Dunes by Radclyffe. The seventh in the award-winning Provincetown Tales. The pasts, presents, and futures of three women collide in a single moment that will alter all their lives forever. (978-1-60282-573-4)

Holy Rollers by Rob Byrnes. Partners in life and crime Grant Lambert and Chase LaMarca assemble a team of gay and lesbian criminals to steal millions from a right-wing mega-church, but the gang's plans are complicated by an "ex-gay" conference, the FBI, and a corrupt reverend with his own plans for the cash. (978-1-60282-578-9)

History's Passion: Stories of Sex Before Stonewall, edited by Richard Labonté. Four acclaimed erotic authors re-imagine the past...Welcome to the hidden queer history of men loving men not so very long—and centuries—ago. (978-1-60282-576-5)

Lucky Loser by Yolanda Wallace. Top tennis pros Sinjin Smythe and Laure Fortescue reach Wimbledon desperate to claim tennis's crown jewel, but will their feelings for each other get in the way? (978-1-60282-575-8)

Mystery of The Tempest: A Fisher Key Adventure by Sam Cameron. Twin brothers Denny and Steven Anderson love helping people and fighting crime alongside their sheriff dad on sun-drenched Fisher Key, Florida, but Denny doesn't dare tell anyone he's gay, and Steven has secrets of his own to keep. (978-1-60282-579-6)

Detours by Jeffrey Ricker. Joel Patterson is heading to Maine for his mother's funeral, and his high school friend Lincoln has invited himself along on the ride—and into Joel's bed—but when the ghost of Joel's mother joins the trip, the route is likely to be anything but straight. (978-1-60282-577-2)